Wild Honey is Elizabeth Walker's third novel following the success of her previous two books, *Dark Sunrise* and *A Summer Frost*.

The wife of a successful banker and mother of two children in East Yorkshire, she devotes much of her busy working life to writing and is currently working on her next novel.

D1471221

By the same author

Dark Sunrise
A Summer Frost

ELIZABETH WALKER

Wild Honey

GRAFTON BOOKS

A Division of the Collins Publishing Group

LONDON GLASGOW
TORONTO SYDNEY AUCKLAND

Grafton Books
A Division of the Collins Publishing Group
8 Grafton Street, London W1X 3LA

Published by Grafton Books 1986

First published in Great Britain by
Judy Piatkus Ltd 1985

ISBN 0-586-06713-2

Printed and bound in Great Britain by
Collins, Glasgow

Set in Times

Chapter One

'It's going to lose! Damn the animal, it's going to lose!' Sheppard dropped his race glasses and let them dangle, staring incredulously as the little filly, distinguished as much by the desperate exertions of her jockey as the orange and white of the colours, wavered and fell back. All around in the stands people were moving and talking but the Sheppard party stood ominously quiet.

'Nowhere,' said Sheppard, his voice hard with contempt. 'The filly hadn't a chance.'

The trainer, a plump man with a battered trilby hat and a nervous expression, began to apologise. 'If you remember, sir I did say she was a little backward. Perhaps if we left her till next season – or we could try her again when the ground –' he fell silent. The writing was on the wall and there was nothing to be gained by crawling. The big, square man glared at him beneath bushy eyebrows and a thatch of springy black hair. 'I've had enough of next times, Carter,' he said, not bothering to lower his voice. 'I don't waste time with people who can't produce results. That filly should have won by a mile and I don't like being made a fool of by a tin-pot –'

'Darling,' broke in his wife, pulling insistently at his arm. 'Mr Carter has a runner in the next race, and I expect

1

he has to see to it. Perhaps we can talk about this later.' She directed a meaningful stare at Carter, who wisely seized his chance, touched his hat and left. Sheppard turned his wrath upon his wife.

'What the devil d'you mean barging in like that? To hell with his other runners, if he'd given them less attention and mine more we might have won something.'

People were staring at them openly, for William's words could be heard halfway up the stands. But people always stared, whether there was a scene or not, and to Jenna it was of little consequence. She gazed across the racecourse, her face still and lovely, while her husband listed Carter's deficiencies in cruel detail. She might have been quite alone for all the notice she took of him, or anyone else for that matter, even the photographers who lined the paddock rails like a firing squad.

'Will you listen to me, Jenna? I tell you I'm finished with him. I've asked Stephen to get this man Hennessey that everyone's talking about. If anyone can make those nags run he can, or so Staveley was saying.' He dropped the peer's name with an assumed casualness that made Jenna's lip curl. William loved titles. He owned two studs and countless horses, some fifty of which were in training, and yet he would accept the advice of a man like Staveley, who owned one dubious gelding, because he also had a title. Anyone he recommended was bound to be useless, she thought nastily, remembering the way Staveley pawed her whenever they chanced to be together. Jenna was a woman who liked her own space.

She turned and said to her husband, 'Why can't we send them all to Downing? He knows what he's doing and we're used to him. We don't have to keep them in Yorkshire.'

William shook his head impatiently. The southern trainer took care of many of their runners but he was a safe, unimaginative man and besides, William liked to see his horses on tracks close to home, which meant a northern trainer.

'We'll see this man Hennessey. Stephen's arranged it for after the next race. And for God's sake be polite to him, Jenna, I don't want you doing your iceberg act. Sometimes I think the only people you're nice to are the ones I'm bawling out. I don't know what's got into you these days.'

'Don't you?' Jenna's head turned slowly and scanned the people starting to throng the stands again. There she was in the blue hat, plump and pink like a blonde and blue-eyed doll. William's latest toy. A wave of misery rose within her and took her by surprise, so that suddenly she was blinking and clenching her fists in the effort of suppressing tears. Stupid to be upset about it, stupid and futile. William always had something going, she should have learned that by now, and it didn't affect her at all. He had the decency to be discreet and in a strange way it was unrelated to the way he felt about his wife. If she let him know she knew and she minded the affair would be done with in an instant, and a week or two would pass before the next one began. He loved her really, Jenna was sure of it, but it wasn't enough to stop him.

'Jenna? Are you all right?' William was staring at her, and suddenly imagining what it would do to the money-grabbing little bitch in the stands who thought his wife didn't understand him, she rested a gloved hand on his shoulder and let herself lean against him for the briefest possible second.

'I feel a bit faint,' she said weakly, her throat aching with unshed tears. 'I'd like to go home now, please, William.'

He patted her shoulder, saying, 'Go and sit in the car for a bit, you'll feel better then. I have to see Hennessey, as I said.'

'But I want to go home!' insisted Jenna, longing to lift her elegant umbrella and smash it over his insensitive head.

'Go if you like. I'll come later.' At once she knew what he was planning; a sweating, gasping, wallowing hour with that woman. She had breasts like footballs and thick, short legs, she was a pit pony where Jenna was a thoroughbred and who knew which would stand the course. Still, Jenna was not ready yet to withdraw from the race.

'I'll stay,' she said finally. 'Then we can go home together. Look, they're ready for the off.'

All conversation was suspended as ten three-year-olds careered down the track, to the accompaniment of a rising crescendo of noise. Jenna watched with slight interest as in the final furlong horses crossed and crossed again, ensuring a tedious wait for the result as the stewards demanded an enquiry.

'Carter lost anyway,' said Sheppard with revolting satisfaction, and Jenna nodded.

Perhaps it was only fellow feeling but her heart went out to the man, nicotine-stained as he was, because his life was on a down-swing and would shortly reach the bottom. A rich man is very like a god, she thought, he has power to save or damn.

Sheppard took her arm. 'Come on, I said I'd meet Stephen in the bar. You can have some champagne, it'll perk you up.'

Jenna agreed. At least champagne put the world at a tolerable distance, for a little time anyway. She began to step through the crowd and as always, paths opened before her. There was an aura about her, an untouchability, that owed only a little to clothes and jewels. She was the sort of woman that wears diamonds as if they were beads and silk as if it were rags, her brilliant St Laurent cape swirled round her in emerald folds but if she took it off you knew she would cast it on a chair and forget it. Sheppard walked behind, relishing the stares his wife received, the indifference of her long, leggy stride. There was no-one ever like Jenna. He loved the way she treated money, as if it were nothing. When he gave her a ring, however priceless, he knew she would leave it on a washstand, attendants returned them to him in the confident expectation of a tip. Jenna had style, there was no doubt about it, and if she was difficult into the bargain, cool and distant and sharp, it was a small price to pay. Like most things, he could afford it.

She wandered past the winners' enclosure, casting a dispassionate eye at the milling horses. No-one yet knew who had won and no-one was confident enough to instal their horse in the first position in case they had to make an ignominious retreat moments later, but they hovered nonetheless. One sensible trainer had chosen to pretend he was third, and when the result was announced was able to move up two places with expressions of modest surprise, thus causing the opposition to appear vulgarly optimistic. He was a tall, fair-haired man, thin and rangy, with at present a smile of diffident charm as he accepted the praises of his owners.

'Who is that?' asked Jenna, pausing to allow her husband to catch up.

'Tall thin chap?' That's Dan Hennessey. There you are, told you he was good.'

'He only got it on an objection,' snapped Jenna and swept into the bar.

Sheppard's assistant, Stephen, a precious young man with a cottage in the grounds and a boyfriend, obtained the champagne. He was a marvellous employee, attentive and aware, always remembering vital things like

5

umbrellas and capable even of buying Jenna's clothes if she felt unequal to the task. Being Mrs Sheppard meant a wardrobe as extensive as the queen's, and far more flamboyant, and Stephen loved to pick things that he knew were just what she'd like. His own taste ran to tight cream trousers and cravats, but when on duty he wore a suit. William thought it proper.

'Jenna's not feeling well,' said Sheppard and at once Stephen was all concern.

'Come and sit down, love,' he urged, taking her by the arm and pushing her to a seat behind a pillar. 'No lunch you see, it's the blood sugar level. I'll fetch you a sandwich, sit there –'

'No, Stephen, please –' but it was too late, he'd gone. And it was pleasant to sit in the faded plush of the members' bar sipping champagne and watching people. For once she felt inconspicuous, though she was far from being so, a slender, lovely woman in amazing clothes, whose head drooped on her neck like a weary flower. William was talking to someone or other, he always knew everyone at race meetings. She noticed the trainer, Hennessey, come into the room, looking round presumably for William. When he saw her he approached at once.

'Mrs Sheppard? I was looking for your husband. My name's Hennessey.'

She looked up at him and administered a thin, discouraging smile. 'He is expecting you,' she said coolly. 'Sit down, he'll come over in a moment.' She extended a hand to the chair opposite and after a moment's hesitation Hennessey sat. He waited for her to say something and when she did not he cleared his throat and commented, 'I gather he wants to move some of his horses.'

Her head inclined very slightly. 'So it seems.'

'I think I should warn you that my yard's full at the moment. I can always squeeze in something good but I don't take rubbish.'

'Are you suggesting that we own rubbish, Mr Hennessey?'

He opened his mouth to say that such a thought had never entered his head and then stopped himself. Damn it, the woman was being as cold as she knew how and they'd asked to see him, after all. He was damned if he'd grovel for the privilege of a smile, he'd rather stay poor.

'I don't suppose you know, Mrs Sheppard, but owners have strange habits,' he said carefully. 'People like you have paddocks full of yearlings and all the nice juicy ones, with the breeding and the prospects, go to their usual trainers. People like Downing, they get the top class stuff. For people like me, people who don't matter, you look under a dock leaf and find this wizened little runt with three-and a-half legs and a liver complaint and you very, very kindly let me have a go with it. I wouldn't know it was a horse if you didn't tell me. Then, when it doesn't win so much as a seller, you say there you are, that proves it – only the big men understand racehorses. It's like trying to train Bernard Levin for the Olympics.'

Jenna stared at him, her cheeks faintly flushed. 'You are very rude, Mr Hennessey.'

'But honest, Mrs Sheppard.' He leaned back and tucked his hands behind his neck, staring at her with calm blue eyes.

'Have some champagne' said Jenna weakly, picking up an empty glass by its stem and tinkling it against the bottle.

'Thank you.' He took the glass and their fingers touched. Jenna withdrew her hand as if she had touched something sticky.

Just then Stephen bustled up with a plate of smoked salmon sandwiches, prettily arranged on a bed of cress and cucumber fingers. 'Here you are, love' he said cosily

7

and set them on the table. 'This will make you feel better.'

'I won't eat them, Steve, you know that,' objected Jenna, but to please him she picked up a triangle and toyed with it. 'Here, Mr Hennessey, help yourself. You'll need your strength if you're going to be rude to my husband.'

Stephen bridled. 'I hope you haven't been upsetting, Mrs Sheppard,' he said aggressively, and Hennessey grinned.

'As if I'd dare,' he said smoothly and Jenna looked at him from under her eyelids.

The confidence of the man! She felt a sudden desire to get the upper hand so she said waspishly, 'On the subject of your training standards, I understand you have Lord Staveley's horse in your yard.'

Hennessey had the grace to look embarrassed. 'Well I do and I don't,' he admitted.

'Whatever does that mean?'

'I keep sending him home, he keeps sending him back. I'm getting quite fond of the old crock actually, even if he would be better off in cans. I agree with you, he's useless.'

'And so is the horse,' added Jenna, wide-eyed, and Hennessey choked on a smoked salmon sandwich.

Stephen was rounding up William like a sheepdog working a fell.

'Mr Sheppard – may I introduce you – Daniel Hennessey.'

'How do you do.' Hennessey stood and the two men shook hands. They were about the same height, a little over six foot, but Hennessey was much the lighter of the two, an athlete meeting William's powerful bulk. Next to Hennessey, William looked fat, whereas in fact he was not. It was simply that Hennessey carried no surplus flesh at all, he was muscle lying flat against bone.

'I was explaining to your wife,' Hennessey began, 'my

yard's full at the moment.'

'Darling, he says he can take good horses but he doesn't want any of our lousy ones,' added Jenna.

William looked taken aback, and Hennessey stared at the floor, his face giving no clue to his thoughts.

'But – I don't have bad horses,' said William in a puzzled way.

Hennessey looked up. 'Not bad, no. But there are horses with prospects and horses without and half the time I don't think you know which is which. Your wife thinks I'm talking through my hat, but take that filly today. Nice little thing, no world-beater and I'll make her win for you, but you can do better than that. You sold a colt last week you should have kept. At the moment you've got a good, sound middle of the road string of horses when you could be up with the best.' Hennessey sipped his champagne and watched Sheppard's face, seeing no hint of surprise or annoyance on the firm, well-fed features. The face of a man who could not be touched, for whom the antics of the insignificant trainer before him were barely interesting. Out of the corner of his eye he could see the woman, her face remote, her fingers toying with the stem of her glass. She might not have been listening at all, yet he knew she heard every word that he said.

'I don't mind a man being frank, Mr Hennessey,' said Sheppard, reaching into his pocket for one of his hand-rolled Swiss cigarillos. He suspended conversation while he performed the ritual ignition, removing the reed from the centre of the cigar and tossing it on to a table, searching his pockets for the monogrammed gold lighter. The trainer was not offered a cigar and the omission was deliberate. William had no objection to plain-speaking experts so long as they remembered who was boss. But he knew when it was in his interest to charm and all at once he smiled. 'I do believe you're right,' he said smoothly. 'These last couple of years I haven't been able to keep as much of an eye on things as I'd like and it's beginning to show. That's the way with bloodstock, your mistakes take a while to reveal themselves.'

'Training is rather more immediate,' said Hennessey. 'They either win or they don't.'

Sheppard laughed. 'But the excuses go on for ever. Look, I've four horses I'd like you to take, the filly that ran today and three others. If you can knock them into some sort of shape then we may be able to talk further.'

'Can I pick the other three?' asked Hennessey, meeting Sheppard's gaze.

'No. I won't send you rubbish.'

'Then I repeat, I reserve the right to turn away bad horses.'

'You're very sure of yourself, Mr Hennessey.'

'And you like to win. If you want your wife to collect trophies as lovely as she is then you have to give me the horses. Your business is money, Mr Sheppard. Mine is racing. All you have to do is take my advice, I'll do the rest.'

Still Jenna's face remained smooth and untroubled. What was she thinking about wondered Hennessey, aware that at last Sheppard was annoyed.

'I'll send you four horses and I'll defy you to find a bad one amongst them,' he declared, glaring.

'I hope I won't,' said Hennessey with a ghost of a smile. 'But you must excuse me Mr Sheppard, Mrs Sheppard. I have a runner to see to.' He put his glass on the table a fraction from Jenna's hand, turned on his heel and began to weave a path through the crowded bar. A tall, contained figure nodding here and there to people he knew.

'I told you I wouldn't like him,' said Jenna and Sheppard glanced down in surprise.

'Don't you? He's bloody sure of himself, I'll give you that. But whether you like it or not he's the man. I've thought for some time that the whole thing needs pulling together, but there are very few men who can look at a yearling, judge its future and be right.'

'I don't think he's one of them,' said Jenna sourly. 'He only thinks he is.'

Sheppard slipped a hand under her elbow and drew her to her feet. He had the daunting ability to divide his life into compartments, when he was in one he behaved as if those before and behind did not exist. It was impossible to have wide-ranging conversations with him, his vision was a single, powerful spotlight, illuminating for a moment and then passing on. The subject of trainers was closed.

'Darling, you're not well,' he murmured, twining a tendril of hair back into the heavy bun at the nape of her neck. 'You look tired, and it's time you went home. I'll get Stephen to go with you, I'll make my own way later.'

'What will you do?' asked Jenna, looking him full in the eye, but he was all bland innocence.

'I have to arrange things with Carter. Tell Elsa not to worry about dinner, I'll have something out. Off you go now, and make sure you get an early night.'

He bent to kiss her but Jenna turned her cheek. Sheppard sucked in his breath in annoyance. 'Damn it, Jenna, can't you be pleasant for once?' he hissed, his fingers digging into her arm.

'Not today William,' she murmured and pulled herself free with a jerk.

On the way to the car the loudspeakers gave the result of the last race. To her chagrin, Hennessey had won.

Jenna sat bleakly in one corner of the Rolls and watched the countryside pass by. Stephen sat in the opposite

11

corner and watched her, sensing the depression that covered her like a blanket.

'I don't think we're going to get on with Mr Hennessey,' he said at length.

Jenna roused herself. 'Probably not. Anyway I can see he and William being at loggerheads the moment something doesn't come first. For all his promises Hennessey can't win all the time. No-one does.'

'Then we won't have to put up with him long,' comforted Stephen, and rested his small brown hand on Jenna's white one. She turned to look at him and her face crumpled. 'Oh Stephen,' she sniffed, reaching for a tissue in her bag. 'Why does he have to do these things?'

Stephen glanced swiftly towards the glass screen between them and the chauffeur and pulled it shut. 'Be careful, lovey, we don't want a scandal,' he urged, but Jenna was in control of herself again.

'It's all right, I'm not making a fuss. It's just – she's not even particularly pretty!'

Stephen looked wordlywise. 'They don't have to be, you know. She's a vulgar little tart, all boobs and bottom, and every now and then that's what he wants. Like whelks at Blackpool, and greasy fish and chips. He'll have his little fling and come home to you as happy as can be. Is there any reason for you to be upset? The thing is Jen, it's only bodies. Doesn't mean anything. OK, in the past when squires fathered babies all over the place, fidelity was a good idea, but it's unnecessary today, for you as much as him. Though I don't recommend you go exploring, love, you know our William's temperament. He's devoted to you and always will be.'

Jenna tore at her tissue, snapping, 'If he was really devoted to me he wouldn't do it! He should have some self-control.'

'That's what my mother used to say to me,' said

12

Stephen, with an exaggerated, nancy-boy pout. '"Stephen, you should have some self-control".'

Jenna was amused and exasperated. 'That's different.' She didn't know why it should be different, but somehow it was. For Stephen barely knew half the men he slept with, but for her, and William, it ought to be more than that. But rich men make their own rules and as William was not all things to her, she was not likely to be all things to him. She sighed, but managed a smile. 'You're right of course, it's not important. I'm just being silly. Look, we're nearly home, I hope those children have behaved themselves.'

The Rolls swept between pillars bearing huge, curlicued gates with gilt tops, and on up a long, gravelled drive. The house was wide and welcoming, in yellow sandstone with a greenish roof, falsely hinting at age. The structure was no more than two years old and held every gadget and convenience known to man, including an indoor swimming pool, sauna, small gym and a video room in the basement. Jenna stepped out of the car and tripped lightly up the steps – made of stone recycled from a demolished stately home and thus authentically indented – past George, the butler, and into the hall.

'Hello, George. Mr Sheppard won't be in for dinner I'm afraid, do apologise to Elsa for me. Where are the children, do you know?'

George, over sixty and portly but with the remnants of a military posture, murmured, 'I'm afraid, madam, that they're in the video room.' His expression was one of deep disapproval and Jenna went cold. He only ever called her madam when there was trouble. 'Is it those films again? George, I told you to stop them! Didn't I make myself clear?'

The butler's outrage bubbled beneath his surface restraint and two spots of colour stained the plump cushions of his cheeks. He was clearly very distressed.

'Madam, I do not appreciate having shoes thrown at me. I do not relish being told that I am a relic of a bygone age, a traitor to my class and a refugee from *Uncle Tom's Cabin*. I do not want to be told that I should do unmentionable things to Elsa, who as you know is a woman of principle who has sought shelter within the safety of these four walls, and what safety can there be here for any of us when boys of fourteen – fourteen, madam – utter words that I should be ashamed to repeat at my age. When I think of the position that young rip is destined to hold I fear for the safety of the country, madam, we should thank our stars that at least our royal family seems to be uninfected by this disease that is sweeping through the youth of today –'

'I give thanks daily, George, I really do,' interrupted Jenna, but George was not to be stopped.

'When I think of the foul thoughts that go into their minds from these films, madam, I don't know where to turn. They are children, madam. Children!'

'Yes – yes – yes, George, I know. Look, I'll go and talk to them. Please, I don't know what I'm going to do, but something. Honestly. I'll come and see you later George, now, why don't you have a cup of tea and a sit down. You can watch the racing results. By the way, we lost.'

His face fell still further and even the crisp white horseshoe of hair that surrounded his scalp seemed to droop. Jenna could tell she had put the lid on his terrible day, but George would insist on betting whether their horses had a chance or not. She resolved to make it up to him, a day at the races for him and Elsa perhaps, there and back in the Rolls. For them it might still seem a treat.

She went to the basement stairs and descended as slowly as she could. This was the worst part of being a second wife, the discipline. There was no way you could tell them off without sounding like Cinderella's step-mother, and the fact that you were not their real parent gave them countless rounds of ammunition to fire at you. Bringing in William was an admission of defeat and she never did it. Besides, he'd probably think it funny.

The video room was almost a padded cell, with dark blue carpet and suede on the windowless walls. Racks of tapes lined the room, the camera and recording equipment stood to one side and there was a single locking cabinet, now standing open, which held William's collection of 'adult movies', kept for stag evenings with business colleagues. Coke cans and crisp packets littered the floor and Tony and Rachel sprawled in chairs, legs dangling over the arms, watching the television. They did not hear Jenna come in and she stared, transfixed, at the screen. Two figures, wearing only hoods and liberally daubed with blood, stepped from their graves and raised ghastly faces to the camera, coming closer and closer until you could see the ravages of beetles and worms – Jenna gave a stifled shriek and pulled the plug from the wall.

'Right you two!'

The shock of her appearance did not give them sufficient time to hide their alarm behind expressions of bored resignation, and Jenna felt a flicker of relief. Sophisticates they might think themselves but not so hard that she couldn't put the fear of God into them.

'Has George been telling tales?' asked Tony defiantly. He was a lanky youth who would one day be good-looking, but at present he had spots.

'I don't need George to tell me what you've been doing,' said Jenna. 'I've just seen for myself.'

'If my father watches them so can we,' announced Rachel, and tossed back her shock of electric blue hair. It was a vivid reminder of another unsupervised afternoon when a twelve-year-old with too much money had wandered off alone. William had been furious and refused to be seen with her, which was nothing new. He found his children a nuisance and let them know it.

Jenna perched on the arm of Rachel's chair and brushed a hand through the spikes on the child's head. 'Did you like watching those things?' she asked gently. 'Didn't you think they were horrid?'

Rachel shrugged. 'Don't know.'

'I bet you feel dirty,' went on Jenna. 'I only ever watched one and I felt as if I needed a bath.'

'But you're such a prude,' sneered Tony. 'You don't like anything.'

Jenna flushed. 'I don't like grubbing around in the filthiest corners of other people's minds. And neither should either of you, and if you do like it then I'm ashamed of you. I'm burning those tapes, since you two can't be trusted, and if I catch either of you watching anything like it again then so help me I'll – I'll –'

'What? You can't do anything to us, you know you can't.' Tony was jeering at her and for a moment she longed to hit him.

'Oh yes, I can,' she said grimly. 'I can send you to school again, the old one, I'm sure you remember it. And I warn you that no amount of wailing will bring you home this time. I'm tired of being nice to you Tony and having you spit in my face, I'm tired of the way you stick your claws into George and hurt his feelings. What's more I'm tired of the way you lead Rachel into your messes, and if this is the sort of person you are then I don't want you around.' She was breathing hard and she saw that she had gone too far. Tony had turned pale and his lip was quivering, and she knew why. Here he was crying out for attention and she threatened to send him away.

You wouldn't! You wouldn't!'

God, but rowing with children was frustrating. They drove you to do your worst and then made you feel cruel

16

because you had done as they wished and treated them as adults. On an impulse she knew she might regret she went and put an arm round him, feeling his shoulders shake.

'Not yet I won't, silly. But I might if you go on like this. I know it's my fault for leaving you alone, but your father – anyway, it's going to be different. Weekends together, that's what we should have. Look, we'll have a proper, organised punishment. You both go and apologise to George and Elsa –'

'We didn't say anything to Elsa,' objected Rachel, but Jenna quelled her.

'You said things about her, and nasty things too. I don't like you for it, either of you, and you must apologise. Then you burn these tapes – all of them – and wash the Rolls. Good open air exercise, that's what you need.'

'But it'll take hours,' complained Tony. 'It'll be dark.'

'I only hope the creatures of the grave don't get you,' said Jenna unfeelingly. 'Come along and get on with it.'

That night Jenna lay in bed and could not sleep. Eventually she got up and wandered aimlessly from room to room, looking out into the night from the windows but seeing only the dark. The master suite was on the first floor of the house, stretching the length of the wide, parquet corridor. Two dressing rooms, two bathrooms – one big, one pocket-sized – and an enormous bedroom with doors leading out on to the verandah. When Jenna designed the room she had felt rich and extravagant, but beautiful as it was it no longer gave her any pleasure. A silk tapestry hung on the wall, glowing in ruby and sapphire, and the carpet was a sea of cream in the midst of which stood the fourposter bed, a vast platform draped with curtains of braided, plum-coloured velvet. William loved the room, right from the carved oak chest covered

17

in griffins and grapes to the exquisite tiny chinese vases that nestled, almost overlooked on a slim shelf below the cornice. To Jenna it felt like a sultan's seduction chamber.

The problems and anxieties of her life buzzed at her like mosquitoes on a hot night. She knew she had to spend time with the children. Hers or not, in the four years she had known them she had come to feel at the very best responsible and probably rather more than that. William ignored them for they were a relic of his embarrassing first marriage and he wanted none of it.

William Moreton Sheppard, husband and millionaire, and one was as important as the other. A man who saw no need to obey the rules by which others lived their lives. It might be that Stephen was right and they were silly rules, but even after all this time his betrayals still hurt. In a way though it was largely her fault, for she did not please him in bed, and she knew it. Try as she would when he reached for her she tensed, holding herself like a board as he wooed her. He did not try to hurt, but when he kissed her breast an image of his teeth on her nipple made her cringe, when he reached between her legs she stiffened in fear of his nails. And the fear made her dry, so that to love her at all William had to smear himself with cream and that was awful. Embarrassing. It was better once he was inside, for then it was almost over. Sometimes he asked her to be on top, and she hated it, hated the way he stared at her face as she struggled to please him, knowing she wasn't doing it right, knowing that what he really wanted was a woman with breasts that swung in his mouth, a woman who climaxed thrice nightly. Once, after endless champagne, she had collapsed on the bed and let him love her, and while the world spun round and round and round she had felt something – a moth's breath of pleasure came and passed her by. And in the morning she was sick and her head ached as if her brain was being drilled, so the moment had hardly been worth it.

Jenna wandered out into the corridor, ghostly in her white silk nightdress, as tall and graceful as a Stubbs painting of a racehorse. There came a rumbling and a clattering in the hall below and she gasped, thinking of burglars. But it was only William coming up the stairs, shirt undone, the hair on his chest beaded with sweat. When he came closer she caught the unmistakable tang of sex.

'Why – Jenna. Couldn't you sleep, my darling? You're cold and you must take a pill. Come here my angel.' He took her in his arms, drunk and with the scent of that woman still upon him. Jenna turned her head and the dark curtain of her hair hid her face.

'What is it? Why won't you kiss me?' He sounded hurt.

Suddenly Jenna had to say it, resentment and hurt babbled to the surface and made her foolish. 'How much does it take to make you happy? You've had that woman tonight, God knows what you've been up to, and now you want me as well. I won't William. I hate it when you touch me, I hate it!' She put her hands up to fend him off but even her palms recoiled at the touch of warm flesh.

William was mouthing her neck, he was pushing aside her nightgown to reach for her breast. 'No, you don't, I love you,' he was murmuring. 'The others aren't anyone, you're my Jen-Jen, lovely, lovely Jen-Jen. You're mine.' Moving with the clumsiness of drink he wrenched at the nightgown and the fabric parted. Jenna dragged herself away and tried to pull the film of silk back over her breasts. In the bright light of the corridor her limbs appeared pale and elongated, and as she lifted her arms every rib and vertebra was clearly visible. The breasts she was covering so anxiously were no more than hiccups in the fleshless expanse of stomach and chest, her skin was stretched tight as a drum. No wonder her clothes hung so

19

beautifully, they were draped on the body of a woman who has consistently and religiously starved.

'I want you! Cuddle me, lovey, let's have a kiss and a cuddle.' William was insistently bumbling after her as she retreated along the corridor. Jenna thought momentarily about giving in, getting it over and afterwards having a bath, but a shudder went through her. She could not! She turned and ran for her dressing room, slamming the door and locking it behind her.

'Go away! You're drunk and horrible and you make me sick. Go away!'

A foot crashed hard into the door and the frame trembled, but it was mahogany and could withstand more than this. 'You frigid cow, open this door! Open it I say, you're not a bloody nun, you're my wife. Open this door!'

But Jenna only crouched on the floor and waited, and after a time her husband shambled off to bed.

At breakfast Jenna sat alone. Neither Tony nor Rachel believed in rising early on Sundays and William was still asleep, sprawled on the bed in his underpants. So it was simply Jenna, sipping a small glass of orange juice and crumbling half a piece of toast. As usual she was immaculate, in silk blouse and crisp trousers, a cashmere sweater draped across her shoulders. Less usual were the shadows beneath her eyes and the faint tremor in the fingers that shredded her toast, lifting not a morsel to her lips.

In the distance she could hear the clatter of the telex in William's study and as the door to the kitchen opened and closed with George's forays into the house, the abrupt life and death of a radio programme. She sat alone in the breakfast room and felt a deathly quiet.

Eventually she would have to move, that was certain,

though she doubted if her legs would obey her. There was lead in her veins, crawling through her blood vessels until it could set in a lump around her heart. Never in her life had she felt so hopeless. At last George came to clear her plate away, and she had to get up. That was the thing about servants, you lived your life according to their routine rather than any of your own. It was a tyranny of sorts.

'I've made Mr Sheppard's breakfast tray, ma'am,' said George and Jenna nodded.

'I'll take it up. Leave the children, if they eat anything now they won't want lunch.' And in the Sheppard household Sunday lunch arrived at 1 pm precisely whether they wanted it or not.

William was awake when she went into the room, lying hunched against the pillows looking pale and rumpled.

'I've brought you some orange juice, coffee and toast,' said Jenna quietly and set the tray down carefully on the gleaming polish of the bedside table.

'Thanks. God, but I've a head this morning. Are there any aspirin?'

'I'll get some.' Jenna went into her bedroom and fetched them from the cabinet. They stood amongst the sleeping pills and tranquillisers, the ranks of bottles a mute reproach.

'William, I want to talk,' she said, dropping the pills on to the tray and seating herself on the end of the bed. 'Do you remember what happened last night?'

Her husband was swallowing his pills, washing them down with orange juice. 'I was drunk, darling. Nothing so terrible, it happens once in a while. You don't have to look as if you've witnessed a murder.'

She shook her head angrily. 'It isn't that! I don't really think it's you at all, it's – it's me. William, I think we ought to get a divorce.'

That did stop him in his tracks. He put down the glass and turned to look at her.

'A little extreme, don't you think, after one minor bedroom dispute? Or have you suddenly fallen in love with someone else? Forgive me for asking, but is it anyone I know? Not George, surely!'

'Oh, don't be facetious. Of course, there isn't anyone else. I married you because I loved you and I still do, but – things aren't right between us. If it wasn't for that you might not need these women. I hate it, I absolutely hate it, I can't bear to think you've been touching them!'

William reached to take her hand but she pulled violently away. 'You imagine a lot more than there is, you know,' he said in a reasonable tone. 'I suppose you're upset because you're not a very physical woman yourself. I've always known you disliked sex, and I try not to bother you too much, but just as I need a game of squash occasionally, so sometimes I need a woman. You wouldn't like it if I continuously made demands on you, would you?'

Jenna clenched her long fingers into fists and thumped them on the bed. 'That's just it! I don't like it either way, so isn't it better if we divorce? You could find somebody who would – I don't know what you do with these women, but whatever it is you could marry someone who would do it. And I – wouldn't have to know.'

William swung his legs out of bed and strolled over to the window. He wore only his underpants and the heavy bulge of his genitals attracted Jenna's eyes. If only that part of him did not exist, how much simpler life would be, but from that to the thick covering of hair on chest and limbs, even on his back, he was a male. Only a proper woman could satisfy him.

Suddenly he turned. 'There's one thing you forget, Jenna,' he said calmly. 'I will never, ever divorce you. I made that quite clear when we married. I won't embarrass you by talking about love, and you might be forgiven for thinking that a man divorced once would think little of doing it again, but you're wrong. I intended never to remarry, until I met you. Apart from the appalling legal mess if I divorced at this stage in my life, there is also – I like having you as my wife, Jenna.'

'Why do you like it? I'm not even nice to you.'

'Why should you be? You are Jenna, unique, an original. Like a beautiful, fragile glass. What would you do without me to take care of you? I'm the only one who can do it. I've always known there was no cuddling you, Jenna, you'd break, look at you now, you are breaking. Special things need special care, I've known that since the first time. But drink makes men foolish and last night I forgot myself. I'm sorry.'

Jenna hid her face in her hands. She wished he had not spoken of that night, it was something she tried not to remember. 'I'm not normal,' she whispered now. 'I know I'm not.'

William came and stood in front of her, pulling her hands from her face and kissing them. 'I wouldn't want anyone normal.' He let her hands fall and went to the breakfast tray, pouring himself a cup of coffee. 'So there you are, Jenna,' he said, the subject clearly exhausted. 'I make very few demands of you but I will not stand by while you wreck both our lives, when there is nothing at all the matter. You are my wife and you will always be my wife.'

She tried to laugh but it was uncomfortable. 'How very final that sounds.'

'Isn't it just. So we need never bother about anything so silly again. Look, I must get dressed and get to work, I have to make the arrangements about those horses. We leave for Kentucky on Friday, is everything under control?'

23

'What? Oh yes, of course. But William I don't think I should come.'

He lowered the coffee cup from his lips. 'Really? Why not?'

'I thought so even before – everything. It's the children. I've been neglecting them terribly lately, they've been watching those horrible films again, and Rachel's hair – after all they're away at school all week and it's only the weekends. I feel I ought to be here at weekends. For a few months at least.' And it would mean peace and isolation. Time to gather her thoughts. In a tight little gesture that was witness to her agitation, she toyed with a strand of hair.

'You're wasting your time,' said William coolly. 'They are unpleasant, undisciplined and weak-minded. So was their mother. The best thing we can do is send them both back to full boarding and forget them.'

'Oh don't be so ridiculous,' snapped Jenna. 'They're only undisciplined because no-one disciplines them, and apart from that they're young and they think we don't care. I feel if I give them some time now, then perhaps next year we could send them both away. I mean, it's not as if we haven't tried it with Tony. It would be a repeat performance to send him back now, and I simply couldn't stand it.'

Her husband put his cup back on the tray and went into the bathroom. 'It isn't for you to stand,' he called above the noise of the shower starting to run. 'They're not your children and I have never asked you to be responsible for them.'

'Since you won't be, I must,' retorted Jenna. 'Besides, I don't want to go to Kentucky for two months. Suppose I come out for a week or two in the middle? I should hate to miss autumn in England.'

William considered. Kentucky oppressed Jenna

because of the crowds of people she attracted. They were swept into a social whirl in which she starred, but in which her remote, private self felt beleaguered. Left in England she would read and shop, and go for long, exhausting walks on the moors, returning calm and bright and happy. Meanwhile he in Kentucky could have a bit of a fling. They would have to be that much more private in future if Jenna was going to take it so hard. Also he could spend only as long as he wished at the Sales, which in fact was less time than Jenna would permit. She would hang around for hours, peering from catalogue to horse and back again, but as for William, he preferred the racecourse. He did not deal in promises.

The children were not a factor that he considered. Years since he had consigned them to a compartment labelled 'Expensive Mistake' and he saw no reason to let them out. He tested the water in the shower and called out, 'All right – but remember what I said.'

'What's that?'

He stood in the doorway, naked but for his wedding ring. 'We will never, ever talk about divorce again. Tell George to check the boiler please, this water is far too hot.'

Chapter Two

The leaves of early autumn, not yet brown, scuttered around the yard and made the horses dance. Hennessey peered at a suspect hind leg and swore when it refused to stand still.

'Make him behave, Bert,' he snapped and the diminutive man at the head muttered 'Yes, guvnor,' and tried to control his charge. When the horse still swung this way and that Hennessey sighed, straightened, and went to the head collar himself. 'What are you, some kind of nut?' he demanded, glaring into the limpid brown eye of the horse. Then he returned to his study of the leg, now so still that it might have been stuffed. The lads grinned knowingly at each other and stored the tale to boast of in the pub. Every one of them believed that the guvnor was in league with the devil.

An expensive saloon car was pulling in at the gate, and glancing up Hennessey knew that it had to be an owner. He cursed again, he hated them dropping in unexpectedly. 'Go and see what they want, Geoff,' he said to his head lad, but the man stayed where he was.

'But guvnor – it's Mrs Sheppard,' he said uncertainly, and every head turned to watch the long, jean-clad legs climb out of the car. From the rear doors there emerged a lanky teenage boy and a girl – he supposed it was a girl – with hair so stiff and blue you could brush the yard with it.

Jenna stood for a moment, taking in the rambling, much amended house with its peeling paint, and the rows of immaculate boxes. The day held a chill and she pulled her coat around her, an enormous corduroy jacket from which her neck rose like a flower stem, weighed down by her coils of hair.

'Mr Hennessey,' she said expectantly, and began to stroll towards him. He put down the horses's foot with resigned patience and went to meet her, resisting the urge to dust his hands on his trousers and clear his throat.

She was the first to stop, simply waiting for him to come to her. God, thought Hennessey, the woman knows how to put you down. Owners were a nuisance at the best of times, but self-important ones were something else. He stomped towards her, saying brusquely, 'Can I help you? We're rather busy today I'm afraid.'

'Then I shall try not to take up too much of your time.' All at once she smiled at him, and he blinked. When this ice maiden smiled she was dazzling.

'Er – your husband isn't with you.' A feeble remark, she would hardly conceal him in the boot of the car.

'No. He's spending some time at one of our studs in Kentucky, and he has asked me to call on you from time to time to see how you are getting on. I have brought the children, though. Rachel, Tony, come and be introduced.

They slouched over, the picture of reluctant embarrassment. A young yellow labrador bounced around them, dropping his ball with optimistic persistence and smiling.

'Come here, Casey, you're getting in the way,' said Hennessey, but the girl, Rachel, said breathily, 'He isn't being a bother, really. I like him.'

27

'Rachel's very fond of dogs,' said Jenna. 'She'd like one of her own, but she's away at school all week.'

'What sort of dog would you like Rachel?' asked Hennessey, a smile softening the heavy grooves from nose to mouth.

Rachel blushed scarlet and muttered. 'Any sort. Even a mongrel, though my father doesn't like them.'

Tony snorted. 'Typical. He only likes thoroughbreds.'

It was the woman's turn to flush and Hennessey wondered at it. The boy had touched a nerve. For an instant she looked slightly uncertain and he said, 'Perhaps you'd like to look at the horses. I think I've got time.'

He regretted the concession the moment she lifted her eyebrows and said with a tinkle of ice, 'That *is* good of you, Mr Hennessey. I thought we weren't to be allowed a treat.'

'I do usually like my owners to telephone. It causes fewer problems all round.'

'I suppose it must, if you have something to hide.'

He stopped and gaped at her. 'And what might I be trying to hide, may I ask? Charging you full whack and keeping the nags in the coal shed, is that the sort of bloke you think I am? Because if so –'

Jenna laid a hand on his arm. 'I'm sorry – I'm sorry. I didn't mean that the way it sounded. But you see, we've had a lot of trainers, Mr Hennessey and – Tony, tell him about that man in America.'

It was a funny story about a man who only ever talked to people before ten in the morning because he was drunk and speechless after that, but the gauche tale Tony mumbled was neither funny nor entirely understandable. But Hennessey grinned and chuckled as if it were.

The lads all stood staring as they processed around the boxes. 'You don't have very many horses,' said Jenna doubtfully. 'I thought you said you didn't want any more,

28

or were you just being rude?'

'Yes, partly,' said the man and Rachel giggled. 'But it's more than that. This season I've had around thirty-five horses, thirty-nine with your lot. Now, each one of those animals deserves every bit as much care as every other one, whether it belongs to the fishmonger, to you, or even to Lord Staveley. That's his over there, head like a hammer and brainless. Nice old chap though.'

'I like Lord Staveley,' said Rachel. 'Jenna hates him, but he's nice. He treats me like a baby and gives me sweets and does rabbit tricks with his handkerchief, but I think he's sweet.'

'Jenna doesn't like him because he's nuts about her,' chimed in Tony. 'She hates anyone who falls under the spell.' He made Svengali like hand movements and Jenna swiped at him.

'Don't be silly,' she said in quelling tones.

Hennessey thought it was time he broke up the family wrangle. 'As I was saying,' he said firmly, 'I cannot look after more than forty horses properly. It wouldn't be so bad if they didn't have to race, but unfortunately the owners seem to think that's the idea.'

Jenna grinned. 'How much nicer it would be without us,' she murmured, and shot him a sidelong glance. Hennessey simply grunted.

They came to the filly that had failed the previous week. 'Any prospects?' asked Jenna. 'She looks a little on the light side to me.'

'Bit strung up. We'll see how she does on less work.' Hennessey reached in his pocket and gave the horse a tidbit, running a hand down her neck. 'I like training fillies,' he said absently. 'They need such tact.'

'And are you a master of tact, Mr Hennessey?'

She was taunting him, her head thrown back. He wondered if the weight of her hair made her neck ache.

'Like you, Mrs Sheppard, I turn it on and off at will,' he murmured, and moved on to the next box.

They stood looking at a big, rangy colt with ballooning muscles. 'Put some money on him on Wednesday,' said Hennessey. 'He should walk it.'

'I don't bet,' said Jenna. 'Besides, don't you think you're a trifle over-confident? After all, there are other horses in these races and it must be so embarrassing when after all your promises he trails in last.' She said it because he annoyed her, but the words were instantly regretted. She was making an enemy of this man and it was foolish. The muscles in his cheeks were tense, but when he spoke it was with soft control. 'I wonder you don't train the things yourself, Mrs Sheppard, since you are obviously such an expert. Or even ride them and do the job properly. Eight stone four should do the filly, I'm sure you won't find that a problem.' It was a veiled insult, for she was a tall woman, but Jenna only laughed.

'Seven stone actually. I shall leave the racetrack to the professionals, but I should love to ride work one morning. What time do you set out?'

He blinked at her and said bluntly, 'You can't weigh seven stone, you're far too tall.'

In answer she swung her coat wide and let him look. She wore a tight white T-shirt tucked into her jeans and he stood and stared at her concave belly and slender waist, so narrow she looked as if she might snap. Outlined too were the tiny breasts, each with its round little nipple, like a cherry on a cake. His face did not change but he was conscious of a rising tide of heat.

'All right, you can do the weight,' he said brusquely. 'If you mean it you can come at eight next Tuesday, but there's no point in killing yourself just to score a point.'

'Oh, Jenna can ride,' said Tony. 'She's better than any of us, especially Rachel, who's scared. Aren't you Rache?'

30

The girl blushed scarlet and Hennessey said, 'She probably hasn't been taught properly. Nobody likes to feel they're out of control.'

'I couldn't make it stop,' mumbled Rachel and Jenna felt a pang of guilt. It would only have taken a little effort to find a suitable pony for Rachel, but in the early days of her marriage there had been so much else to think about. And now the child had a fear she might never overcome.

'It was a horrible pony,' she admitted. 'Anyway Mr Hennessey, thank you for your time. We have to go now and do something about Rachel's hair.'

'Disconnect it from the mains I should think,' said Tony, and even Rachel laughed.

'If you come again I won't recognise you,' said Hennessey gently. 'You'll have to tell me who you are.'

Rachel's blush deepened to purple at the unexpected attention and Jenna ushered her brood to the car. 'I'll see you on Tuesday, then,' she called as she settled herself behind the wheel.

'No later than eight,' said the trainer, and was back with his horses before the car had even left the yard.

Even as the Sheppard car drove off there was a buzz of excited chatter.

'Please, Mummy, can I have one of those for Christmas?'

'Christ did you see that shape? Like a bleeding whippet.'

'If that's a whippet then I'm a three-legged carthorse.'

The conversation died as Hennessey approached. 'You can belt up, the lot of you,' he said shortly. 'I don't care what she looks like she's an owner and deserves respect.' He looked at the grinning faces and knew he was wasting his time. 'This morning's a bloody shambles,' he muttered to himself. It was hard to remember what he had been going to do before the woman came. 'Clear up this

31

yard,' he ordered angrily, and marched off to the house.

'Doesn't know whether he's coming or going,' muttered someone. 'And he says he doesn't care what she looks like, his eyes were like organ stops.'

'Not only his eyes boyo,' said someone lewdly, and there was a burst of laughter, quickly subdued.

Hennessey ignored it and continued on to the house. Damn the woman, she upset him every time they met, and not only him, the yard was in turmoil. She was a strange sort too, gentle and hard by turns. Sighing, he shrugged off his coat and hung it on a peg that already held a mackintosh and a leather headcollar, and added his boots to the pile that had sat on the muddy floor for longer than he cared to remember.

Lilian was hunched at the kitchen table. Fresh from the crystalline glamour of Jenna Sheppard he was shocked anew by his wife. Shocked and moved to pity.

'Have you eaten anything?' he asked softly, but she neither moved nor spoke. Working with the ease of long practice he put eggs on to boil and shoved bread only slightly blue with mould into an ancient and crumb-infested toaster. He supposed they should have a housekeeper, but he couldn't afford it. Besides, Lilian hated strangers.

When the breakfast was ready he set his wife's before her and then settled to eat his own.

'She was lovely,' said Lilian suddenly, and Hennessey jumped. It was days since she had offered an unsolicited comment. He pulled his thoughts together.

'Mrs Sheppard you mean? I suppose she looked better from a distance. She's too thin and too cold.' He never made the elementary mistake of praising another woman to his wife.

'Her clothes were nice.'

'She was only wearing jeans.' That and a clinging white

T-shirt. His flesh stirred, but then he thought what an odd thing it was to have done. Almost as if she had no personal interest in her body, and could therefore show it off as casually as if it were a dummy in a shop window. The emotion had been on his part, there was none on hers. He sliced the top from his egg and neatly disembowelled it. He hated boiled eggs, but they were easy.

'You could have a new dress if you liked, Lilian. I'd take you to town if you wanted. You could buy yourself something.'

She lifted her head and stared at him with dark, shadowed eyes. Her hair hung lank and greasy and there was a coffee stain at the corner of her mouth.

'Eat your breakfast. There's a good girl.'

Obediently Lilian began to eat.

After a while she said, 'Those children. Were they hers?'

Hennessey was sipping his coffee and sorting through entries. He glanced up. 'I don't know. She treats them like hers but they don't call her Mother. Was Sheppard married before do you know?'

Lilian looked vague. 'He might have been – I don't remember' Should I remember, Dan? I'm not sure.'

He reached across and touched her hand. 'Of course you shouldn't. I just thought you might have read something, you know how magazines dredge up things about these people. It doesn't matter.'

But she was brightening. 'I'll look through some. People gave me hundreds when I was in hospital, there must be something. There will be.'

Hennessey was cautious. 'There might not be anything. Don't be upset.'

'Oh there will be. I know it.' She sprang up, again with an alarming, jerky suddenness, and ran from the room. Her husband began to clear away.

She had been pretty when he married her, in a doe-like, downy way. Her hair was soft and fine, he had not known it could lie on her head like wet seaweed. Such a shy, pretty girl and so devoted to him. They had known each other forever.

He had given it so little thought. But he must have thought, it was simply that time and the reality that was now had blotted out the dreams of time past. It had seemed such a sensible thing to do. What had he hoped for when he asked the slight, pretty girl to share his life? Comfort in his home, that had certainly been a factor, a permanent, steady base from which he could go out and tackle the important things in life. Ambition made it difficult to be single, there was no time in the day for endless, repetitive courtings to get yet another body into his bed. And they hung around in the mornings too, getting in the way of riding work.

But he had loved her then, he was sure of it. Loved the shyness, the anxious good manners, the way she tidied his dressing table in just the way he liked. That had been one of the first things to go of course, the tidiness. At first he thought she was ill, physically ill, because she always seemed so tired, she could hardly drag herself upstairs. And when she was there she lay in bed all day, day after day, barely speaking. A silent, fading creature, he had imagined that if he did nothing then one day she would fade quite away and be gone – no more than a rising dent in the mattress. And go she did, but only into hospital, to emerge months later, still strange, still vague, and her memory patchy from the ECT. She was better today though, she really seemed improved. If the fascinating Jenna Sheppard could do that much for him then he'd welcome her despite himself.

*　　　*　　　*

34

The early morning sky was grey and threatening rain, you could smell it on the breeze that ruffled the horses' rugs and blew their tails into plumes. Hennessey sat his horse with practiced ease, his body automatically controlling the animal's nervous fidgetings while his mind was filled with Jenna. He was letting the woman try to kill herself. When she drove into the yard it was all planned, the quiet gelding was ready, the programme thought out: a walk to the gallops, half-speed canter, then stand aside and watch while the serious work took place. But somehow when she stepped out of the car, those long, long legs unending in skin-tight, creamy jodphurs, her hair tumbling in glossy, expensive curls past the shoulders of her quixotically aged bomber jacket, he was filled with a desperate urge to see her face down in the mud. Nobody should be that beautiful, that self-confident, that rich. The lads all gawped at her, some grinned and shuffled their feet, but they might not have existed for all the notice she took.

'Good morning, Mr Hennessey. I'm sorry I'm so late. Did you think I wouldn't come?'

'I thought you might be late, actually. All that dressing must take such a time.'

Her eyebrows rose very slightly. 'I can hurry when I want to, Mr Hennessey.'

He snorted. 'That is a relief. May I suggest you hasten towards Money Market and apply yourself to the task of riding him? He's been waiting quite some time and he lacks the gift of patience.'

The lad holding the horse looked aghast. 'Here, guvnor, she can't ride this,' he said anxiously, but Hennessey froze him with a look.

'You ride Flagship Bert,' he ordered, and a worried looking Bert did as he was told.

Jenna took her time stuffing her hair into a crash helmet. It had not occurred to her that he'd give her a horse like that. He'd meant her to ride that old plug, which was going a bit far the other way, but this! Her stomach was churning like a washing machine and she knew she was in for trouble. After all it was not as if she ever meant to be late, she just always was, and now the man was making her pay. The horse would kill her, she was sure of it. Black, enormous and dancing on spindle legs he looked a different breed from the placid and amiable Flagship now allotted to Bert. But after all, did it matter if he finished her off? Even the children might be glad to have her gone and for her it would mean freedom from the horrible cloud of depression that hovered on the fringes of her mind, waiting to engulf her if she once relaxed her guard. The thought was a soothing one and her guts began to settle.

Hennessey was waiting, tapping his leg with his stick, although the effect was somewhat spoiled by the efforts of Casey to attract attention to his ball, picking it up and dropping it hopefully. In the end the trainer threw it for him, cracking his face in a reluctant grin. Jenna smiled also. He tried to be nasty but it really wasn't in him.

During the trek to the gallops Hennessey said, 'I think you've over-estimated yourself, Mrs Sheppard. Money Market's a hard colt to hold, look, he's all over the place. Bert, come and change with Mrs Sheppard.'

'Thank you, Mr Hennessey but I'm quite all right,' called Jenna with a casualness she did not feel. The colt was ducking his head and swinging his back end into the road and it took all her skill to keep him in line. But she would not be put off and given that seaside donkey, she would not.

'Don't blame me if he chucks you off,' warned Hennessey.

'You're not worried about me, are you?' queried Jenna, tossing a teasing, sexy smile at him, the best she could manage while in fear of her life.

Hennessey noted her white knuckles and felt helpless. This woman was something else.

By the time they reached the gallops he had decided to let her go through with it. She would only get off if they rowed about it, and he was not prepared to give his lads the thrill. He would send her off upsides a slow horse and pray they would catch her at the end, and anyway if she did kill herself it would only mean ruin. Her husband would never forgive him.

'If he starts to get away from you let him run,' he warned Jenna. 'Don't mess with him or he'll buck. Walk down and canter back, off you go.'

Jenna looked very pale and a wisp of hair floated into her mouth. She pushed it away and then clutched at the reins as the horse plunged. She wanted very much to quit, but Hennessey said nothing and keeping her face smooth and calm she turned the colt and headed into the wind.

It took a long time to walk down the gallops. All she could hear was the wind howling across the turf, laying even the short blades of grass down before it. There was a smell of earth and coming rain, the clouds scudded across the flat horizon like angry, over-stuffed pillows. Her heart thudded in time with the jigging of her horse while behind her, respectfully silent, rode Bert. Suddenly she had an urge to talk to someone and she swung in the saddle.

'This horse will cart me, Bert,' she said ruefully.

Bert urged Flagship beside her. 'Don't let him get hold of the bit,' he advised. 'Once he's into his stride you'll never hold him, so snatch him up early on. He bucks a bit, though.'

'So Mr Hennessey said.'

They rode on a few yards and then she said, 'Is he a good trainer do you think? It seems a fairly small yard to me.'

Bert grinned. 'Well it might to you, ma'am, seeing as you're with Mr Downing and Mr Priestley. But you see the guvnor takes care of his horses. Won't take just anything and what he does take, he looks after. Gets a lot of crocks does Mr Hennessey. If anyone can get them winning he can.' He suddenly saw the opportunity to transform his little world, and leaning across to her he said confidentially, 'If I was you, ma'am, I'd give Mr Hennessey a really good horse or two. There's a Northern Baby colt coming up, even the Arabs is fighting for it. Win the Derby with that Mr Hennessey could. And the Arc. If Mr Hennessey had a horse like that there'd be no stopping him –'

'Thank you, Bert, but I think it's early days for things like that, don't you?' said Jenna with a smile. 'If Mr Hennessey can do something with the horses he has now, well, we might give your idea some thought. It's kind of you to mention it.'

Bert flushed at the hint of patronage in her tone. 'You mark my words, he'd win the lot for you,' he reiterated and swung his horse round. 'This is where we start. Right. I'm off.' He gathered his reins, hitched his bottom out of the saddle and was away.

'May the Lord have mercy on my soul,' murmured Jenna, as she began her turn and was nearly cannoned out of the saddle by the colt's bound forward.

He was away before she could think, head up, legs streaking out in front of him. Mindful of Hennessey's words about bucking she set her weight against the bit, kept her head down and tried to catch her breath. It was thrilling! They zoomed past Flagship as if he was standing still, she could feel the power of the massive hindquarters driving the colt's back legs almost beyond his shoulders at every stride. The mane tangled in her mouth, she shook her head and spat, grateful for the goggles that shielded her eyes from the wind. In the distance she could see the other horses bunched and waiting, and realised in a moment she would have to stop. She knew she couldn't, she was nothing but a passenger, a leaf riding the storm. The horses before her began to spread out across the track and she had a sudden vision of a ghastly, bone-shattering collision. There was nothing for it but to stop. Making a huge effort of will she stood in the stirrups and leaned on the reins, knowing that the moment she raised her centre of gravity she was in immediate peril of falling off. The colt's stride shortened, for a wonderful moment she thought she had done it, but then came the buck. Head down, bottom up, and Jenna was sailing through the air to land with a thud on the ground. She lay there, winded, and savoured the knowledge that she was alive. Even the mud tasted sweet on her tongue.

Hooves sounded close to her head and with an effort she pulled herself on to her knees, hands on the floor, head hanging.

'So you're not dead then.' Hennessey had seen her lying deathly still and his heart had quailed. He dismounted and stood by her. Jenna looked up at him, like a lamb waiting for its bottle. Her face was thick with mud and when she pulled her goggles off they left two white circles in the grime.

'That was – absolutely – fantastic!' she panted, and her grin was as wide as the sky. She was like a woman after orgasm thought Hennessey, and his surge of lust made him shudder. God, he needed a woman.

He reached for her arm and hauled her to her feet, staggering, her legs weak and wobbly. 'Are you hurt?'

'No, no, I'm not. I don't think. Has the horse stopped yet?'

'Two of the lads are chasing him. He can't come to much harm up here. Look, I've got better things to do than fuss over you, go and sit in the hedge until it's time to go back. We'll pop you on Flagship and Bert can walk.'

She nodded, too used to people doing her favours to query the arrangement.

She settled herself amongst the hawthorn prickles and felt the cold creep from toes to hair, but it could not extinguish her glow of achievement. Hennessey was intent on his horses, watching them work in twos and threes. The older ones were sensible and most did no more than they must, but the youngsters and the hotheads needed riding. The trainer juggled with lads and mounts, making sure that there was no repeat of Jenna's spectacular performance. Not knowing one horse from another she was quickly bored and after a time she dragged herself out of the hedge, shook the leaves from her hair and sauntered over to Hennessey, her helmet dangling from one finger. He watched her approach out of the corner of his eye but sat his horse impassively.

'That looks a useful sort,' she remarked as one of his three-year-olds finished his pipe-opener looking fit to fly.

'Leg trouble, needs soft ground,' he commented shortly. 'He's racing Saturday, if it rains you should back him.' He wished she would go away, she made him uncomfortable.

'I told you, I never bet.' She trailed a hand down the shoulder of Hennessey's mount, a long slender hand, almost transparent in places with each tendon and muscle clearly visible.

'You should,' murmured the trainer. 'It's something else you might enjoy.'

She glanced swiftly up at him but he was looking at his horses. What would happen now if she ran her hand up his thigh? He turned his head to look at her and she was suddenly embarrassed, although everyone always looked at her and she thought little of it. On the beach in Italy this year she had wandered in and out of the sea as unselfconscious as if she was alone, while cameras clattered like a train going continuously over points. Almost every country in the world had a picture in some magazine or other, the elegant Mrs Sheppard, arrow-slim in her strapless, bright white swimsuit, wearing a pendant with a single, tear-shaped emerald. She had at once depressed the bikini market and promoted a craze for beach jewellery, and not for a moment had she shivered as she was shivering now.

'I'd like to go,' she said then. 'Can I go back now, please?'

'If you must. Here Bert, let Mrs Sheppard have Flagship. She can ride back with Geoff, he's finished.'

Bert slipped off the horse and led him over. Jenna was about to accept his leg-up when she took stock of the fact that he was thin, tired and at least a foot shorter than she. 'How will you get back?' she asked.

He shrugged. 'Walk, I suppose. It's not that far.'

'Then I should be the one to walk. I shall enjoy it.'

Bert looked uncertain. 'The guvnor won't like it.'

'Tell him I insisted. Give me your leg.' She tossed him into the saddle and started across the grass without a backward glance. She had hardly covered a hundred yards before Hennessey's horse caught up with her.

'Where do you think you're going?'

Her glance was cool and a little surprised. 'I am walking back, Mr Hennessey. Bert looks a look down I think, it leads one to wonder what it is you do to your staff. The horses look much healthier.'

'So they bloody should, they eat more. Bert looks tired because he's wasting and I should like to remind you that I give the orders around here. If I say he walks then he walks!' He struggled to slow his mount down to her pace, wondering why on earth he was making such a fuss. All at once Jenna stopped, so suddenly that he rode past her and had to turn round and come back. He was acutely conscious of the lads standing in a group with their eyes glued to the pair of them.

'We're not getting on very well, are we?' said Jenna.

'You're – I'm not very good with owners. Especially rich ones.'

She shook her head impatiently. 'I'm not a rich owner, my husband is. It isn't my money. Look, I enjoyed myself today and I'd like to come again, but I can't if it upsets you. It doesn't matter if I walk or Bert does, except that I shall enjoy it more. I've nothing else to do. Can I walk home by myself Mr Hennessey? Please?'

Her face was turned up to him, the mud dried to smears. He reached down and ran his thumb across her cheek, crumbling a pale bath through the dirt.

'You have my permission, Mrs Sheppard,' he said softly. Then, as she turned to go, he called, 'Will you come next Tuesday?'

She looked back, surprised. 'If I may.'

'Then don't be late.'

Lilian Hennessey sat in her kitchen and pasted another cutting into her scrap book. Only a brief note this time, and a little picture, of Jenna Sheppard on her way to a charity lunch. She gazed from the fuzzy newsprint, so cool and perfect, smiling only enough to show that her teeth matched her pearls. Lilian smiled back happily.

'I think she's wonderful.'

Hennessey snorted. 'She's certainly very rich.'

'Like something from another world. She's a fairytale come true.'

Lilian leafed through the pages, looking at Jenna alone or on the arm of her husband, in a ballgown or at the races. Dan watched her, wondering what he should say. There was no doubt that Lilian was very much better, but the improvement had come so suddenly that he hardly believed in it. Yesterday she had cooked supper and this morning she had cleaned up the kitchen. Grease still coated the Aga but she had swept the flagged floor and tidied the pantry. To Dan it seemed like a miracle, but a strange one, connected as it was with this absorption in the life of Jenna Sheppard.

'She's only human Lilian,' he ventured. 'I'll bring her in next time she comes.'

Lilian jumped. 'No! No, you mustn't. I'd be embarrassed and it would all be spoiled. Promise you won't, Dan?'

He nodded, secretly relieved that he did not have to explain his wife to Jenna. 'All right. I promise.'

Lilian smiled at him shyly and continued to turn the pages of her book. 'He was married before you know. He calls it a youthful mistake. They say he never talks about her because he's in love with Jenna. Well, anyone would be.'

'He's gone off to the States and left her behind. Doesn't seem very loving to me,' said Hennessey sourly.

'She'll be looking after the children.' Suddenly she put the book down and reached for her husband's hand, saying impulsively, 'You see, Dan, that's what makes me think we have something in common. She's so rich and lovely, she adores children, but she can't have any of her own. It must be dreadful for her! And when I see her being so brave about it all, when I'm – well – it makes you realise that it isn't so awful after all.'

Hennessey looks bewildered. 'What do you mean, Lilian? How do you know she can't have children?'

'It says so here, look.' She pointed to an article in her scrapbook. "*Early in her marriage Mrs Sheppard was a frequent visitor at a well-known Swiss clinic, noted for its work on infertility. So regularly did she attend that her*

43

husband rented a villa in the area, and they were seldom away from it for more than a few weeks at a time. Sadly the Sheppards have not been granted the blessing of a child, but Jenna devotes herself to the children of her husband's first marriage finding solace in their lively company. It is ironic that the woman who has everything is denied the one thing that she wants." They call her "Poor Little Rich Girl."'

Hennessey leaned over to read the article for himself. 'I wonder if it's true,' he said doubtfully.

'I'm sure it is. I've been thinking, Dan, do you think I should go back to the doctor? He said there were more things to try.'

'I know he did, love, but – suppose it didn't work?' He remembered all too well the terrible monthly glooms that had blighted their lives in the past, preceded by a euphoria that bordered on the hysterical. But if it meant the resumption of some form of married life it was not to be sneezed at. Then he paused, and a thought came to him. Did he want to return to closeness with Lilian? That had been his avowed aim for so long that he had ceased even to think about it, but now the possibility arose he found himself cautious. Their relationship had changed so much since those early days, their inequality of aims, achievements, even personalities had become so marked. He was the capable, efficient, stable one, she the dim shadow, like a backward child that needed his care. Sex with her seemed almost unthinkable.

He needed something though, that much was clear, for he was in danger of losing his judgment. Increasingly he found his thoughts clouded by the Sheppard woman, and it was hardly surprising. What man wouldn't find her desirable? Long and slim and cool as a glacier, but underneath a hint of flame. If he and Lilian managed to get something going again surely he would feel more in control of himself.

44

Lilian was playing with the scissors, opening and closing them with precise concentration. She was wearing a clean blouse and she had washed her hair, hinting at the girl she had been when they married, but with subtle differences of emphasis. Her eyes were shadowed and her skin looked thick and coarse. He thought of loving her and winced.

'I do want to try again, Dan,' said Lilian and raised her hand to look at him. For a dreadful moment he wondered if she could read what he had been thinking, and his eyes slid away.

'You don't want to try adoption.'

'They wouldn't take us. Not after – not with me being ill.'

He sighed. 'No. I suppose that's true. Well then, if you think it will be all right, we'll go ahead. I'll take you to the doctor tomorrow.'

'Yes. Yes, let's.' She sat for a moment and then burst out, 'I just know it's going to be all right this time! I will have a baby. Everything's got better since she came, she's like a good luck charm.'

A terrible sense of doom came over Hennessey. He felt as if his life was cartwheeling out of control. 'I'll go and check the horses,' he muttered and stumbled into the yard.

Jenna sat slumped in her chair with her eyes closed, listening to the lifesaving sound of Stephen mixing a cocktail. 'The trouble is,' she murmured, 'we've done everything and none of it took very long. Perhaps if we had to go to a tennis court or drive to the swimming baths it would be different, but this place is like a sports complex. We were finished by lunchtime.'

'They really enjoyed it though,' said Stephen, handing

her a frosted glass.

Jenna sipped gratefully. 'Did they? I think they'd have been much happier left to themselves, watching porno movies and brooding. And I know this afternoon was a disaster, Rachel sulked becuase I wouldn't buy her a see-through blouse and Tony thought it was sheer meanness not to let him have a scramble motorbike.'

'I'm afraid, dear, they're used to getting exactly what they want,' said Stephen, sinking into the chair and swinging an elegant ankle. 'You know you spoil them.'

'Well, it's got to stop. But what do we do tomorrow? And next weekend? And the one after that?'

'As for the one after that, you'll be in Kentucky, but I do see your problem. I always told you motherhood was overrated and now you see how right I was.'

Jenna grinned. 'I have always thought so Stephen, my love. It's William who has ideas of founding a dynasty, which is ironic when you think that I'm the one with the conscience as far as bringing them up is concerned. Except that they're not his ideal material, he might be different if they were. Do you think they'd like to take up stamp collecting?'

She looked so desperate that Stephen laughed. 'Frankly, my dear, I am quite sure they would hate it. They might show a momentary interest if you provided them with a couple of penny blacks to start them off, but apart from that – no.'

'Well, what then? Clothes and vice are not suitable hobbies for children. Of course, Rachel does like dogs – oh God, Stephen, do I have to get a dog?'

He was aghast. 'I hate dogs. Messes on the carpet and hair on the furniture. And it would fall to me to look after it when you're all away. If you must you must, I suppose, but please, only as a last resort.'

'You know I think I'd quite like a dog,' said Jenna. 'Dan

Hennessey's got a nice one, a Labrador. I could take it on walks.'

'Darling, you are not the doggy type,' objected her companion.

Jenna was nettled. 'I'm not the anything type. If I want a dog I shall have one regardless of whether it fits in with everyone's idea of the sort of thing I should or should not want. If the world wants to see me as a fashionplate it is no business of mine. I do not have to live up to their expectations.' She slumped back in her chair, the dark eyes flashing.

Stephen poured himself another drink, wondering why he should have touched a nerve with a remark so innocuous. 'I'll be going in a minute,' he said. 'I've someone staying.'

'Have you? I'm sorry if I snapped, Stevie. It's been a trying day.'

'I know, but I really do have someone staying. Have you heard from the lord and master today?'

'Yes, he rang about an hour ago. Seems quite happy.' The conversations with William were always without flaw, he was as efficient at phoning his wife as in any other sphere of activity. He enquired how she was, how things were going, moved on with a brief resumé of his own activities and ended by saying how much he missed her. It was no guide at all to his real state of mind, though oddly enough Jenna thought he did feel the lack when she stayed home. There was no-one in William's life with whom he could relax, except Jenna. One of the painful side-effects of riches was that even friends always had an axe to grind, perhaps they might want to borrow a villa, or they needed an introduction, or at the very least wanted a racing tip. Only Jenna asked for nothing. She had it all.

Stephen left and Jenna went to watch television with the children. Two more days to Tuesday she thought, and caught herself up. How foolish to be so thrilled by a simple ride. She thought of Dan Hennessey and smiled, it was funny watching a man of such obvious independence doing his best to be polite. A kind man, but not a soft one. Nowhere in him was the ruthlessness that was so much a part of William, who valued his own way above everything. She disliked that in her husband, but at the same time she was attracted by it. She gained something from being the beloved of a rich and powerful man.

The television film ended and she said brightly to the children, 'What shall we do tomorrow?'

'Don't know,' mumbled Tony.

'I've got to do my homework,' said Rachel. 'So's Tony.'

Jenna was at once filled with towering gratitude. Of course! Homework! How could she have forgotten such a wonderful invention. 'Right then, homework in the morning and a walk after lunch,' she declared and thought to herself only one empty day before Tuesday.

Chapter Three

It was never Jenna's intention to be late, but as she herself said, she always was. Minutes drifted past while she sat at her dressing table and let her mind wander, valuable seconds were used up in last-minute conferences with George. So it happened that despite being up at dawn she arrived at Hennessey's yard at ten past eight. Everyone was standing waiting.

She flung out of the car and dashed over to the horses, then slowed to a halt under the combined weight of their accusatory stares. Her fingers played uncertainly with the strap of the helmet she carried.

'You're late,' said Hennessey. 'Again.'

'I did try,' she apologised. 'I don't know where the time went –' she looked as bewildered as if she expected the recalcitrant ten minutes to crawl out from under a stone and Hennessey suddenly found himself grinning.

'Well, don't let's hang about now,' he blustered. 'I haven't got corn growing in Egypt.'

Jenna was putting on her helmet and surveying the leggy equines before her. 'What have you got for me today? Not Take-You-Down-A-Peg I hope.'

'We haven't got a horse called that,' said Bert, who regarded himself as on special terms with her since last week. 'You had Money Market.'

'Oh yes. So I did,' murmured Jenna but Hennessey would not meet her eye.

'You've got My Demand and he isn't very demanding,' he said briskly. 'Eats, sleeps and runs, that's all he does. One-paced, but as long as the others are slower that's all that counts. You'll like him.' He walked across to a nondescript brown horse with a bit too much flesh and Jenna followed. She gathered the reins on the horse's neck and crooked her knee for a leg-up. Hennessey toosed her effortlessly into the saddle and went over to his own mount, a retired steeplechaser with so much heart that he didn't notice his legs were worn out.

They set off for the gallops at what should have been a sober pace, were it not for the plungings and fidgetings of the hotheads in the string. Hennessey brought up the rear, resisting the almost overwhelming desire to ride next to Jenna. When he touched her his fingers felt hot. She had legs so long that when he made love to her she would lie under his body like a beautiful starfish, he would taste her hair and the scent of her sweat – he stopped himself with a shudder. There was no use thinking of it now.

Lilian had been to the doctor. She had pills and charts and a thermometer, and every day they went through the morning ritual of the temperature, waiting for the magic rise that signalled an instant demand for sex. It seemed so clinical somehow, and he was not at all sure that he even wanted a child. But if it helped Lilian he had no right to refuse.

If only she could achieve it without him. In the past, before she was ill, the sex had been good, somewhat ordinary perhaps but he had never once failed. When the depression engulfed her everything changed, she lay like a corpse beneath him or clawed and bit like a demented

50

she-wolf. He hated it, and it was the nearest he had ever come to hating her. Oddly enough, once sex no longer featured in their marriage he felt happier. She was the supplicant, he the provider, lending his strength to her weakness and asking nothing in return.

There had been women, old girlfriends mostly that he met at the races, but he hated himself for needing them. After all it was not Lilian's fault that she was as she was, it was not her fault that he could no longer desire her. He was sure that if he could manage the first time the problem would resolve itself, but the heat which he felt for the Sheppard woman was but ashes for his wife. So he stared at Jenna's small, tight bottom as it rode along in front of him and stored the resultant lust.

Jenna was feeling happy. Early autumn was a beautiful time, rich harvest before the cold. Her horse swished through the thin scattering of leaves on the road and the smell of horse and morning air made her blood run clear and fast. It was kind of Hennessey not to have been cross. On a sudden impulse she swung clear of the string, waited until Hennessey approached and then fell in beside him.

'I wanted to ask you something,' she began.

'Oh yes?' God, but it was hard to be polite to a woman when you have just been imagining the most torrid sex with her. That lovely, soft-skinned neck – his horse bounced forward and he quickly caught it up.

'It was only – well – what did you do when you were fourteen?'

He blinked at her. 'Do?'

'Yes. Do. In your free time. You see, Tony and Rachel have been a bit neglected recently and now their father's in America I wanted us to have time together. But I don't know what to do. They don't seem to have any interests at all, so I wondered – what did you do?'

Hennessey laughed. He was less good-looking when he

laughed thought Jenna, but far more approachable. 'It's not something you can do as a family, I'll tell you that,' he chuckled. 'As far as I can remember at around fourteen I lusted hopelessly after women. Everything else was a tedious interruption.' And nothing's changed he thought to himself and laughed again.

'Tony is well up on that,' said Jenna ruefully. 'He has piles of dirty magazines under his bed and I pretend I don't know about them. Perhaps I shouldn't leave them there but – do you think I should?'

Hennessey considered. 'Unless they're really grim then yes, I should. It's his bedroom, after all.'

'That's what I thought. But what did you do when you weren't getting overheated?'

'How nicely you put it, Mrs Sheppard. I rode horses. All the time. My father let me ride in point to points and so on, and I was desperate to be a jump jockey. Too big for the flat you see. And it took my mind off sex.'

'I don't think Tony rides that well,' mused Jenna, 'But then he hasn't had the practice. Mr Hennessey, do you have any horses that would suit –' but she stopped and blushed and shook her head. 'I'm sorry, that's an impertinence.'

'No, it isn't.' Hennessey reached out and touched her arm without realising what he was doing. 'He could come on Sunday afternoons and I'd school him over fences. I could borrow a horse from someone for a few months –'

'Oh, as to that, buy one for him,' broke in Jenna. 'I'll pay anything to keep him occupied.' Very gently she detached her arm from Hennessey's clasp and he unwillingly put his hand back on the reins.

'We'll do that then,' he said. 'You'll come on Sunday.'

She drew in her breath. 'Yes. I'll come.' Their eyes met. Both of them shivered.

It was nearly ten when they rode back into the yard.

The work had gone well and Hennessey was pleased, mentally turning over the race entries for the coming week. He'd declare most of them he thought, though not Dapper Dame, he'd hold her till next season. She might come as a three-year-old but he doubted it. A well-bred tortoise. Best to tell the owners now and get it over with.

A man was hovering near the gate, camera in hand. He began snapping the moment the string came into view, upsetting the horses and making the lads curse.

'What the devil do you want,' demanded Hennessey, swinging his horse in front of the camera and effectively blocking his view. 'You don't take pictures of my horses, fella, not without telling me who you are.'

The man shuffled round the horse's tail and Hennessey swore and dismounted. He grabbed the man by the arm and rammed him against the wall. 'I said stop! What the devil do you want anyway? Who are you?'

'Steady on, steady on, mate.' The man cradled his camera like a baby. 'I'm only after a few pictures of Mrs Sheppard. No harm in that is there? She doesn't usually mind.'

'How did you know she was here?' Somehow it alarmed him to think of men like this plotting her every move.

'Rang the house, didn't I? They'll often tell me. Old man Sheppard likes to see her in the papers, makes him feel good. She sells newsprint, she does. Here! Jenna! Take your hat off, love.'

Jenna behaved as if she hadn't heard, leading her horse into its stable and chatting to the lads as if the photographer didn't exist. When she took off her helmet it was in her own good time but the photographer caught the moment, snapping the picture under Hennessey's outstretched arm as he tried to prevent him coming through the gate.

'If you say where my yard is I'll sue you,' threatened

Hennessey. 'I can't have weasels like you crawling over the place. These horses are valuable, I've security to think of.'

'Then you'd better start locking things up, mate. Anybody could have walked in here while you were having your little trot. Be seeing you.' The man waved to Jenna, who didn't notice him, and dashed to where his car was parked under the hedge. Hennessey watched him drive off, his mood clouded. The man was right of course. Now he had the Sheppard horses he would have to start locking doors and employing nightwatchmen. It was a bore but the stable was in the public eye and there was no way he wanted a doping scandal or, God forbid, the theft of a horse. The thought made him ill and rushed into the yard, wandering about wildly counting heads.

'Whatever's the matter?' asked Jenna as she was about to get into her car. He stopped and grinned sheepishly. 'Nothing. Yet. You're an awful lot of trouble, Mrs Sheppard.'

'But am I worth it, Mr Hennessey?' she teased, and slipped behind the wheel. 'See you on Sunday.'

The following day, all the popular dailies featured a picture of Jenna, her hair tousled and her cheeks flushed.

'Doesn't she photograph well?' enthused Lilian, cutting the biggest for her scrap book. The caption read *Beauty and the Beast* although not an inch of horseflesh could be seen.

'What? Yes, she does.'

Lilian's temperature was up this morning. She had made up the bed with stiff, clean sheets and placed the leaflet with suggested positions on the bedside table. It was like going to the dentist thought Hennessey grimly, and it had as much to do with passion as a medical. But Lilian was doing her best, she had cooked him bacon and ⌐reakfast. He supposed it was her idea of the proper diet for a stud.

'Lilian, do you ever think you might have married someone else?' he asked suddenly.

She looked at him in surprise. 'No, never Dan! I need you. I couldn't do without you. Why, all my life you've been around, I always knew I'd marry you.' She smiled at him happily and he felt mean. Of course she wanted him for more than his sperm. He was her – nurse. Just as her parents had cared for her, so now did he.

He stomped into the yard, resolved to check up on security. As always the stables were immaculate, for he liked his staff to think that he noticed everything. It was impossible, but as long as they believed it they were unlikely to neglect their expensive charges in even the smallest detail, convinced that he knew if they left even one marble of dung hidden under the straw. But he seldom went into the lads' quarters, for it was their own place and he respected it. Today though he was looking at windows and locks.

The lads lived in the top half of the barn, in wooden floored rooms with the bare minimum of furniture. It was not luxurious but it was adequate, and they only stayed there until they could find a place in the village. At the moment there were seven living-in, but they made mess enough for twenty. Clothes, boots and beer cans lay scattered around, and from evey side there stared pictures of Jenna Sheppard. Hennessey clutched at his hair. He was going mad, he was sure of it. Everywhere he looked the woman was there, in the house, in the yard, on the horses and now coming at him from the walls. There she was in a swimsuit, lean and straight and lovely. He felt himself harden and thanked God he was alone. At least it meant he could still do it, all it needed was the stimulus.

Looking furtively around to make sure he was not watched, he carefully detached the picture from the wall, folding it and slipping it into his pocket. Then he moved all the others up to fill the gap. If the lads could have her as a pin-up and centre their lonely fantasies around her, then so could he. That decided, he went round checking the windows and noting the need for padlocks.

That night, Lilian went to bed early. 'I'll have a bath and wait for you to come up,' she said pointedly. 'You know what day it is, don't you?'

'Yes. Yes, I know,' said Hennessey, looking at her from under his eyelids. She was wearing a jumper and skirt, and through them he could see the bulges of flesh around waist and hips. It was the body of a woman who never takes exercise, flabby and dead white. Her breath smelled faintly of onions. When she went out of the room he subdued a rising tide of panic, there was no way he could make love to her tonight. There was half a bottle of whisky in the cupboard and he poured himself a tumbler, forcing it down like medicine. If he could relax it would be all right, tension was the enemy. That and the cold, sick feeling he had in the pit of his stomach.

After a while the whisky began to warm him, and he took the picture from his pocket, spreading it on the table and staring at it. Did she know the fires she lit in men she had never met? Did she understand how much power it gave her? He began to imagine taking her into a quiet room. He would first remove the pendant, it would fall to the floor with a soft thud. Then he would kiss her throat, sliding the straps of her swimsuit down and tangling his hands in her hair –

'Lilian,' he called, 'are you ready?'

'Yes. Come to bed, Dan.'

He slid the swimsuit round her knees and bent to kiss her belly. She moaned and reached for him. Well, he was ready now as he would ever be. He downed the last of and jumped to his feet, feeling himself rasping against his trousers. Racing upstairs he dashed into the bedroom, casting off clothes with barely a glance at Lilian, laying naked in bed with the sheet to her chin. But he could hardly ram himself into her without a word or a gesture of love. Gritting his teeth he climbed into bed and began at once to nuzzle her neck, catching the scent of her onion breath above the toothpaste. Oh God, he wouldn't be able to do it. He sucked at a nipple and tasted soap, he reached between her legs and his fingers caught on hair like wire. It was awful! Oh Jenna, Jenna where are you he begged, but there was no sound but his own harsh breathing. The image of her long, slim thighs floated into his mind. When she spread her legs to welcome him she would smell of roses. With a rasp of thankfulness he straddled his wife and pushed himself strong and hard into her waiting body.

Jenna was also in bed, curled up with a book and a glass of milk. It was pleasant to nestle against the pillows, listening to the noises of the house. When the children were away at school and she was alone but for George and Elsa, like mice in the basement, it seemed to become her own place, whereas when they were all there together it was just a house, on which everyone placed their mark. Through the uncurtained window she could see but one light, that of Stephen's cottage. She had glimpsed the latest boyfriend today, a long-stayer of some two weeks. It was strange but though she thought Stephen looked like a homosexual, if you knew what to look for, the boyfriends never did. Did they not like women at all, she wondered? If not why not? This man was short with thick, strong arms and he had looked at her and smiled. If Stephen was a woman for him what was wrong with the real thing? She lay and pondered with the insatiable curiosity of women everywhere as to what they really did.

The telephone next to her shrilled in its well-bred way and she waited a moment before she picked it up. It would be William.

'Hello,' she said and knew the urge to hang up and pretend they'd been cut off. Her mood was so pleasant and warm, and William was going to spoil it.

'Jenna.' He spoke softly and she knew there was someone there. Why did he bother her when he had some slut close to hand?

'Are you missing me?' he asked and Jenna paused before answering. He never usually asked her that.

'I am a little,' she admitted, but her tone was distant. 'The house seems very empty with the children away.'

'You can always come out, you know. I should like you to.'

'I wonder why? Where is she now darling, nibbling your left ear?'

William sucked in his breath in annoyance. She knew him better than to think he'd keep anyone in the house.

'You're being ridiculous, Jenna, and I dislike it. I won't have you talking like this. When we spoke before we said everything there was to be said and the subject is closed. Do you understand me?'

A sigh crossed the thousands of miles between them and he felt suddenly confused. 'Jenna –' he began, but she cut across him.

'Actually, William, I wanted to change my flight anyway, and come out a few days later than planned. Hennessey's racing our filly and I'm taking the children to watch. I promised.'

All thought of conciliation left him. 'I won't have it,' he snapped. 'I have a right to expect my wife to be beside me and I will not come second to those appalling brats. You are not their mother and they have no right to your

58

attention, whereas I do. You will come out as planned, Jenna!'

She held the receiver a little away from her ear and winced. There was no way she could go back on her promise now and she would not, but William in this mood was frightening.

'Don't shout at me,' she said her voice trembling slightly. 'I can't bear it when you shout at me.'

William was taken aback. It was most unlike Jenna to quail. 'I'm sorry – I didn't mean to sound overbearing,' he said stiffly.

'It was my fault. I didn't explain – I thought you'd like me to see how the filly runs. After all, there isn't much of the season left and I'd like to see if Hennessey's made any difference to her. Shall I come out on the Monday?'

If he said no, they would be at daggers drawn and she might not come at all. She was perfectly capable of it. Now it was his turn to sigh. 'All right, darling. But please, when you are here, try for a little warmth, Jenna. Surely I have the right to expect that.'

She suppressed a stinging retort and instead said, 'Monday it is, then. I'll look forward to it.'

'Will you Jenna?'

In reply there was a gentle laugh, followed by a click as she replaced the receiver. William stared at the dead phone in his hand and then hurled it against the wall.

Hennessey looked at the boy's tense face and felt a pang. Had he been like this once, declaring his feelings for all the world to see despite his earnest attempts to hide them? Tony was strutting like a turkey cock, snapping at Jenna and Rachel, fooling nobody.

'I've only got him on trial,' said Hennessey soothingly. 'If you don't like him I'll send him back. Looks a good sort, though.'

The short-coupled, bouncy animal before them stamped his feet and jingled his bit. 'Will I have to jump him?' asked Tony.

Hennessey considered. If he said no, then Tony wouldn't and the fear would linger for a week. If he said yes, it would be over in a moment. 'You can pop him over one or two,' he said and saw Jenna's hands clasp themselves together.

When Tony went to put his helmet on Hennessey walked behind Jenna and murmured, 'You're as nervous as he is. Don't worry, I won't kill him.'

She turned quickly and gave him a rueful smile. Her scent drifted to him and his heart missed a beat and for a moment he could do nothing but look at her.

'Can Casey come?' asked Rachel.

'Er – I don't see why not,' said Hennessey. 'We're only going into the paddock.'

'How much land do you have?' asked Jenna.

'About fifty,' he replied calmly. 'I rent it from my father, he farms next door. He'd like me to take over the farm really, but I've no interest. It's the training I like, it's what I'm good at.' He seemed so much in control of himself that Jenna wondered if she had been mistaken before. He had looked – wanting.

'Don't you have any ambitions? William always has a dozen.'

He laughed incredulously. 'What for God's sake? He already owns the world.'

'Oh you know, Derby winner, biggest electronics manufacturer, most profitable stallion, that sort of thing. He's never satisfied.'

'I don't suppose anyone is. Yes, I have ambitions. I want Classic winners, all trainers do. Which is why we are in league, he and I, in that one instance we are going in the

60

same direction.'

'Will you get there do you think?' Jenna looked at him curiously.

He concealed the hard purpose with a joke. 'With his money and my talent, how can we lose?'

The paddock was large, about four acres, with small schooling fences at one end and a couple of steeplechase brushes at the other.

'I used to have jumpers, when I first started,' Hennessey explained. 'I'd done a bit of riding and I had the contacts. And I have the odd flat horse go on over hurdles.'

'None of ours I hope,' objected Jenna and he grinned.

'Nothing so low-class for a Sheppard horse. They're all brilliant.' He was mocking her and she turned her shoulder to him, watching Rachel play with the dog. She seemed a child today, when sometimes she could be as hard and knowing as a girl from the streets. Jenna hated that. It was one of the things she vowed to change.

Tony was trotting round the field and Hennessey left Jenna's side to go to him. 'How does he feel?'

'Takes a bit of a hold,' gasped Tony, whose teeth where being rattled through his skull.

Try and relax a bit. You make him think there's something to worry about,' suggested Hennessey, inwardly wondering if the nag was too much for him. Jenna would hate it if he fell off. All the same, millionaire's son or not this was a boy like any other and he would not benefit from coddling. 'Take him once round the field,' he suggested. 'At a canter.'

Tony's white, set face made him hide a smile, but the boy did not hesitate. He steered down the field, relaxed his hold and was away.

'My God, he'll be killed!' moaned Jenna.

'Tony! Tony!' wailed Rachel.

'Shut up both of you and let him ride,' snapped the trainer, sinking his hands into his pockets and scowling. If the lad kept yanking the reins like that he would be bucked off.

To everyone's relief matters improved as the gelding settled into his stride. Tony relaxed and sat still, and it was an almost presentable twosome that swept past and round again.

'Can he stop?' asked Jenna doubtfully.

'He will when they run out of steam,' said Hennessey.

'Dan! Dan!' called a voice. 'Telephone for you.'

Jenna turned and looked at the small, dumpy woman calling from the gate.

'Hell,' said Hennessey. 'Keep an eye on him for me, I'll be back in a minute.'

He jogged off towards the house, his long legs covering the ground with the ease of one of his racehorses. Rachel and Jenna stood and concentrated on Tony, sure that if they stopped watching for an instant he would be off. But this time round he was riding with confidence, and pulled up in front of them puffing.

'That was super,' he gasped. 'Where's Dan?'

'Mr Hennessey has gone to the telephone,' said Jenna pointedly. 'Be polite to him please, he's being very kind. He's left me in charge so you can trot in figure eights till he comes back.'

'I'd rather try those fences,' said Tony eagerly.

'Not till he comes back you don't, they're huge.'

'Are they?' Anxious young eyes stared down at her.

She said hastily, 'They take care over big ones. That's why he has them I expect.'

Just then Hennessey jogged back over the field. 'What, standing around already? You'll freeze him to death. I want a trotted circle, into a canter, take hold of the mane and try that fence. If you pull his mouth I'll belt you one, so remember to hold the mane. Off you go.'

Tony set off, his face chalky. Nobody said a word until he was heading for the fence when Hennessey bellowed, 'Kick him on, kick him on!' and Rachel squeaked and clutched the dog. The horse took it perfectly, but not so Tony, landing with a thump in the saddle with both irons gone and a deathgrip on the mane.

'Do it again,' intoned Hennessey and Tony scrambled back into position and set off.

'Who was that woman?' asked Jenna, simply for something to say. She imagined it was his housekeeper or something.

'What? oh that was Lilian. My – wife.'

There was an unhappy silence. He glanced down at Jenna but her face was calm and still, the smooth untroubled mask she kept for strangers. 'I didn't know you were married,' she said lightly. He had a desperate urge to deny Lilian and say that it was all a mistake, but Rachel was there, and besides, it was Lilian. That shy and trusting smile. It wasn't her fault.

'She's very shy,' he said defensively. 'Doesn't like meeting strangers.'

'What, not ever? How very difficult.'

'It is sometimes.' There, he had betrayed her and he hated himself for it. Lilian had no-one if not him.

Tony was bouncing round and round the field, negotiating the jump with increased confidence, if not increased skill.

'I think that's enough,' said Hennessey and called him in. 'Now you can groom him, Tony. Rachel can help.'

'But – don't you have lads to do that sort of thing?' asked Tony, looking affronted. 'I'm sure my father pays enough.'

'He pays for his racehorses, not for your toys. It's Sunday and there's no-one working except me and I didn't ride him. Get going.'

'I don't know what to do,' said Rachel and looked almost tearful. Hennessey dropped a hand on her shoulder and squeezed. 'Then I'll show you. I like your hair that colour, I forgot to say. Makes you look more human. Pretty.'

Rachel blushed a fiery red and looked helplessly at Jenna. She laughed.

'Darling, when a man pays you a compliment you must always thank him, otherwise he won't do it again. You can say "thank you" and smile, or just smile and incline your head – that's being very gracious – or if, as in this case, you think he's getting a bit carried away you tease him a bit. "Didn't I look pretty before, Mr Hennessey? You said I did. Don't you tell the truth, Mr Hennessey? What a lot there is that you don't tell me. And to think that I trusted you so!"'

Hennessey said, 'Ignore her, Rachel, your mother's a flirt.'

'She's not my mother!' It was said with violence and Hennessey saw a swift shock cross Jenna's face.

'And it's your loss, Rachel,' he said with quelling emphasis and this time it was Jenna's turn to blush.

Once the children had been set to grooming, Jenna and Hennessey wandered round the boxes, looking at the horses. She would not stand still, but wherever her restless movement took her he followed. At last he said, 'We've looked at them all twice. I'm getting giddy.'

She sighed and stuck her hands in her pockets. 'Aren't they finished yet? They're taking ages.'

'I thought that was what you wanted. Look, I'm sorry I can't ask you in – as I said, my wife –'

'Doesn't like strangers. Am I so strange, Mr Hennessey?'

He reached for the collar of her coat and turned it

down, letting his thumb trail along the line of her jaw. He could feel the tremor that shook her muscles.

'Like a bird of paradise. You brighten people's lives.'

She pulled away, going again to a box and looking distractedly inside. 'Rachel doesn't think so.'

'That's children for you. They're never grateful.'

'I always think it would be different if they were my own. Perhaps it wouldn't. Hennessey, do you ever think it would all be right if there was just someone – anyone – who stayed constant? Everyone's always changing. There isn't any – firmness. Anywhere.'

He stared at her pale profile and knew the urge to hold her. 'I don't think we're supposed to find that in life. I never have. And after all, we manage, we learn to be on our own. It's like trains, sometimes when you're with someone you seem to be running side by side, but then you find you're going to different places. If you meet them again you've changed or they have. Nothing stays the same.'

Jenna's eyes sparked with tears. 'It's very lonely.'

'Oh Jenna –' His face was inches from her own, she could feel his breath on her cheek. And then Tony said, 'There you are, you two. We've finished. He looks a picture, come and see.'

They did not jump apart but stood as if frozen. After several seconds Hennessey turned and followed Tony.

All at once he was acutely aware that he had been about to kiss Jenna Sheppard in full view of the house. If he had wanted to wreck his life there would be no more effective way of achieving it. That child had upset her and she needed comfort, but not once had she invited seduction. Except that she did so with every smile and gesture. Suppose she told her husband – or if Lilian had seen it – he went cold. It was time he got a grip on himself and stop this foolishness.

Jenna trailed behind, equally disturbed. She was taking advantage of a kind, married man. Long experience had taught her that given time most men would make a pass at her, and in general she made sure that they did not get the opportunity. It was embarrassing for both of them. But this time she had felt such a desire to be held and comforted and it was only weakness that made her embroil this man. He was married, and she of all people should know how hard it was when a husband strayed. When they admired the horse she stood well away from him, and soon called the children to the car.

'You'll come on Tuesday.' Hennessey caught her eye over the children's heads.

Jenna's gaze slid away. 'Not this Tuesday, no.'

'Why not?'

She shrugged. 'I've other things to do. Besides, I've had enough of horses.'

'But we're coming to see the filly run on Saturday,' interrupted Tony. 'You promised, Jenna.'

'Did I? But are you sure you really want to go? Oh all right, all right, all right!' She covered her ears with her hands at the howls of protest and Hennessey felt a wave of relief wash over him. Surely he could make up the ground on Saturday.

On the way home, Tony said, 'Does he fancy you, Jenna?'

'Don't be silly. He's married.'

Tony laughed dirtily. 'That never stopped anybody. Will you go to bed with him?'

'Tony! You have a revolting mind and what's more you don't understand what you're talking about. I hate it when you behave like some ghastly pimp.'

'What's a pimp?' asked Rachel.

'Never you mind. I'll come to the races but you can go by yourselves next Sunday. I'm not coming.'

'That proves it,' declared Tony. 'He did make a pass at you. What'll you give me not to tell Dad?'

'Really, Tony, you have a hectic imagination,' said Jenna in a bored voice. 'Why you think I should like to stand getting frozen while you gallop round a field is beyond me. I only came this time in case they had to bring you home on a rail.'

'I thought it was so we could have a lovely time as a family,' said Rachel nastily, and Jenna rounded on her.

'What is it with you? I do my absolute best and all you can do is be hurtful and unkind. I'm not your real mother, I know I'm not, if I was I wouldn't have to put up with half the horrible things you come out with.' The car swerved dangerously and Jenna dragged it back to the right side of the road.

There was silence from the back. 'You're not usually so touchy,' said Rachel in a small voice.

'We're sorry we upset you,' said Tony grudgingly.

Jenna swallowed the lump in her throat. 'And I'm sorry I got so cross. I'm trying hard. So is Mr Hennessey, and he's got less reason, and why you can't be nice –'

'I won't tell Dad,' promised Tony.

'There's nothing to tell!' shrieked Jenna and the car skidded into their drive, narrowly missing the gatepost. When she drew up before the door she sat holding the wheel and rested her head on her hands.

Jenna's racegoing clothes varied from designer tweeds to silk and lace. For an outing with the children she selected clothes which she considered to be motherly, namely a brown cord suit and cream blouse. The suit screamed 'style' from its short boxy jacket to its full, deep pocketed skirt, and when she added high-heeled ankleboots and coiled her hair into a bun secured with pins of real gold, she looked like a sex queen playing school marm. Rachel took one look and glowered. 'I wish I'd kept my hair blue,' she mumbled.

'But you look lovely, darling,' declared Jenna, realising for the first time that next to her Rachel was a mouse. 'How about some mascara, she suggested dubiously.

'Oooh, can I?'

'Yes.' It was definitely unsuitable for twelve-year-olds, but she could not endure an afternoon of sulks. From mascara they graduated to a touch of lipstick and blusher, followed by a raid on Jenna's jewellery case and wardrobe. Rachel emerged rather highly coloured, wearing a knitted red hat and matching six foot scarf, four bracelets and a brooch.

'You look super,' said Jenna and Rachel grinned at her reflection in the mirror. Thank God William wasn't here to see, thought Jenna and steered her little flock towards the Rolls.

Stephen was coming in as they left. He glanced at Rachel and his eyebrows lifted. 'Good heavens. Jenna love, there are limits.'

'How narrow-minded of you, Steve. Is your friend still staying?'

To her amazement, Stephen blushed. 'Yes, yes – just for a week or so. It's all right, isn't it?'

'Nothing to do with me. Do please ask Elsa if you'd like anything cooked, she doesn't have much to do during the week.'

'Darling, that's sweet of you,' enthused Stephen. 'Though how you can justify keeping a cook to butter crispbread and scrape raw carrots is beyond me. It's making her depressed.'

She has lots to do at weekends,' objected Jenna. 'The children eat like kings. But we have to go, Steve, tell Elsa I said it was all right.' She waved a hand and joined the children in the back of the Rolls.

It was a dull afternoon and the racetrack was not yet crowded, but nonetheless Jenna attracted her usual comet's tail of photographers and the curious. The children trailed along beside her looking embarrassed and very young. Both of them beamed with relief when they saw Dan Hennessey.

'Mr Hennessey,' called Tony. 'Over here!'

Hennessey schooled his face into polite warmth and strolled across from the paddock. He looked very professional in his green and brown tweeds, his racegoing trilby tipped rakishly over one eye.

'No need to bellow Tony,' he admonished. 'I couldn't exactly miss you.'

Tony glanced ruefully at the goggling crowds. 'It's always like this with Jenna. I hate it.'

'It was your idea to come!' objected Jenna and fiddled with the clasp of her bag. The usual serene calm of her features was absent, she was flushed and slightly ruffled.

'We've got an hour before the race,' said Hennessey. 'I've one other runner to saddle, why don't you all come and help me? The owner isn't here.'

'Yes, please,' said Tony and Rachel bounced with excitement. Jenna shook her head.

'I won't, I'll only make you uncomfortable.'

'What will you do?' Hennessey's voice held a soft throb, but she would not look at him.

She shrugged. 'Have a drink. Wander about. There'll be someone I know. Oh look – there's Lord Staveley.'

Tony gave a whoop of amusement. 'You'll love that. Here he comes, Jen, passion on two legs.'

'Jenna! How wonderful to see you here. And Tony and little girl Rachel.' The florid, toothy face with its big nose and receding hair advanced upon them.

Jenna smiled weakly. 'Hello, Rupert.'

'Didn't think I'd see you with Bill in the States. Well Dan, how does it feel to have one of the world's great beauties at your side?' He put his arm round Jenna's shoulders and gave her an affectionate squeeze.

'You're supposed to say "thank you" for compliments,' said Rachel demurely and Jenna bared her teeth in what should have been a smile. 'How right you are, Rachel. But Rupert is all flattery.'

'Nonsense! I bet Dan hasn't known which way is up since you appeared on the horizon, have you, Dan?'

Jenna looked at him and noticed that he looked oddly pinched and white. 'At least I don't maul her all the time,' he snapped. 'Take your hands off her, Rupert, you can see she doesn't like it.'

Staveley was too dim to listen. 'Nonsense! Jenna and I are old friends.' He leaned over and gave her a smacking kiss on the cheek. 'Tell you what, my darling, let's you and me have a drinkie and a chat. You can look after the sprogs can't you, Dan? Here Tony, buy some sweeties for you both.' He fished in his pocket and extracted a fiver which Tony accepted with alacrity.

'I'll come back as soon as I can,' said Hennessey to Jenna. She met his gaze.

'Thank you.' Then they were parted as Staveley dragged his prize to the bar, intent on sitting her down so he could stroke her knee.

Hennessey's horse came third. Jenna missed the race, trapped in the bar by Staveley who was getting more and more drunk. When Hennessey came to look for her he could see she was on the brink of making a scene as Staveley breathed brandy fumes on her neck and played with the buttons of her blouse.

'Mrs Sheppard.'

Jenna looked up with a relieved and radiant smile. 'Mr Hennessey.'

Staveley caught her waist as she stood, saying, 'You can't steal her, Dan, she's mine for the day!' but he found himself meeting Hennessey's cold glare. The man looked murderous.

'Leave her alone, Rupert. You've had enough cheap thrills for one day.' He put his own arm round Jenna and guided her through the people that thronged the bar.

'Thanks,' said Jenna gratefully. 'He was getting drunk and stupid. I don't know why, but I find him so hard to deal with, he doesn't believe I don't like it.'

'No brains, that's his trouble,' grunted Hennessey. He suddenly felt reckless. It seemed to him sometimes that he was always hedged in with rules; whenever he did something he had to weigh it against who would, or would not approve. There was a time to forget the rules, and here was Jenna. She needed him, she was happy at his side, and for his part he was weak from wanting her. 'Look,' he said, 'I've left the children with the lads, a bit more fun for them I thought. Let's go and back something for the next race.'

'I've told you, I never bet.' But Jenna was all at once girlish and silly, alone with him here. The photographers had wandered away and she felt somehow free.

'I do. Let's go and play.' He grinned at her and she felt her head spin. Too much of Lord Staveley's alcohol.

They made their way into the Silver Ring and along the lines of bookies. 'Honest Joe – We Never Welch.' 'Smith's of Gateshead – established one hundred years.' It was very crowded, people milled around like cattle. Hennessey took her hand and led her up and down, looking for the best odds.

'You put it on,' he urged, and slipped a tenner into her hand.

'But I don't know how!' In the crowd, pushed so close to him, she felt anonymous. No-one was watching here.

'Just say "Five quid each way, Donegal Lady." Try it.'

She tentatively waved her money at a beery, red-faced man with a silk cravat, whose board gave odds of ten to one. He took her note and when he gave her the ticket she put it into Hennessey's top pocket.

'It looks safer there.' As she pushed it down she felt his hand in the small of her back, drawing her to him. They stood, bodies touching, in the midst of the throng.

'Does this happen to you a lot?' murmured Hennessey in her ear.

She gulped. 'Not often, no. Never in fact. What do you want, Mr Hennessey?'

'I should have thought that was obvious.' It was delicious and mad and he could not stop himself. He pressed her closer for the race was running and all heads were turned to the horses.

'You are the most desirable woman I have ever seen,' he whispered, and crushed her hips into him. 'Oh Jenna, Jenna, I want you.'

She threw her head back and stared into his eyes. 'You don't understand – you wouldn't like it. They all think it would be so marvellous, but – men don't like sleeping with me.'

He looked down at her, bewildered. 'What do you mean? Who doesn't?'

'I tell you it would all be a miserable flop.' Tears sparkled on her lashes but the crowd was roaring and they could talk no more. She pulled away from him and gazed blindly at the backs of the people in front. The noise rose to a crescendo of yelling and then died to a murmur. Everyone began to move away.

'It's won,' said Hennessey and his voice was thick. 'Collect your winnings, Mrs Sheppard.'

'It was your money. You go and get it.' The tears were on her cheeks now.

'Jenna –' he took her arm. 'I've got to talk to you. I've got to see you alone.'

'There's no point.' She pushed her hands into the pockets of her skirt and began to walk back to the members' enclosure.

'There is a point! I don't know what you're talking about but I do know that it matters. I want so much to make love to you, I've got it so bad I can't think straight. You don't know what it's like to want something so much –'

She turned then and faced him. 'Why should I not know? I can feel some things and I do this. What I know as well is that it's all fake. You've no idea how disappointed you'd be. Wouldn't you rather leave it like this than go on and find it was all a sham? Because it is, you know.'

Hennessey was white with exasperation. 'Will you tell me what you mean,' he insisted, looking around wildly. Tony and Rachel were making their way towards them. 'Damn,' he muttered. 'I've got to saddle your filly but after that I want to talk. Here, take the ticket and go and get the money.'

He stuffed the slip into her hand and pushed away into the crowd. Jenna stood with it limp in her fingers and sent Tony to claim the winnings.

The filly won by a neck. Jenna smiled and smiled, and thanked everyone in sight, well aware that it meant more to almost everyone than it did to her. Hennessey looked preoccupied and grim, his eyes drawn to Jenna and then flickering quickly away. There was champagne to buy and they both drank as if it were water. Tony and Rachel each had half a glass and became giggly.

'Tuesday,' muttered Hennessey. 'Will you come?'

She looked vague. 'On Tuesday? No, no I can't. I'm flying to Kentucky on Monday.'

'How long for? I have to speak to you, I won't be put off.'

'It's only two weeks, but – I can't see you. Please, there's no point, I told you.'

Lord Staveley was rolling towards them, towing a friend, and Hennessey knew that it was hopless.

'I'll ring you,' he hissed, 'when you come back.'

She nodded, absently, and extended a hand and a smile to the newcomers.

Chapter Four

As the little plane circled prior to landing, Jenna could see set out below the neat squares and rectangles of the stud. It was all so formidably well planned, the road was straight, the fences were straight, and the house presided over ranks of long, straight barns. But the horses softened the scene, racing away from the roar of the plane's twin jets. This was the moment Jenna hated, the swift dip and plunge on to the short grass airstrip. Oddly enough she always trusted airline pilots, anonymous supermen rarely seen, but gum-chewing Arnold, who had two children, a divorce and corns, seemed far too human to inspire her faith. As the grey–blue grass rushed up to meet them Jenna silently prayed.

William stood waiting at the edge of the strip, relaxed in open-necked shirt and slacks. He was flanked by Gerard, his creased and weathered farm manager of many years' service, and Harold Warburton, one of William's several business executives, all of them unnaturally suave. Jenna knew both men quite well and was not surprised to see them. Her husband liked to greet her in consort, it bestowed favour on the men he allowed to accompany him.

'Hello, darling.' William came towards her with outstretched arms and Jenna went into them, turning her cheek for his kiss. She released herself at once and held out her hand to the manager. 'Hello again, Gerard. It's lovely to see you looking so well. You too Harold, how is Marjory?'

They both smiled with real pleasure, flattered that she remembered them. When they went home tonight they would tell their wives, 'I saw her. She asked after you' and there would be no doubt at all who they meant. Everyone began to walk to the house, their feet crunching on the stiff, short, vitamin-rich grass that was the bone and muscle of the priceless stock in the paddocks.

'Are you tired?' asked William. 'We've been invited to the Maclarens tonight and I should like to go. Just a small party.'

'Then of course we shall go.' She smiled at a black maid standing by the door. 'Perhaps Shirley would unpack for me. How are you, Shirley, and the children?'

William had to admire her. Jenna captured hearts without even trying, following a lifetime's training of memory and manners. It was superficial but it was not studied, and the spell she wove survived even her periodic bouts of icy withdrawal, when no-one could speak to her and her smile was gone. It was odd that a woman who could charm so easily should have no close friends. Those who tried to get to know her, and there were many, would find themselves confronted by a polite, impenetrable wall.

William led the way into the huge, airy sitting room, with panelled walls, parquet floor and a vast fireplace for the log fires of winter. On average they spent three months a year here, but the place was always held ready for a visit. They entertained a lot, rewarding friends and business colleagues with a stay at the Kentucky stud. Then the lavish, many-roomed house came into its own and the Sheppards hosted their parties with elegance and style. There had been fewer recently though, and it was because of Jenna, who would not entertain women for William to seduce. She sometimes wondered if anyone ever said no, for William's money and the aura of power seemed irresistible. Even when their husbands knew or suspected, they would still sneak away into the swimming pool changing room with William, while Jenna pretended not to notice.

'Drinks everyone?' William went to the trolley and poured martinis.

Almost every other house in the county had a bar, as vast and lavish as they cared to make it, and to Jenna's way of thinking in dubious taste. Wherever she was in the world she remained cool and English, and William loved it. She was a woman apart and she had a glow for him that no-one else possessed, brighter now in the light of their parting. He was like a man who owns a Stradivarius, struck anew by its beauty every time he opens the case. When the glasses emptied William did not refill them and the visitors took the hint.

'Be seeing you, Mrs Sheppard.'

'My pleasure, ma'am.'

Jenna smiled and remained seated.

When they were gone William poured two more martinis and held one out to his wife. 'I'm sacking Gerard,' he said casually, because the thought was in his head.

She was taken aback. 'What? But – why? He's been here since the stud first started, he knows more about it than anyone.'

'And he's set in his ways. Don't worry, I'll pay him well enough. It's time we had a new man with new ideas, I've already made the appointment.'

She swallowed. 'It will finish him. This place is his life, William, you can't.'

'Damn it, Jenna, I wouldn't have told you if I thought you'd be sentimental. Racing's a business and breeding's a business, I have to make business decisions. Gerard's out. We'll give him a gold watch or something, he'll like that.'

'He'll throw it back in your face.'

'Not if you give it to him. Tell me, how are the children?'

She felt confused. 'Oh God, I don't know –'

'The children, Jenna.' One thing was certain, he would not be taken to task on his business dealings. He allowed Jenna a lot of leeway but in this he always held firm. She would learn not to be so soft.

'All right, the children! Tony's riding at Hennessey's once a week and Rachel goes with him. I'm thinking about getting her a dog.'

'But that's ridiculous. She'd be incapable of looking after it and the task will fall to you. Besides, we're away too much.'

Jenna ran her finger round the rim of her glass. Her head ached and the thought of going out weighed heavy. 'I thought it might be good for her – but we can talk about it. What time's this party?'

'I thought we'd leave around nine.'

He sat on the arm of her chair and rested a hand on her shoulder. 'How have you been, darling? Have you missed me?'

She glanced up. 'Yes. Yes, I think I have. But I was right to stay home you know, the children are nicer already.'

'I've missed you, Jenna.' William slid his hand down the front of her crisp linen shirt and immediately she tensed.

'Don't. Not here.'

'Then come upstairs. I want my wife's beautiful body.'

78

It occurred to Jenna to wonder what he wanted it for, since he satisfied himself sexually elsewhere. To establish territorial rights perhaps, he liked to use the things he owned. 'I'm sorry, William, but I don't want to. I'm tired after all I think.'

'Come, darling, not so tired, surely?' He reached again into her shirt, feeling for her breast. Jenna never wore a bra, there was no need, but she caught his hand and held it away from her skin, muttering, 'I don't want to. Not now, please.'

It was too much. How could she sit here, so lovely, so much the woman he wanted, and refuse him? He jumped to his feet and stormed over to the drinks trolley, although he still had his glass almost full. When he realised this he cursed, picked up the ice bucket and flung it against the wall. It was a plastic affair with a little bell on top and it jingled merrily, bringing Caspar, the butler, into the room.

'You – wanted something, sir?' He looked dubiously at the spreading carpet of ice.

Jenna sat still and impassive.

'No. Get out of here, damn you.'

He waited until the man was gone and then announced, 'You'll go back to see the doctor. He said it would get better, but you're worse than ever. I want a son, and there's no way to get one if you won't have sex.'

'You have a son already.'

'He's not the son I want. Surely Jenna you can see how important this is?'

He held out his hand, imploring her to listen to him.

'I don't want a baby. And I won't go back to that doctor, it was worse than anything having him fumble around inside me – I hated it! Besides, what did he say? "Doubtful fertility." That means no.'

'Not to me it doesn't. If you would only try, Jenna –'

79

She got up then and went to the window, looking out across the paddock to where the mares stood, slack bellied, submissive, their manes tossed by the wind.

'I have tried. It's always the same. If you knew what it felt like you wouldn't do it to me. After all, I'm not asking you to stay married.'

He came up behind her and put his arms around her waist, holding her stiff body as close as she would allow. 'I've told you we will never divorce. If you can only accept that then perhaps you'd see that you have to try to make things better. You have to see a doctor, it's not normal –'

She dragged away from him shrieking, 'I know I'm not normal! You said you liked me this way, but now you want to pack me off to some foul man who gets his thrills from poking things into me and –'

'We've tried four doctors and you've hated every one,' said William and slumped into a chair. 'I've been too soft with you and now you won't even try. Accept it, Jenna, we have a fortnight together and we are going to make love. It isn't a lot to ask, surely?'

Jenna shook her head. 'I think it may be too much.' Her face was bleak

The Maclaren house was a scant two miles across the lush, horse-rich pasture. In Kentucky, William's wealth was not so outstanding, for although the richest among rich men, there were those here who could hold a candle to him. House-parties abounded but servants did not, and it was not unusual to accept a drink from a tray and find it held by the man who dug your garden or cleaned out your pool, and in addition dropped snippets of gossip to the newspapers.

Lights lit the driveway and hung from the trees, giving the lie to William's tale of a small party. Cars like small buses stood in ranks before the fountain, and the spotlights that turned the showers into rainbows glinted also on the chrome teeth of expensive radiator grilles. Still, Jenna was dressed for it in white Kenzo silk and diamonds. She was used to Kentucky style.

'Jenna! How wonderful of you to come.' Lula Maclaren advanced on her with widespread arms, and Jenna submitted to her perfumed embrace. Aged around fifty, Lula dressed like a twenty-year-old and dyed her hair for fifteen, but she was kind, if a little snobbish. William was often available but it was a *coup* to attract Jenna and she knew it. 'Come along in, my dear and see who you know. The Petersens now, and Netta Golberg – it must be almost everyone here.'

Jenna agreed and treated the guests to a restrained nod. There was that blonde, big-busted creature William had toyed with in the past, and judging by her smile in the more recent past at that. The humiliation of it almost choked her. Did he think she didn't know? Lula caught the direction of her eyes and said at once, 'Come upstairs, sweetheart, and do your hair. You can tell me where you found that fabulous dress, I'd adore it except it would never cover the bumps. How do you stay so slim, it's a scandal!' She guided Jenna towards the stairs and she went, unresisting. As they stepped on to the landing and out of sight a woman's voice floated up from below.

'Jesus, but she treats us like dirt. Think it would kill her to smile once in a while?'

Jenna's cheeks flushed deep pink and Lula became flustered. 'Take no notice, darling, she's a jealous hellcat.'

'Another one of William's conquests, I take it. Don't look so bothered Lula, I don't mind that much.'

The older woman peered at her in concern and suddenly Jenna realised that she really did care. It brought a rush of tears and at once Lula guided her into a bedroom. 'Now, now, lovey, there's no need for this. They're all the same, why, if I told you the times Zeke's made a fool of himself over something you shouldn't touch without washing your hands –'

'But all the time, Lula? It's a different one every five minutes.' She sank on to the bed and sniffed into a box of tissues.

Lula hunted round the room for a cigarette, lit it and hitched her plump bottom against the edge of the dressing table. 'William worships the ground you walk on, honey. He'd do anything for you.'

'Except give up his women.'

'Well, if you're as rich as he is it's all too easy. Men never did have any self-control, sweetheart. Say, I've often wondered, how did he get his money? He didn't make it in horses, that's certain.'

Jenna laughed and blew her nose. 'You needn't rub it in, Lula, we know the string's had a bad season. He started in electronics. When he left school – it was a second rate public school – that means private, I know it's stupid but there it is – he went to work for the father of Ralph Perkins, a schoolfriend. It was a little firm, rather humble, making computer parts. Not going anywhere much, it was before the boom. You know William, it wasn't long before people were doing things his way and he and Ralph fell out. The upshot was that Ralph washed his hands of it and went into insurance – he's still selling policies I think – and William married the boss's daughter. He was twenty-two. After that he could do more or less as he liked, and somehow he came across a man who had invented a new type of hearing aid. Everyone uses them now but at the time it was absolutely revolutionary. And what I think happened next was that William got hold of the patent, I don't like to ask how, and sold production rights to Japan. Then he bought out his father-in-law's firm and started expanding. Somewhere along the line he had two children, but the wife was disposed of before Tony was five. I don't know why he didn't let her have them because he couldn't be less interested, but that's William for you, he will never lose even a point. She's living on the Isle of Wight now, we don't hear from her.'

Lula looked astonished. 'And from that he made – everything?'

Jenna nodded. 'He's an incredible businessman. Quite single-minded.'

'So where do you fit into the picture? Your father was never in trade.'

Jenna rose to her feet smiling. 'My father was an ambassador. But come along, Lula, I've sniffed quite long enough. Let's go downstairs.'

The middle-aged face was in wrinkles of concern, in stark contrast to its bright make-up and girlish hair. 'Don't let them get you down, honey,' she murmured, taking Jenna's arm. 'My, you could be my daughter, you know that? If anyone upsets you just you tell me and I'll give them a piece of my mind!'

'That's sweet of you.' Jenna smiled at the thought of she, mistress of the icy put-down, relying on Lula Maclaren for protection, but it was indeed sweet of her.

The party passed in a haze of alcohol and cigar smoke. Supper was served by the pool, an enormous spread of salads and cold meats, hot dishes and puddings. Everyone ate except Jenna, who nibbled at some cheese.

'Eat something, honey, come on, fill your plate,' urged Zeke, but Jenna shook her head.

'It's lovely but I'm not hungry, really.'

William slipped his arm around her waist. 'I've given up persuading Jenna to eat, Zeke. Like a finicky racehorse, that's Jenna.'

'Too highbred,' laughed Zeke and William bent his lips to Jenna's long, slender neck. 'And very, very beautiful.' Everyone was watching them and he felt a surge of pride that of all these people he had the most money, the most talent and the most beautiful woman. And not beautiful alone but – classy. He stared at the blonde girl he had bedded last week and again stroked Jenna's skin with his lips. His wife stiffened but only he knew it and the girl flushed and went quickly out. He would buy her a present tomorrow and when Jenna went home he'd treat that bottom as it deserved.

'How's your English horses coming along? Heard you had some trouble earlier on.'

William clicked his mind into gear and answered his host's query. 'We've had a poor season. But I've a new man now, name of Hennessey. Jenna's impressed by him, aren't you, darling?'

'What? Hennessey? Yes – yes, he seems very competent.'

'I'm thinking of making him my racing manager. He's an awkward sort but I need someone to pull the operation together, both in the States and at home. He seems very promising.'

Jenna put her glass down. 'He wouldn't do it.'

'Whatever do you mean? Why wouldn't he?'

'Because he likes training racehorses. I've no doubt he'll pick yearlings for you and he's got some firm ideas on breeding, but you'll never get him to trail all over the world for ten months of the year. Not his scene at all.' She spoke with conviction and Sheppard glanced at her sharply. 'You know a lot about what he will and will not do. How much have you seen of this man?'

'Not a lot. As I told you, Tony rides there. And we went to the races when the filly won. You talk to him, and see if

84

I'm not right.' Did she sound normal? To her own ears it seemed strained but William said no more.

She drank a little more champagne and wandered round the pool. The cocaine users were a laughing group sprawled on some cushions and one girl, very high, lay naked to the waist while a man nuzzled her breasts. Jenna looked and turned away, her face a mask. 'English cow,' someone muttered.

She walked quickly back to William and whispered, 'Let's go home. This party's getting out of hand.'

'Is it?' He looked hopefully around and saw what Jenna had seen. He was a little drunk. 'You should go and have a good look,' he said with a leer, 'you might pick up some tips.'

Her head snapped back and her eyes grew huge. 'I think I'd better leave now,' she said breathlessly, 'to let you indulge your filthy habits. I'm sure you can find someone to take you home, perhaps that tart who's being keeping you company.' She turned on her heel and made for the door, but William was following.

'You can't make a scene here, Jenna.'

'Can't I? What sort of scene is that over there, then? It would be all right I suppose if I let you maul me in public but I don't think I can stoop to your level.'

'If you would let me maul you in private it would be an improvement,' snapped William and Jenna swung back her hand and hit him, hard, across the face.

They both stood, stunned, while around them the party stopped.

'This will be in the papers,' muttered William. It was one sort of publicity he could do without.

'I'm sorry. I don't know what got into me. Let's go home, please William.'

Whitefaced, with the livid mark of her hand across his cheek, William took her arm and led her out. Chatter

85

broke out behind them.

Tonight they had driven themselves and Jenna was thankful for it. William bundled her into the car like a sack of washing and then drove without speaking for some miles. Then he pulled off the road and switched off the lights.

'We'll do it here.' He shrugged out of his jacket and began to unfasten his trousers.

'What? No, we won't. Don't touch me, William, I'm not in the mood –'

'When are you ever. I've been too soft with you in the past and it's time you learned that you are my wife. I own you and I have the right to use your body.'

She was huddled in the corner, hiding her eyes. She hated to look at him naked, it seemed to her the ugliest, the most frightening thing imaginable. When he flung her across the seats she kept her eyes closed but when he stabbed into her body they opened and she screamed.

'You're hurting me! No, William, please!'

'I should think I am hurting you, what do you mean by shaming me in public. Scream you bitch, scream, let's see how superior you feel now.'

But she did not scream again. He gripped brittle bone and stared into her lovely face, contorted now with pain. She was so tense that he had to drive himself into her and the thrill of it was immeasurable. This was his woman, desired by every man and he alone had the right to subjugate her. As he soared to intense, delicious climax the eyes staring up at him clouded. Her head lolled. She was unconscious.

She lay in the big, soft bed and wondered where she was. It was not an unusual feeling, for she travelled so much that she sometimes forgot which country she was in, let alone which hotel. But this was not an hotel, there was the Mexican painting she had bought last year, and that was her dress, all bloody now, draped over the chair. The Kentucky house, that was it. She struggled to sit up and at once William rose from his seat by the window and came over to her.

'Are you all right?' He looked tense and drawn. Jenna stared at him and let her mind touch on the memory of last night. She shuddered. 'I didn't meant – Jenna, we have to talk.'

'There's nothing to say. I don't even want to think about it. Could you ring for some coffee please.'

'In a moment. You realise that the story of last night will be in every newspaper in the world? Everyone will think we're on the brink of divorce. I don't imagine you will exert yourself to apologise, but –'

'Me apologise! I hardly think I have anything to apologise for,' said Jenna, and turned her head restlessly against the pillows, her dark hair tangling.

'I don't expect my wife to indulge in scenes,' said William. 'And if you say divorce once more I will slap you till you scream. I'm sorry I hurt you, but God knows you drove me to it! And now you've had a sleep and you feel better. We're going out today and we're going out together, we'll ride round the farm first and put paid to the gossip here, and then we'll attend the lunch party at Walter Kershaw's. And damn it, Jenna, you will hold hands with me and smile!'

'I don't want to smile and I won't come with you.' Jenna leaned across and touched the bell herself, knowing that Shirley would come at once with a tray.

William crossed to the door and locked it. 'I'm warning you, Jenna. I allow you freedom that I permit no-one else. But I will not let you go and I will not be denied access to your body. Christ, you complain that I'm unfaithful but

87

you force me to rape you! What do you want, Jenna?'

Shirley's soft knock sounded on the door. 'Go away!' bellowed William and there was a pause. 'Mrs Sheppard?' quavered Shirley, and William flung open the door, plucked the tray from Shirley's hands and flung it with a crash into the hall.

'Now will you go away,' he yelled again and slammed the door in the black woman's shocked face.

Jenna pulled herself upright in the bed, new points of discomfort making themselves known all over her body. She was still losing blood, so it must be her period, a rare event since she could go for months without any loss at all. At least it meant William would leave her alone.

'I hate sex with you. You hurt me,' she said grimly.

William crossed to the bed and caught at her hand. 'Last night was the only time I have hurt you.'

'And once before,' said Jenna.

'Jesus Christ, Jenna, virgins expect to hurt! I was as gentle as I could possibly be. If you knew the way some men treat their women you'd be bloody grateful that I'm a reasonable man.' He rested his forehead on his hand for a moment and tried to gather his wits. He was in danger of losing control. 'Darling,' he continued in a calmer voice, 'we'll say no more about it. I'm sorry I hurt you but I insist that you come out with me today and do as I wish. Then when you go home you must go and see a doctor.'

Jenna swung her legs out of bed, moving stiffly. Her stomach was groaning with cramps, and dark bloody blotches covered her nightdress. 'I'm going home today.'

'Damn it, you are not.'

She looked him full in the face then, and she was deathly pale with shadows like bruises beneath her eyes. He knew he would always want her.

'Arnold can fly me to the airport.'

He let her go past him to the bathroom and when she

had shut the door he said, loudly, 'Jenna, I'm afraid Arnold won't be able to take you. I shall sack him first.'

There was a pause. 'Then I will go by car.'

'There will be none at your disposal.'

'Then I shall walk.'

'I suppose you might if you had any shoes.'

Jenna flung open the door and stared incredulously at him. 'You really mean this, don't you? It's ridiculous! You will go to any lengths at all to stop me going.'

Her husband stared back at her, his face harsh. 'You are so right, my darling. And today you will come out with me and let the world see that our marriage is safe and secure. Because it is, you know. You can go home in ten days' time as we agreed, and in those ten days I will not touch you. There, that's good of me, isn't it? But when I come back to England, Jenna, my love, my dearest angel, I will not be at all patient. So, off to the doctor with you.'

She felt so tired. Tired and drained and hopeless. There was never any point in fighting William once he made up his mind to win. Very slowly, moving as if drugged, she held out her hand to him.

The strange, sleepwalking mood persisted through the day. She rode beside William across broad green acres and automatically greeted the people they met. It was a beautiful place and it soothed her, the stands of elm and ancient oak a testament to permanence. She looked at a yearling running free, his stride long and raking, and she said, 'Hennessey would like that one.' Her husband glanced at her, surprised. How could she behave so calmly after the worst battle of their entire married life? For himself his nerves felt raw.

There was an uncomfortable moment when they met Gerard in the barn. He beamed at Jenna in undisguised dazzlement, and conducted her from box to box as if he were honoured by her interest. She felt like Judas Iscariot, and the eyes she turned on William were accusing.

'You don't have to,' she said as they left. 'If you appointed a racing manager he could direct things and Gerard could still stay on. He's wonderful with the stallions.'

William looked thoughtful. 'Perhaps you're right. I'll think about it.'

Her smile was like sunshine after rain, and when she went up to change for lunch – a long-sleeved dress to hide the bruises – he thought to himself that things seemed almost normal.

At lunch, too, she was serene, and William let it be known, discreetly, that their public row had been followed by a private, and passionate reconciliation. It was true, in its way. It was accepted because the Sheppards were a charismatic couple, an image of unity, wealth and beauty far and away above the marriages of real life. No-one wanted to believe the dream could break, they preferred to see them as golden and inviolate, in much the same way as William himself viewed things. There would be no scandal, just an interesting sidelight on love in the surtax bracket.

Chapter Five

The house seemed very quiet when Jenna returned to it. In Kentucky, there was always noise and movement, whether to do with the stud or with the parties William organised for the world to see his wife. Back in England it was a dull, jet-lagged Wednesday with the children at school and her nerves too jangled to settle to anything. There were letters and messages, and a heap of appointments and invitations to reply to, yet as always the day she returned home would be a wasted one. In her mind she was neither in one place or the other, the routine of home would be strange to her until ratified by a night in her own familiar bed. There was no message from Hennessey. Perhaps her absence had cooled him she thought, and her own heart sank a little. Everything changed.

She lunched on a bowl of thin soup and a roll, watching lunchtime television. It always amused her to see how restrained the home-grown product seemed after the American variety. Strange that from the same stock two such differing cultures could grow, like parents producing two children, one of them a millionaire bookie, the other an Oxford don. William would be happy to live in America all the time she thought, and stirred her soup without enthusiasm. She would hate to leave the small shabbinesses of England.

George came in to take her tray, indicating by the lift of an eyebrow that he disapproved of her lack of appetite. 'Elsa is making chicken in cider for supper, ma'am. Free-range chicken and special farmhouse cider. Going to a lot of trouble Elsa is.'

Jenna tried to smile. 'How very kind of her. I'm sure I shall enjoy it enormously.' She wondered how on earth she was to dispose of the massive helping Elsa would provide. Rachel's dog seemed more and more inviting at every turn.

'By the way, ma'am,' said George. 'Mr Hennessey rang on Monday, he wants to discuss Mr Tony's riding. I told him you would be home today, and he will telephone this afternoon.'

Jenna's heart leaped into her throat, and she swallowed it down with what she was certain must be an obvious effort. 'There – hasn't been any trouble, has there, George?' she asked, and knew that her cheeks were pink.

'Tony didn't go on Sunday, ma'am,' he said dolefully and Jenna's eyes widened.

'Didn't go? But why not?'

George's face was assuming its frozen look, and Jenna groaned. Trust Tony to play up the moment her back was turned. He was like a toddler crying, 'Mummy, look at me,' and if she did not look at once he would throw his toy away and sulk.

'You're sure he went to school?' she asked suspiciously and the ghost of a grin crossed George's face. 'I telephoned, ma'am. I like to think we learn by experience. Both he and Miss Rachel were in class on Monday morning.'

She breathed a sigh of relief. 'Thank God for that. I couldn't face another week like the last time, I thought I would go mad. I think that headmaster did, I have never seen a man so angry.'

The butler's expression said very clearly that if he had had his way Tony would have been offered up to the headmaster like a lamb to slaughter. They were all too soft with him. After hiding for a week in the school potting shed, with the school, Mrs Sheppard, everyone but Mr Sheppard going frantic with worry, and then to be taken home and asked what was the matter – it was plain stupid. A good hiding would cure that young rip, and he should have got it.

'He was very impolite, ma'am,' said George and Jenna almost groaned.

'I'll deal with him,' she said wearily. 'As soon as he comes in on Friday. And George, thank you for putting up with him, I know it isn't easy. I should hate it if you came to feel – well – that there was no future for you here. You know how much I value you and Elsa.'

The butler softened visibly. As he and Elsa so often said to each other, it was Mrs Sheppard they worked for, a lovely lady for all her funny moods. Any of the others, well, they wouldn't give them the time of day, but Mrs Sheppard – never forgot to say thank you she didn't.

When he had gone Jenna was in turmoil. Ordinarily she would have gone for a walk and expended her charge of nervous energy on miles of muddy tracks, but there was no way she could go out now. Hennessey might ring. She stared at the phone by her elbow. There it sat, squat and silent, perhaps if she willed for it to ring it would. He had promised. But if she took the call here, in the small sitting room, George might hear her, and with William's secretary working through the papers she had brought home she could not closet herself in the study. Her bedroom then, but the thought of sitting there all afternoon and staring at the walls had the appeal of life in a cage. She would have liked to ring Tony's housemaster and explain her worries, but if she did that Hennessey might phone and the line would be engaged. She glowered again at the telephone hating it for tormenting her.

On sudden impulse she ran upstairs and went into her dressing room. Vast doors swung aside on three of the four walls to reveal rack after rack of clothes. One cupboard held only shoes, another hats and gloves, another a mountain of nothing but lace slips and panties, for Jenna did not possess a bra. A maid came in three times a week to keep her wardrobe in order, taking away garments for mending and cleaning, sometimes doing a slight alteration that Jenna had requested. At the end of every season something was discarded, if only to make room for the new, but as yet Jenna had not undertaken her end of summer clear-out. It was a chore she always performed herself, for she found it useful to keep fresh in her mind the clothes she possessed. Her style was her own and she planned and experimented in the privacy of her dressing room.

She was pondering over a white summer dress frilled with broderie anglaise which she felt was too girlish for her nowadays but which might appeal to Rachel in a year or two, when the telephone rang. She stood frozen to the spot, the colour surging into her skin. Two, three, four times it rang and then she raced into the bedroom and grabbed it, still clutching the dress in her other hand.

'Hello? Jenna Sheppard here.'

Hennessey's breath suddenly felt short. She sounded so cool and controlled, he had forgotten her English lady-like voice. 'This is Dan Hennessey.'

She sat on the bed, her legs like jelly. 'Hello, Mr Hennessey.'

'I told you I'd ring.'

'Yes. So you did.'

'I want to see you. Alone.'

94

'Yes.' It was almost a whisper.

'Oh Jenna . . .' murmured Hennessey, and the longing in his voice made her weak.

'Mr Hennessey,' she said shakily, 'I wonder – would you come to supper tonight? We can talk about Tony, and the horses, and – everything. Just talk.'

'I don't want to come to your house.' He would take a man's wife, but not under his roof. It seemed obscene, somehow.

'Please. My cook's making a huge meal and I can't possibly eat it all myself. If you came around eight we could talk. About Tony.'

'Right now I don't give a damn about Tony. Will you be alone?'

'Sort of – there's George, the butler, and my cook, and William's assistant has a house in the grounds. So you see it would all be very –'

'Frustrating,' put in Hennessey, and suddenly he laughed. 'All right, Mrs Sheppard, I'll come. Eight o'clock was it?'

'Yes.'

'I missed you.'

'Oh – I'm sorry, I'm not managing this very well. I never felt so nervous in my life.'

'You don't sound it.'

'Don't I?'

'Oh Jenna . . .' He knew if he didn't hang up soon they would go on burbling at each other all afternoon. 'I'll see you tonight,' he said firmly.

Jenna took a deep breath. 'Yes. All right.'

'Goodbye – Jenna.'

'Good – bye.'

When she replaced the receiver she realised she had been standing clutching the dress the whole time. Her fingers had cramp and she had crushed an artificial rose on the bodice. When she tried to smooth it out she found that she was trembling.

What do you wear to receive a man you know intends to seduce you? The problem perplexed her for the rest of the day. Should it be the demure little dress with the Peter Pan collar, like Wendy in Never-Never land, or the shoe-string strapped kneelength tunic that made her look like a better-class gangster's moll? In the end she chose a sort of floorlength Japanese housecoat, made of silk and embroidered with dragons and fish, with narrow sleeves, a high collar and tiny buttons all the way down the front. She left the neck unbuttoned to just above her breasts, and then on impulse undid it to the waist and pulled it wide. She stood before the mirror and stared at herself, seeing nothing at all to desire. In clothes, yes, even she could see that she was lovely, but this naked, pallid body, with her nipples almost livid against her skin – no man could really want it. She pulled the coat closed and buttoned it once again, her spirits plummeting to the depths. This with Hennessey would be awful.

He arrived prompt at eight. George opened the door to him with avuncular pleasure, he liked Mrs Sheppard to have company, she was too much alone.

'Mrs Sheppard will receive you in the library,' he murmured, and proceeded with measured tread across the hall. Hennessey followed, taking in spindle-legged antique chairs, a cabinet of priceless glassware, Stubbs paintings of horses. But when George opened the library door he saw only Jenna.

'Mr Hennessey. I'm so glad you could come.' She stood before the fire, her face framed by heavy bands of hair.

'It was kind of you to invite me. I hope you're not too tired after your journey –'

'No, no. One gets used to it, I think.'

The door closed behind George and they both fell silent. Jenna looked confused.

'Why don't we have a drink?' suggested Hennessey.

She smiled in relief. 'What a good idea. They put some champagne to cool somewhere – yes, here it is.' With cork already removed by a thoughtful George she had only to pour it. Hennessey took a glass and sipped, leaning one elbow on the mantelpiece. Jenna sank into a chair, hunching her knees nervously.

'Don't you think it looks a bit suspicious? Champagne?' he asked curiously.

Jenna looked up, surprised. 'Oh no. I always drink it. Anyway, as far as suspicions go, everyone knows I'm not – that sort of woman.'

'Aren't you?'

Her eyes slid away. 'George tells me Tony didn't come on Sunday. Did something happen?'

'I'm not sure. He was a bit peeved when you went to America, I think. Swore at me a couple of times, that sort of thing. I belted him one.'

'You what?' Jenna was poleaxed.

'Yanked him off the horse and clouted him. He snivelled, then got back on and rode. I was a bit sad not to see him last Sunday, because we were getting on quite well towards the end.'

There was a discreet knock at the door and George came in. 'Supper is served in the dining room, ma'am,' he announced.

'The dining room? George, we shall rattle around like two peas in a dustbin! Oh all right, if we're impressing people so be it. Mr Hennessey, prepare to be impressed.'

'Prepare to be put down you mean,' said Hennessey, with a sidelong look at George, who was playing the old retainer to perfection.

To George's surprise Jenna giggled. 'You must be nice to Mr Hennessey, George,' she said, her racehorse walk taking her to the door. 'Because he whacked Tony last weekend and I know you've been longing to do it for years.'

'Not at all, ma'am,' denied George but he looked at Hennessey with respect.

The Sheppard dining table was built to seat thirty people, and its gleaming expanse reflected the crystal of three vast chandeliers. At one end there huddled two place settings, each complete with three wine glasses and a forest of cutlery.

'I think we're having a banquet for two,' said Jenna and this time it was Hennessey's turn to laugh.

'This is bloody ridiculous, especially since I'm not even wearing a dinner jacket.'

'At least you're not in your racing gear,' comforted Jenna, eyeing his pale tan suit appreciatively. The light cloth draped over muscle and long, strong bone, yet he had a slightly rumpled look that spoke of a man who dressed without much thought.

'We trainers do have some clothes,' objected Hennessey, seating himself in the vacant place at the head of the table and unfolding a napkin the size of a tablecloth. He had trotted out his only non-racegoing suit for this occasion.

'Mr Downing doesn't. However much we pay him he always wears the same suit, either with or without trilby.'

George left the room and again they both fell silent. Hennessey reached out and touched her hand. 'Don't be nervous.'

'I can't help it. This was a terrible idea, we can't talk here.'

'Wait till the meal's over. If we gobble everything in sight we can hide in the library.'

'I never gobble.'

'I don't suppose you do. You know, if anything was to put you off being rich this would be it. Your butler's like a benevolent gaoler, if you don't behave he'll tell the governor and you'll lose your visiting privileges.'

She nodded. 'It is a bit like that. You get used to it. And here he is again with the rations.'

George put down two plates of exquisitely presented smoked salmon and prawns. Hennessey began his with relish while Jenna ate two prawns, a mouthful of salmon and nothing else.

'Don't you want it?' asked Hennessey, whose opinion of wealth was being mellowed somewhat by the best meal he had tasted in his life.

'I'm not hungry. Could you eat some of it, otherwise George will be cross.'

'You're not serious?' He looked at her quizzically and she blushed.

'They don't think I eat enough. Look, we'll change plates, you can keep your knife and fork.'

'Why shouldn't I use yours?' His face was intent and he was not thinking of food. Somehow he had hold of her wrist beneath the table and his fingers followed the lines of tendons and veins.

'If you wish,' she said breathlessly. 'But do please hurry, George will come back.'

He released her wrist and began to eat. 'This sauce is amazing.'

When George returned he looked from Jenna's clean plate to her demure expression and snorted, 'Really, madam!'

'George, you are never satisfied,' she complained, but he whisked the plates away muttering, 'Anyone would think I was born yesterday!'

Hennessey's head was bowed and he shook with mirth

as George grimly served him the chicken in cider. 'Are you sure you have enough, sir?' he asked pointedly, heaping the plate high.

'She begged me to eat it, George,' objected Hennessey. 'I had to.'

George put his spoon down and stood for a moment looking at him. He seemed very sombre and at once Hennessey stopped laughing. There was something here of importance. 'Mrs Sheppard starves herself, sir. We all have to try and stop her.'

'Now you're being silly,' said Jenna and there was an edge to her voice. 'Go away, George, we can manage.'

Moving with punctilious correctness, the butler replaced the spoons in the dishes and withdrew, for all the world as if on the parade ground.

'You've offended him,' said Hennessey.

'He gets above himself.' Jenna pushed a piece of chicken round her plate with a fork.

'He was right, wasn't he?'

She stuffed the chicken into her mouth and mumbled, 'No.'

'Why do you want to be so thin? Another stone and a half wouldn't do any harm.'

'I am perfectly healthy. I shall probably live for ever.' She speared a piece of courgette and chewed on it distastefully.

'You should have been a jockey,' said Hennessey, watching the muscles in her throat as she swallowed. 'Then it would pay you to starve.' The food was delicious but his appetite was gone. Pushing his plate aside he stood and bent over her chair, touching his lips to her throat and holding her hands away as she moved to repel him. She was forced back into her seat, her head flung back, and Hennessey arched over her, absorbed in the sharp, moist pleasure of mouthing her flesh.

100

'Stop it!' Jenna pulled her hands free and struck at his shoulders. At once Hennessey drew back. He took his seat again, flushed and breathing hard.

'I told you it wouldn't be any good,' said Jenna, and she was as lost and tearful as a little girl. It made him ache to watch her.

'Then we won't do it,' he murmured, and she looked up in quick surprise. He assumed a calmness he did not feel, saying, 'I wouldn't do anything you didn't want.'

Her expression had shocked him, she was like a woman expecting torture. And now there was such tension in her that he felt he need only rest one finger on her arm and something would snap. Gradually, as he watched her, she began to relax. At last she sighed and screwed her napkin into a vast, crumpled ball. She threw it at him and he caught it, screwed it tighter and then with a flick of his wrist hurled it to the farthest end of the table.

'Eat your dinner,' he said and picked up his knife and fork. Bemused and uncertain Jenna did the same.

For the rest of the meal they made stilted, uncomfortable conversation and as soon as they had eaten enough to satisfy Elsa they went back to the library and the champagne.

'Leave us alone, George,' said Hennessey as they passed him in the hall. 'I want to talk to Mrs Sheppard in peace.'

The butler looked taken aback but Jenna merely said, 'Not another practicing megalomaniac.'

The door shut behind them. 'Is your husband the other one?'

'Yes.'

The ice in the bucket had melted in the heat of the fire and the champagne was warmer now, the bubbles less sharp. Hennessey sipped from his glass and then handed it to Jenna, who hesitated, and then sipped also.

Hennessey took off his jacket. 'It's hot in here.'

'Yes.' She sat on the edge of her chair, holding the glass and shaking.

'There's no need to be frightened of me.'

'I'm not frightened of you.'

'Yes, you are. When I touched you just now you behaved as if you thought I was going to kill you.'

'You took me by surprise, that's all, and – oh God!' She was crying and the champagne was spilled on her dress. Hennessey took the empty glass and set it down, then stood, staring at her bowed head. He longed to take her in his arms and knew that to do so would be the end.

'It's sex, isn't it?' he said softly. 'That's what frightens you.'

She raised streaming eyes to his and at once he reached for a handkerchief. Her nose was running. She mopped up her face, mascara coming off all over the white linen. 'Your wife will suspect something when she sees this.'

'You keep it. Why did you ask me here tonight? If you don't want to sleep with me.'

He asked such direct questions that Jenna was embarrassed. 'I didn't – I thought – I did want to sleep with you. I did, I truly did. At the races, I felt then, for the first time ever, it was something I wanted to do. With you. I felt – sexy. And then, in Kentucky, my husband – it was awful. I'm so bad he hates it. Says I've got to see a doctor.'

'And will you?'

Jenna shuddered. 'I thought I'd rather try you.'

He laughed as if it was the best joke he had heard in years, and he pulled off his tie and flopped down in a chair. Jenna watched him miserably. She should have known this would be a disaster.

'The Hennessey sex clinic. And I thought I had the problem. It seemed to me that I was asking one hell of a lot from a woman who doesn't need a thing, especially not me. Do you know, Mrs Sheppard, I've had it hot and strong for you since the first moment I saw you. I've never known a woman turn me on the way you do. I'd go through hell fire for an hour in bed with you, and whatever you say, I don't think you have any idea what that's like for a man.'

'I don't understand men at all.'

Hennessey stared at her and then went to the light switch, clicking it off so that there was only a dim glow from a little table lamp and the fire. 'Tell me about your sex life,' he said. 'I won't touch you, especially not here. You know I won't tell anyone.'

'How do I know?'

He leaned over and took her hand, lifting it briefly to his lips. 'Because I'm me.'

Jenna got to her feet then, crossing slowly to the fire. She curled on the rug and stared into the flames, her profile perfect and lovely in the firelight. The cords of her neck were rigid with strain. 'There's nothing to tell. I slept with William two weeks before we were married. I was a virgin. Then we got married. Since then we haven't made love a lot. There doesn't seem much point when I hate it so. He has his women, and I – have nothing.'

'What do you want to have?'

She shrugged. 'A normal marriage, I think. A husband I can love. It isn't very loving when you can't bear a person to touch you.'

'If I touched you now, could you bear it?'

She quivered, almost imperceptibly. 'Not if it was – sexual. Perhaps if I was very drunk.'

'If it wasn't sexual. If I touched you and you knew that it wouldn't lead to anything, that I wouldn't try to –' he searched for a euphemism and decided against it '– get inside you.'

Jenna flinched as if he had hit her. 'I don't know. But

103

you would, wouldn't you? They'll do anything.'

'What does your husband do?' asked Hennessey, and Jenna turned and faced him, almost desperate.

'He hurts me! I know it's my fault and he says I should relax, but I can't when he hurts me so. I know he doesn't mean to but it doesn't make it any better, and now it's got so bad I can't stand it! Hennessey, Hennessey, what am I going to do?' Her fingers clawed in the neat coils of hair and he went to her, taking one of her hands and kneeling beside her in the firelight.

'Hush, hush, hush,' he urged, 'there's nothing for you to do, my angel. It will come right, I promise.'

'Will it? I don't think so.'

'I can try. You've just got to let me.'

She sighed and looked very hopeless. 'We couldn't anyway. There's nowhere we could go. I couldn't bear some sleazy motel or the back of a car.'

'What about a nice, empty cottage, complete with locks on the doors and a bed? It's a holiday cottage, on my father's farm. I keep an eye on it for him during the winter. You can't drive to it you see, you either ride or walk.'

'They don't leave the sheets there all winter do they? They'd get damp.' The sudden transition to anxious housewife made Hennessey blink. Perhaps she did take some part in the running of this mansion after all.

'All right, so we have to provide the sheets. What do you want, a butler?'

'I could bring a blanket. You're not very domesticated, are you?'

'Be nice to me, I'm your tame sex object, remember?' He brushed her nose with a finger.

'Which is what I am to you,' she said firmly, and got to her feet. 'Can you help me pin my hair up, please? George will be shocked otherwise.'

He stood behind her and poked pins aimlessly at the thick, black coils. 'Come with your hair down,' he advised. 'I'm not very good at this.'

'No.' More or less finished, she turned to face him. 'Hennessey, are you going to get enough out of this? If you can't – you know.'

It had also occurred to him that he was building up frustration enough to choke him. He looked at Jenna and thought about what was beneath all those little pearl buttons. 'I'll risk it,' he murmured and his voice was thick. 'Friday. Two o'clock.'

She nodded. 'Will you draw me a map?'

'Mrs Sheppard, give me credit for some sort of planning. I did that days ago.'

He held out a little sealed envelope, and she took it, looking very shy. After a moment he turned on his heel and went out.

Tony and Rachel were weekly boarders at a school some ten miles from home. Although nowhere near progressive, it cherished post-war optimism about creating 'rounded personalities' which in practice meant that games weren't compulsory. It was co-educational, which Jenna felt to be good, having herself been subjected to a convent school where a man was never seen unless he was a priest. Nonetheless it was an environment chock-a-block with opportunities for rebellion on a disastrous scale and following George's warnings she thought a visit might be worthwhile. Besides, it occupied a long, tense Thursday.

The headmaster welcomed her to his office with all the ruffled charm of one who is greeting the school's chief benefactor, and an amazing beauty at that. He poured her an innaccurate sherry and wiped up the drops with his handkerchief, but he did not seem surprised to see her. Jenna's vague anxiety began to solidify into real concern.

'I'm glad you came,' began the headmaster, seating himself at his desk. 'I was going to telephone you today in any case. We've had some trouble with Tony.'

'Has he run away?' asked Jenna in a faint voice.

'Not this time, no. Anyway in my experience they always turn up in the end, cold and hungry but nothing worse. No, I'm afraid Tony has been glue-sniffing.'

'Glue sniffing? Good God.'

'And I am led to believe by some of the other boys involved – Tony has said nothing you understand – that your son has supplied various other pills and potions which the boys have been taking.'

'Rachel isn't involved is she?' asked Jenna.

'Fortunately not. Can you tell me, Mrs Sheppard, where he might have obtained things of this kind?'

Jenna stared at him helplessly. Oh God, why did she feel so guilty when she, at least, had done nothing – but it was always her fault, everyone made sure of that.

'I don't know. But of course we have several houses – I don't think it's difficult for children to get hold of these things, especially in America. But I thought he understood about drugs.'

'Mrs Sheppard – forgive me – but is there some trouble at home? Tony did say something to the effect that there was no point in worrying about what happened to him since no-one else did. Why should he say that do you think?'

She gave a little, forced laugh and sipped at her sherry. It was too sweet, but it strengthened her. 'Because I went to America for a fortnight. I admit, we've neglected them a bit lately, we travel so much you see. But I am only in England now because I felt we should be together more. Their father's in Kentucky just at the moment. Mr

Perkins, what are you going to do to Tony?'

'I have considered expelling him. He was the ringleader, and the other parents are naturally very concerned.'

Jenna gulped. If Tony was expelled from here William would insist he was sent back to full-time boarding and it would be a disaster. If there was one thing William's son had in abundance it was the stubborn desire to win at any cost, and sometimes it was better not to start the fight. Jenna felt the beginnings of panic at a situation she could not control. 'You haven't – definitely decided?'

'No.' After all, they were building a new swimming pool and the appeal letters were about to go out.

'Can I talk to him please?'

'By all means. I have a class to take for Latin now, so you can use my office. I'll ask him to come up. I wonder if you would give my wife and me the pleasure of entertaining you for lunch?'

Jenna declined graciously, her stomach tight with nerves, and sat and waited for Tony. Her gloves were screwed into a tight ball, and she smoothed them out only to crush them again moments later.

'Oh. It's you.' Tony looked very young and his skin had erupted again. She made a mental note to take him back to the skin specialist.

'Surprise, surprise. You look a bit tired, love.'

'So would you if they'd been giving you the rubber hose treatment.' He twisted the headmaster's desk lamp round, mimicked a Nazi voice and thundered, 'Talk you beastly infant, talk, or it'll be the worse for you!'

'Mrs Sheppard? Tony? Are you all right?' The headmaster's secretary poked her head round the door, looking like an anxious horse.

'He's playing the fool,' explained Jenna with a slight smile, and the woman withdrew. 'Do behave, Tony, I'm supposed to be tearing you limb from limb.'

But he only flung himself into Mr Perkins' chair and made it spin. 'Is he going to throw me out?' he asked, braking with his feet on the desk.

'He's threatening. By the way, did I ever tell you what happened to Mark Spitzberg? Nice boy, used to play the guitar, do you remember him?'

'Course I do. His father had that yacht we stayed on once, it was good.'

'That's right. We don't go any more of course, the family's a bit upset. Mark killed himself with an overdose of heroin.'

Tony assumed a look of bravado. 'Always was a twit. Wall Street's answer to Bob Dylan. Come off it, Jen, I'm not that stupid. It was only a bit of a lark.'

'Into which you led others. I'm not getting excited about the Evostik, though I should have thought you a bit too old for playing sticky games. What does concern me is what else you were swallowing and more to the point, why on earth did you do it?'

He shrugged, still with his air of unconcern, but he was suspiciously bright-eyed. 'Don't know. Bit boring here, really. Anyway, why should you care?'

'I don't know why, but I do. It worries me dreadfully to think of you doing something like this when you ought to be working for O levels for goodness sake. You know your father. There's no guarantee that he'll set you up in business. I haven't said this to you before but there's a good chance that by the time you're eighteen you'll be on your own. Financially I mean, there'll always be me.'

'But not him.' His voice was very gruff.

'No. And I want you to know that it isn't your fault. It's because of your mother. You and Rachel are two wonderful people, I've always thought so from the day we met. If your father can't see that, well, it's his problem, not yours. Wrecking your life won't make it any better.'

Tony began to cry and Jenna offered him her handkerchief, a paltry lace affair that was no use at all. He sat in the leather chair and shook with grief, clutching her handkerchief with huge, big-jointed hands, the hands of a man stuck on the thinly muscled arms of an adolescent. She wanted to cuddle him but held herself back, as she always did with her husband's children over which she had no rights at all. Suppose it was the wrong thing to do? Even if it was she wanted to do it and she suddenly rose up and swept round the desk, engulfing Tony in a perfumed embrace. 'There, there, love, it isn't so bad. If you promise to be good, I'll make them keep you on. I'll give them half a swimming pool, the head was itching to ask me, I could tell.'

'I don't want to stay here. I want to come home.' He was snivelling wet marks into the cream lapel of her jacket.

'But why, lovey? You think home's boring, you always say so.'

'No, I don't. Anyway I could go and work for Dan Hennessey, I could be a jump jockey, it's what he used to do. I'm sick of slaving away at things I don't like.'

'What things?'

'Well – chemistry.'

'Oh. Are you falling behind?'

'Yes!' It was said with such a wail of self-pity that it made Jenna grin, and she smoothed the soft brown hair under her hand. Foolish to think that life's problems were always enormous, this one might well be solved by a little extra tuition.

'Do you need to do chemistry? I seem to remember you could do art or something instead.'

'Only the duffers do art. Stinko Phillips says I'm not trying and he keeps giving me conduct marks, but it's so boring no-one could do it.'

109

'Do you want me to engage a couple of German scientists to help out at weekends? I'm sure NASA would let the odd one go,' offered Jenna, her voice soft with tenderness and mirth.

'It's not funny. I don't know what to do. I'd better leave.'

'You will not. I'll talk to Mr Perkins about it. By the way, you upset Dan Hennessey when you didn't turn up. He thinks you don't want to come any more, just when he says you were doing so well.'

'Did he say that? Really?' Tony's tear-stained face lit up.

'Yes,' lied Jenna happily. 'Says you've got real potential. He won't admit it to you, of course, he's not that sort.'

'I should think he isn't. His lads worship him you know, they think he's a magician. You should make Dad give him some decent horses, he could win the Derby.'

'You've been talking to Bert,' smiled Jenna. 'Anyway, don't breathe a word but your father has got plans for him. Nothing's settled, so don't even tell Rachel.'

'I won't.' He moved awkwardly in Jenna's embrace and she took the hint and released him, settling herself again in her chair.

'Do you like Dan Hennessey, Jenna?' asked Tony and she felt herself start to blush.

'He's – he seems very nice,' she said in a strained, unnatural voice.

'He's nuts about you. Keeps asking leading questions to make us tell him things. Mind you, I'm not surprised, his wife's absolutely weird!'

'I'm sure she isn't,' said Jenna in quelling tones, willing him to tell her more and Tony kindly obliged.

'She came out while we were there and it was the weirdest thing. He talked to her as if she was a half-wit.

110

"Don't stand there, Lilian, you will get cold. Go and put a jumper on, go on, Lilian" and she said "Yes, Dan" but when she came back she hadn't got a jumper and she had more goosepimples than an albatross. He didn't say anything, just gave her his coat. Looked a bit sick, though.'

'I should think he was cold,' discouraged Jenna, but her heart bumped in her chest. She did not need to feel guilty, it was only to be expected if his wife was peculiar. Then the thought struck her that much the same thing could be said of William. It depressed her utterly.

Driving home from the school she wondered if she ought not to go tomorrow. After all, she had nothing to lose but an afternoon of potentially dreadful embarrassment. After all this time surely she ought to accept that she was a woman who did not want or need a sex life, whose mistake had been in marrying at all. Unless – unless she could somehow nurture the feeling that came over her when she and Hennessey were together, the tight, throat-catching excitement. She had felt it last night too, but only for a second. Then it had been engulfed in her stupid fear, that now they were alone he would hurt her, when she knew he would never do such a thing. Not willingly, at any rate. But then William never meant to hurt her . . . and if she cared anything for Hennessey's strange wife she would stay at home. But she knew she would not, and the enormity of her selfishness made her ashamed.

She turned her thoughts to the children, the proper subject for her consideration after a visit to school. Tony was to be punished by an hour's chemistry tuition each evening for a month, not with Stinko Phillips but the young and enthusiastic Cambridge graduate the school had rescued from a lifetime's weedkiller research with ICI. Even in his brief ten minutes with Jenna he had

111

expounded on the carbon ring, so something might come of the exercise. It had proved expensive, for the headmaster now held an extremely large cheque.

Before leaving she had popped into Rachel's class and had been gratified by the undivided attention of ten twelve-year-old girls, with every eye glued to her clothes and hair. Rachel nearly burst with pride, but said menacingly, 'I've told everyone you're going to get me a dog.'

'Er – well –' Trust Rachel to trap her like this. 'I was going to talk to Mr Hennessey,' said Jenna lamely. 'To see what he thinks.'

'That's our racehorse trainer,' said Rachel to her audience. 'He's brilliant.'

'And what do you know about it, miss?' Jenna challenged and Rachel went pink.

'Everyone says so. He'll probably win the Derby.'

'I think they usually run horses,' said Jenna acidly and everyone giggled except Rachel. Jenna felt mean. 'But you're right, darling,' she amended, 'we'll talk about the dog at the weekend. Take care.' She withdrew, aware that she had not come up to expectations. Motherhood was definitely not one of her strong points.

For Hennessey too the day was proving endless. He had a runner at a local meeting and he was not optimistic. The owner had bred the animal himself and refused to admit that it had all the speed of a sedentary snail, and Hennessey only stabled it at all because he also trained the man's other, better horse. But he could not afford to waste time on no-hopers, and this afternoon would be the moment to declare it. When the yard was struggling, then he took anything, but now he had to concentrate on results. Which was sad, because the owner was a kindly soul and it was no crime to like your horses. Perhaps he'd take it home as a pet, like a rather large hamster. Except hamsters run faster thought Hennessey ruefully, shoving the car down a gear and overtaking in the face of an oncoming lorry. Since he gave up riding races he used the road to dice with death, with the result that very few people ever accepted his offers of a lift. Most went once, just to see if it was true, but after that they could be seen trudging home in deep snow rather than set foot in Hennessey's car. The exception was an elderly blind owner, who maintained ingenuously that journeys always seemed to pass so quickly with Mr Hennessey for company.

Today he would have liked someone to talk to, for it would have taken his mind off Jenna. He would determine not to think of her and the moment he relaxed he would catch himself wondering what she was doing. Would it never be tomorrow afternoon? Lilian was in one of her meek, meticulous moods, buying his praise by attention to detail, as if you could truthfully praise someone who has cleaned the cooker to perfection and omitted to mop the sludge from the floor. It annoyed him but he was pleased to be annoyed, letting her inadequacies pile up so he could justify himself. As long as she didn't know then none of it could hurt her, and after all, neither he nor Jenna wanted to break up a marriage. This was a safety valve, made necessary by the unforeseen complications of life. What they gained from their time together could be used as a pitprop to shore up the rickety walls of convention. Besides, as things stood, there would be no ultimate betrayal, they would simply meet and talk and touch a little. But his heart began to pump hot, tingling blood through his body and he stamped on the accelerator forcing the speedometer needle up towards its furthest stop.

113

Chapter Six

Honeypot Cottage was in a dell some three miles from Hennessey's stables. To reach it Jenna had to park her car in a hedge on a narrow country lane and then trudge for half a mile through nettles and the stalks of last year's ragged robin until she could see it at the bottom of the hill. The walk relaxed her, she was able to imagine that she was doing no more than enjoying the air of a crisp, autumn afternoon. Surprised rabbits scuttered into the hedgerows and a flock of crows rose from the trees, cawing at her. When she slithered down the muddy bank to the cottage she was pink-cheeked and sparkling.

Hennessey had taken the more usual route, riding his 'chaser along the old green road that led past the rickety garden gate. Few people came that way, especially in winter, and as the horse cantered stiffly down the soft, springing turf he wondered if it ought to be this easy. No-one questioned his sudden desire for exercise since he often rode over to see his parents, or round the farm, finding it a useful excuse to escape the house, and Lilian, when it wasn't a racing day. Yet to him every action seemed highly suspicious, from tightening the girth to donning his decent anorak. He discouraged Casey from accompanying him though, and the labrador sat hangdog in the yard. Hennessey wanted no unnecessary complications on a day which was quite complicated enough.

There was a stone lean-to against the wall of the cottage. Built originally as a stable it had been used as a pigsty, coalhouse and woodstore, but now it reverted to its original function. It was a little low for the old horse but as long as he behaved sensibly he should not crack his head. Hennessey latched the door and deposited saddle and bridle in the kitchen.

The house had the cold, deserted feel that comes from air too rarely moved. Hennessey wandered round but it only took a moment. Downstairs there was the kitchen and the sitting room, wood-floored with a big open grate, while upstairs there was a bathroom so small you could hardly turn round and two little bedrooms. One held an old-fashioned double bed, stripped down to its mattress ticking but still with a big round bolster for a pillow. This would do he thought, and wondered how it would appear to a woman accustomed to servants and Waterford crystal. He began to fear that perhaps she would not come.

As he descended the stained wooden stairs he heard her come in.

'Hennessey?' she called. 'Are you here? I saw the horse.'

'Yes. I'm here.' The joy of it took him by surprise. She looked – wonderful. Her hair was caught in a band at the back of her head and it swung like a skein of silk. Those long, long legs were encased in jeans and she wore a fluffy pink jumper and an anorak. The blanket was rolled under her arm. 'I pinched it from the Rolls,' she said nervously. 'I felt so guilty.'

He grinned. 'So did I. Not enough to stop me coming, though. I don't think anything could have stopped me.'

'What a pathetic pair we are.' She wandered round the

115

room, looking out of the window, but there was no view, only the grass and bushes of the hill.

'Come upstairs,' said Hennessey.

'In a moment. I wondered – is there anything we could drink?'

'No. I thought about it, but if we're going to do this then let's do it sober. One bit of honesty won't hurt us.'

She glanced swiftly at him. 'You really do feel bad about this, don't you? I thought somehow – men didn't.'

'Perhaps it's different if you make a habit of it. Look, I'd love to talk all day but it won't make it any easier. Upstairs, Jenna. Now.'

An agonised expression crossed her face and she twisted the blanket in her hands. Hennessey went to her and took it, then held her wrist and led her to the stairs.

The little bedroom seemed crowded with only the two of them in it. Hennessey spread the dark red blanket on the bed and began to take off his clothes. Jenna stood by the window and would not look at him. If he took everything off she would be down those stairs and away she thought, but when she turned and saw that he was naked she did not run. His body was covered in light brown hair, but she averted her eyes from where it was thickest. He stood before her and unfastened her coat and when he slipped it to the floor she felt the heat of his hands through her jumper. There was a tingling in her nipples and they felt stiff and taut. 'Take your jumper off.' There was no running away now.

She turned her back to do it, stretching her arms and tossing her head to release the curtain of hair. When she turned back to him, slowly, her arms were crossed over her breasts.

'Let me see,' murmured Hennessey, but she shook her head, letting her hair hide her face. But he took her hands and held them wide, staring at a body that was like the

116

skeleton of a bird. Thin, so very thin, he feared that when he held her he would crush those fragile bones, but he longed to touch.

'Oh, Jenna. My Jenna. You don't eat, but you're beautiful,' he murmured.

'I haven't any breasts.'

'Yes, you have. They're like perfect little apples. I adore your breasts, when we went to the races I could see your nipples through your blouse and it was all I could do not to touch them.'

'Don't you want – big ones?' Jenna peeped out from behind her hair.

'What I want is you. Take your jeans off you gorgeous woman.'

She felt suddenly very feminine and stepped out of her jeans like a deer coming out of the forest to drink. She kept her eyes away from him though, and stared at the floor, while Hennessey allowed a slight groan to escape his lips. This was exquisite torture. Her belly was so flat that her pelvic bones stuck up like sails, and her pubic mound stood high, like a hill crowned with a black and mysterious thicket.

'Come and lie with me,' he whispered and again took her hand. 'Come and lie down with me now.'

They lay on the bed and he touched her, his hands stroking arms and legs, belly and thighs. They did not kiss and he made no move to cover her, they simply lay face to face, looking into each other's eyes and touching. She found it strange, not pleasant but not entirely without pleasure either. Sometimes her flesh jumped when he touched a spot and then he touched it again, firmly, as if quieting a nervous horse. He's breaking me in she thought, and a giggle rose in her throat. But as he touched and went on touching she began to wish he would touch further, and raised her own hands to stroke his chest. He was breathing quickly now and a thin film of sweat coated the fine brown hairs. He had flat, smooth chest muscles, lying on the bone like slates on a roof. She closed her eyes and mumbled something unintelligible.

'What do you want? If you don't tell me I won't know.' He was whispering in her ear but she would not look at him. Instead she caught his hand and put it against her breast, and with a short, breathless laugh he rolled her nipple between finger and thumb. Jenna moaned, writhed, and her eyes flew wide open.

'What's the matter? Did I hurt you?' Somehow he had progressed to nuzzling her neck.

'No, no. It's all right. It was – nice.'

'Then I'll do it again.' But he was nearing the end of his tether and he knew it. Just as Jenna began to sink into a bath so warm and thrilling that the room seemed to spin he pushed hard against her thigh, buried his face in her shoulder and climaxed. A sad little murmur escape Jenna's lips.

'I'm sorry. I've made a mess of your blanket.' Hennessey was panting but he sounded unembarrassed. When she looked into his face he seemed younger, the lines less pronounced.

'Oh Daniel,' she whispered, and planted a tiny, feathery kiss on the corner of his mouth.

'Oh Jenna,' he murmured, and gathered her to him, letting their bodies touch from shoulder to toe.

When at last they parted and he began to get dressed it was she who said, 'Do we have to?' It was cold without him near her.

'Yes, sweetheart, we do. Come again Monday.'

'All right. I'll see you Sunday too, for the riding lesson. Oh Dan, I forgot to tell you. Tony's in the most awful trouble, he's been taking drugs at school.'

'Drugs?' The shock on his face almost made her laugh.

118

In her world it was no unusual occurrence for a boy to do this sort of thing, but in his it was plainly earth-shattering. 'For God's sake, Jenna, what sort of drugs?'

'I don't know and I don't really think he does. Some pills and things he got in America. I've had a talk to him and he says he's learned his lesson –'

Hennessey looked menacing. 'Does he now. I shall have a few words to say to him about it, I can tell you. Drugs! Anyone would think the boy was an idiot.'

'Yes, I know, but there's another thing. Rachel –'

'Not her as well. Damn it, Jenna, what are you bringing up, future members of a Triad gang?'

'Quite possibly, but Rachel's only apprenticed at the moment. She wants a dog.'

'Don't tell me – a drug-sniffer.'

Jenna giggled and threw a shoe at him, but he caught it and made as if to swipe at her naked bottom. 'Don't! Don't, Dan, please.' For a second she seemed really frightened. He dropped the shoe and instead came to her and planted a gentle kiss on her lips. 'Of course I won't. Silly baby. Why don't you get her a dog?'

'Oh, William's not keen, and neither is Stephen, he says he'd have to look after it when we were away and he loathes them. A complete cat person is Stephen. So I thought I'd talk to you about it.'

He was pulling on his trousers and didn't speak for a moment. Then he said, 'You could have Casey, if you liked.'

'What? But he's your dog. You like him.'

'Yes, I know, but – my wife doesn't. I neglect him a bit, he can't come out to the gallops of course and on racing days he doesn't get a walk at all. I'd look after him when you weren't here, it would be a very good arrangement. I'll tell her on Sunday.'

'Then you'll have two of us under your spell.'

'I think you are the one with the magic.' He felt the urge to love her again, but he knew it was too soon. She was soft and pliant now, she trusted him, but it was a new and fragile flower. He must be patient. He would lose everything if he did not have patience.

There was a breathlessness about Jenna that weekend that both the children noticed. Even Stephen, coming in and out of William's office, acknowledged a change.

'You seem as if you're expecting something,' he ventured.

'Do I?' It was true, life did suddenly seem full of promise. But it would never do to say so to Stephen. 'Well, we are getting a dog. Dan Hennessey's going to let us have Casey for Rachel, she doesn't know yet. It will be lovely.'

'When did you two sort this out between you?'

Her heart paused in its beating, and then went on. 'When he came to supper on Wednesday,' she said smoothly. 'We'll tell her this afternoon, when we take Tony riding. And you needn't think it will fall to you to take care of it because Hennessey will have him back when we travel.'

Stephen was looking at her very intently. 'That does sound nice. But why are you holding Tony's hand today? He can go in the Rolls. I didn't think you liked standing around in the cold.'

Jenna laughed, a little uncomfortably. 'I don't want to miss the handing over ceremony. Besides, Tony's difficult if I don't go.'

'He is always difficult. This dreadful macho style, it's more than I can stand.' He raised a weary hand to his brow in an affected gesture.

Jenna felt it was time to move to the attack, it was never

120

wise to let Steve get you on the run. 'I imagined you'd like it,' she said waspishly. 'By the way, is your friend still staying?'

'Oh yes. We're getting very cosy, just the sort of thing you hate.'

'Me? Why should I hate it?'

'Because you are always so grand, my sweet. It's your style.' He drifted into the office, closing the door with a sly smile and a whiff of his rather cloying aftershave.

Jenna shivered. What would Stephen do if he found out what was going on? Would he feel duty bound to drop a hint to William? The thought turned her cold. What William would do to her did not bear thinking about, but the damage he could inflict on Hennessey – the wrath of a rich man knows no bounds. He had once felt slighted by a yacht manufacturer in Newport New Jersey, and he had calmly set about spreading rumours and financing research until the man's design was so discredited that his firm collapsed. It had cost a fortune, but for William it was worth it. Jenna wondered why she had said nothing at the time. But then she had not known it all at the time, these things took years before the whole picture emerged, and by then outrage seemed belated and ridiculous. The odd barbed comment and she had let the matter rest. William would ruin a racehorse trainer almost without trying.

She resolved to be very much more careful in the future, no more casual confidences. The price of deceit is that one must weigh every word before speaking, and little as the burden seems at the start it grows heavier with every passing hour.

The children were above themselves at lunch, flicking peas and ignoring Jenna's reprimands. She began to feel helpless in the face of their thick-skinned ebullience.

How did you control people who were too big to hit and too small to understand reason? Perhaps she ought to ban the afternoon's outing, but they would be furious and besides, she wanted to go. She wanted to go very much. So she endured it, trying to ignore the pointed precision with which George set down dishes and removed them, every gesture eloquent of disapproval.

'George thinks we're out of hand, don't you, George,' taunted Rachel, sticking out her tongue at the ramrod, serge-clad back.

'George is right,' said Jenna. 'You wouldn't behave like this if your father was here, so why do you do it now? It isn't fair.'

'Poor old Jen-Jen,' said Tony and spun a spoon like a wild propeller across the polished table.

'Don't do that! Look – any more of this and I'll leave you two behind and go to Hennessey's on my own. Then *I* can ride the horse.'

'And have besotted Dan Hennessey put his hand on your knee. Do you like it, Jen, does it give you a thrill?' The boy looked like a satyr thought Jenna, young but infinitely cruel.

'You're horrid,' she said shortly, and rose to her feet, her meal untouched.

'Mrs Sheppard – please.' George was trying to stop her leaving.

'I'm not hungry, George. No-one could be with the children being so awful. They can eat on their own, I'm going to get changed.'

'All right, I'm sorry,' said Tony grudgingly.

'So am I,' sang Rachel in a totally unsorry voice.

'Well, I'm still not hungry. If you want to come you must hurry, otherwise I shall leave you behind.' She stepped past George and into the hall.

'You should be ashamed of yourselves,' said George in

a voice vibrant with wrath. 'Mrs Sheppard has eaten nothing at all today, and Elsa spent half the morning preparing food she thought would tempt her. And you two – I will not serve you. I will do a great deal for Mrs Sheppard but I will not do that.' So saying he marched towards the door and the kitchen annexe.

Rachel looked shocked and frightened. George had never done this before. She glanced doubtfully at Tony who exuded defiance, and then slipped from her place and ran after George. 'I'm sorry, George,' she faltered. 'Really. If you give me a plate of pudding I'll take it up to Jenna. She might eat it.'

George's face softened as he looked down at her. 'Very well, Miss Rachel. It's raspberry meringue. But can I trust you not to eat it, I wonder?'

'I won't touch a single raspberry, which shows how sorry I am.' Rachel loved raspberries and George knew it.

'Elsa might have some left for tea,' he said forgivingly, and patted the rather sticky hand that rested on his sleeve. She was a nice child was Rachel, and would be very much nicer without the influence of that brother of hers. If someone didn't take him in hand soon – George stumped off to the kitchen to fetch Jenna's pudding.

But when Rachel took it up Jenna would not eat it. A few raspberries and a mouthful of meringue, simply to please, and there it was left on the side tempting Rachel's resolution.

'Don't you want it?' she asked wistfully, her face the picture of longing.

'You can have it if you like.' Jenna was threading tiny knots of pearls through her earlobes, and had pinned her hair in a plait around her head.

'I can't, I promised George. Can I have my ears pierced, Jenna? They'd look super.'

'When you're sixteen and not before. You'd look like a

gypsy.' She stepped into a pair of brown cord dungarees, which should have looked extremely odd when topped by her elegant head, but because it was Jenna they did not.

'I'll never be able to dress like you,' complained Rachel, averting her eyes from the temptation of food. How Jenna could look at it and not eat was beyond her.

'Yes, you will. Not the same I hope, because you suit pretty, frilly things. They look awful on me.'

'Nothing looks awful on you,' grunted Rachel, thinking that Jenna was luminous today. Her skin was glowing and her eyes had a sparkle that might have been due to the lunchtime conflict but she doubted it. Rows usually had a dulling effect on Jenna, dragging her face into tense, unhappy lines. Rachel gave it no particular thought for the world of adults was of little interest to her. Like all children she noted only the things that affected her own small concerns, and when one day she emerged from self-absorption like a butterfly from a chrysalis she would recall events in the past and wonder how she could have been so blind.

When at last Jenna drove into Hennessey's yard they were, as usual, late. Hennessey came out of the house with Casey at his heels and looked pointedly at his watch.

'You can blame the children,' said Jenna with a weary sigh. 'They've been awful.'

'Have they now?' Hennessey strolled over towards them and Tony automatically removed his hands from his pockets and ceased lounging against the car. 'I've been hearing things about you,' said Hennessey, stopping a scant six inches from Tony's anorak zip.

'Have you, sir?' He was very red.

'Oh yes. And before we go any further there are a few things I should like to say. Seems to me that you are in a fair way to becoming one of life's many failures. I can usually spot them, stupid, big for their boots kids who can't work at a thing. I don't bother with them long, there's no point. Are you that sort of kid, Tony?'

'No, sir. I didn't mean – I explained it to Jenna.'

'Don't try and hide in mummy's skirts, boy, it's pathetic. I know you can twist her round your thumb. She forgives you because she loves you, but I don't have that problem. All I see is a self-important young thug who needs putting in his place. What makes you think I want to see you here when you can't even be bothered to telephone to say you can't come? D'you think I've nothing better to do than hang around here waiting on your pleasure? Do you?'

'No, sir. I'm sorry, sir. Jenna said –' he ground to a halt, almost tearful.

'Don't call me, sir, it doesn't wash. You're not in the bleeding army. Now, unless I have some guarantees from you I am going to hand you that horse and tell you to take it away. This instant. You can worry about it, feed it, stable it, exercise it. I don't think I want to bother.'

Topy gaped, envisaging being left with a horse on the end of a leadrope and nowhere to go. He'd have to put it in the garage. 'I – I'm sorry I didn't come,' he said breathily.

'Dan, leave him alone –' urged Jenna, but he didn't turn his head.

'And now you can apologise to your mother for letting her down so badly. She goes away for two weeks and you're taking pills at school. I bet you had a crack at Daddy's booze cupboard too.'

Tony's cheeks flamed and Hennessey knew he had scored a hit. 'You're an overgrown baby, Tony Sheppard,' he said softly. 'And if I hear any more tales about you and your clever little pranks I will come back and knock your head from your shoulders and that's a promise. Now, apologise to your mother.'

'I'm – I'm sorry, Jenna,' mumbled Tony, scarlet to his

125

hair, and when this did not relax Hennessey's menacing stare he added, 'I won't do it again. Any of it.'

'Thank you, Tony,' said Jenna in a stifled voice.

'You can tack the horse up yourself,' said Hennessey. 'And get it right.'

'Yes, sir. I mean – yes.' Tony walked quickly away, breaking into a run the moment he was out of reach of Hennessey.

Jenna let out her breath in an enormous gasp. 'That was absolutely awful! He's not that bad, Dan, he really isn't.'

'Isn't he? Unless someone rides him hard now he's certainly going to be. Doesn't that husband of yours bother with him? If he was mine I'd have him running so fast he wouldn't have time to get up to tricks.'

'Daddy doesn't bother with us at all,' said Rachel in an offhand way. 'The only person in the world he likes is Jenna.'

'Don't be silly, darling,' said Jenna mechanically. She felt very tired all of a sudden and sank with a bump onto a moss covered seat at the side of the yard.

'Jenna? I mean, Mrs Sheppard? Are you all right?' He had thought she seemed pale.

'Yes, I'm fine. A bit tired, that's all.'

'She does this when she doesn't have anything to eat,' chimed in Rachel. 'She left her lunch because Tony was being a pig.'

'So were you,' added Jenna, who had had enough of sibling righteousness, always evident when the other one was in hot water. Rachel bent down and hurriedly patted the dog, hoping to avoid drawing further fire.

Hennessey went to Jenna and put a hand under her chin, turning her face towards him. 'You'll kill yourself,' he said shortly.

'Of course I won't. I just – never feel hungry.'

'You never listen to what you feel, that's your trouble.

126

I'll make you a sandwich.'

'I'd rather you didn't. You're just the sort of man who'd make doorsteps.' As she gazed up at him he slipped his thumb into the corner of her mouth and she gasped as it met her tongue. It was a gesture so sexual that she felt naked, although Rachel was talking to Casey and did not see.

'I will do my best,' he said softly and let her go.

He came back a few minutes later with an inch thick ham sandwich and a preoccupied air.

'What's the matter?' asked Jenna, biting into the sandwich. He had put mustard on it and she coughed, feeling her eyes begin to water.

'Nothing. Lilian. She's – brewing.'

'She's what?' Jenna mopped her streaming eyes and held on to her nose which felt as if it was breathing fire. 'This mustard is lethal.'

'Sorry. It's probably matured, we've had it ages. You see, she – started her period this morning.'

'Oh.' Jenna felt rigidly embarrassed. 'Do you think you ought to tell me things like that? I shouldn't like it if William –'

'I don't suppose you would. I only mean that she knows she's not pregnant, and she was sure she was this time. We've done the lot, tests, operations, hanging from the wardrobe, but for some reason she thought this time was it. God knows why, we only did it once this month. First time for ages, too.'

'Hennessey! You can't give me a rundown on your entire sex life! It's – indecent.' Her mouth was distended by a thick lump of sandwich and he laughed at her.

'You look like a hibernating dormouse. Why shouldn't I tell you, I know all about yours. It's only fair.'

'Yes. I suppose it is. But I never thought – how it was for you hearing it. I only knew how it seemed to me telling it. I

127

don't know what to say.'

'Nothing to say. We have our problems too. I never knew a woman so desperate to have a baby, her whole illness stems from that one single thing.'

'What illness? You never said she was ill.' Jenna was beginning to see that there was a whole section of Hennessey's life into which she had never bothered to look.

'I thought it was obvious. She's been in a mental hospital twice, for depression. Been better lately though, until today. D'you know what she told me?'

Jenna stared across at Rachel kicking stones for the dog. She wasn't enjoying this conversation. 'What?'

'That you couldn't have a baby either. It was in some magazine or other.'

'Was it indeed?' She was discouraging.

'Is it true?' He had to know, whether she wanted to tell him or not.

Jenna got to her feet and wandered over to where one of the horses was standing with his head over the half-door of his box. She fed him the rest of her sandwich.

'Don't do that! It's bad for him.'

'No more than it is for me. Do you think we'd better go and help Tony, he's taking ages.'

'No. Don't change the subject, I want to know.'

'And you always get what you want. All right then, yes, it is true. But I don't mind about it. As far as I can see babies grow up into terrible adolescents and the two I have at present are quite sufficient. It's William who wants the baby.'

'What for, for God's sake? He takes no notice of the two he's got.'

'Substandard models, I'm afraid. He despises his first wife and he takes it out on the children. Ours would be different, you see, the perfect baby. He and Hitler would have had a great deal in common, producing pure Arians

128

by the dozen.'

'It sounds revolting. Tell me, Jenna, why doesn't it bother you when it reduces Lilian to a jelly?'

She shrugged. 'Perhaps because I have before me two examples of real children and very wearisome they are. And you can't have babies without sex, and I don't —'

'Like sex,' finished Hennessey. 'I'm not sure I want to go on with this. I don't want you having his children.'

'I'm not likely to have anybody's children, I don't ovulate if you want to be technical about it. Oh look, here's Tony. I never thought I would be glad to see that child.'

Tony was leading his horse towards them, tacked up but with something strange about the martingale. 'I don't think it's quite right,' he said nervously.

'That's your funeral. Get up and take him out to the paddock,' stated Hennessey.

'But —' began Jenna, but Hennessey glared at her. 'You can't let him ride like that,' she hissed. 'He's got it crossed. He'll fall off.'

'Will he now?' said Hennessey and turned to call Rachel. 'Are you coming? You can bring Casey but don't let him run round the field.'

They processed towards the paddock, Jenna already stiff with cold. It was ridiculous being kept in the yard like this, William wouldn't stand it for a moment. What a strange woman his wife must be, cowering behind closed doors and brooding about babies, when she had a man like Hennessey to love. No wonder he had to turn elsewhere. Despite the cold she felt a warm glow stir in the pit of her stomach. Even with all her hang-ups, she had satisfied him. It lent a swagger to her step and when they stood together at the paddock rails she let her hand trail against his thigh. Hennessey stared rigidly ahead, but muttered, 'Don't! I can hardly walk as it is.'

Jenna giggled and strolled behind him brushing shoulders with assumed casualness. Hennessey longed to kiss her, to push his tongue into that moist and scented mouth – there was a yell and Tony and the horse parted company.

'Tony!' shrieked Jenna and raced across the grass. The boy began to get up, but when Jenna reached him he lay down again and let her cradle his head. When Hennessey arrived, at a much slower pace, she was murmuring, 'Have you broken anything? Can you move your legs?'

'If he doesn't move them in double quick time I'll know the reason why,' said Hennessey. 'For God's sake, Jenna, you didn't make half this fuss when you fell off, why expect less of him? Get up, Tony and sort out that martingale. The poor nag doesn't know which way he's going.'

'I couldn't work it out,' explained Tony, climbing stiffly to his feet.

'You'd better try a bit harder then, otherwise you're going to be on the deck rather often today. Off you go.'

'You made that happen,' accused Jenna when Tony was out of earshot, trying to unravel the knitting he had created under the horse's chin.

'I let it happen, you mean. Look, find somewhere out of the wind, I'll sort him out. Now I've got him nicely cowed I can afford to butter him up a bit.'

'It's horsebreaking, all horsebreaking to you, isn't it? That sandwich was your equivalent of a linseed mash!' She was cross and amused at one and the same time and he adored her.

'Go and do as I tell you,' he said softly. 'And you can read this as well.' He held out a sheet of flimsy telex paper, crumpled from his pocket.

'I didn't know you had a telex machine,' said Jenna, taking it with interest.

'Vital equipment that is. "Horse lost, suggest knacker, regards Hennessey." You'd never get away with that on the telephone.'

That did make her laugh. She was still giggling when she and Rachel settled under the hedge and clutched Casey as a hot water bottle. Jenna spread the telex on Casey's warm back and began to read. It was from William.

'Intend buying Caruso yearling at Sales, limit £1.2 million. Your opinion valued. Will you train, reply soonest. Also sending home-bred Royal Diamond colt selected by my wife. Request my son despatched to nearest suitable riding school, warmest regards, Sheppard.'

'Oh, William, I don't know what I'd like to do to you,' murmured Jenna, folding the telex to a parcel the size of a postage stamp.

Rachel wasn't listening. 'Couldn't we have a dog like Casey,' she asked plaintively. 'He's so lovely. He could sleep on my bed and be my faithful companion for ever and ever, he'd pine away when I died.'

'You're not having anything sleeping on your bed,' said Jenna. 'He can sleep in the hall and eat burglars.'

'Oooh, does that mean I can have one? Please Jenna, does it?'

'It means possibly. Wait and see.' She didn't want to talk about dogs, she wanted to think of this from William. She was not surprised by the horses, the Royal Diamond colt was the one she herself had seen, but she was no judge. William was flattering her. The Caruso colt though, that was something else, a bigger investment than ever before. William was aiming at the top. And then that nasty bit at the end about Tony, trust William to try and do it this way. She felt a smouldering anger at him and

131

resolved to give him a piece of her mind on the telephone this evening. Except it would mean admitting that Hennessey had shown her the telex, and William might ask questions. She had better overlook it, just to be on the safe side.

By the time Tony had finished his circuits and bumps Jenna was frozen to the bone. Her teeth were chattering and however hard she tried she could not help but shiver.

Hennessey took one look and said, 'Come into the house, I can't let you freeze to death. You children see to the horse.'

'I don't think I want to,' said Jenna when they reached the back door. 'Not if your wife –'

'She's got to learn to behave.'

He conducted Jenna past the coats and boots and bridles and opened the door into the kitchen. It grated on broken glass. Jenna peered under his arm, but because the room was unfamiliar she could not at first see what was wrong, except that the walls seemed very bare and the floor very cluttered.

'Oh my God!' said Hennessey and stepped into the room. His boots crunched their way across pottery and books, plants and pieces of bread.

'What – what's happened?' asked Jenna.

He spread his hands wide. 'Lilian. She does this sometimes.'

Jenna looked at the empty shelves and swinging cupboard doors and realised that his wife had taken everything and smashed, crashed and hurled it to the floor. It was as if a whirlwind had been in the place, or – a madman.

'She's broken – everything.'

'Yes.' There was a tremor in Hennessey's voice as he bent to pick up the clock, a little, wooden-cased antique given to him by his father. 'This is ruined,' he said, feeling the case come apart in his hands and hearing the twang of

132

springs. 'I don't mind about the rest, but the clock – it was beautiful.'

'It might mend,' said Jenna. 'I have a man who does odd jobs for me, let me take it.'

'It's not your problem. Anyway I think it's past repair.'

'I can try,' said Jenna and took it in her hands. Some of the carving on the front had broken off and she rested the clock on the table and scrabbled around on the floor looking for the bits.

'I'd better find Lilian,' said Hennessey, and went out of the room. Jenna wondered what he would do to her. If someone had wrecked her home like this she would almost want to kill them, yet Hennessey seemed hardly angry at all. Perhaps he was stunned.

When she had found everything she could of the clock she rescued a spider plant, two cups and some books from the mess and began to sweep the rest into a monstrous pile. There was a jug from the dresser, pretty in pink and white, now in a thousand useless pieces. Not a plate was left intact, nor any food, it was all torn up and thrown on the floor. Footsteps sounded in the doorway and she looked up quickly. Thank God it was only Hennessey, she could not bear to face his wife. How do you speak to someone who has done something like this?

'She's asleep,' he said bleakly. 'Curled up with your scrapbook.'

'My scrapbook? What do you mean?'

'She keeps pictures of you. Newspaper cuttings, that sort of thing. It makes her happy.'

Jenna leaned on her broom and stared at him, her thoughts spinning wildly.

'Dan,' she said slowly, 'is your wife totally mad?'

He almost grinned. 'It may look like it, but she isn't. It's simply that – she wants a baby. When it all goes wrong she gets depressed and frustrated, angry if you like, and then

133

– this sort of thing happens.'

'Other people don't do things like this when they can't have what they want,' said Jenna uncompromisingly.

'I bet some of them do. I wonder how civilised your William is when things don't go his way?' He saw a quick flush stain Jenna's cheeks and felt better. Sheppard's reputation for lacerating reprimands was well-known, whether the person concerned was at fault or not. 'So you see it's not really so odd,' he finished.

'If you look at it like that I suppose it isn't.'

Hennessey let himself sink wearily into a chair. Where do you begin to sort out a mess like this? How, on a Sunday, could you buy so much as a loaf?

'I'll go home now,' said Jenna. 'Thomas can come out with the Rolls and bring you a few things. He'll clear this lot up. If you like – if you want – I can sort it all out for you. New dinner services, that sort of thing. I'd let you have a bill.'

'It's all so easy for you, isn't it?' said Hennessey bitterly. 'Nothing happens that you can't cope with. Send the Rolls, open a shop, buy a shop if necessary, it can all be put right with money.'

Jenna was affronted. 'Honestly, Dan, everyone always thinks my houses run themselves! All right it takes money, but someone has to choose the things, engage the staff, order napkins. Yes, I can sort it out and the reason is not only because I've the money but also because I've had an awful lot of practice!'

'Don't fight me, Jenna, I'm not in the mood.'

'No. I don't suppose you are. We'll go now but I will send Thomas and the Rolls. Will you – will you come tomorrow?'

He glanced up. 'Tomorrow? Yes, of course I'll come. I'm sorry, I'm not –' he waved a hand vaguely.

'No. see you tomorrow then.'

134

'Take the dog. You might as well, she's broken his bowl.'

Jenna stood for a moment, knowing there was no way she could give any sort of comfort. Then she gathered up the remains of the clock and quietly let herself out.

Sometimes, although you have only done something once it becomes part of your past and assumes a permanence that is not real. So Jenna felt as she took the thinly-marked track to Honeypot Cottage, placing her feet where they had fallen only once before but in her heart treading a path well-known. He had been in her mind all night and all today, her morning had been spent in caring for him. She was showing off a little, and she knew it, sending an earthenware dinner service of just the right chunky style, exhorting her clock-man to be finished in days. He would see how Jenna Sheppard could do things, he would discover she was not the useless ornament he imagined. One tiny corner of her mind acknowledged that it gave her pleasure to outshine his wife, but it was not a thought she took out and exposed to the light of day. It was belittling to wish to put down someone so far beneath her touch. If only she knew why on earth he had married her.

He was stabling his horse when she arrived and she smiled and called, 'Hello.'

His smile was thin and humourless. 'Hello. Thank you for the things.'

'Did you get them all right? I am glad. How is your wife today?'

He sighed and said wearily, 'I don't want to talk about it, especially not with you.'

'That's not what you said yesterday, you were busy giving me the details of her reproductive cycle, unasked I

135

might add.' She was sharp with annoyance.

'That was yesterday. Let's go inside.'

He knew he was in a vile mood, but there was nothing he could do about it. His world was not as he wished it to be. He wanted to rage at Lilian, hit her for what she had done, but how could you hurt someone so vulnerable? She hurt herself more than she ever hurt him, her misery was so thick you could feel it. She had cried a river this morning. So he turned his anger upon himself and upon Jenna, because she was beautiful and capable and rich. Also she was taking over his life, all right he needed help but he did not need to be sent whole canteens of cutlery. Knives and forks didn't break for God's sake. It outraged his independence and she could not see.

They went up to the bedroom without speaking, and almost against his will Hennessey found himself wanting her. The need seemed almost desperate, he felt that he might explode in some terrible, terrifying way if he did not love her.

Yet he knew that above all else she needed time. Was she right then, that men forgot everything when they needed a woman? No, he forgot nothing, not one spark of the anger that smouldered in his guts. When she stood in the bedroom and unfastened her shirt he bent his head at once and sucked at her nipple.

She was taken by surprise and stood staring down at his bent head, feeling little shocks go through her as he teased her with his teeth. It frightened her to feel it, she felt pushed alone towards the edge of a cliff.

'Don't,' she murmured, and tried to pull away, but he held her close with his arms around her waist. 'Don't!' she cried again, pulling back against the grasp of his teeth. It hurt, but as yet not unpleasantly.

He stopped then and made her take off her jeans. 'Get on the bed,' he ordered and reluctant but eager, she obeyed. When he lay down beside her she turned to him, lips parted, but what she intended to say was never spoken. With almost a groan he kissed her, letting his tongue sink into the warm softness of her mouth, kissing as he had not kissed in years. For Jenna it blotted out the world, she was conscious of nothing but the dark, breathless feeling of his tongue on hers and her response deceived him. He forgot himself. Suddenly Jenna felt him, probing, thrusting between her legs, trying to invade her body. Her hands pushed at him, her muscles convulsed and she let out a strangled shriek.

'For Christ's sake! Jenna!' One moment he had been holding a woman, the next a block of concrete. The muscles of her belly were so hard he felt he could have stood on them to little effect.

'I'm sorry! Don't touch me,' wailed Jenna, and she pulled away and hunched her knees up to her chin.

'I'm the one who should be sorry,' muttered Hennessey, stroking the curve of her back. 'I never realised – is this what you're like with him?'

She was crying. 'Yes. It's been worse than that lately. I thought it would be different.'

'It would have been if I hadn't been so cross with you. Why the hell did you have to send me a ton of stuff? It's like a bloody hardware store at home, what the hell do you mean trying to take over my life?'

She turned towards him then, her eyes wide. 'I wasn't! I thought you'd be grateful, having such a useless sort of wife.' He flinched and she muttered, 'I didn't mean to say that.'

'I told you, she's ill. Don't be unkind to her, Jenna, she can't fight back. Oh, I know you wanted to show me how well you could do it but – it's my home. Nothing like your home. What in God's name am I going to do with a set of candelabra? I'm not flaming Liberace!'

137

'They were pretty. They're only pottery ones, they match the dinner service.'

'I'm sending them back. Christ, Jen, I'm sorry, I know you meant to help. And I'm sorry about just now, I shouldn't have tried so soon. Does your husband still go on when you tense up like that?'

She got off the bed and fumbled in her coat pocket for a handkerchief, blowing her nose and wiping her eyes. Her hair covered the awful thinness as if embarrassed to let it be seen. 'He goes on regardless. He orders me to relax, but when I'm like that –' she shrugged, and it was wordlessly pathetic.

'I don't know how he can do it.' He had felt how she was, the man must have to force himself into her as if storming a castle. Perhaps Sheppard enjoyed it, hearing her scream. Hennessey felt like murder. 'Come back and I'll cuddle you. Just cuddle, nothing else.'

'I think I'd rather go home.'

'Please, Jen. I'm sorry I was angry. I'm often like that when Lilian – has one of her moods, not fit company for man nor beast. I can't be angry with her, you see.'

Jenna sighed and went to sit on the edge of the bed. Hennessey toyed with her hair, pulling long strands of it into the air and letting them fall, burying his face in the thick black coils.

'I know I went over the top,' she admitted. 'It was part thank-you for everything. Tony's thrilled with you because you gave him a word of praise, he's completely forgotten all the perfectly dreadful things you did to him. I actually liked him yesterday evening. And Rachel is besotted with that damn dog, who was sick on the carpet from overfeeding. It was awfully kind of you, Dan.'

He said nothing but lay, propped on an elbow, playing with her hair. His face had a closed, inward look and she knew he was thinking thoughts he did not intend to share.

138

She suddenly felt very lonely, and said in a slightly too loud voice, 'By the way, what are you going to do about those horses? William rang me and said he hadn't heard from you.'

He roused himself to answer her. 'It's a bit difficult really. I don't like Caruso stock, lacks guts. Your husband wants to win the big ones, and for that you need a horse with some fight in him. From the breeding, this one might have what it takes physically, but as far as his mind goes, he might not want to push himself that hard. And when you're paying that much you shouldn't have doubts. I shall tell him but if he still wants to go ahead, then yes, I'll train it. I can't afford to be that scrupulous, though if it doesn't come good I'll probably wish I had been.'

'Yes. William can be very unforgiving. Still, there's the other one, the Royal Diamond colt. Don't you like him even?'

'Hard to say since I don't know what you go for in horses. My guess is it's a big fat pet or a leggy neurotic, and I don't like the thought of either. In horses that is, I'm a bit more broadminded in bed.' He bent his head and kissed the point of her hip, bone covered with the thinnest of skin.

Jenna quivered. 'It's a lovely horse. At least, I thought it was at the time, but I only saw it in the field and I said casually to William that I thought it was the sort you'd like. Now I can't even remember what colour it is, but it must have been nice for me to say it. William's buttering me up, you see.'

'Christ. Most men buy bunches of flowers. Anyway, why is this sugar daddy such a sod to Tony? Why on earth should I send him to a riding school?'

Jenna signed. 'William hates Tony, I think. I pretend he doesn't but it's true. Like an idiot I told him that Tony enjoyed coming to you and William is trying to stop it. He

139

knows I won't arrange it so he's trying to do it through you. Very devious is William.'

She saw Hennessey's puzzled expression and laughed. 'I'm not very biddable, you know. I sometimes think William finds me awfully hard to handle because he doesn't often stand up and fight, he does things like this. I can be very difficult when I feel like it.'

He sat up and nuzzled her shoulder. 'Do you feel like it now?'

'I'm – not sure.'

'How about now?' He was caressing her ear with his tongue.

'Mmmm,' she murmured, and turned her head towards him. He wouldn't hurt her now, she could tell, look he wasn't angry at all. It shook her to find that her tension evoked a new and different response, almost without trying she found her body retreating from panic. As his mouth touched hers she subsided back on to the bed.

Chapter Seven

Lilian wandered round the kitchen setting out all the new things with an almost childlike pleasure. She thought it was sweet of Mrs Sheppard to send all those presents, but she was like that, kind to others. The moment she realised what a terrible thing had happened she sent all this to Lilian.

In her mind Lilian did not think that she herself had caused the destruction. If Dan had asked her and kept on asking she might have admitted it, but in an indirect way – 'who did it?' 'Lilian.' If he did not ask then she spoke and behaved as if it were an unforseen calamity, possibly an earthquake, for which sympathy was an appropriate response. It surprised her that Dan did not see this. When she had lived at home with her parents and she broke something they always understood that it wasn't her fault. They comforted her in case she felt upset at the loss, which was often the case. They put her to bed and made her milky drinks, and so should Dan. But he didn't understand, which made it all the more pleasing that Mrs Sheppard clearly did. Lilian rubbed the candlesticks with a soft cloth and set them on the dresser.

When Dan came in he said, 'I'm sending them back. We don't need them.'

'But they're from Mrs Sheppard! I like them.' She set her face in a stubborn mould and glared at him.

'I'll buy you something else for the dresser,' wheedled her husband, knowing how determined Lilian could be at times.

'I don't want anything else. She gave them to me and they're mine.'

He stood and looked at her for a moment, remarking that she almost seemed cleansed, now that her tantrum was over. The brooding was gone, the whites of her eyes had lost their yellow tinge and she no longer hunched her shoulders when she moved, as if nursing a pain in her chest. Even the tears had passed, like a tropical storm. Rather than spoil things he would send the candlesticks back tomorrow he thought, and crossing the room to his wife he gave her waist a squeeze. 'We'll see. Why don't you get the tea now? I'm starving.'

It occurred to him that he ought to feel guilt in touching his wife when he had spent the afternoon with Jenna, but all he felt was peace. His mind was clear and thoughts slotted into place so easily that it seemed he could solve the problems of the world, given a sheet of paper and half an hour's silence. He made a mental note to tell Jenna how good she was for him, this morning he had been clogged with frustrations, he had achieved nothing except the suppression of the lads, who crept around with their heads down hoping to avoid his notice. He had bawled Geoff out for calling the vet to a leg without asking, although on another day he would have been every bit as furious if Geoff had referred to him first. Now, because of Jenna, he could set about his work with calm purpose, and his first task must be to apologise. It showed weakness to kick others for one's own failings.

He thought of what his father would make of all this, and it brought a rueful grin to his lips. Of Presbyterian stock, Andrew Hennessey lived by a code that was as rigid as it was selfless. A farmer all his life, he was revolted by the casual cruelties that others practiced in their live-stock, letting familiarity dull their sense of another's pain. He believed, and he taught his son, that there was no excuse for unkindness. And in a way Dan was still follow-ing his teaching, although he doubted that his father would agree. Life with Lilian was so very, very lonely. If Dan was to be kind to her then he had to look elsewhere for release, and where he looked was Jenna. He had not realised how much he needed someone to talk to. A strange woman, Jenna, who kept a part of herself alto-gether secret while seeming to be quite honest. But then perhaps he did the same. There were barriers which he could never lower, things he did not admit even to himself. And wrong as it was to take pleasure in Jenna, it hurt no-one at all, so there could be no reason to stop. If there had been reasons by the dozen he could not have done it, she haunted his mind like a living, breathing ghost. They would meet again on Friday, at the races. He could live until Friday.

Hennessey had three runners that Friday and all the owners were present. Jenna had the unfamiliar sensation of being one of several, for no other trainer in her employ had ever done other than put her first. Today she realised that as Hennessey said but she had not believed, for him every horse was as important as every other, no matter who it belonged to. It was something she did not like.

They stood in an excited little group, talking and sipping their drinks. Jenna was polite but withdrawn, watching as the others hung on their trainer's words, her expression one of detached interest, like a visitor at the zoo. And the cooler she was the more they pandered to

143

her, constantly flattering and courting her attention.

'You must know more about this than even Mr Hennessey, you have so many horses,' ventured Harold Carstairs, who owned a chain of supermarkets but knew when he was outclassed.

'I would hardly dare to say so,' murmured Jenna. 'In fact Mr Hennessey doesn't approve of my choice of horses at all.'

'Let's say I reserve judgment,' said Dan with a smile, but she would not meet his eye.

'I think I read somewhere that your husband is at one of your studs in America,' began Mrs Wildenhall, a short fluffy lady who found Jenna terrifying and showed it by becoming excessively vivacious.

'Did you?' replied Jenna with ice in her voice.

Suddenly Hennessey was annoyed. Here she was, with more than any of them and she could not be polite. Her world was divided as his could never be, two sorts of people, those she cared for and those she did not, and for one she would do everything and for the other nothing at all.

'Come along, Mrs Sheppard,' he said crisply, 'you can help me saddle a horse, you might at least find that interesting. If you'll excuse us.' He hooked a hand under her elbow and removed her from the circle before she had time to think of a reply.

'What on earth do you think you're doing?' she demanded as soon as they were out of earshot. 'I don't want to go anywhere near your blasted horse.'

'Is that so? Well, I can't stand watching you be as cold as you know how to those harmless people. Why will you one day charm the birds off the trees because it suits you to hear them sing, and the next freeze them all to death? It doesn't hurt to be kind, Jenna, they were thrilled to be talking to you.'

He was glaring at her and she felt very small. 'Don't shout at me, people are looking. Anyway, you were being horrid. I don't like it when you ignore me.'

'I didn't ignore you. And it's no reason to take it out on them, you're not a child.'

'I'm not the sort of person you think I am, either. Do you know what happens if people like me chat nicely to people like them? They ring you up for weeks after and want you to open their supermarkets, turn up at their fêtes, go to their houses for dinner. And if you do, they ask you to join the board of governors at their pet school. Sooner or later you have to be rude, so I make it sooner.'

'That's rubbish. If it did happen all you need do is set one of your flunkeys on them and you'd put them off telephones for life. If you want my opinion you've been spoiled, Mrs Sheppard, and it hasn't done you any good at all.'

She felt an upsurge of anger so strong that it almost choked her. She knew that if she didn't get away she would murder him, and she turned and ran towards the door. Hennessey looked after her for a moment and then followed, moving through the watching heads with an unreadable expression.

He caught up with her near the stables, where she was standing disconsolate, unsure of what to do. There were fewer people here, mostly stable lads and trainers.

'Jenna! Are you all right? You're not going to cry, are you?'

'Cry? If I'd stayed there another minute I'd have hit you and that would have looked good in the papers. If I'm a spoiled brat what are you, you conceited, arrogant worm you, letting them fawn on you as if you were the fount of all wisdom. I hope everything loses, and then I can watch you squirm.'

'Bad-tempered bitch,' said Hennessey and popped a

swift kiss on the top of her head, leaping backwards immediately as she raised her fist to strike.

She watched him laughing at her and she wanted to scream. Instead, she arranged her face in smooth lines and held out her hands. 'I'm sorry, Dan. I will be good,' she said demurely and he took hold of her fingers. She went close to him, raised his hand as if to brush it with her lips and sank her teeth into the pad of his thumb. He gasped and swore, and she moved away with a smile. 'Now I'll go and be nice to them,' she purred, and strolled away, inwardly shocked rigid by her behaviour. She was turning into a vicious woman and it wasn't like her. She was goading him to something but she did not know what.

Ever since that last afternoon she had felt so restless, she was hot and cold and she did not know how to cure it. Now they were fighting and it was all her fault, which was unfair when there was nothing she could do about it. Something had happened to the control mechanisms and try as she would they refused to work. When Hennessey came back into the bar it was to find her chatting with rival verve to Mrs Wildenhall, her glass going repeatedly to her lips as she agreed rather wildly that Marks and Spencer knickers were wonderful value.

'You never wore a pair of Marks and Spencer knickers in your life, Jenna, and I should know,' said Hennessey and Mrs Wildenhall gasped and then giggled.

'Been haunting the washing line again, Dan?' retorted Jenna, but her face had flamed. He couldn't let everyone know just to get his own back, it was going too far. She raised her eyes to his in mute entreaty and he stared thoughtfully back.

'Come and talk to your jockey,' he said and Jenna muttered, 'Yes, Dan,' and followed him meekly.

'Are you going to apologise?' he asked grimly as they trod the turf towards the paddock. The horses were already parading, their tails hanging like spun silk, the grooms looking uncomfortable in suits or underdressed in jeans.

'They should have a uniform,' said Jenna.

'What? Who?' Hennessey could not follow her changes, she made him feel giddy.

'The grooms. They never look right. Oh, of course I'm sorry, Dan, I never meant to do that. I've never done anything so awful in my whole life and I don't know why I did it then. Did it hurt?'

'Of course it bloody hurt! You've got teeth like a cannibal.'

They stood on the smooth turf and waited for the jockey to appear. It was cold and Jenna shivered a little, turning the collar of her short mink jacket up under her chin.

'If you ate more you wouldn't always feel so cold,' said Hennessey.

'I am trying. I ate a boiled egg for breakfast today. It was ghastly.'

'I don't like them much either. God Jenna, I'd give anything to be in bed with you now.'

She blushed again and said almost tearfully, 'So would I. I think that's why I'm cross, because we can't.'

A wave of feeling came over Hennessey as he gazed down at her, so svelte yet with a little-girl look of confusion and shame. He wanted to laugh and cry and make violent love to her, but all he could do was settle her jacket more closely under her chin. 'Monday', he whispered, and she nodded.

The jockeys came into the paddock, walking stiff-legged and brisk. They were such small, muscley little men, some with the bland faces of youth, others with the marks of years of wear. For the Sheppard horses Hennessey always employed the best, on this occasion a freelance of considerable experience.

'How do you do,' said Jenna politely and the man touched his cap. He was more interested in Hennessey who could tell him how to win the race. The owner was no use at all.

'Get him away fast and get him on to the rails,' said Hennessey. 'He can't run in a straight line to save his life and if you take him up the middle we'll end up on the mat. He's got a fair turn of foot so you can make a late run, but watch him, he doesn't run straight under pressure. We'll settle for a place.'

'Will we?' asked Jenna.

'Christ, yes. The others are good horses. If I'd had any sense I'd have sent the bugger home the day he arrived.'

The jockey allowed the vestige of a smile to cross his starved and sunken cheeks. He led a difficult life and it took a lot to amuse him for he lived a stone under his natural weight, travelled thousands of miles a year and had rheumatism in his hands. Also it was the end of the season and he needed a rest.

'I'll see what I can do, sir,' he grunted and Jenna shrugged and sighed. All the other trainers noticed and felt a lot happier, that was one owner who did not expect to win.

When the horses went down to the start she and Hennessey made their way to the stands. Carstairs and Mrs Wildenhall were there, and they stared at the approaching pair with such frank curiosity that Jenna felt embarrassed.

'They think we're having an affair,' she muttered.

'They're very nearly right.'

She smiled then, to think how unlikely it was that she, the woman who hated sex, should be having an affair. Well, almost. It made her feel sexy, and she greeted her fellow owners with unusual warmth.

Only minutes passed before she realised her mistake. No sooner had the horses left the starting stalls than Carstairs began reading the race, in what he thought was Peter O'Sullivan style. 'There he is, tail-end Charlie. Sunburst in the lead, followed by Tea-Towel – yours is last Mrs Sheppard. Challenged by Heraklion –'

Meanwhile Mrs Wildenhall kept up non-stop commiserations. 'Poor Mrs Sheppard. Never mind. Better luck next time. My horse doesn't always win, well you have to accept the rough with the smooth, don't you.'

On and on they went while Jenna and Hennessey stared resolutely through their glasses and made their own assessments.

'Boxed in,' muttered Jenna.

'He's OK for a bit. Look, there he goes, good man, Len.'

'And you're bringing up the rear,' boomed Carstairs.

'Poor Mrs Sheppard,' shrilled Mrs Wildenhall.

'Christ, look at him wander,' moaned Hennessey, as the gelding followed a wavering course to the post. He was beaten half a length into second.

Jenna and Hennessey exchanged glances. 'Not bad,' she acknowledged.

'Be nice to the jockey, he worked for you. That horse should have been born a tram.'

'I beg your pardon?' said Mrs Wildenhall, looking puzzled.

'Then it could have run on rails,' explained Jenna patiently but the woman still looked blank.

'Better luck next time,' boomed Carstairs. 'Can't win 'em all.'

'No. Indeed.' Jenna and Hennessey left with relief to welcome back the sweating, twitching horse.

'Very well done,' said Jenna to the jockey. 'You rode a magnificent race.' She beamed at him and the jockey blinked. It was not often they were so pleased to come second.

'Pleasure, ma'am,' he replied. 'Does hang left a trifle.'

'He does indeed. I'm delighted that you did so well.' Another dazzling smile and the jockey staggered off to the weighing room, his little frame loaded down by the tiny saddle.

'Workmanlike sort. We should use him again,' said Jenna.

'Teach your grandmother to suck eggs,' said Hennessey, and she grinned. Nothing annoyed him more than to be told his job, she must remember that.

The remainder of the afternoon was somewhat trying, but fun all the same. As Hennessey predicted but Carstairs refused to believe, One Stop Shopping came nowhere. No sooner had they survived his gloom than they were faced with Mrs Wildenhall's euphoria when her filly won by a neck. She screeched so much that it gave Jenna a headache.

'I really do think I should go,' she said at last. 'The children will be home this evening. Thank you so much for a lovely day everyone.'

'Oh, Mrs Sheppard – I wanted to ask you something,' said Carstairs, his face flushed with alcohol. 'I've got a new shop opening in Burnley soon and although my wife usually does the honours I thought this time if I could prevail upon you – nothing to it really, it's just like launching a ship.'

'You don't chuck bottles of champagne through the window, do you?' queried Jenna. 'I've launched two oil tankers and a ferry, as it happens, and honoured as I am that you should ask me, Mr Carstairs, I am really far too shy. The last time I had to make a speech I fainted. Please forgive me.' She spoke with finality and avoided Hennessey's eye.

'I thought you were shy from the way you were talking,' gushed Mrs Wildenhall and Jenna said, 'Er – yes. I really do think I must go now. Goodbye everyone.'

'Sunday,' said Hennessey. 'Tony's riding.'

'Yes. If I can. Goodbye.'

She drove home in the Rolls thinking how wonderful life could be sometimes, with excitement and fun and someone to share the laughter. She would take her camera on Sunday and take some photographs of them all, she had let that hobby lapse of late. As the car turned into her drive she was thinking with some appetite of dinner, for the children would be home and Elsa would be letting caution fly. She ran up the steps and into the house, calling, 'Anyone home? We got second.'

Casey bounded towards her, barking and squirming with delight. She pushed him away from her tights, saying, 'Down! Down Casey!' in mock anger, for it was pleasant to be greeted with such verve. It made you feel wanted. George came down the stairs, moving with unusual haste, for he also liked to be in the hall to welcome her when she came in.

'Second George,' repeated Jenna. 'I hope you had an each-way bet.'

'Yes, madam. I'm afraid that Tony is unwell, I wonder if you would go and see him before I call the doctor.'

'Unwell? Oh no!' She raced up the stairs, nearly breaking her neck as Casey tangled his legs with hers, sure in her mind that Tony had done something dreadful to himself. When she raced into the room and saw the swellings under his chin she felt speechless with relief.

'Don't look so pleased, it's mumps. The whole school's got it.' He moved his head with difficulty.

'I thought you'd had it. Or was that Rachel?'

'Rachel. Still, it saves me from chemistry.'

'No, it doesn't, you don't feel ill with mumps. I shall ask

151

that nice young man to set you some work.'

Tony grunted and hunched a shoulder. 'He already did, actually. It's in my bag. But now I can't ride.'

Jenna thought of the long, empty Sunday ahead and felt her spirts sag. 'No. I'll phone Hennessey. But the horse will still be there when you're better. Can you eat or is this terminal?'

'I can manage soft things I think. Some soup, a creamy pudding, that sort of thing. Tell Elsa.'

'Ask Elsa please, you mean. Have you got anything to read?' Her mind's eye saw his pile of dirty magazines and she wished she had removed them.

'I've got a book, thanks. Can I have something to drink?'

'I'll send up some lemon barley water. You look lovely, like a pet chipmunk.'

She left and went to her dressing room, reflecting that she always felt totally loving when people were ill. It touched some vein of sympathy that was hidden under normal circumstances and made her tolerant and patient and warm. It was sad about Sunday, though perhaps it was as well. To meet and not touch was like torture. If only, if only it could come right, if she could hold him as he should be held and find release. Rachel burst into the room and she jumped.

'If Tony's off school can't I be as well? They don't know I haven't got mumps.'

With a sigh Jenna turned her thoughts back to the tangled and thorny thickets of teenage life.

It was raining on Monday, a cold lashing rain that made Tony glad to be in bed. When Jenna told him she had to go out he was curious and in the end she lied and said she was going to the doctor for a check-up. She drove away with an odd feeling inside her, partly excitement but tinged with fear. She wanted so much from today.

Despite boots, anorak and hat she was wet through by the time she reached the cottage and Dan was already there.

'I lit a fire,' he said when he saw her. 'Dry things out a bit. Everyone thought I was mad going out in this.'

'Yes. We are mad, I think. I had to lie to Tony.' She pulled off her hat and her hair tumbled around her.

'How is he? I hope to God you haven't brought mumps, I'd never forgive you.'

'I think he's OK, a bit bored. What's so terrible about mumps?'

Hennessey grinned and gestured towards his flies. 'Makes your balls fall off. So come on, let's make the most of them before the worst happens.'

She blushed and giggled, suddenly shy. He came and stood very close to her. 'Your hair's wet,' he whispered. The room was dark but for the flickering of the logs in the grate, and the rain lashed on the windows, making the house seem a refuge from the storm.

'Let's stay down here.' Jenna was taking off her clothes, and her hands were shaking. Just to be with Dan stirred her, it was as if her body remembered what he did and cried out in yearning. There was a moistness between her thighs.

When she was naked she swept her hair back and faced him, so long and pale and slender that it made him weak. 'Do it properly,' she whispered.

'Not if I have to hurt you.'

'But I want it. Even if it hurts I want it, I can't bear – not.'

And he wanted her so much he could hardly breathe. When they sank into the circle of firelight it was like sinking into a deep and secret pool.

Never before had she felt like this. When his lips touched her throat she gasped at the thrill of it, as if her whole body was charged with a current named desire. When he reached for her breast she writhed under his fingers, for it was almost too much to bear.

'My love. My little one.' He was above her now, gazing down into her beautiful face, and for one second, as he touched her, a shadow came into her eyes. But then her legs were parted, she had opened like a flower to welcome him and he was home.

Suddenly she was at a place she had never been. He had taken her to a new country and even the colours were changed, echoing what she had seen before but striking new chords of feeling in her soul. She clung to the man who had carried her there, afraid but sure he would not let her fall and he held her and took her with him, faster and faster until at last – the world came to an end. Her cry was like that of a stricken doe.

'Jenna. Jenna darling, did I hurt you?' He lay on her body, still within, bonded to her by sweat.

She opened her eyes and gazed up at him, aware that her nails had raked his back like talons. 'I never thought – I could feel that. Like pain. But not. Like dying.'

'Like freedom. Jenna, my Jenna, you touched my soul.' There were tears on his cheeks and she took them on her fingers and put her fingers to her lips.

'I want all of you. I don't want you to leave me.' She wrapped her legs around him and her body gave a little convulsion of joy. 'I've wanted this since the day I saw you and I didn't know what I wanted.'

'I knew. I thought it would send me mad.' He was in heaven and he knew it, taking handfuls of hair and smothering his face with the glory of it. As the dark afternoon drew to a close he loved her again.

*　　　*　　　*

What should have been an end became a new beginning. There was no hope now of retreat and they could only go on, but what was ahead they did not know. They had stepped out of time and if they knew that it could not be forever, that was something they would rather forget. Hennessey came to hate racing days, for then he could not see Jenna. If she went to the races with him and they talked and laughed, he would look up to see the eyes of others. Was it so obvious then? Perhaps so. One day they went with Lord Staveley, on an ordinary day, and for no reason at all that Dan could see Staveley drew him aside and murmured, 'Take care, old chap. Devilish sticky fella to cross is Sheppard, there's not many live to tell the tale. Adores his wife you know. No need to explain, dear chap, I know I'm probably seeing things that aren't there, but take a warning from a friend. Step lively.'

So he and Jenna did not go racing together, and the days hung like lead in his hands.

As for Jenna, she blossomed like a flower in the desert after years without water. The world was made new for her, even the silk of her dresses felt freshly gentle on her skin. How had she never noticed how good the world smelled? Of earth, and grass, the smell of coffee or new baked bread. No longer did George nag her to eat. She ate little, she would always do so, but it was a rare day now when she ate nothing at all. And because she was happy she could let warmth spread, spending hours playing Scrabble with Tony, taking Rachel and Casey for walks. Even to William she was gentle, answering his questions over the phone without rancour. All was well so long as he did not come home.

She must be careful though, of Stephen. When he saw her in the garden taking photographs of the dog, happy in herself and in her task, he said, 'Anyone would think you were in love, Jenna.'

'Don't be silly, Stephen. It can only be with Casey, he's a gem.'

'Nasty, smelly animal. Go on, love, tell me. I'll keep your secret.'

As if there was anyone she needed to tell. It was her own, precious thing, and the world should not look at it. Anyway, she wasn't in love. It was just – Dan, and that was different.

'Go away, Steve, I'm busy. Or better still hold Casey over there while I set this up.'

'You can trust me you know.' He spoke with unusual sincerity, but Jenna turned her shoulder. It might be true, but his willingness to hear was not matched by hers to confide.

'There's nothing to tell,' she insisted, and a gentle flush stained her cheek. Stephen went resignedly to hold the dog.

The centre of the universe was their cottage, a place of wonder and discovery. In the long, dark afternoons of autumn they talked and made love until they could love no more, yet still they were reluctant to go.

'I wish we could live here for always,' said Jenna one day, threading her long legs back into her tights.

Hennessey was lying on the bed, watching her. 'Would we be happy do you think? Together? We're different Jen, very different, but like this it doesn't show.'

She turned then delicious in jumper and tights, as if auditioning for Peter Pan.

'How are we different? In superficial things like money, yes of course. But in the things we want and need? I don't think so.'

He sat up and began to look for his socks, the muscles of his back making hard ridges against his spine. 'I want a top-class stable full of classic horses. You don't want that. I come from solid, respectable farming stock that would rather die than sell half an acre of land, and you – where do you come from? You never say.'

Jenna swept her hair over her face and brushed it vigorously. 'Nowhere very important,' she said in a muffled voice.

'So tell me. Little beggar girl from the backstreets of Naples, come on admit it.' He swept the hair aside and peered in at her, popping a kiss on the end of her nose. He knew only too well that there were many things she hid from him.

'No, nothing like that. My father – he was an ambassador. We went everywhere with him, mother and I, two years in Rio, three in Madrid, we were upmarket gypsies. I was an only child. Sometimes I went to school, sometimes I had a governess because – I was pretty, you see. Men followed me. When I was ten a man tried to get me in his car outside the school. He asked me and when I said no he made a grab, and I screamed and screamed. When people came he drove off but they caught up with him. He was arrested. It made my parents very nervous and I was never allowed to go anywhere alone, ever. And when I was twelve – but you don't want to hear all this.' She gave him a humourless smile and reached for her jeans.

'Go on Jenna. I want to know.'

'There isn't any more. Nothing important.' She did not want to say, she had said too much already.

He caught her arm and gently pulled her to him, holding close. 'Tell me. I won't mind.'

'But I will,' she whispered. 'Oh, it's nothing very terrible, not by today's standards. It seemed so at the time though. I hated telling people, I never did. You see, when I was twelve my father ran off with a Spanish countess. The scandal was terrible, it caused a diplomatic incident. And my mother was – devastated. I can see now why he did it, this woman was terribly glamorous and passionate,

157

and my mother wasn't like that at all. An English county lady, very sweet and kind, but not sexy in the least. Solid tweed suits and twinsets, that was my mother. She trusted my father implicitly you see, and that made it worse. It was weeks before she really believed it had happened and after that she never trusted a man again, not even the caretaker or the plumber. I was sent to a French convent and they spent six years trying to persuade me to become a nun. Even I began to think I'd look rather nice in a habit but my mother thought that was going a bit far. When I left we had an apartment in Paris and my mother saw that she could get back into the swing of things if she started taking me about, so one minute I was in the convent and the next in this frantic social whirl. It was dizzying.'

'Wasn't your mother worried about what would happen to you? You're a beauty Jenna, and at eighteen, in Paris –'

Jenna giggled. 'I was never alone for a minute. Which was just as well because there were hordes and hordes of men, it was terrifying. In a way I loved it, the clothes, the excitement, but after the convent – I couldn't enjoy it the way others did somehow. I always felt apart. And people said I was cold.'

Hennessey held her tighter in guilty remembrance of the time when he too had thought that. 'What happened next?'

'I met William, we fell in love, we got married. And my mother now lives in earthy seclusion on a farm in Brittany, William bought it for her. So it all ended very respectably, you see.'

She pulled away and went back to dressing. There, that was over. She felt better now that he knew. In all her years at the convent she had dreaded anyone asking about her father, she would ignore someone for months rather than respond to a query. Sooner or later they learned not to ask because it paid to be friendly with Jenna. There was glamour in being witness to her complete self-sufficiency and everyone had always known she would make a brilliant marriage. The triumph when she netted Sheppard was as much her friends' as her own.

'So what are you then?' challenged Hennessey, pulling on his jumper. 'Nun, English lady or Parisian flirt? You could be all of those things.'

'I don't need you to tell me I'm paranoid about men. I've always known that. Anyway, I'm cured.'

'Are you?' Hennessey was staring at her and his face was very still. She did not know what he was thinking.

'Why did you marry your wife?' she asked suddenly. The question was one they avoided. They never asked such things, either of them, for in a roundabout way it meant 'Do you love me?' and that could never be answered. But she had to know.

Hennessey cleared his throat before he spoke, but still his voice sounded thick. 'She was pretty. And sweet. I needed someone. Her father's farm's next door to ours and everyone thought – I thought – that if we married it would make a good size holding. Her father gave me my start in training, before I moved to where I am now, so you see, when it came to it, I owed them something. And she loved me. I thought I loved her. Perhaps I did and perhaps I do. I try always to behave as if I do, because she deserves that. It isn't anything to do with us.'

Did he mean that or did he only wish to mean it? 'Do you make love to her?' she asked shrilly, because again she had to know.

Hennessey sighed. 'That's a foolish thing to ask.'

'Is it? But it makes my flesh creep to think –' she shuddered, eloquently, and Hennessey caught her shoulders. 'I try not to, Jenna. Sometimes – yes I do. She wants a baby and I have to. It isn't often.' And always I

159

think of you, he added silently, and knew that it was not Jenna he betrayed.

She pulled away and began to gather her things, hat, scarf, coat.

'Thursday,' said Hennessey.

'No. I can't. Tony gets suspicious.'

'I don't care what Tony is, you have to come. Please Jenna.'

'No. Make love to your wife instead.' She dragged the door open and flew down the stairs and out of the cottage, tearful and sick. Like Goldilocks after eating all the porridge she thought as she blundered her way along the muddy, brambley path.

'Jenna! Jenna!' He was following. Tears began to blind her and her hair was tangled across her face. She stumbled against a bush and in a second was held fast by her hair. When he came to her she was sobbing and her nose was running.

'Make it let go,' she gasped, wrenching at her hair.

'I love you, Jenna.'

'You can't say that, it isn't allowed. I won't come again, it's all gone too far.'

'If I don't come I'll call at the house. I won't let you stop, I can't.'

'My husband comes home next week.'

There was silence. 'That's no reason to stop,' he said at last.

'Isn't it? I'd feel like a prostitute.'

'I don't care. I didn't go through all this to hand you back and let him make a meal of you. Like a defrosted chop. He can't love you like I can, you know he can't. It need only be once a week, Jenna, and then you'll go away on trips and things – then we can stop. But not now. I won't let you.'

She had stopped crying and was untangling the length of her hair. 'It's wrong, Dan.'

160

'We're not hurting anyone. If it makes us nicer at home then it's right. Come on Thursday, Jen darling, you must.'

She smiled up at him, a watery, unsure smile. 'Last time before William gets home.'

'Let's make the most of it.' He took her wet, smeared face in his hands and kissed her.

Thursday was a bitter-sweet time, when they loved as if the world was theirs to keep. When Jenna rose to get dressed, Hennessey said, 'God made a mistake somewhere. Why weren't you born the girl next door to me?'

'I'd have despised you for a ploughboy,' smiled Jenna. 'Anyway, we're different, you said so.'

He pulled her to the bed again and kissed her. 'Say you love me. Just for today.'

'It would only make you sad. It doesn't help.'

'I could wish your husband dead.' There was a huskiness in his voice that made Jenna shiver.

'There would still be your wife. Please be careful, Dan, they must never ever know. It would be so awful.'

'Would it? Yes, it would, for Lilian. It would finish her. But Jenna, I wish you were mine!' He held her so tight that the breath was squeezed from her, and when at last he let her go he looked white and ill.

'When will you come again?' asked Hennessey as she put on her coat.

'I don't know. When I can. Not often.'

She seemed so calm and so sure of what she should do that it enraged him. 'I wish this hurt you as much as it does me,' he muttered. 'You go back to your money and your foul, stupid husband and you leave me bleeding. I could kill you Jenna!'

She jumped as his voice rose to a shout. That was men for you, even Dan, dear kind Dan, had in him this

161

horrrible, terrifying violence, suppressed but never vanquished. 'I'll come when I can,' she repeated, and fled. Hennessey groaned and sank wearily on to the bed.

Chapter Eight

Kentucky had not been good for William. He looked tired and sallow, his skin lacking the bloom of health. Too much good living thought Jenna, with the scorn of the natural ascetic. There were problems too at the stud, for the yearlings were not making the prices they should and one of the stallions was seriously underbooked, which had forced a reduction in stud fee. Not a happy trip in fact.

In a strange way Jenna was not upset to see her husband, and that surprised her. She had not thought this new confidence could stretch to encompass William, but she had not felt a twinge of guilt when she raised her cheek for his kiss. They were formal, a little constrained, like fencers looking for an opening, not with intent to wound but only to explore. Yes, she had been busy, especially with Tony ill, oh, and she was seeing that doctor. One afternoon a week, the day varied. It was doing her a great deal of good.

William smiled and enfolded her in a hug, but she let him know by a tiny stiffening that she expected him to go no further. He felt a stab of familiar, helpless rage. Should he demand compliance and know himself a brute, or accept her denial and with it her victory? He never knew how to cope with Jenna.

'The Royal Diamond colt should arrive next week,' he said with assumed casualness, and despised himself for courting her goodwill. But it was worth it when she smiled and said with warmth, 'It was sweet of you to send him. Tell me, what does Gerard think of his prospects? I'd feel a bit happier letting Hennessey have him if there was someone else's good opinion to defend myself with. You know how particular he is about his horses.'

'Hennessey will train what we give him or I'll know the reason why,' said Sheppard, evading the question. 'He's getting above himself, he even finds fault with the Caruso yearling.'

'Yes, I know. I'd believe him if I were you, he knows what he's doing.' Jenna drifted across the room, her black silk dress hanging straight as water. She looked – priceless, thought William, and snapped, 'How is it that Hennessey is always right and the rest of the world wrong? Everyone knows the colt is superbly bred, they don't come any better. He's getting it and I expect results, I'm owed them if only because of his cheek.'

She withdrew from the argument, saying, 'You're probably right. Tell me, how is Gerard?'

Trust Jenna to notice what he didn't want to say. Best to get it over with, she would only pick away until she found the truth. 'He decided to leave', he announced. 'I told you he wouldn't like the changes, and so it proved. I paid him well, naturally.'

'Naturally.' Contempt lent an edge to her voice. 'Trust you, darling, never to let little things like promises get in the way of your life. Or Gerard's. That man has given you his all for years, couldn't he at least have been allowed six more months? I might have forgotten by then.'

'I didn't promise anything, and I told you, he quit. Jenna this is none of your business. I don't interfere in the running of the houses, and I don't expect – but I don't want to quarrel.' He went to her and rested his hands on her shoulders and she at once moved away.

'Tony will be down for dinner, he's nearly better. I should tell you that he's still riding at Hennessey's. I saw no reason to stop it.'

William was aware of a thick choking sensation, as if he was breathing through a fog. Why, with Jenna, could he never achieve what he wanted? All his life since before he could remember he had schemed and worked and planned to come to the position he was in now, with power enough merely to ask and have his wish come true. If he was hungry he ate, if he needed a woman he bought her, even a man's ruin could be accomplished in the space of an afternoon. Yet his wife, the person in the world that was closest to him, opposed his every whim.

'Why can't you once put me first, Jenna?' he asked in trembling tones. 'I give you everything and you give me nothing at all, nothing I tell you!'

She was looking at him with cool, infuriating detachment. 'I see no reason to take from others to give to you. It's hardly as if you're short of anything. How will it benefit you to make Tony miserable?'

'That isn't the issue at all. I simply wish to avoid cluttering a business relationship with a trainer with personal involvement, it makes life impossible. When the time comes, as it always does, to explain exactly where the man's duties lie, how will it be to have Tony bleating, "But he's nice!" Hennessey's no fool Jenna, he knows that it pays to be chummy with the family.'

Jenna had the depressing feeling that although William wasn't right he sounded as if he was, and nothing she could say would alter it. There were always two ways of looking at things, one from the standpoint that people are entirely motivated by their feelings, the other that no-one does anything except for personal gain. Neither was wholly correct, but there was truth in each. When Hennessey was kind to Tony he knew he was pleasing Jenna, and when he disciplined him, although he had the boy's welfare at heart, he was also relieving Jenna of a task. And he gained by her approval, so both motives were satisfied. As with William, in sacking Gerard he was benefitting by a commercial decision, but also allowing himself the pleasure of the exercise of total power. That was William's vice.

The door of the sitting room opened and Tony came in, the swellings under his chin reduced from balloons to mere tennis balls.

'Hello, Dad,' he mumbled grudgingly, and Jenna noted that he had put on a frayed grandad shirt that must have been skulking around in his wardrobe for years. Trust Tony to seize the chance to annoy.

'What are you wearing?' asked William with menace, and Jenna laughed.

'Don't rise to the bait, darling, it isn't worth it. You look ghastly Tony, but I imagine that's the idea. We're drinking Bucks Fizz, would you like a taste?' She was adopting an enlightened attitude to drink and children, but she had the disquieting feeling that she might merely be producing alcoholics with finer than average palates.

'God Jenna, you spoil him,' snapped William, and suddenly she turned.

'You've been in this house one hour and you've been ghastly for fifty-nine minutes. Do you have to be so horrid? This is our home and we live in it, quite happily when you're not here, we'd be even happier if you didn't come jackbooting in and try and take over our lives. It isn't – necessary.'

Father and son stared at her. It was a rare day that Jenna flared, they were not used to it. Even at her coldest she was always in control and now neither of them knew what to say. Fortunately George appeared in the doorway, by his very blankness of expression indicating that he had heard every word.

'Dinner is served, madam,' he intoned, and they went with relief to eat.

Jenna was sorry for her temper. 'Let's start again,' she begged, touching William's hand as it rested on the cloth. They were eating in the breakfast room, its summer yellow cosiness more suited to family meals than the imperial majesty of the dining room.

'Yes let's,' said William, and a smile lightened his face. He was tired and disorientated and wanted nothing but Jenna to be kind to him, which was surely little enough for a man to expect? He felt hard done by and said with conscious pathos, 'I have a headache.'

'Do you, darling? I'll fetch you an aspirin.'

As always the desired response, and William began to feel better. The meal was excellent and when Jenna returned she brought with her a vitamin pill as well as the aspirin and he began to feel cosseted and loved. He could almost ignore his silent, resentful son.

'I think it's time we had a party,' said William as the pudding arrived.

'What sort of party?' In the past Jenna had organised barbecues, pyjama parties, buffets, meals for two hundred and intimate select weekends for a dozen guests in the luxury yacht class. She was an expert at parties.

'Just an ordinary party, we could invite anyone who's in England, half won't be at this time of year.'

'Tony and Rachel's friends as well?' queried Jenna.

'God, no. I want the house to remain standing for a little longer, thank you.'

'If we had a disco in the games room we could invite half a dozen,' offered Jenna, who knew only too well that Tony's silences on occasions such as this did not signify

167

consent. He would get his own back somehow.

'We wouldn't want to come to one of your lousy parties,' mumbled Tony.

'Hard luck, it's compulsory,' retorted Jenna. 'I'll let you choose the disco music.'

'I suppose it wouldn't matter,' agreed William grudgingly. Tony was good at compiling party tapes, it was one of his few talents. 'But no Saxon.'

'Or Motorhead,' added Jenna.

'Nothing but Beatles and James Last, I know,' said Tony with an upward roll of the eyeballs.

'And some sad, romantic stuff to make all the divorcees jump into the pool,' giggled Jenna. '*You Don't Bring Me Flowers*, that always gets them.'

'You're a sadist,' said William, thinking that there was very little music that touched Jenna. Her emotions were far too deeply buried for that.

'Invite Downing,' he added, 'he's not too happy at the moment, sees Hennessey encroaching on his territory. He can stay the night. Invite Hennessey as well though, then they'll have to be polite.'

'Can we have Doctor and Mrs Leeming?' asked Tony innocently. He had never forgotten the time Mrs Leeming had become very drunk and undressed before the assembled company, to be bundled out by a furious Doctor Leeming just as she was in the act of removing her knickers.

'No,' said Jenna firmly. 'We don't know them any more.'

'Prude,' said Tony and Jenna blushed, wishing for once that William would tell him off. That he didn't probably meant he agreed.

She was suffering the usual sense of failure when it suddenly occurred to her that it didn't apply any more. She was as sexual as any of them, at long last she knew what it was all about. And if she still didn't like the idea of people undressing in public that was her right. In all probability Mrs Leeming's strange habits were entirely due to frustration, anyway. The thought made Jenna giggle.

'Let's make it a firework party,' she said happily. 'I know it's a bit early but that won't matter. We can get someone in to do a display and we can serve hot food and punch. But we'll put black tie on the invitations, otherwise everyone will come in jeans.'

'I'm coming in jeans anyway,' said Tony.

'For once you'll be presentable, my lad, or I shall know the reason why,' said William. 'Go away, Tony if you've finished and leave Jenna and me in peace.'

Tony looked daggers and Jenna sighed. He and William annoyed each other simply by existing and neither ever let the chance of a barbed remark pass unnoticed. It was almost a habit with them, but an unhealthy one. She watched with increasing depression as Tony slouched to the door.

'I thought we'd go to Queensland after Christmas,' said William, leaning back in his chair and lighting a cigar. 'I have to check up on things there.'

He owned a small Australian printing firm and used it as a base for antipodean asset-stripping. They had a small beachhouse which was sufficient for a month or so, but Jenna would not buy anything larger. To her mind Australia was too hot and the people too anxious. Time and again she had been penned into a corner by a man intent not on seduction, but impressing her with his knowledge of Shakespeare. All the Australians she met were intimidatingly well-read and convinced that even England's dustmen were devotees of Milton. She knew that somewhere there did exist the men they were all apologising for, beer-swilling illiterate mysoginists to a paunch, they paraded in droves on the beaches, but she

169

was confined in a rarefied prison. Things had become worse since William insisted on sponsoring a theatre, simply because he liked his new-found image as a cultural benefactor, and they were besieged by would-be playwrights. Their effusions ranged from Equus with kangaroos to gory enactments of Australia's penal history. 'Culture is becoming very horrid,' she had commented once, and scuttled on to the next plane home. She felt a glum sinking of her spirits and unfairly blamed Australia. Still, she had survived it before and would do so again.

'Do you want me to come?' she asked.

'Of course I do,' said William, a note of warning in his voice. He had expected this and prepared now to do battle. But Jenna disarmed him.

'I'd like to come as a matter of fact. As I told you, I'm seeing this doctor and she thought that after Christmas I might be all right. The Australian trip would be a lovely time to start again don't you think?'

'Jenna!' William reached for her hand. He looked amazed. 'Darling, you don't know how much I've wanted to hear you say that. Of course we can start again, it can be a second honeymoon.'

Jenna gulped, remembering the first.

'I wanted to say,' William went on jerkily, 'about Kentucky. I was – unkind – and I'm sorry. Truly sorry.'

Despite herself Jenna was touched, for William never apologised, except in a superfical way for arriving late at a function when he had made no attempt to be on time. He did not need people's forgiveness. She stood up to go to him and bent to press a kiss to his cheek. 'All forgotten,' she murmured and felt his arm round her waist. Still, instinctively, she tensed. 'Let's go to bed,' whispered her husband. 'Let's have our new beginning early.'

Familar panic made Jenna's heart start to pound and her hands fluttered in their desire to push this man away.

'But darling,' she said shakily, 'the doctor doesn't want anything like that until the treatment's finished. She says that something as long lasting as this can't be cured overnight. Actually she offered to see you and explain, because she says an understanding husband can make all the difference.'

'No, no, that won't be necessary,' said William crossly and Jenna gulped. She had been gilding the lily with a vengeance and it would have served her right if William had called her bluff. It wasn't that this thing with Hennessey was in any way important, how could it be, but she owed it to Dan to keep it on a little longer. He had done so much for her. This way things were neat and as honest as they could be when one is deceiving one's husband and when it was all over she and Hennessey could go back to their respective marriages purged of their obsessions. Wasn't that worth the odd lie?

'What's this doctor's name?' asked William, releasing her and fishing for one of his odd, thin cigars.

'Doctor – Innes,' she gasped, sinking into a chair and wondering how it was that a woman of principle could turn into a natural liar almost overnight.

'In York is she?'

'No, no – Harrogate.' She noticed she was twisting her rings furiously and at once linked her hands on the table in front of her.

'I hope she knows her stuff.'

'Oh, she does, she does! I feel much better already, not so – tense. And I'm sure it will be all right in Australia, different atmosphere and everything. Doctor – er – Innes is a pioneer in the field.'

'What field's that then?'

'Oh, you know, sex and – things.' She was exhausted. It would almost be easier to give in and tell the truth she thought, nothing could be worse than this network of lies.

Other women confessed to affairs, although of course they were not married to William. He would finish Hennessey. Her eyes drifted upwards and met her husband's speculative gaze.

'I think I'll go and lie down,' she said jerkily. 'I have to relax a lot. Yoga. Meditation. That sort of thing.'

'What, all at once?'

'All new methods. Pioneer work, you know.' She stumbled from the room and even her legs were shaking. If William suspected nothing it must be because he thought she was mad.

On a blustering afternoon she lay in Hennessey's bed and told him about the party.

'Will you bring your wife?' she asked teasing the hairs on his chest with her fingers.

'Would you mind if I did?'

Her fingers jerked and gasped. 'Bitch. I don't know why you hate her so. You get all the best bits.' He bent his head and caught her skin in his teeth and Jenna squeaked.

'You should divorce her. She's batty.'

'No she isn't. Look, I won't bring her if it'll make you feel any better. She wouldn't come anyway. In fact I don't think I will.'

'You've got to, it's a three-line whip. Downing's coming, so William can stage a confrontation.'

'What the bloody hell for? God, Jenna, if anyone ought to get divorced it's you, your husband's power mad.'

'Money makes people like that, look at Henry the Eighth. Anyway he wouldn't let us divorce, it's the one thing he always says. He couldn't bear to watch me go off with someone else you see, and then there's the money. It would cost a fortune.'

'What would he do if he found out about this?'

mumbled Hennessey and Jenna moaned beneath his kisses.

'He'd finish you, that's for certain. Don't Dan please, I really must go.'

'Later. Sex is good for you, Jenna, your breasts have grown from apples to oranges.'

'It's all the food I'm eating. I shall be like a house-end soon.'

Hennessey laughed and pulled her to him, cradling her buttocks in his hands. 'I'll start to complain when these don't fit any more, you must have put on all of four pounds. Has your husband noticed?' He asked the question casually but they both knew he had been angling towards it for hours.

'No,' said Jenna shortly and began nuzzling the hollows of his neck, pressing herself against him in obvious encouragement. He was not to be diverted, however.

'Do you make love with him? Jenna I've got to know.'

'Why? I put up with your wife, why shouldn't you put up with William? It's only fair.'

'Like hell it is. Don't tease, Jen, this is important. It matters to me.'

She pulled away then and sat up, flushed and cross. 'You don't own me. No-one does. I don't have to answer to you for the things I do. You know I hate what you do with your wife but you still do it, you've no right to ask me questions.'

'You asked me. Do you, Jenna?' He caught her wrist and held her on the bed. 'Is it night after night of sex, making up for lost time, like Sleeping Beauty and a middle-aged Prince Charming, teaching you all the foul tricks he's learned from his tarts? Is it?' He sounded vicious and he looked it, the heat of anger staining even the whites of his eyes. It frightened her and she stopped playing.

'We don't do anything,' she muttered and ducked her head into his chest. 'I said the doctor thought I shouldn't. I'm seeing the doctor now as a matter of fact.'

Hennesey blinked at her. 'And he believed you?'

'Oh yes. He wasn't too pleased, but then who would be? He's sleeping in his dressing room till I'm better.'

'You lying bitch.' He said it without thinking, meaning to be playful if he meant anything at all. To Jenna, haunted by her own duplicity, it was too much. She had done it all for him and he at least should understand.

She pulled away, shrieking, 'What the hell is it you want? It's you I'm doing it for and it's more than you do for me. But I've had enough of this, I hate you Dan Hennessey, and I won't come again. Why should I lie for you, I don't need you any more. And I will sleep with my husband and I'll do every horrible thing I can think of with him and you can lie awake at night and wonder what it's like. Or bash away at your nutty wife of course, though I doubt if that's much fun. What's she doing now, smashing up the house again?'

He lunged across the bed and caught her arm, spinning her round to face him. She knew she had gone too far when she looked at him but she stood and shivered and took back not a word.

'You foul-mouthed, faithless bitch. You're rich and you're beautiful and you're cruel. Your husband's right to hang on to you, you make a lovely pair, neither in the least bit interested in the weak or the sick or the helpless.'

'How right you are,' said Jenna, and her voice cracked. She pulled away to hide the tears and began to struggle into her clothes, fastening buttons wrong and tangling the arms of her jumper.

'You don't care about anyone but yourself. You'll cheat on anyone if it suits you and never think twice. What will I be to you in the future? That funny little man

Hennessey, good in bed but my dear, all he talks about is horses. Will you tell everyone how wonderfully therapeutic I am? Frigid ladies thawed to order.'

'Shut up,' sobbed Jenna, trying to put on her coat through a mist of tears. He came and helped her, still naked, the white mark of swimming trunks still visible from the summer. He hunted around in his mind for something else to hit her with, watching her blunder round the room stuffing things into her bag. 'And you can tell that son of your's that he isn't welcome any more. I don't want him and I don't want you. If you came I wouldn't be here. I wish I'd never met you, Jenna, you're – you're –' but his throat was tight and he could say no more.

She fled from the room, her feet rattling on the stairs and then the front door banged. He stood at the window and watched her struggle up the path, her hair whipped by the wind into a curtain that hid her face. Then the bushes closed behind her and there was nothing but the chirping of a bird sitting amidst the tired hawthorn leaves. She wouldn't come back. She was gone.

Hennessey sank on to the edge of the bed and buried his face in his hands. 'Oh Jenna, Jenna I love you,' he whispered, and tasted the salt of his tears.

When he got home he found Lilian in the kitchen waiting for him.

'Dan look what's come,' she said excitedly. 'It's an invitation. The Sheppards have invited us to a party.'

Her husband said nothing but went to the sink and filled the kettle.

'Can we go, Dan? Please? I thought at first I wouldn't, and then I thought that isn't fair, making you go everywhere by yourself. I can buy a new dress and everything.'

Gradually her words and her excitement began to filter through to him. He turned and looked at her, bright-eyed, flushed and happy. 'Do what you want, love. I'm tired.'

'Are you Dan? You look a bit pale. Go and lie down, I'll wake you for evening stables.'

'Why don't you do it for once? You've watched me long enough, God knows.' Today he had lost interest even in his horses.

'Don't be silly, of course I can't. I'll tell Geoff you're ill, he can do it. Look at this card, it's properly engraved and everything.'

'God Lilian, will you just shut up!' bellowed her husband, and flung out of the kitchen and up to bed.

In the morning it was too late. She had sent the reply.

When the Sheppards gave a party the whole county knew about it, from the police directing the traffic to the photographers haunting the gates and the curious there just to watch. Everyone knew that the fireworks alone had cost thousands, that the pool was to be lit by underwater rainbow lights and that the games room had been turned into a cave, with acres of black sheeting and nylon cobwebs. What no-one suspected was that Jenna was almost paralysed with nerves.

She stood in the hall, glorious in a midnight blue dress made up of a myriad tiny pleats, each one with a silver thread running down the crease. When she moved she sparkled like stars in a night sky, her head tilted slightly by the thick coils of hair, also interlaced with silver. Suppose, after all this trouble, he didn't come? From the moment she received the reply she had known that this must be the best, the most expensive, the most impressive party that had ever taken place. All right he was bringing his wife, but that was to be expected. He would hardly climb all the way down. If they could just meet and say sorry, that was all she wanted, at least for Tony's sake, for he expected to start riding again very soon. So she justified herself, and her heart bounced in her throat as each car drew up to the door.

William stood beside her, looking his best in dinner jacket and white ruffled shirt. He loved to see Jenna on nights such as this, she was in her element as hostess, far more than ever as a guest. She gave more easily than she took and she found comfort in being in control at a party, moving from group to group and room to room with clearly defined duties other than enjoyment. The notion that he only gave parties as a setting for Jenna occurred to William, and he cherished it briefly, thinking that he would tell someone that later on, and let them spread it. A nice touch.

When almost everyone had arrived, but not the Hennessey's, Jenna left the hall and strolled around, talking and making sure that glasses were full. Every turn she made brought her eyes across the door and still he did not come. She knew she would die if she waited much longer, it would almost be better if she knew he would not come, although then she would certainly die. What a foolish state she was in. Her eye lighted on Stephen, and she saw that he was watching her. She smiled and he came across to her side. He looked strange and sexless in his dinner jacket and he wore a new ring with a dark red stone.

'A success already I think.'

'Do you? If only it doesn't rain on the fireworks.'

'Relax, it's not like you to worry. Are you sure it's just the fireworks?' He was looking at her with his ingenuous, little-boy charm which she knew to be skin-deep if that. Stephen was no-one's fool and no-one knew what he really thought. She gave him a nervous glance and he touched her arm. 'Don't take it so hard, love. Believe me, it isn't worth it.'

'Really, Stephen, I don't know what you mean.'

At that moment the door opened and in came Hennessey, followed by his little, brown-haired wife. Try as she would her cheeks became hot.

'Don't you?' said Stephen, and Jenna stepped away from him towards the newcomers.

'Mr Hennessey. How kind of you to come. I'm so pleased at last to meet your wife.' She looked not once at him, but instead gave her hand to the woman at his side. A little woman, obviously shy, with wispy hair and a blue tulle dress that didn't suit her. She took Jenna's hand and shot her a glance that held something akin to terror. It gave Jenna pause.

'I know this must all seem a bit overwhelming,' she said on impulse, 'but William always goes over the top. You can wander round just as you like, the whole house is open. Go and look at the disco in the games room, the children have turned it into a cave, complete with plastic skeletons. We'll be eating at around midnight, after the fireworks, and anyone still here at seven will get breakfast. George, a glass of punch for Mrs Hennessey, please. Be careful, it's very strong.'

Lilian took the glass, gasping, 'You're very kind.'

'Not at all. Just as long as you enjoy yourself.' Jenna took her leave with a smile, and drifted away across the hall, stopping to exchange a word with an elderly couple in the corner.

'She's wonderful,' said Lilian to Hennessey, but he did not reply. She glanced up at him and saw that his face was white and set.

'Don't you feel well, Dan?' she asked and he came to himself and smiled.

'I'm OK. Come on, let's go and see what's happening.'

The fireworks began at ten and everyone muffled up in furs and woollens to line the terrace outside the swimming

178

pool. Anyone who did not want to brave the night air could stand against the huge sliding windows that bordered the pool and watch from there but as Jenna said, you did not get the lovely smell of gunpowder, leaves and the night. She herself stood in her mink and watched the rocket stars arc across the sky and she smiled and smiled and smiled.

The wind blew and a little spatter of rain touched the upturned faces. A few more people went indoors, leaving only the hardy on the dark terrace. Jenna sensed someone behind her and knew that it was Hennessey.

'I didn't think you'd come.'

'My wife wanted to.'

'I wanted to say – about Tony. I haven't told him you don't want him to ride anymore. I can't.'

'You know I didn't mean that. I was angry.'

'Yes. As long as that's all right then. I'm sorry I was mean about your wife. She's very scared, isn't she?'

'Terrified. It was good of you – before.'

'Not at all. It costs me nothing, as you always make so clear. If you'll excuse me I'll go and see to the food.'

'Jenna –' He put out a hand to detain her but she evaded him and left, her high heels clicking on the stones. His heart thundered in his chest as he turned back to the fireworks, and when it started to rain in earnest he stood there, staring, until a waiter asked if he was all right.

When he went in he saw that Lilian was talking animatedly to a grey-haired woman in a severe green dress. He went across and at once his wife said, 'Dan, this lady runs a children's home for babies that aren't – well –'

'The mentally handicapped,' said her companion without any embarrassment.

Lilian nodded fiercely, and caught at her husband's sleeve, like an anxious child herself. 'Nobody wants those babies, Dan. I thought, couldn't we –?'

'No,' interrupted Hennessey, and met the eyes of the grey-haired woman in silent entreaty.

'They don't go for adoption,' she said with understanding.

'How do you know the Sheppards?' asked Dan, to cover Lilian's hurried fumbles for a handkerchief. God, couldn't she forget about babies for one evening at least?

'Jenna is our patron,' said the woman. 'She takes a great interest, and finances our holiday home. She often visits. Some people have a knack with these children and some don't, and she is very good. Unsentimental you know, the children like that.'

'Mrs Sheppard's always kind,' said Lilian with a sniff, and Hennessey saw that she had pulled herself together. Thank God for that.

'You don't know her,' he said grimly and thought, neither did he. How much more was there to Jenna that she did not say?

He turned to watch her walking from group to group ushering them in to eat. She must have felt his eyes on her because she turned her head in his direction, but looked swiftly past and away. Suddenly desperate, Hennessey knew he had to see her alone.

He settled his wife with her new-found friend to eat at a little sidetable and then started to trail his prey. He lounged against pillars and loitered in doorways, but each time she saw him she moved back into the throng. Then a voice hailed him. 'Hennessey! I've been looking for you, I'd like you to meet Henry Downing.'

With a sigh, Hennessey turned to meet William's bright, malicious gaze.

'How do you do, Mr Sheppard. Henry.'

'You two know each other I see. Tell me, Henry, what do you think of our rising star?'

It was a cruel question and the older man flushed. He

was dressed in his racing tweeds and Hennessey remembered Jenna's comment and grinned. Downing misinterpreted his expession.

'There's no need to laugh about it. I know you're cutting me out,' he said bluntly.

'Balls, Henry, you know I won't train your numbers. You're safe from me.'

'With you getting the Caruso colt? You can say what you like but you're getting it, not me.'

'Tell you what, why don't you take it instead?' said Hennessey airily. 'Mr Sheppard knows what I think. If Mr Downing wants him he can have him, sir.'

William was annoyed. He enjoyed it when they squabbled but not when they took matters into their own hands. 'I've made my arrangements and they stand,' he snapped. 'Mr Downing will have plenty of good horses for next season, he can be assured of that.'

'Thank you very much, sir,' said Downing in a dutiful false gratitude, and to unsettle him still further William threw an arm companionably round Hennessey's shoulders. The younger man felt his muscles tense, and for a moment let his thoughts dwell on what it would be like to hit the plump, complacent face next to his, to let his fist pound into bone and muscle and flesh – '– and I feel sure that Dan and I will be able to work well together, selecting the stock to go on and wear the colours, I'm sure you'll agree, Henry, we need some young blood in the organisation.'

'Of course, sir.' Downing was looking more and more glum and Hennessey suddenly said, 'You had a good win on Saturday, Henry, in fact you've had a fair season all in all. I picked up a full sister to that horse at Doncaster, I've got hopes for her.'

'Trust you to spot that one,' commented Downing. 'Quite a bargain, I hear. Mind, you can tip me when it's trying.'

'You know mine are always trying. Very trying.' He made the old joke and they laughed.

'Tell me, Dan,' said William, moving back to take charge of the conversation. 'How do you organise a betting *coup*? I know all you trainers do it so don't pretend you don't.'

Hennessey moved irritably, for Jenna had come back into the room and at any moment she might go upstairs. 'I don't mess about with races,' he said shortly. 'If they're entered they're in there to run. Believe me, it's hard enough getting them first past the post on any day without worrying about the odds as well. If the owners want to try and make a killing that's their privilege, but as for me, I just run the horses. Of course I tell them if I think the horse will win, it's only fair, but if you say that and it loses, and they've put their shirt on it, well you wish you'd kept your mouth shut.'

Downing grunted his agreement and both men cast sideways looks at Sheppard. They wanted him to go away to let them indulge in a comfortable moan about owners, who were a difficult and unpredictable bunch dedicated to upsetting the training of racehorses. Like most trainers they thought it would be a great improvement if horses were provided on the National Health and owners dispensed with altogether.

'Who did you buy your filly for?' asked Sheppard, sipping his drink with assumed nonchalance. He sensed the two men banding together against him, which was not at all what he wanted. Divide and rule was basic to his organisation.

'I bought her on spec,' said Hennessey, his eyes wandering. 'I'll find someone for her when she's broken.'

'Put her down to me,' said Sheppard. 'I don't care what she cost, if she's got prospects I'll take her.'

Hennessey sighed and briefly turned his attention back to Sheppard, but he was too preoccupied to be tactful. 'I'm sorry, sir, but I won't sell her to you. She's a moderate horse and the races she'll win will be moderate. All right, you could own half the horses in the country, but it wouldn't get you anywhere. As I've told you before, you must be selective, train only the best. Top class horses, top class races, you don't want to waste your time on platers. Anything else is stupid.'

Sheppard stared at him and Hennessey stared back. 'Steady on, Dan,' muttered Downing, unselfish enough to dislike seeing a man ruin himself.

Sheppard turned and called across the room, 'Jenna! Jenna darling, come and hear Mr Hennessey tell me how to make money.' A polite chuckle rose from the assembled company. Jenna drifted towards them, beautiful and disinterested.

'Surely you have enough already, darling,' she commented, and moved into the circle on her husband's arm. She felt rather than saw Hennessey clench his fist and she reached up and tickled William's ear with a finger. 'Is he being difficult, love? I did warn you.'

'So you did. Jenna says it's no use asking you to buy my horses, Hennessey, because you can't leave your wife. She says she's mentally ill. Is that true?'

'William!' Jenna leaped away from him as if stung. 'I never told you that! Please, apologise at once.'

'Been in mental hospital hasn't she?' continued William, an interested smile on his face. 'Fortunately there's so much less stigma attached to it these days, people don't call you mad any more.'

'It was depression,' said Hennessey in a tight, furious voice. 'She's here tonight and I don't want her upset. It was only depression.'

'So, marriage makes her depressed does it?'

Hennessey slammed his glass on to a table. 'Much as it makes your wife lose her appetite,' he retorted and stalked away, slight with fury.

Jenna turned to William, her face shocked. 'How could you? I must go and apologise, it's the least I can do. That was cruel.'

'But necessary,' said William. 'He was getting a bit too self-important. Yes, you go and be nice to him, it will make him feel better. Now Henry, another drink.' He turned to the stunned man beside him.

Jenna found Hennessey on the terrace, still shaking with rage. 'That man,' he burst out as Jenna approached, 'for two pins I'd knock his beautifully capped teeth into his expensive haircut. Christ Jen, how can you stand the bastard?'

'He's on my side,' she said ruefully. 'I'm sorry, Dan. I didn't tell him about your wife, I promise. He has research people to do that for him.'

'Scraping up dirt to throw at people. He's – foul.'

Jenna considered. 'I think the word is unscrupulous. Anyway, now I must go and see how things are in the disco, it's black as night in there.'

'I'll come with you,' said Hennessey, beginning to calm. 'I haven't seen it yet and it must be good, people keep reeling past looking stunned.'

'Yes,' said Jenna doubtfully and since she could see no way of detaching him from her side she made her way in silence back into the house.

'Did you have to climb all over him?' demanded Hennessey as they reached the door. 'And don't tell me you're always like that, he looked so surprised you'd think the princess was kissing the frog.'

'Now who's being nasty?'

She opened the games room door and at once the sound was like a wall. Lights flashed in the gloom, gyrating bodies were wall to wall and in the air hung cobwebs and bones, swaying in the draughts and brushing people's hair.

'Good God,' mouthed Hennessey, and the door closed behind them. There was something strange about the light, it took the colour from people's faces and made them appear as ghosts. It was hardly possible to say who was who, and in the crush couples clung and swayed anonymously.

'I must go and find the children,' yelled Jenna, but Hennessey saw better things ahead. He slid his arms around her and drew her to him, joining the mass of dancers. She pushed him away but he would have none of it, and in the end she slid her arms around his neck and clung.

'I'm sorry, I'm sorry, I'm sorry,' he murmured in her ear. 'I love you and it makes me jealous.'

'You said such awful things,' whispered Jenna, and he nodded.

'So did you.'

The music changed to heavy metal and they could not talk, but when it finished Jenna said, 'We mustn't start again.'

'We have to. I can't stand it on my own.' He was holding her so tight she was almost crushed, and she pulled back and looked into his face.

'I just feel – that it's all going to be wrong. Suppose they find out?'

'They needn't. They won't. Oh Jenna, I want you so much.' He buried his face in her neck, kissing and caressing as if they were alone, and for a moment she let him. It was such bliss to be in his arms again and know herself loved, she could feel her heart swelling with the joy of it. Then she lifted her head and looked straight into the eyes of the man dancing next to them. It was Stephen.

185

She was off and away across the floor almost before Hennessey realised, and he barged after her with scant regard for the people between. He caught her next to the record deck. 'What's the matter? Jenna?'

'Stephen saw. Stephen knows. What shall I do if he tells William?'

'Will he?'

She looked at him with wide and frightened eyes. 'I don't know. Perhaps not. But he could blackmail me or anything. Dan, we've got to stop, it's getting so awful.'

'Do you want to stop? Really? Never be together again?' He stared at her and in the strange light he looked drawn and desperate. She shook her head.

'Let's go and find the children,' she said almost tearfully, and slipped behind one of the curtains and out of a door.

They went into the children's sitting room where tonight tables were laid with crisps and sandwiches, and giant cans of coca-cola with taps on the side stood like cheerleaders at a baseball game. A few teenagers with spiky hair lounged around and a girl was sitting on a floor cushion crying. Her friends clucked and fussed like anxious hens.

Jenna pulled herself together and wiped her fingers across her own cheeks.

'Helen? It is Helen isn't it? Is something the matter?'

As soon as they saw her everyone in the room looked furtive, but Jenna had come to realise that this was a natural reaction to the presence of parents at a party. From smoking pot in the garage to grinding peanuts into the carpet, the kids were bound to be at fault.

'She's quite all right, Mrs Sheppard,' volunteered one girl, ghastly in pink eyeshadow, like a raging case of conjunctivitis.

'But she's crying. Has someone upset you, love?'

'No. No. Honestly,' gulped the girl but the tears welled. Jenna could see that no-one was going to tell her anything and she looked helplessly round at Hennessey. He shrugged expressively and bit into a sandwich. It was peanut butter and he winced and tossed the remains into the wastepaper bin. The aftertaste clung to his mouth and he longed for a decent drink, beer or something. It would have been real, something to take away the strangeness of tonight where everything was different and odd, and he could have everything but the thing he really wanted. He thought briefly of Lilian, left alone somewhere or other, but he lacked the will to go to her.

Jenna had given up on the girl. The problems of youth, even when explained, are so often incomprehensible.

'Dan, I think Tony's done something. He asked her to come but when I asked where he was she howled.'

'Did she? Jen, can't we go somewhere and talk, I'm sick of trailing you round like a poodle.'

'I've got to find Tony. I didn't have time for him today and you know what he's like when he feels ignored.'

Dan watched the worry pull her face into lines and he put a hand to her back and felt her spine through the dress. 'Poor Jen. You're not having a good night, are you?'

'It hasn't been a good three weeks,' she said shakily, and he laughed and hugged her, and saw all the children watching.

'Let's go,' he muttered, and led her out by the hand. For Jenna's sake he had to be careful, she was a princess in her beautiful castle and if William ever knew it would fall about her in ruins. She had risked too much for him already and he owed her his discretion. As they left the room he dropped her hand and walked beside her in respectful deference.

They looked in the kitchen and the study, the library and the billiard room. Jenna flew round the bedrooms while Hennessey waited by the stairs.

'They're not here,' she hissed from the landing, eyes wide and a wisp of hair flying. 'They must be outside.'

Hennessey sighed in exasperation. That boy was more trouble than he was worth and if it wasn't for Jenna he'd forget about him. 'I'll go and look,' he said in answer to her unspoken request. 'You go back to your guests and pretend nothing's happened, though God knows why I'm doing this. The boy does have a father you know.'

'Dan, you mustn't let him know. Really, he'd be furious.' But she knew he didn't believe her. A child raised in love finds it hard to imagine that when the chips are down a parent will turn aside, but Jenna had seen for herself. William revenged himself on Tony.

The night air was blessedly cool after the frenzied heat of the house. Hennessey stood for a moment and let his eyes adjust to the blackness, savouring his solitude. Behind him the music thumped out, there was high, feminine laughter, the tinkle of broken glass. Everyone would say it was a wonderful party.

There was a thin moon, obscured by clouds from time to time, but Hennessey could see enough to pick his way across damp lawns. The garden led down to the river and there was a little boat house clinging to the bank like a snail on a wall, now just visible as a hump against the night sky. His feet squelched in mud as he approached and wet seeped through the thin soles of his shoes. Damn that child, he'd belt him when he found him.

Soft giggles came from the boat house. Hennessey crept the remaining yards and pushed the rough wood door with his foot. The giggling stopped.

'Hello everyone,' he said grimly. The four bodies stretched out on the boards stopped writhing and sat up, Tony's girl dragging her blouse back over her breasts.

There was a love-bite on her neck. The other couple were unknown to Hennessey, but they were clearly very drunk. They all were, their faces slack and flushed.

'What have you been drinking?' asked Hennessey wearily and reached for one of the bottles they had stashed in the little rowing boat at the back of the hut.

'None of your business,' slurred Tony in alcoholic defiance. 'Drink what we want, it's my booze.'

'Tell that to your father. Christ Tony, this is brandy! Are you trying to kill yourselves?'

'We mixed it,' said Tony owlishly and waved an empty champagne bottle, but it fell from his fingers and hit his girlfriend on the shoulder. She yelped, mumbled and scrambled towards the door, only to be noisily sick on the grass. The other girl started crying.

Hennessey sighed and ran his hand through his hair. What was he to do with them, tight as ticks and helpless as babies. 'What's it all in aid of Tony?' he asked wearily. 'OK, today your mother was busy, of course she was busy, you're old enough to understand. Why, if she doesn't give you her individed attention do you play tricks like this?'

'She's not my mother,' mumbled Tony. 'She isn't old enough.'

'Do you want your real mother? Is that the trouble?'

'No!' It was said with vehemence.

A thought occurred to Hennessey. 'Where's Rachel? Don't tell me she's mixed up in your little orgy.'

'Went for a walk. Took the dog and went for a walk.' The world was spinning and Tony lay flat on his back and closed his eyes. Outside the girl was being sick again and the other couple appeared to be falling asleep.

'Where did she go?' asked Hennessey, and then when Tony did not answer he kicked him. 'Where did she go?'

'Ouch! Don't, I'm tired.'

'I don't care if you're Rip Van Winkle, wake up and tell me where Rachel is. Tony, it's two o'clock in the morning and she is twelve years old!'

'Said she didn't like parties. Went for a walk. Dunno where.'

The girl staggered back into the hut, looking deathly. In the light of the one feeble bulb the quartet seemed almost laughable, a caricature of decadence, like children dressed up in their parent's clothes. Hennessey tipped the girl's head back with a finger. 'Does your mother know what you get up to?' he asked and knew the question to be foolish. He wanted to tell the girl how much she was risking, the misery she was creating for herself before she was old enough to understand, but she was too drunk and too ill and besides, there was never any telling them. That was the pity of it. Jenna should never allow such children so much freedom, it was a betrayal of trust.

'Stay here you lot,' he ordered. 'I'll send someone out to you. I'm going to look for Rachel.' He shut the door behind him and ran back to the house, stepping into a puddle in the dark and soaking one foot to the ankle. Damn Tony, damn Rachel, and damn Jenna for letting this happen. The party was roaring and when he crossed the terrace and went in by the pool he saw at least three people swimming fully dressed. Jenna was in the dining room, making elegant conversation. Her eyes met his as he entered, and he crossed swiftly to her.

'Boathouse. Four of them, drunk as they know how. What on earth do you mean by letting kids like that get hold of booze, I'm damned if I'd let a child of mine come to one of your parties!'

The couple she had been talking to looked fascinated, but Jenna merely said, 'Was Rachel there?'

'No. Rachel has taken the dog for a walk, and I am

190

going to look for her. May I suggest you send someone down to the boathouse with some coffee and some towels, and when the kids are presentable and have stopped being sick, send them all home? And stand clear when their parents come round tomorrow.'

Jenna said nothing and went into the hall to speak to George. The shrieking from the pool was becoming deafening, and the thump of music from the disco could be felt in the vibration of the floor. Hennessey went to find Lilian, and opened the library door. In the dim light he could see a couple in close embrace on the sofa and when the man looked up he saw that it was Sheppard. 'Like father like son,' he muttered, and closed the door again. At least that would keep him out of the way for a bit.

He found Lilian wandering distractedly across the hall, and when she saw him her face lit up. 'Dan! Thank goodness I've found you, I don't like this party at all.'

'I think you have to be a fully paid-up member of a coven to be at home here. Look, can you find someone to give you a lift back? I've got to go and look for Rachel, she's gone for a walk of all things.'

'But it's dark.'

He held his temper on a tight rein and forced himself to speak calmly. 'That's why I have to look for her, she's far too young to be out by herself. Find someone to take you home.'

'Dan! You know I can't.' She looked stubborn and helpless at one and the same time and Hennessey felt like screaming. Instead he said, 'Then you'll have to come with me. And don't ask questions, Lilian, I couldn't stand it.'

They drove in silence along dark lanes, circling end-lessly round the house until at last they found her. She sat in a gateway, her arm round Casey, and she was almost dead with weariness. Lilian clucked and fussed, and when they took her home for once looked at Jenna with eyes that accused. It was the beginning of the end of her obsession.

'I'll put Rachel to bed,' murmured Jenna. 'Thanks, Dan.' She too looked exhausted, and there was a tremor in her that he felt when he touched her shoulder, as if all her muscles were rigid with strain. 'Are you staying for breakfast?' she asked. 'We're serving it early. Then perhaps people will go.'

'Don't tell me you haven't enjoyed it,' he said with harsh sarcasm.

'Get stuffed,' snapped Jenna, and turned on her heel.

Chapter Nine

Jenna stood in Hennessey's yard and looked at the two horses, one worth at least a million dollars, the other the Royal Diamond colt, home-bred and unvalued. Here, far from the wind and rolling paddocks of Kentucky her own choice looked small and a trifle showy, with long white socks on both hind legs.

'We thought we'd call the Caruso colt, Fleece and the other, Sharps,' she said nervously. Hennessey had passed no comment yet and she feared the worst. 'They don't look too bad – do they?'

Hennessey shrugged. 'The Caruso's all right – good legs I'm glad to say. I wouldn't think he's an early horse though, he's got some growing in him. We'll take it slowly.'

'What about – my choice?' Jenna felt as if she were asking him to pass judgment on her own worth as a human being, which was ridiculous when it was only a horse. Hennessey sighed and shrugged his shoulders again. 'I suppose we can do something with him. If you discount his curbs, and the narrowness of him, and with his head set on like that he'll never look right, but –'

'Dan! Are you serious?' Appalled, Jenna was peering at the animal as if it had suddenly turned into a monster.

Then she saw that Dan, and all the lads, were grinning. 'Oh.' She turned on her heel and flounced towards the car. Hennessey followed, half-believing she was upset.

'Come off it, Jen – we didn't mean anything – oh.' She too was laughing and she looked so pink and kissable that it was all he could do not to take her in his arms then and there.

'You're rotten,' said Jenna. 'What do you really think of him?'

Hennessey sank his hands into his pockets and looked again at the horse, a far safer prospect. 'Good shape, good legs, look at that second thigh. Flashy but I knew it would be, that's you all over. Neat. Square. Look at his back end, bunchy, and under that fat there's some muscle. Sprint I should think, though his breeding doesn't suggest it.'

'I didn't think he had much breeding,' said Jenna diffidently.

'I was being tactful.'

'Oh.'

'Look,' said Hennessey, 'I've got to go to the saddlers. Why don't you come, I want to talk to you.'

Jenna gulped. 'About the children?'

'Yes. You have to do something, Jen, even you must see that.'

'Why even me? I'm not that neglectful. At least – oh all right, I'll come. I can see you're going to nag until I let you browbeat me with all your educational theories. But may I point out that children are not horses.'

'I'd like to know what the difference is.'

Jenna considered. 'Their clothes cost more, for one thing.'

'I'll send you my saddlery bills.'

'Well, they certainly can't run as fast.'

'You've been meeting the wrong horses.'

194

'And they've only got two legs,' she finished and waved a finger at him. 'You can't deny that, you know you can't.'

'Idiot.' He sword-fenced her finger briefly with his own.

'Dan, people are watching,' said Jenna softly and the laughter faded from his face.

'Yes. Get in the car, love, will you?' He gestured towards his little red sports car and all unsuspecting she settled herself inside.

Hennessey threw two saddles on to the back seat and coiled himself behind the wheel. He started the engine and drove carefully out of the yard. Jenna was about to comment on the loveliness of the autumn colours when Hennessey spun the wheel, stamped on the accelerator and shot down the lane like a cork from a bottle. They rounded a bend, overtook a tractor on the brow of a hill and almost failed to avoid a landrover coming the other way.

'Slow down!' wailed Jenna, when she could find her voice.

'Turn on the radio, then you won't notice,' commented Hennessey, inured to terror in his passengers. They screamed on to the main road, were doing ninety in two gear changes and overtook a lorry, also on the brow of a hill and without slackening speed. They hit the ton on a mile long stretch of dual carriageway.

'Let me out! I don't want to die,' moaned Jenna and Hennessey held on to the wheel with one hand and pressed buttons on the radio with the other, keeping half an eye on the road.

'It's Jimmy Young, listen to that,' he encouraged, overtaking a Mercedes even though they were running out of road. He notched down a gear and pinched a piece of tarmac that rightfully belonged to the mini coming the other way.

195

'You've killed that man. He's in the ditch,' said Jenna in a high, tight voice.

'No he isn't. Christ, Jen, don't be so nervous. Anyway, about the children.'

'What about them. Dan, mind that cyclist! I bet that's the last time he ever tries to turn right.'

'Makes horses terribly nervous, cyclists do. It's the flapping capes. Oh Jen, wouldn't it be nice if we could drive on and on away from it all?' He mocked her with grand romance.

'No! If you want to talk you'll have to stop, I tend to be incoherent when my past life is flashing before me.'

'Mmmm. Let's find a nice, quiet lane.' He turned right down a narrow opening, taking an oncoming van by surprise, but Jenna merely moaned. When they screeched to a halt in a field gateway she found her fingers clamped fast round her seatbelt.

'Is it any wonder your wife's a nervous wreck?' she enquired weakly.

Hennessey grunted. 'I do slow down for her, she really does get frightened.'

'Tell me, how does she register terror? I must take notes.'

He leaned across and took her in his arms. 'Don't talk about her, you know it makes you nasty. Look, you've got beads of sweat running down your throat, let's see where they go to.' He began to unbutton her blouse and she let him, tangling her fingers in his hair as he buried his face in her flesh. It was delicious.

'Let's do it in the car like a couple of teenagers,' he suggested.

Jenna was taken aback. 'We can't! It's far too small. Anyway, it's broad daylight.'

'There's no-one around. Anyway, most people conduct their affairs in cars, it's only really lucky girls that get

196

beds.' He nibbled her fingertips and she giggled.

'You'll have to get a bigger car. And there's another tractor coming, so we can't.'

Hennessey sighed theatrically and conceded. 'All right. But about the kids, Jen, you've got to do something. There is a right and a wrong way to bring up children and you're making every mistake in the book.'

'No I'm not! It's not my fault they're so difficult, they were like that when I met them. And I do try, I involve them and I take them places –'

'And over-indulge them. Then you forget them for days and remember them for minutes, you make threats that you never carry out and you apologise all the time for their father. It's got to stop.'

She looked bewildered. 'But – I can't not buy them things. It would be mean.'

'They don't need pocket-sized televisions, satin jackets or God help you several pairs of denim riding trousers like what all the best poofs are wearing.'

Jenna looked conscious. 'I thought he'd look nice in them. And it saves his jeans, after all.'

'How economical of you. And what on earth were those kids doing at that party? You could have sent them to a friend's house, surely.'

'I didn't want them to feel shut out.' It sounded feeble now.

'So you included them in a fully fledged orgy! That's what I call considerate.'

But she was looking tearful and anxious, pleating the hem of her shirt where he had pulled it free from her trousers. He could not rage at her, and he took her hand. 'So why don't you send them to boarding school? Then in the holidays you could make a terrific effort, take on a student to help or something. It would be far better for them.'

'No it wouldn't! Tony hates boarding school, he ran away from the last one, he was gone ages. And the time before that – he was expelled, you see. Actually I think the headmaster got the thing all out of proportion because I don't think Tony would bully little ones, and he swore he hadn't, but the head simply wouldn't believe him. He was a very difficult man.'

Hennessey looked astounded. 'Jen, he'll end up in Borstal,' he said weakly.

She looked up. 'No he won't! I mean if he mugged someone or something we could always buy them off – couldn't we?'

'What, so he could go out and try again? Be reasonable, Jen, please.'

'I am being reasonable! I'm trying to make him feel loved and wanted, with a realistic idea of his future role in life –'

'Which book did you get that out of?'

'*Childhood and the Adult* if you must know. I think William is an example of a home without a firm male presence – his father died young – and in consequence is taking on a position of unrealistic dominance. Don't you agree?'

Hennessey chuckled. 'No. He's just rich and spoiled, and if it wasn't for you I'd tell him to stuff his horses. I'm not sure I want to be famous any more, actually. Lilian would hate it.'

Jenna pulled her hand free and vigorously tucked her shirt back in. 'We'd better get on, we haven't got all day, I have a lunch appointment. And if you insist I'll look at more school prospectuses, though I think I could write one myself by now. For "relaxed" read undisciplined, for "warm friendly atmosphere" read crammed together like rats in a box because stately homes weren't meant to be schools.'

'Hmmm. Has that Stephen character said anything to

you by the way? Tell me if he does, I'll knock his teeth in.'

Jenna looked at him and shuddered, for he looked murderous. 'He hasn't said a thing,' she muttered. 'He just smiles, knowingly. I hate it. But you can't thump him, you're supposed to be nice.'

'So I am. And to prove it I'll even slow down. By the way, which is your day for the doctor this week?'

'I thought – Wednesday?'

'I'll bring my stethoscope.' He grinned at her and suddenly she was happy. The world did not seem a frightening place, her life did not feel out of control, when she was with him. Unlike William he did not want more of everything, the best of all that was there, for Dan selected and rejected, taking only the things he truly desired at a price he was prepared to pay. Yet she knew that he found her quite expensive, and the currency was lies and broken promises, jealousy and coming hurt. He hated kowtowing to William for her sake.

Hennessey started the engine and pulled out into the lane. Jenna made an undignified scramble for her seat belt. 'I know of a school, actually,' he commented. 'They do riding, some of the boys go in for point to points. He might like that.'

'I thought he wasn't to get any treats?'

'That isn't what I said and you know it. Do you want me to make enquiries?'

'No!'

'Then don't blame me when he ends up in court.' The little car tore back to the main road, sending two pheasant screeching over the hedge and startling a sleeping cow out of her skin.

The weeks until Christmas assumed a pattern of their own. Jenna suspected that William had started another affair, but he was discreet and she found it did not offend her. After all, it could hardly do so when her weekly visit to the doctor in Harrogate took her to Honeypot Cottage and Hennessey. She had thought that in any relationship such as theirs there would come a time when the sex began to pall, and the necessity for being ready and in the mood every Wednesday at two would be like meals set before you when you had ceased to be hungry, but it was not so. They always made love, sometimes quickly, sometimes taking all the afternoon, and never once did it seem other than a wordless, infinitely close conversation. If they felt like it they strolled in the woods, talking and laughing at silly jokes. Sometimes they squabbled but they both took care never to let it go too far, for neither wanted the awful weeks of their separation to be repeated. That had been a miserable time, forerunner of the moment that could not be far distant when they must finish it. Instinctively Jenna went about creating an illusion of permanence at the cottage, bringing flowers and dried leaf arrangements, leaving clean underwear and fresh sheets. The sheets in particular caused her great inconvenience, since she had to patronise an obscure Chinese laundry in a back street in York, but she loved the respectable sensation of sliding into a clean, fragrant bed. Affairs could not be sordid when the sheets were clean.

There was to be a gathering of family and friends at Christmas, including William's deaf and arthritic mother extracted from her nursing home for the occasion. They would have drinks parties and supper parties, visits to church and the Boxing Day meet, all of which required the greatest possible organisation from Jenna. Mindful of Hennessey, she engaged an impoverished undergraduate to keep the children company, and made out lists of instructive tours and suitable trips. When Tony heard he was furious, declared himself totally opposed to babysitters and threatened to poison the student. Jenna wrote and cancelled the arrangement, feeling weary and depressed.

Hennessey was vague about his Christmas. Quietly at Lilian's parents he thought, they never had a tree or anything at home, not since the first year they were married. Lilian didn't want to be bothered, for Christmas was a difficult time for her, heralding as it did the end of another twelve unfulfilled monthly cycles. So Jenna made a little tree out of a fir branch and put it in the cottage, and on it she hung a small square parcel. 'Let's come on Christmas Eve,' she said. 'It will be our own, private celebration.'

Hennessey was touched. For a moment he could not speak, and then he took her hand and kissed it, saying, 'I wish we could change things. It shouldn't be like this and I hate it. You shouldn't stay in that marriage of yours.'

Jenna shrugged and gave a little, false laugh. 'Well then, neither should you. But since we both know that wishing won't change things we both will stay where we are. Actually William and I are getting on quite well together at the moment and when all's said and done we're quite well suited. We like the same films, that sort of thing. Can you say as much for you and Lilian?'

'She's – all right.' As always the urge to protect and defend. Not even Jenna should know that Lilian lay in bed for days, silent and unmoving, only to arise one morning and take up some frenetic activity that petered out half done. She had painted the hallway yellow, splashing paint on windows and tiles, losing heart when it did not seem to look as she had hoped and leaving a wavering line where yellow joined the old, faded blue. It was a mess.

There were fits of dressmaking too, when the sitting room floor was covered in pins and patterns, fabric and zips, acquired with high enthusiasm and abandoned soon after. Before their marriage Lilian had often appeared in garments she said she had made. It was only now Dan realised that behind that trim, capable Lilian had stood her anxious, hard-working mother, nursing, cajoling and finishing the sewing.

The perennial problem was not pleasant, and he preferred to avoid thinking about it. How much nicer to turn to beautiful, sweet-smelling Jenna with her tart comments and her gentle spirit, who had only to glance his way to make the day worthwhile. 'As pants the hart for cooling stream, when wounded in the chase.' They had sung that at school and it was a chase all right, the frantic pursuit of success through the uncertain medium of horses. But he had found his cooling stream and he was drinking very deep.

Jenna went home that day feeling oddly tired. Only to be expected of course at Christmas but it was unpleasant when your limbs felt as if weighted with lead and your view of the perfect evening encompassed only bed and a dreamless twelve-hour sleep. Anaemic possibly, it was time she had a real check-up. She often had to take vitamin supplements as a direct consequence of her diet, and it might be that they were needed again. Although she had been eating better lately, by her own standards if not anyone else's. The moment she got back she ordered a tray of tea in her bedroom and telephoned her doctor, making an appointment for the day before Christmas Eve.

'I don't believe you!'

'I can assure you Mrs Sheppard, there's no mistake. My heartiest congratulations. You are pregnant, about three months I should judge, although it is difficult to say with a

202

woman as slim as you are. I shall give you a diet sheet, I cannot emphasise enough the importance of good feeding during pregnancy –'

'I'm not going to have it.'

There was a stunned silence. 'But – why not?' The doctor had seen her through months of tests and pills, had recommended her to countless gynaecologists, all to achieve the result now evident.

She gathered her handbag, dropped her gloves, picked them up and dropped them again, wishing she had never come into this room where the man before her had somehow caused her to be pregnant. If she hadn't come in she wouldn't have been. 'I must have an abortion. Give me the name of a clinic or something, I simply must.'

'But – apart from anything else Mrs Sheppard, its Christmas. Look, why don't you talk it over with your husband and come and see me again when the holiday is over. I know it's sometimes a shock when a woman has reconciled herself to childlessness and suddenly finds herself pregnant, but you're young and you have no idea of the pleasure a baby can bring. Why, I have four children myself, the youngest is two, would you like to see a picture of him?' With all the verve of a doting parent he whipped his drawer open and presented her with a picture of a grinning toddler, dribbling on to a teddy. She whimpered and thrust it back at him, jumping to her feet and blundering out through the door.

She rushed past the neat, respectful nurse and through the waiting room, wherein sat two besuited businessmen. Heart thought Jenna absurdly, they're going to have heart attacks and I would do anything to change places with them. If I was a man I could have a coronary and be done with it. I don't like my life and I don't like this baby. It isn't a baby, he's made a mistake. Please God let him have made a mistake.

'Mrs Sheppard – your gloves; called the doctor, but she was out into the street and running. Up the hill and round the corner, where in God's name had she parked the car. Her heart was beating a tattoo against her ribs, perhaps she was going to have a heart attack. She leaned against a lamp post and tried to catch her breath.

'Excuse me – are you all right?' A concerned matron, her grey hair in tight permed curls round her face, two vast bags of shopping in her hands. After all, it was Christmas.

'Yes – yes, I'm fine. I was running.' She forced a smile and walked on, her legs unsteady. Where on earth had she parked the car? Her face felt stiff and immobile, her tongue dabbed in and out, dryly licking dry lips. As she walked she rested a hand on her belly and felt it hard and round, defending its secret prize. How could her body betray her so? All these years it had been her servant, as thin and sexless as she wished, and now it had tricked her. As Hennessey had tricked her, forcing that vile, lethal fluid into her time and again and making her pregnant!

Oh God, she had been so stupid. If Rachel had got herself into a fix like this she would have been furious, she would have said didn't you know, didn't you think? And here she was with a baby inside her and she couldn't tell anyone. For a moment she toyed with the idea of telling William: 'Darling, I'm pregnant, isn't it wonderful?' Perhaps a little lying about dates, she supposed it might be possible. She knew it wasn't. Even if he believed it was his, and a little thought would put paid to that, she could not imagine embarking on such a lie, such a betrayal. Whatever his faults William did not deserve to be saddled with another man's child, and the thought of his wrath should he ever find out made her quail. William broke men for imagined insults. What chance had a woman and an unborn child against him?

She supposed she should tell Hennessey, for after all, it

was his fault. Except that he, like her, had been conditioned to thinking that pregnancy was a thing to be struggled for, not achieved without thought or intention. They had come together in mutual joy, they had swum in a crystal pool, and she had only to speak to muddy the water forever. He wouldn't want her now.

He would pretend of course, because that was the man he was, he cared about people. He might even leave his batty wife for her sake, though she doubted it. Men didn't leave their wives for their mistresses, even when the wife in question was able to fend for herself, which in no way could be said of Lilian. Stupid, peculiar woman that she was. Jenna allowed herself a moment's spiteful clawing, venting her rage on the woman who clung to Hennessey like mistletoe to a tree, sinking tendrils into the sap and drawing on another's life. But exchange Lilian for Jenna, move the counters on the chess board and have the white king take the red queen, what then? The game would not be ended. The red king would wreck the board before he lost, and afterwards, in the mess of broken pieces, there would be nothing half worthwhile. Jenna had walked, clear-eyed and smiling, into a trap.

So it was the abortion then. Nothing else to do. Unmake the baby that had crept so silently inside her and now nestled, growing, in the warmth and the dark. In the minutes since she left the doctor's surgery – many minutes she realised, almost an hour – she had accepted that it was truly there. And though she said again what she had said at the doctor's – 'I'm not going to have it' – her heart and the part of her that was already engaged in protecting its young rebelled against the destruction. There must be some other way out, for of all the actors in this drama, the baby was the only one not guilty.

She had been walking aimlessly, moving from street to street and seeing nothing. Her head was swimming, she

205

would give anything to stop, but she was late and she had to get home. She saw a passing taxi and hailed it, sinking into the back with a gasp of relief that was very nearly a sob. Someone would come and fetch the car tomorrow.

When at last she was home she crept like a wounded animal into the safety of her bed. She wanted nothing and no-one, would they all please leave her alone. She was ill, she was weary, her throat ached with silent sobs and after a little, her body aching for rest, she slept.

Waking then, in the quiet of dawn she felt calmer. Thoughts swam into her head, clear and pale, and she took and turned each one, wondering at it. No need to do everything at once, her head told her. Everything is made up of tiny little steps and if I take just a few each day I can find my way out of this maze. There is only one thing that I need do now, and it's a hard thing. I always knew it would be hard and if I do it now, quickly, when there's none of me alive at all except my head, then it will be over. She crept from her bed and went to her writing table, a Louis XIV excritoire that was a present from William.

My Dear Dan she wrote *I'm writing to say goodbye. I'm sorry to give so little warning, but perhaps it's better like this, because after all, what is there to say? Except thank you. I'm not a natural liar you see, I hate myself for the lies I've told and I've suddenly come to realise that whatever it is we have just isn't worth it. I'm sorry, but there it is.*

I'm sure you'll understand. Please don't try and see me again, it would only upset us both, though I imagine we shall often meet casually at the races and so on. I have no doubt at all that you will go on to a fantastic career, with or without our horses, though I hope you will always look upon the Sheppard connection as one of the better things in your life. I'm sorry. Jenna.

Formal, final, excluding. She folded it and placed it in an envelope, and placed the envelope in her bag, safe from prying eyes. Then she sat again at her desk, and saw that her hands were trembling. Suddenly she grabbed another piece of paper and scrawled on it in big letters. *Damn you you bastard, you've made me pregnant. There's a baby growing and growing inside me and I could kill you for doing this to me when I trusted you! I bet you'd feel proud of yourself if you knew, great big, potent man making a barren woman swell, but I hate you! I won't beg you for help, I will manage ON MY OWN and you can spend the rest of your life wondering what went wrong. Oh Dan, Dan, Dan, Dan, Dan . . .* She found that she was sobbing and shaking, she clutched at the paper, screwed it, tore it, shredded it into strands with her teeth. Then, when it was no more than a handful of tiny pieces, like ghastly confetti, she felt calmer. She gathered them into her hands, pressed her hands to her pregnant belly and went into the bathroom. Only when the paper had disappeared down the toilet did the shaking stop, and it took her breakfast tray and a pot of strong coffee before she felt able to face what she had to do next.

Well served as always, her car was once again in the garage, rescued at the cost of the chauffeur's night off. Even in the midst of her turmoil Jenna remembered to thank him and he loved her for it. 'She's such a lady,' he said to George later that day. 'You can't imagine her doing anything cruel or underhand.'

'I don't think Mr Sheppard appreciates her,' agreed George and they nodded, aware as few could be of William's philanderings.

Jenna drove badly that morning, misjudging distances

and braking too late. When she reached the place where the path joined the road she flung out of the car, leaving the door swinging wide. After a few paces she stopped, went back and shut and locked the door. Control. She must strive for control and here, where no-one was watching, was a good place to practice. She strolled slowly down the path, only to find that within a few strides she was running. This must be over soon. She couldn't bear it.

The key to the cottage was always in a gutter, covered by a lump of broken slate. She reached it on tiptoe and opened the door as if she expected Hennessey to be inside, although she knew he would not be coming till afternoon. There on the hearth was her little Christmas tree, brave with its tinsel and it's two little presents. Two. He had hung it there after she left last time. A sob rose gurgling in her throat and she swallowed it down, taking the box from the tree and leaving her letter in its place. Then she went quickly from room to room, collecting things. Shoes, underwear, an umbrella. A book she had lent him, returned, he had only read it to please her. The blanket they had used the first time. She left it, and the sheets, and the little rug she had bought for the floor, there was nothing she could do with things that cried 'here' every time she saw them. Close the door, replace the key, pick up your plastic carrier and know that it is ended. She would never come here again.

On the way home, blinded by tears that would not stop, she knew she had to talk to someone. She would go mad with all this inside her, and apart from all else, she needed help. Then she thought of Stephen, and her tears began to slow. He had said nothing and she presumed it meant support. Perhaps his own vulnerability made him kind to the weaknesses of others. He was away for Christmas, acting out a bachelor charade for the benefit of his family, but he would be back early in the New Year. That sort of man knew all about abortion clinics and so on, he might be able to help. Someone must know what she should do.

Jenna was unused to thinking of herself as strong, perhaps because always in her life there were peope who were stronger. But now with no-one to help her she found a resilience and a courage that she did not know she possessed, holding her upright as she greeted her guests, tilting her head in casual amusement. The house was a brilliant palace of light, a theatre of luxury and merriment, the only sour notes being sounded by the players. Casey had chewed at a rug and William wanted him gone, Tony had given Jenna a set of mildly saucy prints and William was outraged. Throughout it all she soothed and mediated, caught George's eye and remembered to thank her cook and always, always, always kept her hand from straying to that tiny bulge of stomach that had never been there before. But try as she might to pretend that all was well she knew she looked different. The face that stared out from her mirror was chalk white with thick, black shadows beneath the eyes. Did she imagine it or were her rings tight on her fingers? Was that something that happened to you? She did not know. Leave the jewellery in the box, wear the flowing, waistless clothes and paint away the pallor and the marks of tears.

In the dull aftermath of Christmas when the old year is dying and the new one has yet to be born Jenna took the children, the reprieved dog and such guests as remained and walked on the moors in the damp, wintry air. The others dawdled or gave up, but she strode on, the dog at her side, exhausting herself. It was good to be alone here, climbing hills till it hurt, spending such energy as remained on walking. The days were empty, the future bleak, but here on the hills it seemed not to matter. When she was at home she found her thoughts straying to the days that were to come, when her baby was gone, Dan was gone and she was once again back in that time before either of them was known. A sort of panic rose in her throat at the thought of it, which was foolish since if ever she should feel such a thing it should be now, when her downfall was brought closer by every passing day that this thing in her belly fed and grew. On New Year's Eve, Jenna laughed and smiled, and when the old year passed and the new one began no-one thought it odd that her cheeks were wet with tears. Melancholy was expected at such a time, everyone wept for something. William took her in his arms and kissed her, and for once she was glad of it. Human warmth and touching seemed so very far from her.

Stephen returned the next day, pale and rather quiet. That evening, with William safely closeted in his study, Jenna went quickly across the dark lawns and knocked on the door of Stephen's house.

'Jenna.' He was holding a glass half-filled with whisky, and she saw that he had been crying.

'I'm sorry, Stephen, but I've got to talk to you,' she said urgently and pushed past him. The house had the cold, still feeling of disuse and in the sitting room the gas fire popped feebly as it tried to stir the air. She suddenly remembered that there should be someone else here. 'Stephen – your friend?' she asked and he laughed, waving his glass and slopping the drink.

'Gone. Flown away, like all the rest. You know we queers, never the same bedmate two nights running, we don't feel like other people. Animals the lot of us. My mother says so.' He was crying again and Jenna went to him, holding and petting until he was calm.

'Tell me what happened,' she urged, settling him into

his chair like a child. All the neatness had gone, he was slack-faced and pathetic. But he tried for an air of unconcern. 'He wrote that he's going to marry his cousin. Sorry, second cousin. Couldn't face me you see, says it's been going on for a while. As if he couldn't meet me and tell me to my face, that's what really hurts – anyone would think there hadn't been anything between us –'

Jenna gulped and put a hand to her head. 'Will he be happy do you think?' she asked distractedly.

'What the hell do I care if he's happy! Of course he won't be happy, what can that scheming little bitch do for him that I can't, she'll never love him the way I did, she's just out for her two point something brats and her safe little house in Esher whereas I – didn't want – anything at all!' His face contorted with sobs and Jenna knew that if she didn't tell him now she never would.

'Do you want to know what I'm here for?' she asked loudly.

'What? Oh, all right tell me. Does the lord and master want me to do some more pimping for him – sorry, Jen dear, I didn't mean that, I'm overwrought. What is it love, quick, before I utterly disgrace myself.' He mopped at his face with a polkadot handkerchief.

'I'm pregnant. And the father isn't – William.'

'Oh – my – God.'

She sighed into the silence, then put her finger into a small puddle of whisky on the coffee table, licking the amber drops like a child with a lolly.

'I think I'd better have an abortion. I thought you might know of somewhere.'

'You poor cow.'

She shrugged, making a better pretence of lightness than had he. 'I asked for it I suppose. I can't tell – the man – and it would be more than my life's worth to tell William. So I have to. Don't I?'

He nodded, slowly. 'I think so, love. How far on are you?'

'I don't know, the doctor was vague. Three months perhaps. I don't think it shows yet, not to a man. Do you?'

'No. You look a bit grim though, lovey, but people may think it's just insomnia. We can all claim that one. Poor, poor Jen. I knew you weren't cut out for casual screwing and I tried to warn you. You're too – straight.'

'You wouldn't say that if you knew the lies I've told.'

'And now you're in this mess. Oh well, Uncle Steve will get you out. I'll make an appointment for next week, you'll have to go to London for the day, say it's shopping or something. When you come back you can say the trip's made you ill and you can stay in bed for a day or two. And after that darling, you'd better be more careful.'

'There won't be any need. I've finished it.'

'I don't know why you even started it.'

'Don't you?' She didn't know, now. She was adrift on the ocean and her familiar landmarks had gone, lost over a distant horizon. How she had come there and where she was going were things unremembered. She rose wearily to her feet.

'I think I'll go. Thanks Steve. I'm sorry about your friend.'

He stood at the door and watched as she retraced her steps across the lawns. William's creature he had always thought her, dancing in the spotlight on the palm of her husband's hand. Now she was walking off into the shadows, but this time she held a glow of her own.

Jenna stepped from the taxi and blindly shoved some notes at the driver. He had looked knowing and curious at one and the same time when she gave him the address and she wanted to be rid of him. She was shivering with nerves and her fingers felt cold and clammy, clutching the piece of paper with the appointment on it as if her own life was at stake, instead of the life of her child. Her stomach lurched and she wondered if she were going to be sick. On the other side of the road there was a woman with a baby in a pram, although all you could see was the hump of blankets. It could be an ugly baby, deformed, retarded, anything. If it was she would wish she'd done as Jenna was doing now, flushing it out, getting rid of it before it could think or feel.

The clinic was a prosperous grey building with a shiny wood front door. A place of hushed discretion where the nurse did not quite meet your eye. 'Mrs – Maynard' said Jenna, for Stephen had lent her his name for the day. It sounded strange and infinitely false, but not an eyebrow was lifted. She was passed into a carpeted waiting room and sat with her eyes on her hands, trying not to look at the girl in the seat opposite. Younger, poorer, more nervous.

If only Dan were here. The thought popped into her head without warning and it almost made her smile. As if he would participate at the murder of his own child.

It would be beautiful, too, their baby, for they were tall and strong and slender and they would have a baby to match. Women longed to have babies such as hers, all over the world there were people eager to take care of them. The nurse came in and took away the girl opposite. Jenna heard her feet brushing through the pile of the carpet, a door opening, voices, a door closing on silence. She sat and eyed the rubber plant with distaste, a flourishing monument to the abortion trade. Footsteps approached the door, passed it and went on, and Jenna nearly fainted with relief. Safe. They were both still safe. In fact if she opened the door and crept away, they need never find her at all. Hardly had the thought been formed than she was on her feet in the hall, sneaking away like a thief, like a guest who has stolen the spoons.

'Excuse me? Mrs Maynard?' The woman at the desk was looking at her. 'Can I help you?' she asked, the light glinting on her spectacles.

Jenna edged away towards the door. 'Thank you – no – I don't think you can,' she said grittily, sliding round the door, into the street, and away.

Jenna wandered the streets like a lost soul, not knowing why she had done as she did, only aware that she could not have done anything different. What happened now was a mystery. Perhaps if she sold all her jewels, cleared out her bank account and absconded – but then what would happen to her life? Besides, she had not definitely decided to have this baby, she had only decided not to get rid of it, which wasn't the same thing at all. She was waiting for a magic wand, and if none was forthcoming today there might be something of the kind in tomorrow. For now at any rate she could only go home, and as a cold spatter of rain swept down the street she shivered and turned her steps towards the station. William wanted them to leave for Australia at the end of the month.

She fell asleep on the train going home, for despite all the complexities of her situation her pregnant self needed sleep and took it. When she awoke it was to a sense of the unreal, her mind a fog, her trip a dream, her pregnancy a figment of her imagination. She was early and there would be no Rolls to meet her, she would have to get a taxi. Feeling a wreck she pushed at stray tendrils of hair as the train drew into the station.

The platform seemed very long, stretching away into grey uncertainty. At the end, by the gate, there was someone that looked like Hennessey, but of course it could not be. As she approached her step slowed. It was Hennessey.

'Jenna.' He was pale and his hair needed cutting. He

wore his tatty old sheepskin over jeans and a jumper, working clothes.

'How did you know I would be here?'

'George said you'd gone to London. I decided to meet the trains.'

She nodded, without interest, her mind still clouded with sleep and strain.

'Shall we have a cup of coffee?' she asked. 'I went to sleep on the train and I feel a bit strange.'

He agreed and they walked together across the grey asphalt to sit at a messy formica table in the buffet, sipping from paper cups.

'What's happened?' he asked, his eyes bright, acute, knowing her better than she did herself. She shifted uncomfortably in her chair and said, 'Nothing,' in a voice that declared her to mean 'everything.'

He stroked her finger as it rested on her cup, and instinctively she moved away. Dangerous, very dangerous to let him get close to her.

'That was a horrible letter,' he said gently.

She blushed and fixed her gaze on a point behind his head. 'I'm not very good at letters I'm afraid. But I meant it, Dan.'

'Did you?'

She was a cat on hot bricks, looking everywhere but at his face. The canteen manageress was berating a slovenly girl, conformist maturity meeting iconoclastic youth, complete with greasy hair, bitten nails and a resentful manner.

'Do you think Rachel will be like her one day?' said Jenna.

Hennessey followed her eyes. 'Christ, I hope not. She must weigh fifteen stone.'

Jenna blinked and looked again. 'I meant the girl.'

'Oh. Well, she does already, doesn't she? Look Jen, I

don't give a damn about your observations on humanity, I want to know why you decided to kick me in the teeth suddenly, at Christmas, when we were closer than we've ever been. You write me a letter you could have sent to a stranger and expect me to take it all quite calmly. *Please don't try to see me again.* Lady Muck issuing orders to the troops. Now I'm prepared to hear some excuses, otherwise I shall take the greatest pleasure in pushing you over a cliff!'

She looked at him then, wide-eyed. 'Really?'

'No. Oh Jen, I've missed you so. Don't say this is making you happy, you look ill. Damn it, will you tell me what went wrong!' But she shook her head miserably and for something to do he took a drink of his coffee and grimaced. It tasted bad but so did his life since Jenna walked out of it. That was the frightening part, she had taken his happiness and he needed it back, he needed to feel her skin against his and to taste the moist warmth of her flesh. It infuriated him that he needed her so much and he glared at her with such a mixture of anger and desire that she longed to hold him. If he had missed her then she had been lost in the dark without him, but there was no point in telling him so. She remembered her problem and fostered her rage.

'I think William suspects,' she said in clipped tones. 'No doubt Stephen dropped a hint of some kind. Not who of course, I doubt if either of us would be here now if he knew who, but simply that there might be someone.'

'So why couldn't you tell me?' He didn't believe her and it showed.

'I thought you might take it out on Stephen,' she said quickly, making it up as she went along. 'After all, you said dreadful things. Perhaps you didn't mean them. I thought you did.'

'You knew I didn't. Now tell me Jenna, dear Jenna,

what the loathsome William is doing about his unfaithful wife.' He linked his hands behind his head and waited.

'He's – he's checking up on me. I can't get out any more. But apart from that – much more important than that really – when I thought he knew I got such a fright. I suddenly saw what would happen if he did find out. Yes, it was wonderful with you, of course it was, but it's William I love. Really love, not the frothy sort of thing we had. We're not the same sort of people, you and I. He's my husband and I don't want to lose him.'

All the colour had drained from Hennessey's face as she spoke and when Jenna looked at him she felt quite sick. But, to make absolutely sure, she added the final touch. 'And then of course we began sleeping together again. You've no idea how wonderful it is and I've you to thank –' She reached a hand to him, but he struck it violently away. She shivered with fright and bent her head for the onslaught.

'Wonderful! It's wonderful that it's wonderful you can wonderfully screw your husband, how wonderfully pleased I am for you! What a pity that I didn't crawl away into the shadows like some used piece of tissue paper, instead of making a disgraceful scene. After all, you gave me the pay-off, didn't you?' He slapped a little jeweller's box on the table, the solid gold cufflinks Jenna had given him for Christmas.

'Don't you like them?' she asked feebly, thinking that it had taken her half a day to choose them.

'Like them? I'm not some sort of gigolo to be given his reward. My wife gave me the ones I wear and I shall continue to wear them.'

'I should have guessed. They're ghastly.' She never could resist the chance to snipe at his wife.

'But she is an honest woman, which is more than can be said for you.' He was hurt, terribly hurt and the urge was to strike back hard. They were both beginners at rows, and they fought without restraint, going too far too quickly.

'All those lies were for your sake,' said Jenna, her eyes brimming with tears.

'Tell that to sodding William,' spat Hennessey. 'Tell me, what did he give Tony for Christmas, his own first heroin shot?'

And, since William had bought nothing for Tony and it had been left to Jenna to write labels reading *Love from Daddy and Jenna*, she was incensed. 'What did your so honest, so lovely wife give you then? A temperature chart with the relevant dates filled in? You always tell me how much you enjoy those rapturous nights.'

He caught her hand and crushed her fingers, muttering, 'Shut it, Jenna! Shut it before I strangle you.' Her eyes were wide and dark and her mouth was quivering. If only he need not love her so. Gathering his rage he snarled, 'And I'll thank you to return my present. I chose it for someone I don't think exists.'

'I don't have it on me,' lied Jenna. He had given her a tiny Victorian brooch carved in the shape of a love spoon. She wore it now, pinned to the collar of her blouse, and she would not give it back. It was her talisman.

'You can post it.' She would see him in hell first. She got to her feet, pulling her coat close around her throat, but found herself strangely reluctant to leave.

'You will be all right, won't you?' she asked.

'If you think I'm going to kill myself because of you then you're even more conceited than I thought.'

'But – you'll drive carefully.'

'I never drive carefully.'

'No, and you'll kill some unsuspecting child and blame me. That's just your style, it's always someone else's fault!' She flung the final, unjustified insult at him and stormed out on the tide of her indignation.

Later, in the taxi, she found herself shaking. Her hands felt very cold and she knew she was near collapse, but with a great effort of will she forced herself to calm. There was not only herself to think of now, there was her baby.

Stephen met her at the front door. 'Jenna? Are you all right?'

'Yes, thank you. Come into the library will you Stephen? George, a tray of tea if you please, I'm really quite chilled. Thank you.'

There was a fire in the library grate. Jenna sank into a chair and held her hands to the flames, taking comfort in the warmth of her surroundings. Her home might be a place of conflict but it was her own, a refuge in which she could feel safe. As long as William was away of course.

'How are you Jen? You look very pale.' Stephen was on edge, aware that in helping her he had risked his whole career.

'I didn't have it done,' said Jenna calmly.

'What?' He didn't believe her. Just then George arrived with the tea, complete with a plate of hot buttered scones and another of crumpets, which sometimes tempted Jenna's errant appetite. She smiled her thanks and accepted some tea and a crumpet.

'You are joking,' said Stephen the moment George left the room.

'No I'm not. I'm sorry, Steve, but I couldn't go through with it. Because it isn't the baby's fault you see, you can blame who you like but not the baby. And it was a terrible place, a giant dustbin for people's indiscretions.'

'You don't know what you're doing,' said Stephen weakly. 'Are you going to tell him?'

She shook her head. 'I'm not that stupid. Whatever he did to me he'd get rid of the baby, I'm sure of that. My consent would be a very minor matter. No, I think I'd better have it and get it adopted. You could arrange that, couldn't you?'

He thought she had gone mad. He put a hand to his head and tried to gather his wits together, thinking all the time what if Sheppard holds me responsible for any of this.

'Stephen,' said Jenna gently, 'if you don't help me and it all comes out then I'll make sure William knows that you knew and didn't tell him. I'm sorry to threaten but I can't afford to let you back out.'

He could see she meant it and she looked very far from mad. Tired perhaps but in full command, and Stephen bent before the superior force. 'What do you intend to do?' He poured himself a cup of tea and sank into a chair opposite her.

'Just this. I will go on quite normally until it starts to show, I don't know how long that will be, but it might be quite a long time. William and I will go to Australia, I want to get away from here anyway. When I think it's getting obvious my mother will suddenly fall ill, she's in Brittany as you know. I shall go to her. And nothing, absolutely nothing, will winkle me out until the baby is born.'

'Suppose he comes to visit?'

'I shall rely on you to stop him, or failing that, let me know. Then we can take evasive action.'

'It'll never work. Someone's bound to notice.' Stephen felt helpless and besieged.

'Can you see any difference?' She stood up, her skirt falling loosely from the waist. There was a weariness about her that showed in the way she stood. The flesh under her eyes was puffy with strain.

'Like that it doesn't show, but – hold it closer.'

Jenna did so, stared at the neat bulge it revealed, then turned impatiently away.

'I won't wear tight clothes. Besides, just another two months will be enough, if he finds out then it will be too late. You can't get rid of babies then. Anyway, he won't find out, I won't let him. Oh Steve, I know you think I'm being stupid but I simply couldn't go through with it. It seemed so – self-seeking. There was a young girl there, you could see she couldn't cope, she was almost a baby herself and she looked poor and frightened and alone. I'm alone but I'm not poor and I'm trying not to be frightened. My baby is owed a chance of life.'

Stephen stared at her, suddenly aware. 'You're in love with this baby already,' he said with something akin to disgust.

'No I'm not,' denied Jenna, inwardly thinking that if anyone needed someone to love and love her then it was she. For a brief, ungoverned moment her mind constructed a picture of how it might be, now, if Dan was at her side. To her surprise she felt a tear drip on to her hand and she turned quickly aside. 'I think I'll go to bed,' she muttered. 'I'll talk to people tomorrow.'

Chapter Ten

The dark and heavy days of winter weigh upon the soul. Life is ebbing, and even those who know they will greet the spring hear the whisper of death. When the snow fell soft as leaves upon a grave and covered the earth like a pall Hennessey knew despair.

The house was silent and chill because no-one in it had the will to provide light and warmth to chase away the night. Day after short day Lilian lay in her bed, sometimes crying, sometimes staring at the ceiling with eyes that did not blink. She did not wash, she did not speak, and when in an excess of revulsion her husband dragged her to the bath she sobbed and whispered, 'You're cruel. You don't love me any more,' and because he had long ceased to love her he denied it. What was there to love in this log of a woman whose inner torment closed all doors to the world? He did not know her and neither it seemed did anyone else. Doctors could only suggest hospital but when he mentioned it to Lilian she became frantic, clinging and begging that he should not send her away. If only she could have her baby. In desperation he bought her a kitten, but like the dog, Casey, it was adored and then ignored. 'I'm not a child,' she said resentfully and Hennessey winced. He treated her as one. It was easier that way.

Jenna had gone to Australia. He knew because Tony told him when he came riding, disgorged once a week from the Rolls Royce. It made Hennessey burn to see that she had again abandoned the children, leaving them to the doubtful authority of servants. He treasured his outrage and told himself that Jenna was truly heartless, closing his ears to Tony's accounts of telephone calls and telex messages, not to mention the installation of Jenna's elderly cousin with the express brief of looking after the children.

Hennessey himself was bombarded with telexes, but all from William. How were the horses, were they going well, were they all fit. He took a perverse delight in replying as tersely as possible. 'No work. Snow.' And again 'Fleece shinsore. Resting,' knowing full well that he was causing maximum consternation. In the meantime he was engaged in creating, for Jenna and to spite her, two exceptional racehorses. Fleece was a classic hopeful, of that he had no doubt. Whether he had the nerve to withstand the pressure of the racetrack was another matter, but he was progressing nicely. There was a heart-stopping moment when he ditched his rider and bolted from the gallops, charging through an open gate and on to the road. He was caught by an old lady outside the village sweetshop, and Hennessey was treated to a lecture on how to manage horses, which at least made him smile. Two-year-old racehorses are unpredictable babies and there is nothing but a whisker between them and disaster whenever they leave their boxes. However much care is taken they can step on a stone, shy at a blowing piece of paper or cannon into another horse, inflicting God knows what damage to young bones and muscles. But, as his lads said, Hennessey was lucky with his horses. Perhaps that was the trouble, he had wished for such luck and he had got it, and with it the reverse side of the coin. How he longed for things to be different.

He was nearing the end of his tether and he knew it. Day followed weary day, up at the crack of dawn to work horses, back to schooling and leg problems, dark cold afternoons when he sat at his papers and thought about shooting himself. Jenna had been the light in his life, with her he had learned again how to be happy. There was such relief in talking and being understood, relating a funny incident in the knowledge that she too would see the joke. Only now did he know what it was to be truly lonely.

What a bitch. What an absolute total bitch, taking what she wanted and ditching him like a used car, except that the Sheppards traded in their cars and bought newer, glossier, even more expensive models. They did not deserve his work and expertise but he gave it just the same, turning the gutsy little horse Sharps into the best sprinting prospect he had ever known. It galled him to be doing this for her, yet in a different way pleased. When she came home he could stand and say, 'Look what I have done for you,' and know that it would turn a knife in her soul.

He grimaced and got up from his desk, gazing out across a landscape of grim winter fields, dotted with crows. It was strange, this desire to hurt and to hold at one and the same time. She had been right to end it and when all was said and done, it was no crime not to love him. But he had not known she could be so – closed to him, as if once her decision was made he was shut out for ever. And he would wander the world, alone and cold, and never feel warm again. He turned from the window and went to stir the fire, if he went on like this he and Lilian would make a wonderful pair, both as nutty as a fruitcake.

*   *   *

Jenna lay on her sunbed, stretched her endless legs and

smiled sleepily up at her husband. 'I thought you were going windsurfing,' she murmured.

'I thought I'd rather stay with you.' He squatted down beside her, a chunky, hairy figure with the beginnings of a spare tyre bulging over the top of his swimming trunks. Jenna felt her comfort get up and leave, like a cat disturbed by a dog.

'What do you want William?' she asked bluntly.

'You.'

This had been coming for days, heralded by little things. He took care of her at dinner, offering wine she did not want, he walked very close when he was beside her. It was oddly touching, watching a man who had forgotten the rules of courtship striving to play a role he had long outgrown. What William wanted he took and now to ask for something he believed was his already showed a softness she had not known he possessed.

'Let's go in,' she murmured, and swung her legs to the ground, drawing the length of scarlet silk in a swathe around her body. She had started a fashion this year for silk sarongs.

The beach house was large and airy by anyone's standards except William's. It had only four bedrooms, which he described as poky, and they ate in the kitchen, admittedly in a sun-filled annexe but in the kitchen just the same. And there was no pool, only the private beach, which he found embarrassingly frugal. But the lack of space meant no live-in staff, which Jenna liked. The cook came in as requested for lunch and dinner, leaving them to fend for themselves at breakfast and in the afternoons the house was quiet and dark, shielded from the sun by heavy blinds at the windows. Jenna went into the dim shadows of her bedroom and waited for her husband. She felt cold.

'Jenna.' He held out his arms for her and she went to

him, feeling him hard against her pregnant belly. It was unreal she thought as his lips sucked at her neck, unreal and immoral. He pulled at her sarong and found the swelling globe of her breast, cupping it in his hand and squeezing her nipple. Surely he must notice she thought, there was nothing there before, but in his bursting, throbbing excitement William noticed nothing. His hands clutched and probed, as if now that he was allowed to touch he could not touch enough. He began to hurt her, digging his nails into her buttocks until she gasped.

'Be gentle William,' she murmured and he grunted, pushing her backwards on to the bed. He was not gentle, he nipped and squeezed, hurting her only a little but enough for her to cry out at each fresh assault. She twisted her hands in his hair and dragged his head back from her, yelling 'Stop it!' into his flushed and grinning face.

'No,' he said shortly, and straddled her, pushing himself deep inside. 'Does it make you want to hit me?' he demanded. 'Go on, bite me, scratch me, I like it.' And Jenna looked up at him, this man who was staking his claim to her body regardless of her pain and she drew back her fist and punched him hard in the mouth. With a cry that was almost delight he climaxed.

Later, while he slept, she went through to the kitchen to make some coffee. She sat and waited for the percolator to boil, wishing that she could only talk to Hennessey. He would explain things to her because he was a man and knew how men thought, whereas she could only guess at the motives which drove a man like William. It seemed to her now that for William sex and pain had always been inextricably linked. She had thought the first time that he had hurt her because she was a virgin, but now, aware of how sex could and should be, and allowing herself to think whereas before she had closed her mind, she could see that he had meant to hurt her. A man of his experience

226

must have known how tender were a woman's breasts, how much it hurt when a man poked stiff fingers between her legs, yet he had done it and gone on doing it even when she was begging him to stop. It had almost been rape. Afterwards she had shivered and cried and said she could not marry him and he had been frightened. He had coaxed her into marriage and ever after held back when he felt the urge to hurt her. But she had known it was there, and the knowledge had been like a frost, blighting her budding sexuality.

The percolator began to bubble and she turned it down, pulling her dressing gown close about her regardless of the day's heat. William came through from the bedroom. He was calm, at peace, the bruise on his lip showing purple against his tan.

'Darling.' He bent and kissed her cheek. 'That must be a wonderful doctor.'

'But I hit you.'

'I don't mind. Next time make it so it doesn't show.' He grinned as if they were two conspirators in a secret and Jenna thought briefly of all those girls in the past. Did they enjoy the things William did? What did he make them do to them? She thought of whips and leather underwear, the very stuff of personal columns in lurid Sunday papers, and she felt the urge to laugh. Poor William, all these years he had been longing for a wife who would indulge him and instead he had been faced with frigid, straitlaced Jenna.

'I didn't know you liked that sort of thing,' she said, a fist against her mouth.

'Most men like a bit of spice,' said William, and she knew that however desperate and well-nigh dangerous his bedroom practices might be, for William it would go into the box labelled 'spice' where it need not, could not be judged. Her amusement jelled into a lump of cold fear.

He might hurt her baby.

'What are you doing this afternoon?' she asked distractedly, for it was the weekend and all Australia closes down at weekends. William was forced to take up relaxation.

'I think the windsurfing.' He was pouring the coffee, a man radiating content. 'Why don't you come too? You haven't been looking too well lately, the exercise will do you good.'

'I get plenty of exercise. It's just the heat, you know I don't like the heat.'

'It's never bothered you before. Perhaps you need a tonic of some sort, we'll get that doctor chappie out to you. I thought the other day that your hands looked rather puffy.'

'I told you, it's the heat,' snapped Jenna, and resisted the urge to fold her arms acros her belly. There was a gentle fluttering deep inside her and she wanted to cry. 'I don't need a doctor,' she murmured, and her sadness was reflected in her tone. There was no pleasure in anything any more.

William reached for her hand. 'I'm so glad we came away. Just the two of us. Sometimes I don't feel very close to you, and I don't know why. I don't mean – I hope you know how precious you are to me, darling.'

Her smile was strained and unconvincing. 'Of course I know. But it's no reason to keep sending me off to doctors, I'm really quite healthy. I'll have a swim this afternoon and then rest, I'll be better tonight.'

'And so will I,' he promised, and put his mouth to her neck. Jenna had never felt so threatened in her life.

In the dull heat of an Australian afternoon she let the sun dry her and watched William windsurf. He was bad at it, and she feared for his temper. Her swim had been so peaceful, alone in the dark green water of the neighbouring bay. Would it hurt to drift out, out, out to the horizon? Such a gentle end to it all. But at last, for whatever reason, she swam back to land.

William's windsurf teacher, a young Australian who was far more concerned with his effect on her than the progress of his pupil, began to bellow instructions. It aggravated her headache, there since this morning. Couldn't the boy see that William was no more in control of that thing than if it was a half-broken horse?

'Turn the board,' he yelled again, 'and keep away from the rocks.' He himself executed a graceful one-handed turn directly in front of Jenna, but as usual she barely noticed him. Her attention was on William, struggling with a flapping sail far too close to the rocky part of the shore. Then the wind came and the sail filled, but instead of turning, the board sped forward, heeled and tipped William neatly between two rocks.

Jenna sighed, for it was just such a thing that could trigger one of William's nastier moods. Then she realised that he wasn't getting up. She tightened the knot on her sarong and hurried along the beach, aware that only weeks before she would have run. It weighed heavy, the creature within. The Australian was there before her, his board racing across the waves. William lay in the churning surf, his face as grey as seaweed, boiling with fury.

'I've broken my leg,' he hissed between clenched teeth. 'Damn you, boy, I'll take you for every penny you've got for this.'

The lad recoiled as if from a snake. 'I said stay away from the rocks,' he faltered and was rewarded with a brilliant smile from Jenna.

'Of course you did. Go and call an ambulance please, my husband is in pain. It's all right, darling, I'm here.' She felt like a man on death row who hears that the state has today abolished capital punishment.

The fracture was not a simple one and William was confined to a private hospital. For Jenna it was indeed a reprieve, only now that William was safely hidden away did she realise that she had held her muscles rigid for weeks past, enclosing her womb in a straightjacket of tension. Now she could relax, merely ensuring that whenever she visited William it was in a flowing cheese-cloth dress that fell straight from the bust, pretty and appropriate in the Australian heat. William was a difficult and furious patient. Dissuaded from savaging his windsurfing tutor he contented himself with sending vicious messages all over the world, causing consternation wherever they arrived. Long and abject replies were forthcoming, all except from Hennessey, whose cryptic answers only served to inflame the already irascible William.

'That man needs his arse kicked,' he snarled and Jenna felt herself colour. She hated to talk about Hennessey, she loathed it when Tony spoke on the phone and gave her excited accounts of how 'Dan says I'm coming on well' or 'Dan never asks a horse a question he can't answer' and more cunningly 'Dan always wants to hear about you, Jenna.' Did he now. She did not want to hear about him, ever. Her hand closed around the little lovespoon brooch, pinned on the inside of her pocket. For safekeeping, only.

'How's the Kentucky stud?' asked Jenna, which proved to be an unfortunate question.

'Royal Diamond's been kicked by a mare,' said William, pulling against his traction. He wanted Jenna to comfort him, he needed her to do so, and yet she wandered around the room, picking up grapes and looking at his chart.

'I told you Gerard was the man for the stallions,' she said absently, and flicked her husband into annoyance.

'It has nothing to do with Gerard! Anyway I wanted to talk about Tony, his headmaster says he isn't trying.'

He had her interest then. 'When did he say that?'

'I wrote to him. I want him out of that school Jenna and back to full-time boarding, I'm not having him waste his time and my money like this.'

'I'll go and see the headmaster when I get back,' stalled his wife, but William would have none of it. Every ounce of attention that she gave to Tony and not to him was too much.

'You'll find another school and you'll send him. Do I make myself clear?'

He did indeed. Jenna soothed and consoled him, arranged for a video to be brought to his room and crushed fresh grapefruit herself for his drink. As she bent over him, smoothing his pillows, he looked up at her and thought of saying 'I love you' but in the end said nothing. Instead he complained about the service in this place, and insisted that she find him a private nurse.

Two weeks later Jenna telephoned Stephen. 'I think it's time,' she said briefly. That very day a woman in a shop had asked her when it was due. How could she tell, someone who didn't even know her? Could it be that William knew and for some strange reason of his own, said nothing? It was possible. Not like William, though. Besides, people saw what they expected to see and she had always been the wife that William expected. Perhaps even the wife that he deserved.

Stephen murmured at the other end of the phone. 'I'll get in touch with your mother,' he was saying. 'Take care, love.'

'I will. Thanks. Thanks a lot.' She replaced the receiver and went to stand before the mirror in her bedroom, smoothing her dress against her. From the front, nothing, but from the side – she swelled from the navel, as if she carried a neat football within her, an excrescence stuck upon her slender self. Even William must notice something soon, if not her belly then her breasts, full and luscious for the first time in her life. It embarrassed her to see them. When her mother's letter arrived at last she rushed to the hospital, presenting her husband with a face of genuine fear.

'Darling! The most terrible thing has happened, it's my mother. She's had a heart attack of some sort. She's trying not to make too much of it, you know what she's like, but I can tell it's serious. Look, see what she says: *I'm sorry to break into your holiday, darling, but I would like you to come and stay for a week or two. Just you, I don't feel up to a crowd. Perhaps William could come a little later in the year. I hate to be a nuisance but it's been so long since we spent any time together*. William, she thinks she's going to die!'

'Let me see that.' William took the letter and scanned the sheets, fighting the irritation that welled within him. What a time to take Jenna from him, when his leg was broken and he needed someone close at his side. Still, at least he had Nurse Phillips, who tended him with pleasing deference and could probably be persuaded to lend her Australian buxomness to the task of making her employer happy. Besides he liked Jenna's mother, she had been instrumental in persuading her daughter to marry after that first, disastrous night. And she kept out of the way, which was more than could be said of most mothers-in-law.

'When are you going?' he asked, handing the letter back.

'What? Oh – tomorrow, I think.' Jenna felt her heart pounding with the joy of success. If he had said no she would have been helpless.

'Don't hesitate to call in a specialist if you have to.'

He was being generous, and it made Jenna want to cry. 'William, you are sweet. I hate to leave you like this. I haven't really thought but I might take her to one of the Swiss clinics, if it seems necessary. Will that be all right?'

He took her hand and pulled her close to the bed, his head dangerously near her swollen belly. If he touched that hard, round mass he would know the truth. She bent swiftly and put her face down to his, kissing him with true tenderness and passion, the product of her lie.

Brittany was still wet and muddy, a place of winter fields and cows after the Australian sun. Jenna shivered and pulled her fur close round her as the little Renault puttered along the arrow-straight road, that alone shrieking that she was in France. Her mother lived in a rural hamlet miles from the nearest shop, in an old farmhouse that William had offered to do up but which Jenna's mother refused to allow him to touch. So she wrestled daily with wood-burning stoves and sloshed water from a wobbly tap over tiles laid a hundred years before and thought herself happy.

Leggy French chickens clucked in the mud around the door, and Jenna picked her way across the yard in her unsuitable shoes. The door opened before she reached it, and there stood her mother.

'Oh Jenna.'

'Oh Ma!' She fell into her mother's arms and sobbed, a little girl again, bringing her troubles to mummy.

Lady Wentworth was a tall woman with large dark eyes and a delicate nose, but in all other respects Jenna resembled her father, from her elongated limbs to her mane of heavy hair. Her mother was a plump woman, comfortably rounded, with hair of a pepper and salt grey that is the hallmark of English county ladies. French *chic* had passed her by, her skirts were tweed and substantial, her jumpers shapeless and her shoes sturdy brogues that Jenna sent her from England. Jenna loved her enormously.

'Let me look at you. Let me see,' urged her mother as soon as the first greeting was past.

Jenna blushed and looked shy. 'I don't like you to. I've spent so long hiding my bump I'm not used to letting people look, and anyway, it's such a telltale about what I've been up to.'

'You are very like your father,' said her mother with a touch of disapproval. 'As upright as they come in public but in private you waste no time at all in getting into a horizontal position.'

'Mother!' gasped Jenna, half shocked and half delighted. 'If you must know it took me ages. I only wish now it had taken longer. or that I'd been a bit more careful,' she added ruefully.

'Not that it never happened at all?'

Jenna shook her head. 'No,' she said simply and went through to the fire.

Jenna's mother lived in a strange mixture of frills and disarray, every chair sported an embroidered antimacassar and also unfinished knitting pushed down the side. Books and papers lay everywhere, the logs for the fire were laid on the ashes from weeks before and a fat dachshund snored on the appalling handmade rug. But there were polished silver ornaments in the window and a priceless Chinese plate upon the wall, as well as frilly patchwork cushions in piles along the sofa. It made Jenna's artistic soul feel nervous.

'This room needs pulling together,' she said critically.

'Leave it alone, darling, I like it. Yes, I know it would

look fantastic when you finished, but then I'd have to be careful and I shouldn't like that.'

'We do live in our house you know,' objected Jenna.

'Do you? But you travel so much. Sit down while I make the tea, and then we can talk. And please do not suggest that I bring up this baby, I have given up motherhood, I was bad at it.'

'So am I. Actually I hadn't thought of that. No, my poor baby is going to be adopted.'

'Who by?'

'How should I know, by whoever comes along, I suppose. It will be a beautiful baby, everyone will want it.'

Her mother looked at her speculatively. 'Do you want to leave William, darling? And keep the baby? Is that it?'

'Not really, no.' Jenna sighed. 'He wouldn't let me, and I know I'm a coward but when it comes to it I can't fight him. There's no point, he always wins. And he'd ruin Dan.'

'That's the father?'

'Yes.' Jenna said it on a rush of tears and her mother wisely abandoned the subject. Her daughter was tired and tense and unhappy, and she did not need an inquisition. As the weeks passed and the peace of the French countryside became absorbed into her spirit, she would feel calmer and more able to talk.

Gradually, as the damp days of winter began to give way to a hint of spring, a pattern began to emerge. William remained in Australia with his nurse and his leg, letting the sunshine restore him and sending Jenna presents, everything from coral bracelets to surfing prints. Tony and Rachel remained in England, in the doubtful care of a gullible old lady and Jenna stayed in retreat in France, numb with the relief of at last admitting her pregnancy.

The baby was moving within her, a mass of flailing limbs pressed against her waiting hand, and sometimes she found herself crying at the loneliness of it all. At night in her empty bed she needed a man, to hold her close and to comfort and say 'I feel it too.' She needed Dan.

If Dan was here she could admit that she was frightened, terrified of the moment when this baby, now so huge and strong, would force itself out into the world. She who feared pain and found her body a mystery even to herself would have to face, alone, an experience that changed women. Everyone who had ever had a baby remembered it with unique clarity, could recite the chronicle of events without mistake despite the point of the exercise, the baby, being almost middle-aged. And they told her she would forget how bad it was, as if that should console her when in order to forget you had first to suffer. Almost sick with fright she bought a French book on childbirth, compiled for those determined to eschew technology.

'I will now do a double somersault from the high trapeze without a safety net,' muttered Jenna and her mother glanced at the book, wrinkling her nose at gory pictures of distended bellies and vulvae. Jenna gazed in sick fascination. One woman, stark naked, was held by her husband from behind, her whole body arched in tension and pain as she forced the baby out. She could not imagine letting anyone see her in such a position. She could not imagine surviving such anguish!

'I think you had better go into hospital to have it,' advised her mother, seeing how unhappy Jenna had become, even her bump seemed to have shrunk as if once again her daughter was denying that she was pregnant at all.

'No! They all say how awful that is. I'd like to have it here. By myself. In the dark,' she added revealingly.

'But darling – you surely weren't this shy when you – er – became –?' Her mother petered out, blushing delicately.

'That was different. That was Dan.' She took herself off for a walk in the lanes, past the muddy, shuttered farms with their caged rabbits and rickety dogs, their hedgerows alive with birds and flowers long sprayed into oblivion in England. No matter that this trap was of her own choosing, she was trapped just the same. It was terrifying. As March slid into April's balmy days she hid in her rural fastness and longed to be free.

*   *   *

High on the wolds of Yorkshire, Hennessey too sniffed the wind and judged it to be spring. The flat season was under way again, but he had few runners since the ground was like porridge and he would not run anything but mature mudlarks until it improved. Owners were restive and the horses also, eager to stretch winterbound limbs over the springing grass, and insensibly, as he sat his horse on the gallops and let the chill fresh breeze ruffle his hair, Hennessey knew hope. They were alive, he and Jenna, they were still in this world. There had been no true ending.

Tony came as usual that Sunday and at once Hennessey knew that something was wrong. The boy was wound up like a spring, he rode without pleasure and the horse, sensing it, skittered unhappily.

'Hop off for a bit Tony,' said Hennessey afer a few minutes. 'I'll saddle my old fella and we'll go for a hack. Make a change.'

Tony agreed without hesitation, but as they trotted up the lane towards an upland path he seemed to relax a little. When they turned into the narrow track and away from the traffic, Hennessey let Tony ride alongside.

'Good week at school?' he asked conversationally.

'Yes. No. Dan – I don't know what to do.'

'Oh. Well, tell me and I'll see if I can help.' He stretched every nerve to appear non-judgmental, even if it was only until he found out what Tony had done.

'You see, it's Rachel.'

'Rachel!' That was a surprise. 'What's she been up to?'

'I don't know. I mean, she won't say. The thing is, for a couple of weekends now she's been going to stay with a friend of hers, a girl from school. At least, that's where she said she was going, but she didn't. And I don't know where she is going. She takes Casey with her, and some clothes, and she come home on Sunday morning, and Aunt Dorothy's useless and Jenna's away – I don't know what to do.'

Hennessey swallowed and rubbed the back of his neck with a cold hand. 'Christ, Tony. Thank God you told me.'

'I didn't know what else to do.'

'Have you rung Jenna?'

'I can't, she isn't on the phone. She's at her mother's in France, it's really primitive, you have to heat a cauldron thing if you want to have a bath. I suppose I could write but I don't think she'd come. I think she's tired of us or something.'

Hennessey snorted and gave his horse a fright. 'I'll give her "tired". She can be so irresponsible sometimes I could kill her.'

'Dan,' said Tony cautiously, 'are you in love with Jenna?'

There was a silence. A blackbird was singing in the hedgerow, manic with joy.

'I try not to be,' said Hennessey grimly, when the air was thick with things unsaid. 'I imagine she has a lot of people feeling like that about her.' Probably including you, he added to himself.

'I wondered if that might be why she won't come home.

238

I've asked her and asked her but she won't.'

The older man sighed, looking weary and unhappy. Then he smiled, making an obvious effort that was painful to watch. 'None of it's worth worrying about. Tell you what, I'll come and talk to Rachel and that Stephen chappie and see what I can sort out. I'll write to Jenna and explain things for you. There's nothing to stop her coming home, I promise you that.'

Tony looked doubtful but there was also relief in his face. 'Can we have a canter?' he asked and Hennessey nodded, smoothly moving his horse up a gear while Tony flailed and flapped his reins.

'Damn it, boy, you can do better than that. Gather him up. Get hold of his head.' They thundered off up the path, sending rabbits and a venturesome fox diving into the undergrowth.

In the evening, Hennessey's little red sports car raced into the Sheppard drive, spraying gravel on to the lawns. George opened the front door before he could knock.

'Good evening, sir, I heard you arrive. Perhaps I might mention that the gardener does get upset if there is gravel on the grass? I understand it breaks the mower.'

'Does it? Graze geese on it instead, much more sensible. I'd like to see Rachel please, George.'

'Tony did mention that you would call. If you'd like to wait in the library?'

Hennessey stepped into the leather cosiness of the room with a strange feeling of apprehension. He knew Jenna was not here yet he expected her to appear at any moment, and when the door opened and it was Rachel he felt a pang of disappointment.

'George said you wanted to see me, Mr Hennessey.'

'Yes. Rachel, where have you been going?'

The colour flamed in her cheek. 'Tony told you!'

'Of course Tony told me. It's the first sensible thing he's

239

ever done, there may be hope for that boy yet. I'm not sure about you, though. I want the truth.'

She said nothing. She ducked her head into her chest and remained silent, well aware that it was her best and only defence.

'Well. If that's the way it has to be then I'd be obliged if you'd go and fetch Casey. I can't possibly let him live with someone who doesn't take proper care of him.'

Her head shot up, she was at once outraged and tearful. 'I do take care of him! I always make sure I take his food!'

'But where do you take it, Rachel? He's a country dog, he needs good long walks in the fresh air every weekend, and if I'd thought for one moment that you'd –'

'He does get walks! I take him on the moors, it's all right, really it is.' She hung her head again, ready now to tell and in a way glad to do so. There had been stark terror in so easily slipping out of the chains of her life. She had known that no-one really cared.

For some weekends past Rachel had informed her aunt that she was going to visit a friend, had collected Casey and an overnight bag and arranged for the chauffeur to drop her at the end of her friend's street. They often did this when they went to visit people because it embarrassed them to be seen in the Rolls. Then she walked to the bus stop and caught a bus to the hills, getting off on a lonely stretch of road and walking to a little shepherd's bothy, long disused, that stood on the skyline. The first time she had only stayed an hour or so before returning home, but on each successive visit she had stayed longer and longer, brought more and more things until at last it was, as she said 'just like a real home'.

'Isn't this a real home?' asked Hennessey thickly.

The child shook her head. 'Not without Jenna.'

Hennessey turned quickly away, hiding the tears. Damn the woman, she caused so much grief. 'Weren't you frightened?' he asked, when he could speak.

'I had Casey,' said Rachel proudly. 'He looked after me.'

Thoughts of rape, kidnap, murder, all entered Hennessey's mind and he sank into a chair, wondering how he could make the dangers seem credible to the girl before him. Then he realised how unfair that was, the child should not be frightened, she should be protected. Contenting himself with a few vague threats he went off to see Stephen.

'Mr Maynard.' He barged past the unsuspecting Stephen and into the sitting room. A glass of wine and half a pork pie were in evidence, surrounded by a sea of newsprint.

'I was having a quiet evening, as you can see,' said Stephen crossly, gathering things up and plumping cushions.

'I don't give a damn what you were doing. I want to get in touch with Jenna.' Stephen paused in his homemaking, and lifted a quizzical eyebrow. 'How thrilling for her. I shall of course be delighted to forward any correspondence, do sit down, Mr Hennessey.'

The tall, thin man remained standing, but Stephen sat, throwing one leg theatrically over the other in half conscious invitation. Hennessey looked at him and laughed. 'You do take the biscuit,' he said thoughtfully, and Stephen flushed.

'Spare me the macho exhibitionism. Mrs Sheppard is staying with her mother, she is not on the telephone and I am not authorised to give you her address. I am sure if she wished any relationship you might have had to continue then she would have given you her address herself, but as it is I very much regret —'

'When is she coming home? Is it soon?'

'May, June, something like that. No set date as yet.'

'Then I have to talk to her. It's about the children, Rachel's been wandering off by herself and someone has to keep an eye on her, on both of them, and that Aunt's no damn use at all. Look, I know she doesn't want to see me but if I could just explain things to her I know she'd come home.' He swallowed and steeled himself to beg. 'I don't suppose you understand, being the way you are. I loved her so much I – I made it too hard for her. I can see now that she had to finish it, but I hated the way she did it. I suppose there isn't a kind way, if she'd been kind I'd never have let her go. All I want is to tell her that I won't be difficult, I won't make it hard now. She has to come home. The children need her.'

Stephen picked at his fingernails. That very morning William had sent him a telex that accused him of incompetence, there had been too many of those of late. William was not amused by loyalty, he preferred the sound of rolling heads. What other victim had ever had such a chance of revenge?

'Strange that men like you always think we wouldn't understand,' he said slowly. 'We can love you know, although of course without the distressing – end result.'

Hennessey caught the intended implication. 'What do you mean? End result?'

'What should I mean? Except that biological urges have such biological purposes.' He relished the dawning shock on the other man's face.

'Do you mean – are you trying to tell me –' Hennessey licked dry lips – 'that Jenna is pregnant?'

'That would seem to be the logical conclusion don't you think?'

There was a long, tense silence. Then Hennessey sank into a chair. 'Oh my God, at last it makes sense. I thought I was going mad.'

'Personally I wanted her to have an abortion,' said Stephen conversationally. 'She almost did, but women are so unpredictable. The baby will be adopted of course. I must say I have to admire her, I never thought she could keep it from Sheppard.'

'But – why should she want to keep it from anybody? All right, if it all came out it would be chaos, but in the end – I mean, she's going to lose her baby. Our baby.'

Stephen laughed, but not unkindly. 'You flatter yourself, Mr Hennessey. Jenna is a wonderful wife for a millionaire, she fits the role perfectly. But she isn't much of a mother. Neither does she see herself as the wife of a bankrupt racehorse trainer, and honestly I can see her point. And of course it has to be considered that Sheppard might not stop at bankrupting you, there's a man in America now who'll spend the rest of his life in a wheelchair. Nothing to do with us you understand, it just – happened. These things do when you cross a man who can buy what he wants.'

Hennessey was hardly attending. Thoughts whirled like a fog in his head, his chest felt so full that he had to force his lungs to keep breathing. 'Give me the address,' he managed finally. 'Don't worry, I won't say it was you. Just give me the address.'

Stephen wrote it out with a flourish and when he gave it to Hennessey their fingers touched. 'Do please feel free to come and see me at any time,' he murmured and his meaning penetrated even Hennessey's preoccupation.

'You'd do better trying Sheppard, he'll stuff anything,' he said bluntly, and left, leaving the door swinging wide. Stephen went to shut it, feeling cold, lonely and ashamed. He was even unsure that he had done the right thing, now he had time to think about it, for Sheppard could curse today and promote tomorrow, he was notoriously unpredictable. It would have been better by far to wait. Tonight more than ever he missed his lover, he wondered if he could ever think of him without the pain of loss. He went alone and unhappy to bed.

Jenna was out walking when the little red car screeched up to the farmhouse, sending a chicken scurrying for safety in a cloud of white feathers. Lady Wainwright came disturbed and distracted to the door.

'Monsieur –' she began, and then looked at the man before her. 'Oh. You are English.'

'Is it so obvious?'

Lady Wainwright looked from the tousled sandy hair to the crumpled tweeds and said simply, 'Yes.'

Dan slipped his hands into his pockets and stood for a moment. 'I'm looking for Jenna,' he said uncomfortably. 'My name's Hennessey. Dan Hennessey.'

'She's not – she isn't – you can't!' Jenna's mother looked confused and the expression so matched Jenna's that Hennessey felt weak.

'I know all about it. I have to see her, is she in?'

Lady Wainwright felt helpless and angry at one and the same time, angry at Jenna for having put her in this position, helpless in the face of this quietly determined man. 'I don't know what I should do,' she murmured, and clutched her hands together. 'No she isn't in now, she's gone for a walk. Oh come in, come in Mr Hennessey, thought I don't want to talk to anyone who's done such a terrible thing to my daughter.'

'She should have told me,' he defended, in the process of being shooed into the sitting room. He sat down too carelessly and almost squashed the dachshund. 'What in God's name is that? Sorry, old chap, you shouldn't sleep under cushions.'

The dachshund curled a lip but was discomfited when

244

Hennessey tweaked his nose.

'He bites,' said Lady Wainwright.

Hennessey peered at the dog. 'Only Frenchmen, perhaps. Look Mrs – I'm sorry, I don't know your name –'

'Wainwright. Lady Wainwright.'

'Good heavens. Look, do you know what made Jenna behave like this? I tell you she had no right, none at all, and you at least should have made her see that.'

'I? What could I do?' She felt threatened, as she so often did with men.

'You could have made her tell me, of course. We both made this baby, we both have a right to say what shall happen to it!' Suddenly, and without realising that he was in the least upset, he was shaking with pent-up fury. He stood up, determined to get a grip on himself. He must not shout at Jenna, he simply must not.

The window was partially obscured by geraniums in pots, but through the misty panes he could see the yard. Jenna stood there, staring transfixed at his car. She wore a dark blue dress that blew around her in the wind, her pregnant belly clearly outlined.

'Jenna!'

She looked up, saw him, and started to run. He was out of the house and after her before she had gone ten paces, weighed down as she was by the baby within, but she kept on running until he caught her. Her face was deadwhite, her lips almost blue and when he clutched her wrists she hung from them, gasping.

'Let me go! Leave me alone!'

'And let you do what you like with my baby? You bitch, you thrice-damned bitch, how could you do this?' Even as he spoke he was holding her, half dragging half carrying her back to the house.

'It isn't yours, it's mine. I can do what I like. You got what you wanted and I hate you, go away, go away!'

'Never. And stop screaming, you'll make yourself ill.'

'Why should you care?' Tears and hair were almost blinding her.

'I didn't, but I care about the baby. Get in there and shut up. If you go on I might strangle you.' He thrust her at the sofa and stood over her, trembling.

The dachshund slunk away under a table and Lady Wainwright looked from this white and furious man to her sobbing daughter and felt like doing the same.

'Will you please both calm down,' she said tightly. 'I will go and make some tea. Please, Mr Hennessey, Jenna has been under a very great strain.'

'No I haven't. I don't need him,' gasped Jenna, and with a strangled cry Hennessey rushed to the window. He stood and breathed the thick air, fighting for control. When he turned he was calmer, but his eyes glittered strangely.

'Let me look at you,' he said softly.

Jenna turned a shoulder to him. He moved over to the sofa and knelt before her, taking long strands of hair in his fingers and letting them fall. Then his hand strayed to her face but she would not look at him, although she almost cried out when he suddenly cupped her breast.

'Don't touch me' she whispered.

'You are the mother of my child. I can touch if I like.' His hands went to her belly, strong and warm, and when she tried to stop him he pushed her back on to the sofa. She lay there, crying, as he discovered the extent of her burden, feeling the thrusting kicks pressing against his palm. He felt enormous desire and great tenderness, yet when he looked into Jenna's ravaged face he saw only heat.

'It has nothing to do with you,' she said. 'I knew you'd be upset and that's why I didn't tell you. I'm going to have it adopted.'

Hennessey swallowed. 'It's there, inside you. Don't you care for it at all?'

She almost laughed. Not care for it, she who cared so much she had suffered everything to let it live, who would suffer still more to allow it to be born.

But she said only, 'I can't let myself care. You have Lilian. I have William. Nothing's changed. People long to adopt babies, someone will want him.'

'Him?'

'Yes. I think of it as him.'

Lady Wainwright came back into the room, and when she saw her daughter lying with a man's hand on her pregnant belly her own cheeks flamed.

'Jenna please!' she begged, and in a fluster Jenna sat up, dragging at her skirt and pushing her hair from her face. Hennessey moved to sit beside her, and he it was who gathered her hair into his hand and drew it into a long, straight fall down her back.

'You're so beautiful,' he said as if they were still alone.

'Not like this I'm not. I feel a wreck. So fat.' Jenna took a cup of tea from her mother. It was scalding hot, but she sipped just the same.

'Not fat at all. Like a swollen bud, and not so swollen at that. Is it due next month?'

'Yes. How did you know?'

'I counted. Jenna, Jenna – I never wanted this to happen to you. I'm so sorry.'

Jenna put down her cup and said with an assumption of lightness 'I imagine we're both sorry. What a pity we weren't careful. But there's no magic solution so you had better go back to England and forget you ever knew.'

Again, the exclusion. He felt annoyed all over again. 'I'm not going back till it's born. The horses can go hang for a while, I am staying.'

'You're not!'

247

Hennessey picked up his own tea and did not reply. And because neither woman had the strength to oppose him, when they ate their evening meal he was included and when they rose to go to bed he was shown a room across the landing from Jenna's.

In the dark of the night, when the owls were calling in the woods and the moon lit the steps of deer as they trod softly across the vegetables, Jenna went to him. She opened the rough plank door by its old-fashioned latch and crept to the side of his bed, the plain lawn of her nightdress falling like a shroud around her. 'Dan,' she whispered. 'Dan, are you awake?'

In answer he reached out and gathered her to him, pulling her distended body close. They lay for a long time in the quiet and the dark, listening to the owls, and then his need overtook him. At first she was frightened, she was too big, he would hurt her, but he held her on her side and juggled her limbs until he could slide gently between her legs. She moaned and writhed a little, letting him know that it pleased her, and although she did not reach orgasm, when he left her, satisfied himself, she felt warm and almost safe.

'What do you think it will feel like?' she whispered, knowing he was almost asleep.

'Having it you mean?' As always he understood. 'I don't know. I've seen horses. It's painful yes, sometimes very painful, but then they don't understand. Better for people I should think.'

'I shouldn't mind if it could be like this. Private. I don't want to have everyone watching me.'

'You've got to be safe, Jen. You know that. For the baby.'

She sighed. 'Yes. I never thought this far, you see. No abortion, I decided that, but I didn't think of how it was actually going to get out. And when I see how big it is now

– I feel so afraid.'

What did she want him to say? Don't worry, I'm here? When she had made it very clear that she did not want him. In fact what was she doing here, in his bed, except taking her comfort as she always took it, without any thought for others?

'For once in your life you will have to be brave,' he said snappishly, but gave the lie to his words by scooping her into his arms. Jenna breathed the warm sweat in the hollow of his throat and settled herself to sleep.

In the morning Lady Wainwright went to wake Jenna and on finding her bed empty rushed to open Hennessey's door. There they were, the two of them, Hennessey naked and Jenna almost so, her belly and one breast escaped from her nightgown. Her mother's mouth formed a round 'oh' of astonishment and Hennessey, who was awake, sat up and flicked the cover over them both.

'Don't ask me what to make of her,' he said with a shrug. 'Because I just don't know.'

He stayed four days and in that time the life of the house began to revolve around him. It was not that he was demanding, far from it, he simply asked what their purpose was for the day and waited until they thought of one. Then he helped them fulfil it. Somehow the hospital visit that Jenna had been postponing suddenly took place, as did the shopping for baby clothes in the nearby town. Also at his prompting she wrote for school prospectuses for Tony and Rachel, and composed a letter of admonishment to Aunt Dorothy. Hennessey sighed and agreed it would have to do. Jenna's present plight pushed other troubles well out of mind.

He was very anxious about what she would do when the baby started. There was no telephone, it was at least an hour's drive to the town on very slow roads and the hospital was everything Jenna loathed, sterile, impersonal, and keen on knives.

'I will not be cut,' said Jenna, crossing her legs unhappily. 'William would know.'

'If you ask me he's going to have to know,' said Hennessey. 'It's all very well trying to ward off disaster Jen, but sometimes we have to face the music.'

'I've done all right so far,' she objected. 'Anyway, it's as much for you as for me, can you imagine what this would do to Lilian? Me, having your baby?'

He paled visibly and she knew she had struck home. It would send his wife completely round the bend. They both knew he could not really stay much longer, his horses needed him, for good as his head lad was he could in no way replace Hennessey. Also the ground was drying and there were races to run, but even if he knew he had to go, just for the present he stayed.

On the fourth night Jenna could not rest. She had cramp and continually wanted to pass water, feeling the urge the moment she got back from the bathroom. She suspected that Hennessey would leave in the morning, and the thought filled her with a feeling that was close to grief. Yet her physical discomfort almost matched her mental stress and she tossed and turned beside the man who was the cause of it all and cursed him for being able to sleep. Suddenly the bed was very wet. 'Dan,' she said unhappily, 'Dan. I think I've wet the bed.'

He stirred into wakefulness and put a hand on the sheet. 'My God, this is the end,' he muttered. 'You spend all night going to the toilet and then this happens. Change it in the morning, your bed's made up isn't it?'

She agreed that it was and they trailed wearily across the landing to her too narrow bed. No sooner had they settled than Jenna sat up again.

'Dan,' she ventured, 'Dan, I'm leaking.'

He too sat up and put on the light. 'What do you mean, leaking?'

'Like – leaking. Look, I'm wet again.'

'Christ! Where the hell is that baby book?' He leaped out of bed and began to rummage for the book. When it was not forthcoming Jenna started to look too but it took some time to find rammed as it was down the side of an armchair in the sitting room.

'Now we've got it I can't understand it,' complained Hennessey. 'It's all in French.'

'I know what it says,' said Jenna. 'Oh. That's what I thought.'

'You've started, haven't you? Your water's have broken. It's coming early.'

'Yes.'

They looked at each other apprehensively. 'We'd better go to the hospital,' said Hennessey.

'No! No, it's all right. The book says it can take hours and hours. You've got to wait till the contractions are coming really quickly, minutes. I'm not having any.'

'Are you sure?' He studied the incomprehensible book, but became sidetracked by the picture of the woman giving birth, just as Jenna had been. 'God Almighty,' he muttered and without thinking put a protective arm around her.

They made a cup of tea and sat on the sofa drinking it and feeling nervous. Jenna put hers down half-finished and began to wander round the room.

'Mother could always go for Doctor Maçon,' she said thoughtfully.

'You're going to the hospital. Any contractions yet?'

'No – no. I only thought if there was any problem, the car wouldn't start or something. There's always Doctor Maçon.'

251

'I think we should go now,' said Hennessey. 'After all, this baby is about four weeks early.'

'It might not be. I never did have any firm dates. I think it's OK.'

'Suppose it isn't? I'm going to wake your mother.' He went up the stairs and the moment he was out of the room Jenna leaned hard against the wall and panted. That was the third bad one, she had felt sure he must notice. When it had passed she slipped out of the door to Hennessey's car, withdrew the keys from the ignition and came back into the house. She was smoothing the earth on a geranium when her mother came downstairs.

'Darling, you must get dressed and go at once to the hospital. I know you don't want to, but I assure you it is best. Off you go.'

'It isn't time' protested Jenna, but her mother would have none of her stalling. She was despatched to dress, and was obliged to puff her way ignominiously through a contraction halfway up the stairs, with Hennessey above and her mother below, both fretting. Then she was pushed protesting into the bedroom.

'You've got to get dressed,' said Hennessey, unfastening her nightgown.

'I shall do much better at home,' insisted Jenna and found that she was becoming tearful. She sank on to the edge of the bed, feeling unable to cope.

Hennessey gathered her into his arms, as always weak before Jenna's unhappiness, and he felt her belly go rigid as a contraction began. She sank back on the bed, her fingers clutching at his arm.

'Don't fight it,' he urged. 'For once let your body take over. Look, I can see you're fighting it.'

'It hurts!' gasped Jenna. 'God, how it hurts!'

'Stay there,' he urged as the contraction subsided and he rushed down to her mother. 'Go for the doctor,' he advised. 'Take my car. There's no time for the hospital and anyway I think she'll be better here. Be quick.'

Back up the stairs to where Jenna was again wrestling with her pain. 'You've won, you're staying,' he told her tersely, and was rewarded with the ghost of a smile. Then her mother was there, worried. 'I can't find the car keys.' 'They're in the geranium pots,' confessed Jenna and her mother looked blank.

'Deceitful cow,' retorted Hennessey. 'Go on then, look in the geraniums. She's buried them.'

Looking bewildered, Jenna's mother went.

Once the little red car had driven with unaccustomed sloth out of the yard, Jenna and Hennessey were alone but for their book. He pored over it, trying to decide what it said. 'I think you're supposed to walk around,' he advised, and Jenna glanced at it and agreed. So she wandered about between contractions, clutching the bed, a chair or Hennessey the moment one began. They were becoming worse and as each one progressed she would find the breath for a short, anguished scream.

'Dear God, how I wish I could have this for you,' whispered Hennessey, torn between his urge to comfort and Jenna's need for firmness. Left to herself she became frantic, when he left the room for a flannel to bathe her face she followed him saying, 'Dan, don't leave me. It hurts.'

And it did, however much she steeled herself against the rising tide that swept upon her, a vicious tide, with teeth, which each time retreated a little less far. It was worse even than she had imagined, for she had not thought that her body could turn against her so. She, the part that was truly her, cowered in the midst of this labouring body and did not help herself. Instinctively Hennessey comforted her, bringing a small and probably lethal electric fire, lighting only a table lamp to bathe the room in a soft yellow glow. Then he held her and stroked her, coaxing her to join her body in its struggle.

'Let it happen. There's nothing you can do yet, just relax and go with it.'

She lay on her side on the bed, holding his hand. When he moved to reach the book she clutched at him. 'It's all right, I'm not going. I won't leave you. I want to see what it says about delivering the baby.'

He peered at the text, reflecting that they never taught you anything useful at school. What was the French for 'umbilical cord' then? Another pain and Jenna was twisting her nails in the flesh of his arm, the muscles of her neck like ropes. When it was over she lay against him, panting. 'I don't want the doctor,' she muttered. 'You stay with me.'

'The doctor isn't here,' he soothed, wishing that he would come. Jenna's mother was such a vague, negative woman, did she not realise the urgency?

'When he does come he'll give you something to take away the pain,' he encouraged but she buried her face against his arm and said, 'I don't want him.' At that moment he loved her more than he had ever done, her face blotched and sweaty, the soaking nightgown in a knot around her waist. But the pains were coming faster now, they came in waves, one upon the other and Jenna was beside herself.

'Make it stop,' she gasped but he held her as she writhed, saying, 'Feel it, Jenna, think about it. You are opening to let the baby out, let it come.'

She looked into his face, whimpered, and her body convulsed as she began to push. Her arms were round his neck, she clutched at him, her feet scrabbling for a hold on the bed. Hennessey knew the baby must be imminent, he had seen enough animals to know that this was the time. There was the book, open at the photograph of the grimacing woman, who now looked like Jenna. The room seemed hot, sweat beaded the hair of his naked chest, and Jenna's nightgown was getting in the way. He guided her arms out of it, in passing kissing her hand. When the pain came again and he moved to hold her their flesh was bonded with a mutual sweat.

The urge to strain was now so strong that there was no longer any division between Jenna and her labouring body. She was one with it, an animal, in her small dark place that was her own and of her own accord she scrabbled off the bed. At last, with her feet on the floor, she could push. Hennessey held her, whispering endearments, worried to death that the baby would shoot headfirst on to the floor, but that was unimportant, if only it would come out! Jenna heaved, she strained, her breath caught in her nose in a high whine of effort and was released in an enormous cry. She sank back on to the bed as Hennessey reached down and guided his son into the world.

The baby was slate grey and squashed looking. For a moment he thought it was dead, but even as he watched, it stirred, snuffled and began to breathe. He looked at Jenna who lay quite spent on the bed. 'It's a boy.'

'I know it's a boy. Let me.' She held out her arms and took the tiny, slimy burden, still joined to her by its cord. Even to their untutored eyes the baby looked very small.

'We must keep it warm,' said Hennessey distractedly, and went in search of blankets.

Jenna lay and waited for him, her work now over, and felt herself float on a sea of peaceful colours, pinks and greys and deep, throbbing purple. The baby was snuffling again and she pushed herself up a little, bringing him close to her breast, so that when Hennessey returned he found the baby suckling and Jenna almost asleep, linked by the cord that snaked back into her body. He wrapped them

255

carefully in blankets and then, a true Englishman, went to make some tea.

Some babies are born angry into the world, and Jenna's was one of them. What it was that irked him no-one knew, but he had all the vocal displeasure of a Labour politician. No sooner had he caught his breath from being born than tiny as he was he began to complain.

The doctor who had been delayed on another call, was anxious to take both Jenna and the baby into hospital. He was indeed premature and weighed barely five pounds, but he was well, and noisy and Jenna would not go. She did not want to do anything at all but stay in the remote little farmhouse and tend her baby. Outside there was the real world to face and the longer the confrontation was postponed the happier she would be.

But there was still Hennessey, and he would not be put off.

'We'll call him Marcus,' Jenna said contentedly, but his face was grim.

'Why should we call him anything at all?'

'People do keep the baby's proper name sometimes. I can call him what I like.' The angry wails were starting again and she reached out to pick him from his cradle.

'Jenna – suppose we bring the whole thing out into the open? Tell your husband, but not Lilian, I don't think she could take it. We might work something out.'

She glowered, furious with him for making her think about such things. 'What did you have in mind, setting me up in some little lovenest for you to pop in and visit whenever dear Lilian can spare you? I keep telling you, I don't think William's going to like you very much when he learns what you've been doing. And there's Tony and Rachel to consider because nobody else does. Face it,

Dan, you don't want to be saddled with me and a baby, not if it means you lose your horses, and it would.'

He sighed and paced the room, his thoughts going round and round searching for a way out. Not for a moment did he believe Sheppard would totally ruin him, but it would certainly mean the end of any classic hopes. That had been the dream for so many years past that he found it hard to imagine that there would be any point in life if the chance were gone. It was bad enough having Lilian as a brake on his ambitions, but if he were obliged to focus his sights on platers and budget price handicappers for ever he did not know how he would cope.

He turned to face the woman who had brought him to this pass. 'If it wasn't for Lilian, if she wasn't there – would you come? Risk it?'

She shrugged. 'I don't know. As it is the question doesn't arise. Honestly Dan, the only answer is to have him – you know.'

'Say it.'

'No.' She would not look at him. Her head was bent over the baby, as it sucked and gurgled at her breast, and the fine line of her nose and cheek moved him utterly.

'If you're going to do it you'd better make it quick. Shall I ask someone to come and take him? Today?'

Her face turned towards him, the eyes wide and dark with shock. 'You couldn't! I won't let you!'

'Face it, Jenna, you either admit it all, or give him up. Decide.'

'I will – later. Not now.'

He was becoming frantic in the face of her indecision. 'Do you think you can go home with a baby under your arm and say look William, guess what I found? Even if you got away with it, I'd never let you take my baby into that house.'

'So it's your baby now, is it? You'd rather I gave him to

257

strangers than let William have him.'

Hennessey considered. 'Yes, I would actually.' He thought of the big, empty rooms and the deadly silence that pervaded the huge house. Brought in like a lost dog his baby would never know secure, untroubled love. He wanted his son to have the country childhood that he himself had enjoyed, full of horses and hot summer days, snow as crisp as icing in the winter and no choice but to trudge through to school. Too much ease was bad for anyone.

'Jenna,' he said slowly, 'how about – if I take him?'

There was a tense, building silence. When Jenna spoke she did not recognise her own voice. 'You want to take my baby and give him to your wife.'

'Not – exactly. I want to care for him. If I took him you could see him all the time. Lilian wouldn't mind, I'd make sure of that, and she'd never know where he came from. She'd be so much better if she had a baby, and he'd be with me – please Jenna.' Now that it was said he was very much afraid. The thought had been with him since before the child was born, half-formed, half considered and only now admitted. He had wanted Jenna from the moment he saw her, but the baby had been the object of his desire from the time that he first felt it move inside her belly. All right, he was asking a lot, but so was she in expecting him to watch her dispose of his child and take no part in it.

'I wish your wife was dead,' whispered Jenna, and there was venom in her words.

'You wouldn't come to me even if she was.'

'At least I wouldn't be giving my baby to her. She's a lunatic.'

Hennessey could feel his temper going and he struggled to keep calm. 'No she isn't. Everyone thinks she'd be quite normal if she had a baby and we have a baby that's an embarrassment to everyone. You can't deny him a home

258

'simply because you want to deny her a baby.'

'She can have any baby she wants as long as it isn't mine!' Jenna clutched at her child, who moved his tiny head from her nipple and bawled. She bent over him, breathing his downy hair and making it wet with her tears.

'Have you got any better ideas?' There was a silence but for the baby's mutterings. 'So that's agreed,' said Hennessey.

Jenna shook with sobs, her hair hiding both her own face and the baby. He reached an arm to her but she struck at him. 'Don't touch me! I hate you, you bring me nothing but misery and pain. If you must steal my baby then you must but I don't have to look at you, and I don't have to let you touch me! Go away!' Hennessey went.

Downstairs Jenna's mother took one look at his face and poured a glass of plum brandy. 'I think she's a little overwrought,' she apologised.

Hennessey sipped at his drink and tried to gather the threads that made up the fabric of his thoughts. 'God, how I wish things were different,' he said bleakly.

Lady Wainwright took her dog on to her knee and played with his ears, keeping her eyes averted from this man who seemed so large in her little, messy house. 'I do hope you will be kind to Jenna now,' she murmured. 'It would be best if you left her alone. William is a very good husband to her, I always knew he would be. She needs looking after, you see.'

Hennessey considered if that was true. Yes, sometimes she did, but sometimes everyone needs someone to take care of them. It did not mean that they should ever surrender control of their own life. But all he said was, 'He doesn't take care of her. He buys her things, that's all.'

'Jenna needs things, she loves her clothes and jewels.'

'She likes them but she doesn't need them,' broke in

Hennessey. 'At least, she shouldn't need them. Lady Wainwright, you should come out of your rural retreat and take a good look at your daughter. She's grown up. You don't know her at all.' He could have added I am the only person in the world that knows her, so I am the only one that loves her. No-one else can because they don't see her as she is. And always she sends me away.

Downing the rest of the brandy in one fiery gulp he got to his feet. 'I'll have to see to the papers. I don't even know how to register this baby, do you?'

Lady Wainwright sighed unhappily. 'You go to the Mairie in town. But you mustn't use Jenna's real name, use Wainwright please.'

'The baby will be called Hennessey. I'll own up to him if no-one else. Look, I want to sort out a passport and things, I may not be back tonight, don't expect me.'

He took no notice of the drive into town. His movements were automatic and his thoughts sombre. Why had he allowed this to happen? The mess was of his own making and the solution must be his also. Foolish Jenna, to think she could lie there and hope that it would all come right. Still, that was what beautiful women learned to do, let people arrange the world around them only to wonder why it did not make them happy. If only – there were so many if onlys. The fact remained that whatever else Jenna might do she would not give his baby away. He would not let her. That puny, screaming morsel had changed his life, because whatever happened now, whatever else might pass away, his son was his son for ever. Jenna might think she could escape everything unpleasant in her life, but he knew better. Besides, he was sure that in the end he could work it out.

Four muddy French cows meandered across the road and he screeched to an impatient halt. The cows were followed by a Frenchman, toothless and bent, who turned blank eyes to Hennessey and nodded. Hennessey nodded back, whereupon the man waved his stick. Hennessey lifted his hand in reply and the man bowed, at which point Hennessey let in the clutch and roared rudely past. So much for Anglo-French relations.

They took a further turn for the worse at the Mairie. Hennessey's French was bad, the clerk's English non-existent. No doubt illegitimate babies were born in France from time to time but if so the clerk had never heard of it, and refused to believe that such a thing had now happened. Hennessey struggled with his explanations, both he and the clerk convinced that the other was being obstructive. The clerk became Gallic and voluble, Hennessey English and loud. It seemed that they would be there forever, locked in misunderstanding until they strangled each other, and even the couple who had come in after Hennessey backed away a little, as if the entertainment might turn sour. Then Hennessey drew breath and thought for a moment. He extended a hand to the clerk's notepad. The man thrust it across like a challenge and stood scornful as Hennessey wrote *mere* – Jenna Wainwright. *Pere* – Daniel Hennessey. *Bebe* – Marcus Hennessey. The pad was returned and on it lay a hundred franc note. With a snort of disgust the clerk pocketed the money and neatly wrote out the certificate.

Dan staggered out into the road too exhausted to think. He had a certificate of some sort, though what it actually said he could not tell. What to do next? He looked round for somewhere to have a drink while he thought about it.

The Mairie stood to the side of a large central square, dotted with plane trees bright with young leaf. On the far side there was a scruffy French café with a couple of tin tables and a Ricard poster. Hennessey went across and ordered coffee and a cognac, feeling a sense of budding elation. It was legally his baby now, it had his name and the certificate was in his possession. The next step was to have the child entered on his father's passport, and for that he needed the British authorities. Would they let him do it? He wasn't sure. It might take weeks, they might wish to make enquiries, anything. He sat for some time, his coffee long since drunk, the cognac only a remembered glow. The waiter came out of the dark café and whisked away the empty cup and glass. Hennessey braced himself for another fruitless struggle with the natives. '*Ou est le British Embassy, s'il vous plaît*?'

'I beg your pardon, *monsieur*?' The waiter, who might have been the brother of the clerk at the Mairie, looked sardonic. Hennessey felt a fool.

'Er – I wondered if you could tell me where I could make a passport enquiry. I imagine it's the British Embassy, but –'

'The British Consulate. Rue du Faubourg St Honore, Paris. I work in England for some time, you understand. Chiswick. You know Chiswick?'

'No, no, not Chiswick. Yorkshire.'

'You wish to phone the consulate?'

Hennessey thought. Did he wish to phone or would it be better to arrive on the doorstep? Ought he to try and do this legally at all, it might be best to pick up the child, make for the nearest port and smuggle it on to the ferry. Pity it was such a noisy brat. Anyway, he was doing nothing illegal, he was simply taking his own child home.

The waiter waited impassively. 'How do I get to Paris?' asked Hennessey.

Hennessey enjoyed driving in Paris, it was his sort of town. It was like an enormous game, the winners racing away at traffic lights, the losers huddled against the kerb with crumpled wings. But as in all cities it was impossible to park, and after an hour's disgruntled search, made longer because he didn't know the French for 'car park,' he drew in under a disabled sticker, telling himself that if he wasn't disabled now he would be if he stayed in the country much longer.

The British Consulate in Paris is a large, modern office block, and the passport section is on the fourth floor. Hennessey took the lift and approached the girl at the reception desk.

'Can I help you?' She was English. Thank heavens for small mercies.

'Er – I hope so. I want to put my son on my passport. He was born prematurely you see, and we want to take him back to England as soon as possible.' He smiled in what he hoped was a frank and open way.

'You have registered the birth?'

'Oh yes.' He flourished the unintelligible certificate.

'I will contact Mr Cunningham.'

They chatted while they waited for Mr Cunningham to appear.

'Is the little boy well?'

'Very well. I'd have brought him in, but he's very noisy.' Pray that they didn't actually have to see the child. He'd have to borrow one'

'Really? You don't expect that of premature babies do you?'

'He's been very unexpected all along really.'

A dark haired diffident young man came in. 'Mr Cunningham,' said Hennessey and stood up, radiating confident ease. It didn't do to look as if you needed a favour. Again he explained the position, and at once Mr Cunningham assured him that there was no problem at all. These things sometimes happened – nature was so unpredictable – all that was required was the father's passport, his own birth certificate and the child's certificate of registration. It would take perhaps half an hour.

'There is – one slight complication,' said Hennessey.

'Yes?' Both Cunningham and the girl cocked helpful ears.

'The child's mother – and myself. We aren't married.' Consternation registered on the faces before him and he rushed on. 'She's very independent you see, and has always felt that she didn't want to submerge her identity in marriage. Which is all very well until you have babies when you least expect them –' he looked apologetic and resigned at one and the same time.

'Oh dear,' said Mr Cunningham and scratched his head.

'It can't be so difficult – can it?' asked the girl, who read *Cosmopolitan* and would have been a feminist herself if her boyfriend wasn't so against it.

'If we could put the child on the mother's passport –'

'We haven't got her birth certificate.' It was only luck that his own was kept in the same envelope as his passport, simply because it was convenient.

All at once he began to enjoy his role as soulmate to a committed feminist. Given another minute and he would be telling them all about their unconventional lifestyle in a bijou flat in York, with a Burmese cat and Jenna a member of CND. He could see it all. They had probably come to France to attend a peace rally, and what with the excitement of all that chanting and then the midnight vigil, the next thing they knew she was in labour.

'I think the mother had better complete a guardianship form,' said Cunningham suddenly.

'Oh?'

'It simply says that she agrees for the child to be in your guardianship, on your passport. Will that be all right?'

'Of course,' said Hennessey, looking as honest as they come'

264

Twenty minutes later he sat at a table in a backstreet café, borrowed a pen from the waiter and wrote *Jenna Wainwright* in spidery writing on the form. A quick cup of coffee and he was back at the consulate, his liberated girlfriend consigned to a cultural tour of Notre Dame to ensure that the baby absorbed the atmosphere at the earliest possible age.

'Have a pleasant trip home,' said Mr Cunningham, giving him a firm handshake.

'Thanks for all your help.' Hennessey gathered up the papers and ran down the stairs into the street.

He was elated and appalled at one and the same time. It shouldn't be that easy! He could be abducting some baby that had nothing to do with him at all. Still, he supposed that unattached infants weren't lightly come by, even in France.

It was a long drive back and he was drained of all energy by the time he drew up at the farm. It was evening and the shutters were closed, but at the sound of the car the door opened.

'I thought it must be you,' said Lady Wainwright.

'Yes. Is she – are they all right?'

'Perfectly well, thank you. But I've been thinking – I'm not at all sure that this is a good idea.' She stood in the doorway and clasped rough hands, stained from scraping carrots.

Hennessey sighed. 'Do you think I could come in before we start talking about this? I am rather tired.'

'I suppose you might be. Oh yes, come in, I didn't mean to keep you standing there. But Jenna seems so settled with the child, and she hasn't once mentioned you taking him –' she led the way into the haphazard sitting room and stood in unhappy bewilderment.

'Are you saying she's changed her mind?'

'Not exactly. She hasn't said anything.'

Hennessey allowed himself a snort that was almost disgust. Jenna and her mother were two of a kind, ostriches both of them. Did they think he wanted to take the child away? Well yes, he did, because it was his son and he was the only person who could give him any sort of life. And Jenna had known from the beginning that she must lose him. He had a sudden vision of Jenna's dark head bent over the baby's downy one, and his throat closed. If only – but he had thought of everything and nothing else would do. He coughed and said huskily, 'I'm sorry. I know it hurts but I'm doing what's best for the baby. She must see that. And if she'd ever once said that she and I –' he couldn't go and turned aside, shaking his head in apology.

'She and William are very well matched,' said Lady Wainwright on a plaintive sigh.

For Hennessey it was too much. Well matched indeed! If she was really like that arrogant, overfed brute of a man then the last thing she deserved was this baby. He turned and made for the stairs, the weariness falling away as the anger surged. He flung open the door of Jenna's room – and stopped. She was asleep, her face turned towards the cradle, one arm outstretched as if to comfort. The baby slept also, making snuffling sounds like a puppy. Two people that he loved more than anyone in the world.

Behind him, lady Wainwright twittered, 'Don't wake her. She needs her sleep,' and Hennessey replied 'No. I won't wake her.' He knew that if ever he was to take this baby it had to be now. He could not bear it if she asked him not to. He went softly to the cradle and gathered the baby into his arms. It mewed and waved tiny fists, and Jenna stirred a little. Hennessey almost wished she would wake up. But instead she cuddled back into the pillow, the long pale fingers of her outstretched hand curling and then relaxing once again. Hennessey pushed past the woman in the doorway and went quickly downstairs.

'How will you manage? Feeding, his nappies, everything –'

'I bought some things in Paris. And there's all that you have here, she won't want to look at it. I'll get by somehow.'

'What will I say to her, when she wakes up?'

'I don't know. Tell her – oh, for God's sake, she's your daughter and you say you know what she wants! Say whatever it takes to make her feel better.' He felt choked with irritation at this woman and her helpless inadequacy. Was it surprising that her daughter was as she was? He knew he had to get away, now, before Jenna woke, and with the woman like a bat fluttering around him he went to and from the car. When all was packed and the baby settled in a cocoon of blankets on the back seat he turned to Lady Wainwright.

'Tell her – I'll do my best for him.'

'If only I could be sure it was right to let you take him –'

'I'd have taken him whether you let me or not. Goodbye.' He slid behind the wheel and started the engine. Still no outraged cry from the house. As he drove into the lane he noticed that for the first time in his life his hands were shaking.

And when Jenna woke up, she found that her baby was gone.

Chapter Eleven

The racetrack curving away into the distance was like a length of green ribbon in a young girl's hair. Everything seemed fresh and new, even the tired and musty suits that the trainers wore. Hennessey hated the smell of his, recently dry-cleaned when Lilian in an excess of zeal had taken his wardrobe in hand.

Sharps was running this afternoon, in a sprint, one of those races that is so soon over it seems hardly worth the anxiety that precedes it. He was a miracle that little horse, able to blast out of the stalls like a rocket yet with the guts to hold his own in the mêlée that followed. And today the Sheppards were coming to watch.

Unusually for him, Hennessey had two stiff drinks before they came. He mooched around talking to people, his eyes straying always to the entrance. It was nearly three months since he had seen her. It seemed like forever. Such a strange time too, tinged with unreality and reeking of impermanence. But there was no reason why it should not last, or at least none that he could think of. True, the lads were taken aback when he turned up with the baby but he had silenced them. He told them it was a private adoption arranged by a mutual friend, and they seemed to accept it. A few days later he overheard two lads having a chat and a sly smoke in the straw barn.

'Bit odd, this baby the guvnor's found,' said one. 'Didn't think they'd let women like her have them, I mean, she isn't right whatever he says.'

'Bloody peculiar if you ask me,' said the other, taking a long drag on his forbidden cigarette. 'I reckon it's his. Got some girl in the club and took the kid off her hands. Can't say as I blame him, his missus gives me the willies.'

'Didn't used to be like that, though. You weren't here then, but when he first married her, she was pretty. Quiet like, and shy, but pretty. God knows what went wrong. He'll be hoping this kid'll make some difference I expect.'

Hennessey crept quietly away. They were right, and to deny it was a waste of breath. The most he could hope for was that they pretended to believe him, and they were too polite to do otherwise. People outside might also doubt the story, but at least he didn't know about it. The stable was a community turned in upon itself and conditioned to secrecy and subterfuge. The village did not expect to understand the comings and goings of the people there, and the arrival of a wailing infant one rather chilly evening caused little enough interest. Adopted, borrowed, fostered, did it matter if it made that strange Mrs Hennessey happy? Something had to, that was certain. Dan's father summed it up when he looked thoughtfully at his son and said, 'I don't know how you managed it, lad, but it's a blessing that you did. It'll be the saving of Lilian.'

Now, it seemed that he might be right. It had been a nightmare journey, with the baby screaming for the breast he could not have, turning his face away from Hennessey's ineptly presented bottle. When at last they reached home Dan was sick with weariness and when Lilian took charge of the sobbing bundle that plagued him he felt only relief. His wife's face glowed as she held the child, and when at last he began to suck the alien rubber teat, at first cautiously and then gulping at the food, she smiled in the old, peaceful way and said, 'He's beautiful. Thank you, thank you, Dan.' So, both Lilian and the baby were happy. Why then did he feel that it could not last? That he did not wish it to last?

The house was a cage for him nowadays, he paced the rooms as if seeking escape. Lilian had her baby, it was what she had always wanted, but somehow it did not set him free. Was that what he had hoped to buy with this, his most precious gift? An end, at last, to obligation? If so he had been a fool, he was more shackled than ever by his son's need of him. Lilian wasn't right, whatever he said.

He came back to himself and the milling crowd of people, with no-one that he wished to see amongst them. Would Jenna never come? When, finally, she arrived he had his back to the door but he sensed the ripple of interest that moved like a breeze through the crowd. He forced himself not to turn round, he would not look at Jenna on the arm of that man.

'Well there you are, Dan! We've got a box, are you coming up?'

'Good afternoon, Mr Sheppard. Later perhaps, I have to saddle the colt.'

'Not yet, surely. Jenna, here's Dan Hennessey, say hello.'

She said nothing. Thin again, painfully thin, and her eyes like huge pools in her face. She wore deep, glowing pink and a long pink scarf held her hair in place.

'Hello,' said Hennessey. 'If I may say so you look good enough to eat.' Sheppard laughed but Jenna did not.

'I'm afraid you'll have to put up with a rather chilly Jenna today Dan,' he said cheerfully. 'She's got the glooms.'

'Hardly that, darling,' she said thinly. 'I am simply not too keen on spending the afternoon waiting for a two-minute dash when the result is a foregone conclusion.'

'Don't you like to see your horse win?' asked Hennessey.

'I couldn't care less,' she said with utter truth, and turned on her heel. The two men stood looking after her, William with a slight dent in his good humour, Hennessey at last feeling drunk.

'Jenna's not herself today,' apologised Sheppard, which was in itself surprising. 'Her mother's illness upset her and I was away too long in Australia. My leg, you know. I think some home life will do us both good, but she does seem so unsettled – I wonder, Dan, would you mind if she rode out with you some morning? I'm sure it would cheer her up.'

Hennessey tried to swallow and found he could not. He coughed instead. 'Yes, yes, of course. She might like to see our new baby. Marcus. We've adopted him.'

'Really?' Any momentary interest Sheppard might have had ceased the moment he had what he wanted. 'I'll get my assistant to ring you. Come up to the box when you can. Oh, and I want a list of the entries for the rest of the season, Fleece isn't doing enough.'

'He's doing as much as he's going to,' said Hennessey flatly but Sheppard ignored him. Hennessey glowered after his retreating back until a friend nudged his elbow and muttered, 'Never mind Dan, you can always nail the bastard's horses.' He grinned and agreed, knowing that he never could. As far as he was concerned they were his horses, and he generously allowed the owners to come and look at them occasionally. Stupid load of monkeys the lot of them, and Sheppard was the chief ape, with a wife too good for him.

He mooched around downstairs until Sheppard sent a waiter to fetch him up to the box. They were all drinking champagne, Jenna, Sheppard and three or four others, a

271

tiny Japanese couple amongst them. He was polite but restrained, listening all the time to Jenna's conversation while trying to maintain some semblance of one himself.

'Do you think the colt will win, Mr Hennessey?'

'Very possible, ma'am –' Jenna was talking about the children. 'William would like them to board full-time but I should hate that –'

'I understand they have special shoes to run in, too?'

'What? Er, yes, racing plates, very light.'

'– so William insists that I come, even though it is very dull. I find people involved in racing very tedious on the whole.'

Suddenly he could no longer resist. He spun round, cutting off his questioner in mid-sentence and saying, 'Really Mrs Sheppard? Your husband's arranged for you to come riding next week so we can bore you some more. Tuesday all right?'

'What? Not Tuesday, no. I'm busy.'

'Pity. You could see our new baby. Marcus.'

There was a silence. Her eyes bored into him, screaming at him, how can you do this to me, now, with these people around. 'Oh,' she said breathily. 'That would be nice. Tuesday you said?'

'Yes.'

It was time then to go down to the paddock. The horses were parading in the summer sun, restless, eager, and against all the odds Hennessey felt his spirits lift a little. 'Mrs Sheppard chose this horse,' he told the Japanese couple and they bowed and nodded, their faces fixed in smiles. 'She's an eye for a horse,' he added and they did it again, as presumably they would if he told them the world was about to end. He smiled stiffly back and retreated. Jenna stood a little apart and there was nothing to do but talk to her.

'Where did you find those two puppets?'

'Business colleague of William's. Go away, Hennessey.'

'I can't, you're the owner. I wanted to say – he's very well.'

'No thanks to you. How's the lunatic?'

He allowed the ghost of a smile to cross his face but wiped it off immediately when he saw the heat in Jenna's eyes. Push her an inch and she'd hit him.

'She's fine. Much better. You did a very generous thing.'

'I didn't do it, you did. Damn you.'

'Pretend it was your idea, it'll make you feel better.'

She looked at him in patent astonishment. 'Nothing will ever make me feel better,' she said simply and welcomed her husband with a brilliant smile. 'Darling, Mr Hennessey's been telling me that he doesn't want to run Fleece too much in the south because his wife doesn't like him to be away from home. I don't think we can have that, can we darling?'

William looked astounded but Hennessey merely laughed. 'Don't tell such lies, Mrs Sheppard. If you do as I tell you then we'll have him in next year's Derby.' He won't win, he added silently, but at least he'll be in the race. He met Jenna's fulminating gaze with eyes that were calm and level.

They waited until the horses cantered down to the start and then went back up to the box to watch the race from there. As expected, Sharps made mincemeat of the field, and Sheppard was jubilant.

'Well, Jenna, say what you like, Dan can certainly make them win. But you chose the horse, my darling, remember that. Tell you what, Dan, why don't you come to Kentucky with us in a month or two and pick out some yearlings? You and Jenna between you would come up with some stars.'

'Let's see how the season progresses,' said Hennessey smoothly and accepted a glass of champagne. This was a nightmare afternoon, yet he loved it. The air about him crackled with the excitement of Jenna, he had only to let himself look at her to feel dry-mouthed desire. Yet she was so angry with him. He would let her hit him till he bled if only he could help her find release.

When the day was ended the Sheppards returned alone to their huge, quiet house. William was still excited, Jenna sombre. She went to her dressing room and wearily pulled the scarf from her hair. William came to the door.

'Come to bed,' he said simply and she nodded. There was a horrid ritual these days about their sex, and it always involved a small kind of torture. Hidden beneath her lovely clothes were little livid marks, yet she never once stopped him. It was as if she relished the pain of punishment, the physical stabs that dwarfed the torment in her mind. All that she asked was that he did not make her pregnant, and in her present mood it seemed little enough to allow her to take steps to avoid it. Tonight though he wanted something different.

'Let's be kind to each other,' he said comfortably, settling himelf beside her in the high, wide bed. He must be getting old, or perhaps it was his leg, aching now after a day spent standing. Ever since he had returned from Australia Jenna had been far from him, keeping deep within herself and never coming out. He felt the need to reach in and touch her.

'I don't want you to be kind,' said Jenna, tossing her head restlessly on the pillow. 'Do what you like.'

'I like to be kind,' he murmured and leaned across to nuzzle her shoulder, running his hand up her thigh and over the curve of her hip. She shuddered beneath his touch and he was at once reminded of how things used to be. He moved to kiss her, setting his full, moist lips against her dry ones, his tongue probing her mouth inescapably. Suddenly she thought she would choke and she turned her head aside, letting him lick her ear, her neck, fix his mouth upon her breast like a giant, hungry baby. The sobs began to shake her, she found she could hardly breathe for crying and soon even William could not go on.

'Whatever is the matter?' he asked in helpless rage.

'I don't know. I really don't. Oh William, I'm so unhappy!' She needed comfort and it was something he had never learned how to give. He sat up, disturbed and unsure of himself. This raw emotion was an embarrassment to him.

'George will bring you a warm drink,' he announced firmly. 'A cup of Horlicks or something.' He was putting on his dressing gown, taking action.

'I don't want any Horlicks,' wailed Jenna, but since William could think of nothing else to give her, Horlicks was what she got.

On Tuesday, Jenna was late. The string was waiting for her and the lads were bemused, for Hennessey was not angry, only patient. 'She'll come,' he insisted and half an hour later she did, quiet, pale, without apology. As silent as she, Hennessey legged her up on Flagship and they all set off.

It was a day that would soon be hot, and even now the skylarks were singing high above the gallops. The ground was becoming very hard and there were some horses Hennessey would barely work at all. Flagship, now an old campaigner, was one of them.

'Take him slowly Jen,' he urged. 'He's got legs like china. Nice old boy, but he's coming to the end of the line.'

Silent, obedient, she set off, riding neatly but without enjoyment. When she reached the end and the horse was in a light sweat she pulled off her helmet and let her hair blow in the warm breeze as she walked him round to cool him.

Hennessey tried to turn his mind back to his horses, but they seemed worthless in the face of her misery. He had never thought she would take it quite so hard. Lilian, yes, a woman who longed for a baby, she could never give one up, but Jenna, unsentimental, unmaternal Jenna to be so distressed – he had not expected it. Suddenly he turned to his head lad, today riding Fleece. 'Take over Geoff,' he said shortly. 'I'm going back.' Geoff's face became fixed in a blank mask, but as the trainer rode away he allowed himself to curse a little under his breath. The guvnor was heading for trouble and no mistake, even a blind man could see he was head over heels for the woman. What with that, and all the upset at the house – there was going to be trouble, that's all he could say. Look at the lads now, all smirking like a load of Cheshire cats. What was the man thinking of?

Hennessey rode to where Jenna sat her horse and lightly touched her hand. 'Come on,' he said softly. 'I'll take you to see him.'

The rode in silence down the hill until at last he said, 'If anyone else had taken him you'd never have seen him at all.'

'I wouldn't have let anyone else take him. I don't think I ever really meant to.'

'Then what did you mean to do?'

She shrugged, as unsure now as she had ever been. She would have done something.

'You can't have him back. It would kill Lilian.'

'Have I asked to have him back?'

How he wished he could give him to her. They came to the yard, now guarded by timelocked gates and a watchman who was having his breakfast but grudgingly let them in. Hennessey stabled the horses, for once almost neglectful, and went to the back door. 'Lilian,' he called, 'I've brought Mrs Sheppard to see the baby.'

No reply. Jenna stepped cautiously inside, at once realising that she must take off her boots. The floor was scrubbed and all the old muddle of tack and raincoats was gone. Lilian stood in the centre of the kitchen, and like the room itself she was neat, clean and presentable. A plump little body, her face shut against the intruders. 'How do you do,' she said grimly.

'How do you do,' replied Jenna. 'I wondered if I might see the baby.'

'He's having his nap.'

'Oh. Well, I won't wake him, I promise.'

'I prefer people not to see him when he's asleep. It disturbs him.

'Lilian,' said Hennessey in a warning tone, 'I want Mrs Sheppard to see the baby. Come on, Jenna.' He took her arm and pushed past Lilian, going quickly up the stairs. Jenna followed, her heart pounding. On the upper landing there were many doors, much in need of paint, but on one there was a china plate reading *Marcus's Room*. Jenna wrinkled her nose at it and followed Hennessey in.

The room was submerged in nylon frills, they draped the window, the cradle and hung in festoons down the back of a chair. Bottles and jars of baby products were in serried ranks upon a table and the room reeked of soap, the more over-powering because it was stiflingly hot.

'I've told her a dozen times not to make it so warm,' muttered Hennessey and went to open the window. Jenna was not attending. With soft and yearning face she was leaning over the cot.

'He looks – lovely,' she whispered.

'He does when he's asleep. Cries a lot. It upsets Lilian.'

'I knew he would cry. He yells for what he wants, and he gets it.'

'Marcus needs his rest,' said a voice from the door. Jenna did not turn round.

'I haven't woken him.'

'But I think it's time you went.' The antagonism was loud in her voice and Hennessey sighed. 'Lilian, Mrs Sheppard isn't doing any harm. Go downstairs, we'll be finished in a minute.'

In answer Lilian barged over to the cradle and picked up the sleeping child. Jerked awake, he let out a startled yell. 'There! I knew you'd upset him. I tell you, Dan, you should leave him to me, you don't understand babies.'

Jenna stood and stared at her son, almost wringing her hands in anguish. 'Why couldn't you let him sleep? I wasn't doing any harm. Please don't shake him like that, he doesn't like it.'

'I'm the best judge of what he does and doesn't like. He's my baby.'

Dan looked at Jenna's stricken face and took her arm. 'Come on, love. Let's go down.'

They heard the door shut behind them and Lilian crooning to the now screeching child. Jenna's breath was coming in short, gasping pants as she tried to suppress tears. 'She won't let me see him, will she? She won't let anyone see him, she'll keep him in that box of a room and smother him. You can't let it happen, Dan, you mustn't!'

He caught her hands and tried to soothe. 'It's only because she's anxious, she'll get better. I don't know – perhaps she senses how interested you are. It's only natural.'

'Natural! She's naturally bonkers, that's what she is. Tell me, does she even look at you these days? You and I could make love right in front of her and she wouldn't give a damn, she'd be so busy squeezing my baby to death!'

The truth of it was plain even to Dan, but it sparked him to rage. 'Keep your voice down, damn you! Of course

278

she's devoted to him, she's waited long enough God knows. And look at this house, it's immaculate. She's a wonderful mother, and you can't stand it.'

Jenna looked at him consideringly and the cool detachment of her gaze damped his anger. He might have been a stranger. Then she strolled over to the dresser and enumerated the things she found there.

'One fluffy blue rabbit, one rattle, one box of baby wipes, two dummies, a bottle of rosehip syrup and a bib. I take it all your things have been dumped elsehwere. But that's your problem, if you want to live in a giant nursery no doubt you will. You promised I could see him. That was part of the deal.'

He stared at her lovely face and a twinge of excitement ran through him. It was all slipping into place. He had not planned this, no, but he had known that they would come here. It was what he had waited for. He looked dubiously at the floor and sighed. 'I can see it's going to be difficult with Lilian around. It would be better if you didn't see him at all of course, but I don't suppose you'd agree to that? No. Well then, it's back to the cottage, isn't it? It's still empty, we were going to let it but Dad didn't get round to it and I didn't feel like reminding him. Fortunate really.'

'What do you mean?' She looked at him in shock.

'I mean – you and me. I'll bring him, one afternoon a week. She won't like it but I'll insist. And then –'

'– what?' Her voice was thick with apprehension.

'Well. We can talk about that when we're at the cottage, can't we?'

He came and stood very close to her, she could smell horse and sweat. She could sense his desire. Slowly, she shook her head. 'No go, Dan. I've had enough of that game. William and I – we're trying. I don't want any more lies, I've told so many they come back at me out of the walls, I can't remember what's true and what isn't half the time. Please don't ask.'

Without warning he bent and kissed her, his tongue a live thing in her mouth, reaching, probing, demanding her response, and if she was unwilling her body was not. He could still set her on fire. 'Stop it!' She struck punishing fists at his chest. 'You're an animal, Dan, all you want is sex and lots of it. You don't care what it does to me, or to my marriage.'

He was breathless. For once in his life he wondered if he was nearly out of control, a strange feeling and a heady one. 'All I care about – is staying sane,' he said thickly. 'I have to. For Lilian, and Marcus, yes, and for you. I owe you a share of that baby and I intend you to have it. But I need you. Not just for sex, though God knows I want it, but – not to feel lonely. I'm so lonely without you, Jen, and it's sending me mad.' He was tangling his hands in her hair and she wanted to pull away, but he held her and she could not.

'What about me? Everything is the way you want it. Underneath you're just like William, you take what you want without even asking twice. The only difference is that you apologise. If you were as rich as him you wouldn't.'

'I'm not apologising now. Just think Jen, you, me and the baby. Bliss. The way it should have been all along. I won't do anything you don't want, I promise. All you have to do is come and you can hold him and touch him, see for yourself how he is –' even as he spoke he was touching her, sliding his hands beneath her jacket to feel for her breasts.

'What if I don't come? Will you let me see the baby then?'

He nibbled her lips. 'Oh yes. I'll bring him to the front door of your house and I'll hammer on the door and ask your husband if he'd like to come out and see his wife's baby by another man. And if it brings the whole world down around me and you and Lilian and the whole sodding lot of us I tell you I won't give a sodding damn!' His hand gripped in her hair and dragged her head back, he pressed salty kisses on the long arch of her neck and only when Lilian's feet sounded loud on the stairs did he release her.

She seemed unaware that her husband was alone with a woman whose hair was a tear-soaked tangle, and that he indeed had sunk trembling into a kitchen chair.

'He's gone to sleep,' she said contentedly. 'I have to make his bottle for lunch soon so I think you'd better go. You can eat at the pub, Dan.'

'I haven't had any breakfast yet,' he said wearily, but she was uninterested.

'I must get some more vaseline,' she muttered, opening a cupboard in the dresser. Even Jenna, distressed as she was, could see that the cupboard was groaning with jars of vaseline.

'You already have some,' she said in a flat, grey voice.

'I like to keep a stock. I must get some more vaseline. Yes, and I have to make his bottle for lunch. That's right, make his bottle for lunch.'

Jenna turned and made for the door, her back a wordless accusation. 'Thursday,' said Hennessey, and she paused and then went on.

A strange feeling of calm descended on her as she drove slowly home. Her baby was well, he was warm and fed and wanted. In the days after she lost him her breasts had ached with unwanted milk and the pain was more than physical, there was a scar in her that only the sight of her pink, plump baby could heal. Even her jealousy was a small price to pay for relief, and besides, the one she was really annoyed with was Dan. He it was who had stolen her baby and given it to someone he cared for more than her, yet still he wanted her to love him. Well she would not. He was someone she needed because he alone could give her access to her baby and for that sex was a small price to pay. But she could and she would withhold what he wanted more than that, which was herself. He did not deserve her.

William was in his office when she got home and she went in to see him, bending over the dark head and kissing him. 'Feeling better?' he asked absently.

'Yes, thank you. I think I'll go shopping after lunch, I'm in desperate need of some clothes.' For Jenna, a rise in spirits inevitably meant a shopping spree and William smiled at her. Perfect, lovely Jenna that he alone possessed, his woman of fire and ice. His horses might be beaten, his investments could always fail, but no-one had a woman like Jenna. Her legs were endless in the clinging breeches, her heavy linen shirt was damp with sweat. He was about to slide a hand between her legs when his middle-aged secretary came in with some papers.

'Mr Maynard asked me to give you these, sir.'

'Thank you. Please do not interrupt when I am talking to my wife, Stella.'

'Oh – oh. I'm sorry Mr Sheppard.' She retreated, blushing, and Jenna flicked a finger at his hair. 'That was unnecessary.'

'Not in the least. I was about to begin to make love to you.'

Now it was Jenna's turn to blush, for she and William had such a polite relationship that the mention of sex always seemed out of place. It was as if an acquaintance at a cocktail party had suddenly put his hand up her skirt.

'Not here, surely,' she said uncomfortably with a nervous glance at the door. Imagine doing it with that woman

282

sitting there listening, although that was probably what William found exciting. He began pulling her shirt free until he could see her breasts, small and round with large, dark-red nipples.

'These have changed colour,' he commented, holding one between finger and thumb, Jenna gasped and forced herself to stand still. If he dug his nails in now she would scream.

'Let's go upstairs,' she begged. 'Then we can lock the door.'

'In a moment.' William was enjoying himself. 'Was Hennessey there this morning?' he continued. 'That man would give his right arm to sleep with you Jenna, did you know that? When he's near you he can't think of anything else, he watches you all the time. I wonder what he thinks about when he makes love to his wife? I wonder if it's you?'

Jenna shuddered. 'Don't be silly. He only thinks of his horses.'

'Probably makes love like a horse, backwards. Come on, let's do it like that now. You can pretend I'm a stallion called Hennessey. Come on, Jenna.'

He pushed her face forward over the desk and dragged at her trousers. When her pink, narrow bottom was exposed he unzipped himself and entered from behind, in one solid, painful thrust. She bit her lip and clutched at the far edge of the desk for support, feeling his hands cup her breasts under her shirt.

'Would he do it like this?' whispered William in her ear. 'Would you like it?'

Almost against her will the thought entered her head. Hennessey's sandy head in place of William's dark one, his long fingers on her breasts, his thick penis inside her. She groaned and pushed her bottom higher, letting her head hang. Her hair fell over her face and down towards

283

the carpet on the far side of the desk, and William found his breath hissing between his teeth with excitement. Now he had her, now she was truly his, willingly subjugating herself beneath him. A rising tide began in him, he clung, he clutched, he thrust – and as he climaxed he heard Jenna cry out. When he levered himself off her prone body, the papers his secretary had brought crushed beneath her, he saw her holding her breasts and crying.

'I'm sorry – did I hurt you?'

'It's nothing – it's all right.' Neatly encircling each breast was the imprint of five fingernails. She scrubbed at her tears and pulled her clothes roughly back into place.

As so often with Jenna, William did not know what to say, although he wanted to tell her that he never meant to hurt. It was simply that he needed to own her, needed to be sure she was his, and even when they were making love he could feel her separateness. Her innermost core was always her own, and he challenged her for it, only to regret it in later calm. He cleared his throat. 'Jenna – you do know that I love you?'

She kept her head turned away. 'I'm sure you do, darling. Now, if you'll excuse me I must go and change.' She rushed from the room, past the rigid figure of the secretary, prepared to lock herself in the toilet if need be, in search of privacy. This house was a prison, yet she did not even have her own cell.

The children broke up for the holidays on the following day, and Jenna went in the Rolls to collect both them and their vast amounts of luggage. Both children seemed tired and somewhat withdrawn, slumping on to the seat with none of the euphoria Jenna remembered from her own schooldays.

'I thought you might like to go to Scotland,' she said

tentatively. 'There's an adventure school there. It might be fun.'

'It would certainly get us out of the way,' said Tony grimly. 'I know how you hate us under your feet. Where will you and Dad go, Crete?'

It was unusual for Tony to include her in his antagonism and Jenna felt uncomfortable. 'No. Actually we were away so long at the beginning of the year we thought we'd stay home for the summer. Of course there's Kentucky for the November sales and then some ski-ing – and the weather's lovely at the moment, you can't beat England when it's hot.'

'Good heavens, slumming it a bit aren't we?'

Jenna glared at the boy. 'You sound just like Hennessey,' she snapped.

'Will you let us stay at home?' asked Rachel. 'Daddy always wants to get rid of us, I know he's going to send us away to board –'

'Since you haven't yet gone I think you can assume I've put a stop to that,' said Jenna, thinking that William and Hennessey ought to get together on that one single thing. They both nagged her all the time time, but from different standpoints. It was outrageous of Hennessey to think that she could not take care for children, even her own, their own baby!

'Yes, of course you can stay home,' she said abruptly. 'We'll organise lots of things for you to do. I'll make a real effort.'

Tony chuckled. 'Lasting all of a week, we know you, Jen. What will it be, health-giving walks and dancing lessons? We'll do the Wolds Way tomorrow afternoon.'

'Er – I'm busy tomorrow afternoon,' said Jenna, and they both burst out laughing.

'It's a huge walk, silly,' said Rachel and gave her an

impromptu hug. Jenna felt foolish and delighted at one and the same time.

She had never seen the path to the cottage in the full flush of summer growth. Ragged robin marched beside the track and in the shady verge there was the misty blue of celandine and meadow cranesbill. Part of her saw and took pleasure in it, but she was breathless with haste, rushing along as if escaping hell and about to enter heaven. Suppose he had not brought him, her thoughts whispered, suppose he was there without the baby? There was nothing she could do. She felt powerless and angry, excited and afraid and when she reached the cottage and looked for the key she felt numb with shock. It was not there.

'I've been waiting for you.'

She turned and saw him in the doorway. 'But I'm early.'

'I was earlier.' His skin was brown with summer tan, but he looked tired and very strained. There were lines between his brows that had never been there before. He stood aside to let her come in and when she passed him she smelled hoof oil and bran. William never smelt anything but clean. Her eyes blinked in the cool dark of the cottage and there, lying on his back on the rug in front of the fireplace was her baby.

She breathed the scent of his skin and felt a downy cheek against her lips. When a wavering fist poked at her eye she laughed and nibbled at it, letting him clutch at her hair, and when she unwrapped him from his smothering clothes and found his hot round tummy she blew on it and they both chuckled.

'He's wonderful,' she said happily. 'He looks so well.'

'Do you really think so? You really think he looks all right?' He sounded grim and anxious.

'Well – yes. I've been thinking, your wife may be fussy but it's only natural, you said so yourself. She takes too much care if anything, look at the clothes he's wearing. You know, until I saw him I kept having this nightmare that he was crying and crying and no-one would give him anything to eat. But she does feed you, doesn't she, angel?' She buried her face in him again, delighted with the feel of baby skin.

Hennessey sighed. 'She feeds him all right. So you're happy now then, Jenna? You like the way things have turned out.'

'Hardly that.' She sat back on her heels and looked at him, the focus of all her inner rage. 'You've got everything your way now, Dan, if you don't like it there's nothing I can do. After all, you never asked my opinion.'

'Jenna, that is bloody unjust! If you had told me you were pregnant, if you had given me a chance to help and I hadn't, then you might have had cause to complain. But oh no, you didn't need me, you wouldn't let me have any part in it. Until you couldn't avoid it, that is. Even now you grudge me the baby, and damn it all, I'm his father!'

Jenna dropped her eyes. 'So you are,' she said lightly. 'Anyway, I don't mind you having him. I did mind – her – but not now. She loves him. If I keep telling myself that I don't mind.'

'Yes.'

Hennessey felt restless and unhappy. Lilian had been strange when he took the baby, he had told her repeatedly that he was taking Marcus out and she had seemed not to understand. Then, when he had put him in the car, intending to drive to the end of the track and then walk, he had looked through the window and seen Lilian making up a bottle.

'What are you doing?' he asked, going back inside.

287

'I'm going to feed the baby.'

'But he isn't here. I'm taking him out.'

'Yes.' She went on making the bottle. There was no reasoning with her, he knew that of old, and it frightened him. She was supposed to change now, be different, but even with a baby she was odd. He thought of the hours she spent alone in the house with the child and even in the heat of a summer's day he felt cold.

Jenna and the baby were gazing into each other's eyes in mutual fascination, and suddenly Hennessey had to smile.

'You're lovely,' he murmured.

'Who is?'

'Both of you. By the way, is Tony going away during the holidays, he didn't know. I was thinking I might put the nag out to grass for a bit, he deserves a break.'

Jenna grimaced. 'That's a pity. No, they're not going anywhere. I thought an adventure centre in Scotland but they don't want to go. They'd rather let me arrange things for them. You see, the children quite like me looking after them, even if you do think I'm no good at it.'

She was needling him and the pricks were finding the target. 'I don't think drug addiction is a worthwhile accomplishment,' he snapped, and then relented. 'Be honest Jen, you don't keep a close enough eye on them. Money, a car complete with chauffeur, they can get up to anything and you never ever learn. Mark my words, they'll be up to their necks in it within a week and don't expect me to help you.'

'Oh I won't. I should know better than to ask you to do anything, you always let me down!' She uttered the appalling lie and he stared at her in amazement. Then he began to laugh. 'Go on, back that one up,' he urged. 'Tell me how useless I am.'

She was blushing and would not look at him. 'You're

useless. Let's take this baby for a walk, Dan. I'll carry him.'

So they strolled under the spreading branches of oak and sycamore, silver birch and ash. The baby weighed heavy in Jenna's arms and soon she gave him to Dan. He took him with tenderness and care, and Jenna said, 'I am glad you've got him really. You were right.'

Later, they went back to the cottage, the baby long since asleep. Hennessey laid him on the rug again but when he stood up, Jenna was preparing to go.

'I mustn't be late. The children.' She looked shy and uncertain of herself, and Dan was at once reminded of how she had been at first. 'Come to bed,' he said softly. 'I know it seems strange after so long, but I promise it will be all right. I won't hurt you.'

She glanced up at once, realising that he believed no-one had touched her since the baby. 'I must go – really –' she backed towards the door.

'Come to bed. I brought the baby, you come to bed. We agreed.' He caught her arm and led her firmly and inexorably up the stairs.

In the familiar little bedroom Jenna felt weak. It was like the first time, she had the need to hide from him. But he was taking off his clothes, watching her all the time, and she turned her back and undressed quickly, pulling her hair over the scars on her breasts. Then she sat on the bed, her knees to her chin. Hennessey moved to take her in his arms, his hands already going to sweep her hair out of the way and she caught them, saying, 'Let's do it backwards for a change.'

He grinned. 'What, not look at you? No thanks. Anyway, it takes a very sophisticated girl to enjoy it like that and I don't think you would. Another day.'

He bent his head to kiss her and against all her intentions Jenna felt her body arch towards him, her legs

289

spreading themselves with a natural ease that never came with William. Then he drew back her hair and bent his lips to her breast.

'Christ! Jenna!'

'Don't look. It's nothing to do with you, don't look!' She was trying to cross her arms across her chest, but he held her wrists and prevented her.

'I'll kill the bastard. What did he have to do it for, you're his wife! When was it, tell me.' He pushed her back on the pillow and towered above her, furious and terrifying.

'It isn't any of your business,' she muttered. 'I – I liked it. He often hurts me, I don't mind. You should try it, a little bit of pain is good for sex –'

In answer Hennessey let go her wrist and lifted his hand to strike. Jenna shrieked and threw her arm across her face. He dropped his hand. 'And you like it. Does he always do this? Often?'

'He – once he didn't. I cried, I don't know why. It isn't so bad. You see, he feels – it's a fight with him. He has to win and I have to lose, I thought perhaps all men felt like that a bit. And didn't dare to show it. Don't you ever want to hurt me, Dan?'

He looked down at her lovely, fair-skinned face and felt like crying himself. 'No' he whispered. 'Never. I mean, there's a difference between rough, hard loving and – this. Here, let me look at you.' Swiftly and before she could protest he began to study her limbs and body for marks. They were there, pink, barely healed stains, the indentations of teeth on one buttock. When he asked her about that Jenna began to cry. 'It's nothing to do with you,' she insisted. 'Leave me alone. I want to go home.'

'Not yet you don't. If he can do what he likes with you then so can I. Damn it, I don't even hurt you yet you let him do what he wants and make me buy you with promises. I'm going to have you whether you like it or not, Jenna Sheppard!'

He was furious and very aroused, she had to spread her legs wide to let him in, and while he mated with her, for it was hardly love, he stared into her face and hissed, 'Is it better with him? Is it?'

She gripped the muscles of his upper arms, stared back into his face with eyes like the night and said nothing until her orgasm forced her to cry out. He was finished soon after and rolled quickly away. He was breathing very rapidly. 'I can't bear him to have you,' he panted. 'You'll have to stop. Promise.'

'He's my husband, not you.' Jenna was already getting dressed.

'He's a brute.'

'And what are you, to threaten everything so long as I let you screw me? I won't promise a thing, I will do what I have to. And I'll come next Thursday, so you have nothing to complain about. Next time bring a clean nappy for the baby, he's very wet.'

He followed her down the stairs. 'I'll kill him. So help me I'll strangle him –'

'Dan!' She faced him, staring straight into his eyes. He was trembling. 'It's all right,' she said softly. 'When you think about it you'll see it doesn't matter. Anyway, you don't care that he hurts me, only that another man has sex with me. Well I'm sorry, but there it is. You'll get used to it.'

'I will never, ever get used to it.' Hennessey's voice sounded raw. He had a sudden vision of Jenna writhing in pain, pinioned under her husband's cruel body, and he snatched her to him, almost crushing her. Gradually Jenna eased herself away. 'Don't make it hard.' She went to the baby, kissed his sleeping cheek and left. There was no farewell for Hennessey.

He went home a long time later, driven there by a hungry, fist-chewing baby. Lilian was scrubbing the kitchen cupboard and had no time to feed him, so Hennessey did it, finding solace in the eager guzzlings of his son. He loved Jenna so very, very much. Suddenly, in an instant that afternoon he realised that the situation had become intolerable, for no better reason than that he could not bear Jenna to be loved by another man. It was something he had deliberately excluded from his consciousness and even if Sheppard had been kind he would have loathed it. The very thought made his gorge rise. She was his and his alone, and for all their differences they were the same. Like a metal that can be twisted into delicate patterns or used to make something solid, in appearance so different, in essence the same. Yet he was shackled by Lilian and Jenna by Sheppard's money and in any case she did not want him. Never once had she offered to give up so much as a single fur-lined wrap for him, she had never once considered that it might be possible. So, she was venal and self-seeking, without regard for others. Yet if only she would turn to him and say 'I need you' he would give her his all, his prospects, his ambitions, perhaps even his wife's sanity. But it was too little. She did not want it.

On a day that should have been hot and bright, Jenna's carefully laid plans for the children's entertainment fell about her in ruins. They had intended to go to the sea and do some dinghy sailing, learned by them all in Australia, but due to what the weatherman claimed was a swiftly moving low and Tony declared to be gross incompetence on the part of the meteorologists, the day turned out to be grey, wet and blustery. Jenna ran through lists and lists of activities, ranging from educational museum visits to oil painting, but they had done them all. She began to wonder if she should revive the pornographic videos, if only to keep them off the streets.

'What would you like to do?' she asked Rachel, who was less likely to suggest a roulette session than Tony.

The girl considered, her head on one side. 'I'd like to visit Mr Hennessey's,' she declared. 'He hasn't seen Casey for ages.' She was slightly pink and Jenna allowed herself a smile. Rachel was exhibiting all the symptoms of a teenage crush, and for once she found a suitable target. Hennessey would be gentle. Just then William came into the room and looked thoughtfully out at the wind lashing the heads from the roses.

'No sailing then,' he commented.

'No.'

He rested a hand on Jenna's shoulder, as always scrupulously avoiding contact with Rachel. He never touched either of his children. 'We thought we might go and visit Hennessey's instead,' added his wife.

'Will you? I think I shall come, I want to have a look at Fleece. The race is only next week.'

In a few days' time Fleece was to be matched against a field that included two of the best two-year-olds in the country. So far he had managed a first in an easy race and a third in a stiffer one, but he had never been pressed. Hennessey had been building to this, the Ridings Cup, but of late he had seemed disinterested, meeting all William's enquiries with a brevity that bordered on rudeness. It was time the man was given a shake-up.

They all climbed into the vast interior of the Rolls, Tony sullen because his father was coming with them.

'Move over at once, Tony, you're taking up all the room,' snapped William and his son moved perhaps half an inch. There was plenty of room, except that the whole world was hardly big enough for this father and son when they were in the mood to find fault.

'Please don't let's quarrel,' begged Jenna, knowing it was a futile request. It had occurred to her to stay behind but that would mean a missed chance to see Marcus, as well as an opportunity to impress Hennessey with her familial status. Not that he would be impressed if William and Tony fought all the time.

They drove into the rain-soaked yard to see Hennessey trudging past in a stained canvas hat, anorak and gumboots. When he saw William's neatly coated figure, spruce beneath its umbrella, Jenna detected a look that was almost a sneer.

'Mr Sheppard. A family outing, I see.'

'Hello, Dan,' called Tony, attempting to emphasise his friendship but sounding bumptious and young.

'Hello, Mr Hennessey,' added Rachel and blushed to the roots of her hair when he smiled at her. He strolled across and pulled her hat over her eyes. 'Hello, Miss Freckles. Tony.' He said nothing to Jenna but their eyes met and they both looked away.

'We were going sailing but it was too horrid so we thought we'd come and see you,' confided Rachel, emerging from her hat. 'I've brought Casey. I've been walking him every single day and Jenna's been helping me train him. Look. Down Casey, down. Down. DOWN!' The dog turned a deaf ear and wandered off to lift his leg at a post. Rachel grimaced in mortification and Hennessey said casually, 'That shows Mrs Sheppard's been helping you. Here Casey, lie down.'

The dog recognised the tone of authority and at once came and lay abjectly at the trainer's feet. Rachel looked adoring, Jenna amused and William bored.

'Mr Hennessey,' he said with studied patience, 'I wonder if I might have a word with you?'

Hennessey turned and looked at him. 'I'm rather busy I'm afraid. Some other time perhaps.'

Sheppard sucked in his breath and said, 'Now, please, Dan. I'm getting a little tired of your offhand attitude to training racehorses.'

'It's not the horses I'm offhand with, Mr Sheppard,' purred Hennessey. 'But I can see you've come all this way to tell me my job so I may as well let you do it. Do you want to come in the house or shall we stand out here while your wife dies of pneumonia? I know how careful you are of her health.' The shot went wide because William had no idea what he was talking about. So they all trudged into the kitchen, including Casey who left a trail of huge paw-marks on the spotless floor. Lilian was there, looking bewildered and frightened by the sudden invasion.

'Go upstairs, Lilian,' said Hennessey curtly, but she stood and twisted her apron in small, anxious hands.

'How is the baby Mrs Hennessey?' asked Jenna and Lilian turned her doe-like eyes upon her.

'I don't know you,' she muttered.

'Er – yes, you do. We've met. How is the baby?'

Still Lilian said nothing and under Sheppard's amazed stare Hennessey came and guided her from the room, closing the door behind her. 'Do sit down,' he said then, as if demented women were all in a day's work, and obediently they all sat round the large scrubbed table.

'I'll make coffee,' said Jenna, and went to put the kettle on, changing the order to tea when she saw there was only a teaspoon of coffee left in the jar. Oh well, she was taking good care of the baby, that was all that mattered.

'Now, Dan,' said William soothingly, confirmed in his superiority by the shambles around him. 'We have to consider next week's race.' He extracted one of his Swiss cigars and began patting his pockets for a light.

'We don't have to do anything,' said Hennessey and tossed him a box of matches. 'And I don't mind if you smoke but don't drop the ash on the floor, it upsets Lilian.'

Tony gasped and choked on a giggle, but William was amazed. 'I don't know what's got into you Hennessey,' he snapped, 'but you are pushing your luck. Look at the weather today, it could ruin the going and are you considering it? . . .'

'No,' interrupted the unrepentant Hennessey.

'Why not?'

'Because it's rock hard and can only improve. Damn it all, Mr Sheppard, I either train the horse or I don't. If he's fit he'll run, if he isn't he won't. Once he's running he'll either win or lose, unfortunately my crystal ball isn't working or I'd give you the result. If you want my guess it's that he will win if he gets a clear run, because he hasn't the guts to make a fight of it. Now, we could talk all afternoon and still say no more than that.'

'I don't like your attitude, Dan.'

'You don't buy my attitude, William.'

There was a stunned silence, into which Jenna put the mugs of tea. 'Drink this and stop squabbling,' she ordered. 'We'll go and look at Fleece in a minute please, Dan, I know you hate owners but we're a necessary evil. And I know it's raining but – can Tony have a ride? I thought William would enjoy seeing how he's improved.'

Her eyes met Hennessey's and he read all that she wanted to say. Please don't fight, please don't make it difficult. I want Tony to show off in front of his father, he so much wants to impress him. Please Dan, do it for me.

'Er – I'm sorry if I sounded abrupt,' he said stiffly to Sheppard. 'New baby you know, we don't get much sleep. Hop off and get the horse tacked up, Tony, you can take him into the paddock.'

Sheppard, mollified, picked up his mug. 'I should tell you, Dan, that I've great hopes for you. We could make a great team but sometimes I wonder if you want to make it to the top. You've got the ability, no doubt about that.'

'I don't go in for team-work,' said Hennessey and stared blank-faced at the wall.

When they had drunk their tea they trooped into the yard and went to look at Fleece, desultorily chewing hay in an immaculate box. All Hennessey's horses lived like kings with straw to their knees and the boxes whitewashed within and painted without. They were like jewels in an expensive shop, surrounded by leather and velvet. They all wore donkeybrown rugs with yellow edgings, inscribed with the horse's name, and on racedays they wore one kept for best, with the name in gold braid and a curlicued 'H' on the corner. Fleece blinked at them, mild-eyed, and Hennessey pulled the horse's ear. 'Did we wake you, fella?'

'He's very gentle' said Rachel and extended a tentative hand.

'Too gentle. Nothing about him,' said Hennessey. 'Look at Sharps there, head out, terrified he's missing something. That horse wins because he hates to lose, it has nothing to do with how fast he can run. This one couldn't care less.'

'Then you must make him care,' said Sheppard. 'A bit of stick wouldn't do him any harm at all, I thought so last time.'

'Hit him and he'll throw in the towel,' said Hennessey. 'He's not too keen on racing as it is, finds it all very alarming. But we can leather him if you want Mr Sheppard, a really delightful spectacle that would be, jockey bringing up stripes on a natural coward who's better bred than suits him.'

'It would be cruel,' objected Rachel, daring to pat Fleece's neck.

'Don't be silly,' said Sheppard crossly. 'If he wins without the stick then all is well. Otherwise we shall just have to see.'

Jenna laughed. 'We'd see all right. He wouldn't let him be hit, darling, whatever we said. Dan has very strict rules for his owners you understand, they are allowed to cheer when their horses win and that is about all. Oh, and they can accept the trophies. Anything else and he gets very cross, as you can see.'

'You seem to know him very well, Jenna,' said Sheppard softly.

Jenna looked away, startled. In her efforts to mediate she had said too much.

Just then Tony came round the corner on his horse, his face a study in boredom.

'Are you all coming or do I have to wait all day?' he asked with mock weariness, and Hennessey and Jenna grinned and began to walk to the paddock.

'Damn it all, Tony, you'll learn some manners or so help me I'll sell that horse under you,' thundered Sheppard and Jenna flinched visibly. Hennessey stamped on the urge to turn round and murder Sheppard, and instead said tightly, 'I think Tony is very anxious to impress you, Mr Sheppard. He's worked very hard and he deserves some appreciation.'

'When you accept my advice on horses I will accept yours on children,' said Sheppard, and smiled. Now he had the man. Hennessey hated Jenna to be upset, Jenna hated Tony to be uspet, so in order to hurt Hennessey one had first to annoy Tony. When the boy began his careful circles of the field Sheppard wandered off to admire the view.

'Damn the man! Can't he even spare a minute for his own son?' Hennessey was white with rage and Jenna felt near to tears.

'You've annoyed him, it's all your fault. I wish we hadn't come. He's going to be beastly to Tony and I shall have to live with the consequences.'

'Then leave him,' snapped Hennessey, 'or is the money so precious that you can't?'

The wind gusted and blew a shower of warm rain into their faces, whisking Jenna's hat off her head and dancing it away to land on the grass underneath a jump. Her hair, stuffed beneath it, whipped across her face and blinded both her and Hennessey, standing close at her side.

'I'll get it,' cried Rachel and raced after the hat. Hennessey spat the hair from his mouth and bellowed 'Don't!' just as Tony's horse came over the jump. Rachel heard the cry, looked up and saw the horse coming to meet her. She screamed, Tony wrenched at his horse, and in a dull mist of horror Jenna saw Rachel prostrate on the grass, the horse buckling to his knees and Tony like the hat, wheeling through the air without weight or substance.

Hennessey and Sheppard were there before Jenna could force her dead limbs to move. 'Don't touch them,' snapped Hennessey.

'God damn you man, they're my children!' Sheppard was strangely appalled. He went to where Rachel was lying sobbing. 'Are you all right, Rachel? What do you mean by doing such a stupid thing!' The child sat up and sobbed still harder. A large lump was appearing above one eye.

'She didn't mean it to happen,' said Hennessey, calming now he could see that no-one was dead. 'Well done, Tony, you used your head. Which bit hurts?'

Tony was almost grey, his colour collected in little livid stains under the skin.

'Only my wrist,' he whispered. 'I thought I'd killed her.'

'Well, you didn't. You rode well, we'll have to find a race or two for you. Come on, boy, try and move your legs.' Hennessey, in his element, was calm. Sheppard, very far out of it, was not. 'Lie still, Tony, your back might be broken. Jenna, go and get an ambulance.'

'That's not necessary is it? Dan, is it necessary?' She was leaning against the brushwood fence, feeling faint but aware that no-one had time to waste on her. Sheppard loomed into the air in front of her, his face streaked with mud. 'He is my child, I will say if he needs an ambulance.'

'But darling, he's only hurt his wrist. We can take him in the car, can't we, Dan?'

Hennessey glanced up. 'Yes, I should think so. Go and sit down somewhere Jen, you look ghastly.'

'Will you stop ordering the behaviour of my family! Who the hell do you think you are?' raged Sheppard, but Hennessey ignored him, concentrating only on winding Tony's scarf tight round the injured wrist. Fearful of her husband's imminent explosion Jenna gathered Rachel into the circle of her arm and waited until he was finished. 'I'll take the children back to the house,' she said wearily. 'Hurry up you two and William, please don't row. It isn't necessary.' She started back across the field, Tony close beside her.

Sheppard was filled with the impotent rage that only Jenna could inspire, but as she walked away it drained and left him feeling dull and hopeless. He leaned on the top of the fence and watched in silence as Hennessey caught the horse and began to disentangle the bridle. 'I shall never understand my wife,' he said suddenly.

Hennessey looked up, startled. 'She isn't so complicated, surely.'

'I don't suppose you see it. Hot and cold, and always the one you least expect. I find it hard.'

'She's very lovely.' The conversation was weird and unreal, but somehow neither man wanted to stop it. Sheppard looked off into the distance. 'The most beautiful woman I've ever seen. Everyone wants her, including you. I've seen you watching her. You don't know what it's

300

like – you never have her, somehow.'

And Hennessey, who knew exactly what he meant, felt in sudden sympathy with a man he hated. 'She's like that horse, Fleece,' he said abruptly. 'You gain nothing when you hit.' He gathered up the reins of Tony's gelding, swung into the saddle and rode away.

Chapter Twelve

There were voices in the house, talking to her, there was a particular one in the cupboard that kept telling her to go. Where? Where should she go to get away from the voices? Those people in the kitchen, were they real people or the voices? It was hard to tell, though sometimes you could tell the real ones because they didn't talk to you. Only the voices talked to you, they were the only ones who knew who you were.

Of course there were things to do, things she had to do, all the time, otherwise she would forget who she was and the voices would get her. These bottles for instance, you had to keep making those. All the time. And you had to clean, that was important, if you didn't, if you didn't make the bottles and clean, clean, clean they would get you. What would happen if they got you, if you didn't clean the bath four times a day and the voices crept out of the little crack between the wall and the floor and got you? She knew. They would get into your mouth and in through your ears and up your bottom and into that place the men liked and there wouldn't be any her any more, it would be them, all them, and no place for her but a little tiny corner in her head. And she'd have to keep absolutely quiet so they didn't find her there, not a word, not a whimper, or

302

they'd find her. Best to keep away from the voices. Best to keep on making those bottles and when he told you not to you didn't listen, no, because he didn't know the voices were going to get you. He cried a lot these days. Perhaps he did know about the voices, though if he did you'd think he'd say. And the baby cried too, on and on, though he knew she hadn't time. She'd told him, she hadn't time because of the things she had to do, so he'd better be quiet or they'd hear him.

He'd said he was giving her a baby, but really it wasn't one. She knew that. All right, the outside looked like a baby, but inside its eyes, those odd dark eyes, you could see how cross it was, trapped in there. Perhaps that was what happened when the voices got you, in which case she was sorry for it. He at least should understand about the bottles and the cleaning and the way you had to keep away from the cupboard in case they got you, so why did it have to go on crying?

There was a dry feeling in his mouth and his guts were churning. Thank God the jockey looked calm, waiting for instructions with a confidence that spoke of known abilities and luck on your side. Good man this one, with a brain. Bet he didn't marry a lunatic.

'She has lost her perception of reality.' You can say that again. Last night, wandering the house, hour after hour and then not knowing who he was. That had been – awful. Frightening. But at the same time it broke your heart to see her so unhappy, so utterly, totally lost. Better today, though. He had fed the baby and she had changed him, wiping him clean with idiot precision. She took such care of him, such infinite, painstaking care, there was no need to worry. He hoped. Tomorrow, when this race was over, he would think of something to do. Oh God. What?

'Are you all right, Mr Hennessey? You look a little tired.'

He ran a hand across his face. 'My wife – she's not well. Look, the horse will run but he isn't bold. Don't let him get boxed in, he'll flap, and anyway he's got the legs of them, provided you don't lose touch altogether. And for Christ's sake don't hit him, he'll turn to jelly.'

'What if I look like coming second? Can't I try the odd cut?' This jockey was out for his winner's percentage and no accusation of not trying. Sheppard had a reputation for shredding jockeys he thought had thrown in the towel, but Dan was reading his mind. 'Don't touch him. If you do I'll give you worse than ever Sheppard might. Hit him and he'll lose what little heart he has for the job, and that isn't much. Oh, but I'm sick of this bloody caper, I really am.' He raised his eyes to scan the packed stands, the happy summer trippers with their fifty pence bets and the elegant racing connections with their manners and impossible expectations – what did they think he was, a miracle worker?

'Why don't you go and have a drink? Make you feel better.'

'I'm OK. Have you ever been inside a mental hospital?'

'Er – no.' The jockey looked taken aback. But he knew about Hennessey's wife, everyone did. Said nothing, but they knew, and felt sorry. Nothing you could do though.

'I have. Hellish places really, dustbins for unhappiness. I suppose they do cure people but you wonder if they wouldn't rather be dead, some of them. People there have spent their lives inside. They – they want me to have my wife committed.'

To his shame he found he was crying, but there was nothing he could do about it. He wiped at his cheeks and the jockey looked embarrassed. 'Go and have a drink,' he advised again, and saw with mingled consternation and relief that Mrs Sheppard was coming over.

'Dan? Are you all right?'

'And why the bloody hell shouldn't I be?'

The jockey looked from one to the other. There had been talk, and by God she was gorgeous today. White silk dress and long white streamers floating from a tiny hat, perched on a thick chignon of hair. The only colour those huge dark eyes and lips so pale and pink and kissable – the jockey, who would hardly reach her shoulder, tried to concentrate on thoughts of his wife, a solid little woman who was good at making jam. Mrs Sheppard was looking at Hennessey with a soft and anxious face. There was something there all right.

'Will you come and have a drink, Dan? Everyone wants to talk to you.'

He sighed. 'I wonder how many of them will want to chat if he loses. All right, I'm coming. I feel like a performing monkey.'

'More like Daddy gorilla woken from his afternoon nap. But I'll buy you a hat with a tassel if you want.' She was trying to jolly him, but for once it had no effect. She could sense how bad things were with him, but this was no place to fall apart. Was it the horse, the baby or Lilian? Lilian. It had to be. That batty, plain woman could reduce him to this and Jenna hated her for it.

They went up to the box but Hennessey refused champagne and drank scotch instead. There was a tremor in his fingers, but two drinks stopped it, so he had two more for luck. Tony was there with his wrist in a plaster bandage but Rachel had a black eye and had elected to stay at home. 'I wanted her to come with a patch over it, like a pirate, but she wouldn't.' Jenna was too bright, too noisy, too anxious that William should not notice Hennessey's preoccupation. She hung on her husband's arm and touched his cheek, and Hennessey felt a moment's pity for the man. You could see he loved it but why she was kind when in an hour she would be cold was something he would never understand.

Lord Staveley was there too, red in the face and cheerful. 'Good to see you, Dan.' He dropped his voice conspiratorially. 'Between you and me if the colt wins today you're made. Set you up, Sheppard will, he's had enough of Downing. Mean a move, of course, but then you've always known you'd have to move south sometime. Father's still able to run the farm, isn't he?'

'What? Yes, yes. I'm sorry, I can't think straight at the moment. The race you know.'

'Not like you to get rattled, Dan. Still, it is a big day. Seen the odds? He's favourite.'

It was time to saddle the colt and Hennessey made for the door, staggering a little when the floor lurched sideways. God he was drunk, whisky on an empty stomach. He hadn't eaten since – a very long time. A hand appeared in front of him waving a wedge of smoked salmon sandwiches. 'Eat these,' said Jenna tonelessly and he blundered out with the sandwiches clutched in his hand. They tasted wonderful. Gradually the floor began to steady but he still saw the world at a distance, even the horse seemed a long way away.

'D'you think he'll win, guv?' asked the lad, unnaturally spruce in a suit.

'He's got a chance,' said Hennessey and rested a hand on the horse's neck. There was a fine sheen of sweat, but he wasn't too fussed and Hennessey murmured soothing nothings to him. He looked well, there was no denying it, and the lad had made a beautiful job of him, quarter marks and all.

It was time to go. They left behind the purposeful bustle of the stables for the noise of the parade ring. Fleece began to play up, but his lad bossed him and he behaved.

Good class field this, with a collective value of several million pounds and the connections wore nearly as much in jewellery. The Sheppard party came down from the box, led by a jovial William. He strolled across to Hennessey, remarking, 'You look tired, Dan. Don't say you're nervous?'

'Not at all. Glad to see Tony's little the worse for wear, that could have been nasty.'

William glanced at his son and then away. 'Yes. I only wish he could find something to do with his time instead of hanging round the house all day. Born lazy, that's his trouble.' Tony caught the end of the speech and a flash of hurt crossed his face.

The jockeys marched towards them on short, brisk legs, touching their caps to the owners. A strange relationship this, deferential and yet superior, because in the last analysis it was all up to the jockey.

'I've instructed him not to use the stick,' said Hennessey to Sheppard, thereby circumventing later comebacks.

'I only hope you're sure about this,' said William, which reserved his right to tear Hennessey apart if the horse lost.

The girth was tightened, the jockey legged into the saddle and Fleece was away, to win or lose as the fates decided. Hennessey reflected on what a disproportionate amount of money and hope rode on that horse, who at his worst would run perhaps twenty yards behind the winner. A futile exercise, it had to be admitted, a trial of strength between rich men, held at long range. He felt so tired and depressed. People killed themselves by falling under horses, would that be a good way to go?

Painful, probably, and not necessarily fatal. All around him people were tense with excitement and expectation. He could not stay here with them, he would go into the bar and have a drink.

He was almost the only customer, everyone else was watching the race. Blissful silence, in which the pounding of his head could ease. It suddenly occurred to him to wonder how many hours in the future he would spend at racetracks. Hundreds, possibly thousands. Drinking drinks he did not want, talking to people he did not like. Training would be all right if it wasn't for the races, and if Sheppard gave him any more horses he'd have to endure parties such as this almost weekly. He supposed he might get used to it.

The crowd outside was roaring and roaring, he thought of the game young horses that were stretching every muscle to amuse them and it seemed a very aimless way of life. He ordered another drink, and as he was paying he heard hurried footsteps. Jenna, the streamers of her hat swirling around her.

'He won.'

'Oh.'

'William's delighted, he wants to talk to you.'

'Tell him I'm busy. I don't want to talk.'

'Dan, please, what's the matter? It's something dreadful, I know it is. Marcus is all right isn't he?'

He drained his glass and grimaced at the burn in his throat. 'I don't know. He's with Lilian, so I suppose he's all right. Leave me alone, Jen.'

She recoiled, feeling the sudden stab of tears behind her eyes. Weren't they close any more then? What had happened?

'It's Thursday tomorrow,' she said tentatively.

'Is it? Oh, I can't come tomorrow, it's too difficult. Another time. Look, I must see to that horse.' He put his empty glass down on the bar and pushed his way through the crowds of people congregating for their drop of consolation. Jenna followed, her heart bumping against her ribs.

Fleece was twitchy with weariness and excitement, filling the winner's enclosure with stampings and clouds of steam. 'Well done, Dan!' enthused Sheppard when he saw him. 'He walked it, what a horse! You were right about the stick, I'll give you that.' He turned to Staveley, also enjoying the triumph and said, 'Damned touchy this man, won't let me say a word to him about the horses. But they win, eh, Dan?' It was clear that he was setting Hennessey up to be a 'character', a great man with a great man's idiosyncrasies. From now on Hennessey could be as rude, bull-headed and contrary as he wished and William would wear it. 'That's Hennessey,' he would say and store the tales to recount at parties.

Later, in the box, with the rosebowl safely collected and the horse on his way home, William leaned drunkenly on the trainer's shoulder and said, 'I've got a place lined up for you at Lambourn.'

Hennessey, even drunker, replied 'I hate bloody Lambourn.'

'Stuff that! You and me, we can put together the best stable in the country. Eighty horses, that suit you? Choose them yourself. Buy 'em in, money no object, then we can give the Arabs a run for their money. Stephen'll be in touch, you can go and have a look at the place. Needs some work, of course. Anyway, what's wrong with Lambourn?'

Hennessey lurched across to the table bearing the drinks and poured yet another large scotch. 'It's got sodding horses in it.'

'So it has, by God. Your wife is it, doesn't want to move? You can persuade her Dan, she'll go, got a way with women you have.'

Hennessey laughed, and for a moment sounded really amused. 'Have I now? The only place my wife's going is the loony bin, do they have those at Lambourn too? Full of bloody trainers, probably.' He took a long pull at his drink, and thereby missed the shock on Jenna's face. The woman was mad, she had always known it, and there she was on this lovely summer's day alone with the baby. What on earth was Dan thinking of to leave her?

She went across to William. 'Darling, Dan's in no fit state to drive. I want to go home now, so I'll take his car and you can drop him off in the Rolls when you're ready. All right?'

Wiliam beamed at her. 'Yes, of course. Darling, darling Jenna, I love you because you're so beautiful.'

She sighed. No-one would love her if she was not. She went across to Hennessey and slipped her hand in his pocket, neatly extracting his car keys. 'William will take you home,' she said shortly, and avoided his eyes. They might like to compare notes the two of them, these two men with their male concerns which were so far from hers as to be meaningless. But there was Tony, looking bored, and she summoned him with a smile. 'We're going home.' His relief was almost laughable.

As she and Tony drove slowly through the thick race-course traffic, she said casually, 'I thought I'd pop in at Hennessey's to see his wife. I don't think she's very well.'

'Dan was upset about it, wasn't he?'

Jenna glanced at the boy in surprise. 'I didn't think you'd notice. William didn't.'

'Bit thick about people, is Dad. If he saw someone bleeding to death he'd ask if they were all right and if they said yes he'd believe them. Perhaps that's why he's so good with money, it's all there, obvious, no hidden meanings.'

'You're getting very perceptive in your old age,' commented Jenna and Tony looked embarrassed.

'I wish sometimes I didn't see things,' he muttered.

They drove in silence for some miles, only switching on

the radio for the racing report.

'The victory of Fleece in the Ridings Cup this afternoon established him as the leading two-year-old this season, and confirms his trainer, Daniel Hennessey, in his position as racing's brightest star. This man's reputation has been growing steadily over the past two or three years despite being based in Yorkshire, but if he is going to do his horses justice in the future he will almost certainly be forced to move south. Rumour has it that the millionaire owner of Fleece, William Sheppard, is looking to Hennessey to take control of his entire racing empire.'

Jenna leaned across and clicked it off. 'I wonder if he will move.'

'Will you mind if he does?'

She flushed and tried to laugh. 'It's got nothing to do with me, Tony. You'll lose your riding lessons though.'

'Yes.' He sighed. 'Jen, would you mind if I boarded full-time in the future? I know you like to have us at home, but Dan knows about this school where you can do riding, and it would be something to do at weekends. It's not much fun hanging around the house.'

She opened her mouth to speak and then closed it again. Really! How ungrateful could you get. She hoped he hated it, she really did, and he needn't ask her to take him away because she wouldn't. Again the threat of tears and she lifted her chin defiantly, stamping on the accelerator and saying stiffly, 'If that is what you want then of course you may, Tony. Turn the radio on again please, I don't feel like talking.'

They were hot and sticky by the time they reached Hennessey's. The watchman came to unlock the gates and she drove carefully into the yard.

'Mr Hennessey will be coming on later,' she explained to the waiting lads. 'Have you seen Mrs Hennessey today?'

Bert shook his head. 'Not often we do see her, actually. Been very quiet.'

'Oh. Wait in the car please, Tony.' She went to knock at the back door, and when there was no reply she opened it calling, 'Mrs Hennessey? Are you there?' Silence. The skin on the back of her neck began to crawl, and when she stepped inside the effort of will was almost tangible. Everything very clean and tidy, a strong smell of disinfectant catching at the throat.

'Mrs Hennessey? Lilian?'

Outside there was the sound of a horse whinnying, the lads shouting to each other, buoyed up by the afternoon's victory, but in here the quiet was thick as glue. No-one in the sitting room, a bare place of stark white walls and hard chairs. No-one in the cluttered, lived-in study. This was Dan's place, she would not be here. Upstairs then.

Feet sounding loud on the treads. 'Lilian? Mrs Hennessey?' A strange, snuffling sound and her heart leaped. The baby, it had to be the baby. She ran the last few steps and into the nursery, but the cot was empty. The baby was not there.

It was then that she began to be really frightened, to know that something awful was in that house. But where, where was her baby? 'Oh God, please let him be all right,' she whispered, and ran from room to room, looking in beds and under them, but no-one was there. The house was empty. She stood on the landing and tried to stop herself from screaming because after all, Lilian could have gone out or something, it was only her own mind that was turning this into a nightmare. Then again she heard the snuffling, a muffled infant wail. It was coming from the cupboard, the big, square cupboard on the landing. Knowing that if she did not do it now she never would she flung open the door. There, lying on his front on a pile of towels, weak and sick from screaming, was her baby.

She picked him up with hands that shook, she pressed his sodden, infant body to her breast and wept for and with him. He must have been there hours and hours and hours. 'Oh baby. Oh, you poor baby. Never mind, Mummy's here now, she's got you, she won't let you go. Naughty Mummy to let you go, never mind, you're safe now.' He was sucking his fists in hungry desperation and she longed to give him her breast, but there was nothing there for him any more. Refusing to think of the absent Lilian she went down to the kitchen and looked in the fridge. There were ranks, regiments of bottles. 'Good grief. Wait just a minute sweetheart, Mummy will heat one of these for you. It won't take long.'

But while she was waiting Tony came in from the car. 'Where's Mrs Hennessey?'

'I don't know. I found the baby upstairs, he's in a terrible state. I'm going to feed him.' The bottle must be warm enough now. Moving awkwardly because she had never done this before she maneouvred the baby into the crook of her arm and presented the ugly rubber teat. His mouth latched on to it and he drank, making happy little noises as he guzzled.

'He's all wet, he's ruined your dress,' commented Tony.

'He's more than wet. It doesn't matter, I'll change him in a minute. Poor, poor baby, what a terrible day you've had.'

Tony wandered round the barren room, looking at things. 'Where do you think she is?'

'Out, I suppose, though I can't say I'm very interested. How could she leave you, precious? Pop up and see if you can find some clean nappies and one of these suit things will you Tony.'

Obediently he went. She heard him moving around on the floor above, opening cupboards and drawers, going from room to room. The baby had finished his bottle and was lying like a drunk on her lap, replete and incapable. Tony's feet crossed the landing, there was the sound of a door being opened, and then he screamed, his voice falsetto in its anxiety. 'Jenna! Jenna! Come quick!'

She clutched the baby to her and raced up the stairs. Tony was standing in the bathroom doorway, and as she approached he stepped aside. 'I was looking for the airing cupboard. I found it. Look.'

Crouched between the hot water tank and the wall was Lilian Hennessey. At her side was a large bottle of disinfectant. She crouched with her knees to her chin, her arms crossed on her chest, so the blood from her wrists had gathered in the lap made by her skirt. The smell was dreadful, of vomit, disinfectant and blood, but her face, half hidden by her lank brown hair, was that of someone resting.

'Oh – my – God.' Instinctively she pressed the baby's face against her shoulder, in case he should see. She tried to take a deep breath and could not, so took small shallow gasps instead. How horrible this was, and yet not so bad as you might imagine it to be. But she could not bear to touch it.

'Come away,' she said tightly. 'Go downstairs and ring for the police and an ambulance. I will get some things – for the baby.' She backed from the room and Tony followed her, his face grey. Then he raced down the stairs, and she could hear him dialling, making a mistake and cursing himself, then dialling again. She would have to be quick.

There was a small holdall in the baby's room and she grabbed it, stuffing it full of nappies, clothes, anything that came to hand. The baby's carrycot stood in the corner and she placed him in it, pushing extra things round the sides. Then she took first him and then the holdall downstairs and put them carefully into Hennessey's little car. As a last thought she took half a dozen bottles from the fridge and added those too.

Tony was coming from the study just as she finished. 'They'll be here in a minute,' he said with relief.'

Jenna nodded. 'Wait for them. I'm taking the baby home, you can tell Hennessey. He'll understand.'

'But – you can't leave me here!' Tony was incredulous.

'You'll be all right. Bye, lovey. Take care.' She bent and kissed his cheek, then ran out to the car. He stood at the door, amazed, as she drove quickly away.

They contacted Hennessey at the racecourse and William brought him home. The two men travelled in virtual silence, both still drunk, neither wishing for the other's company.

'They said it was an accident?' queried William.

'She's killed herself.' Hennessey knew it as well as if he had seen her in the act. Was that why he had left her today, so she could do it? Possibly. Why else had he said she'd be better off dead? He focused his muzzy thoughts on his particular anxiety. 'They didn't say anything about the baby.'

'Baby? What baby?' William looked confused and Hennessey didn't explain. Oh God, what happened now?

When they reached the house Tony met them, shocked but self-important.

'I found her. Jenna was here, but she went before the police came. She took the baby. She said you'd understand, Dan, but she was odd – I don't know.'

'Come along, Tony, it's time we were going.' William was anxious to be out of this ugly, tragic house, back to the light and warmth of his home, back to Jenna.

Hennessey was looking at him strangely, and his eyes glittered. 'You can't go yet,' he said softly. 'Come into the study. I want to talk to you.'

The police inspector was hovering. 'I wonder if I might

315

talk to you, Mr Hennessey? It seems quite straight-forward but there are a number of points I should like to clarify.'

'When I've talked to Mr Sheppard. We'll only be a few moments.' Bemused, William followed him into the study. Hennessey stood and stared out of the window, then he spun on his heel and confronted the big, fleshy man.

'You ask what baby. That's my baby. Mine – and Jenna's.'

William gaped at him. 'You're as mad as your wife.'

'Not yet I'm not. She had it at her mother's, you remember how long she was away? How upset she was when she came back, didn't you think it odd? She hid it from you – and from me. She was going to have it adopted, but when I found out I took it. Gave it to my wife, I don't think Jenna will ever forgive me for that. You see, I don't want your horses, or your stables, or your money. I want your wife.'

He stared at Sheppard, who took a small, desperate step backwards. 'You're mad,' he said again. Hennessey slowly shook his head. 'Jenna wouldn't – she couldn't – it isn't possible! She doesn't even like sex that much!'

Hennessey shrugged. 'She liked it well enough with me. She's scared of you, in bed and out of it. Right to be really, you do as you like and to hell with who gets hurt. I think that now you'll ruin me, and I don't honestly blame you, if I was you I might do the same. I don't care any more, somehow.'

William's chest was tight, he was finding it hard to breathe. 'I don't believe you,' he whispered. 'Even if I do, I'll not let you have her, I'll kill you first. Jenna. She's my wife. I love her!' He said it as if surprised that it should still be true.

Hennessey sighed. 'I know you do. So do I. She bewitches men, and they don't recover. But you can't make her happy and the tragedy is that she doesn't want me to try.'

'I don't understand.' Sheppard passed a hand over his face, and Hennessey went to a cupboard and poured two large whiskies. 'She's gone you know. Left us both. She's taken her baby and gone, I don't know where. My guess is that when you get home you'll find she's packed her case and cleared out her bank account. Strange really, it ought to have been possible for it not to come to this. The one person I wanted not to hurt was Jenna, but I did. And you needn't look so bleeding grief-stricken, Sheppard, because you were a sod to her. I know!'

Shock was giving way to anger and Sheppard took a furious gulp of his drink. 'Tell you did she, during your foul little orgies? Where did you do it, in the back of that car? I'll ruin you all right, you can guarantee that. You made her do this, Jenna wouldn't – she knew I loved her. All right, I had affairs, but she was so – they don't mean the same for men. I didn't father children!'

'Thank God. You hate the two you've got.'

'You know nothing about it! Can't you leave any of my family alone?'

There was a knock on the door and the police inspector came in. 'Sorry to disturb you, Mr Hennessey, but I have to talk to you.'

'Yes – yes of course.' Hennessey put his glass down and went out. With shaking hands William went across to the cupboard and poured himself another drink, but he could not touch it. Instead he sank into the battered leather chair, his face crumpled and he began to sob, quietly at first and then with more and more force. Gradually, as he gasped and wept, he became aware that someone was holding his arm. It was Tony.

'Come along, Dad,' he said in a matter of fact tone. 'We've got to go home.'

William looked up in bewilderment. 'That man says – he says he and Jenna –'

'Yes. I know. Her and Dan. But come home, Dad, please, you don't want people to see you like this. Please come home.' Gently he coaxed William to his feet and out to the waiting Rolls.

Hennessey sat in the quiet house and wondered if Lilian was there. They had taken her body only a few hours before but it did not feel as if she herself was gone. Did he believe in spirits? Hard to say. If she did still exist, somewhere, he prayed that the woman she should have been, who had been trying all these years to fight her way out through the fog, had at last become free. That morning, after the terrible night, he had made a frantic telephone call to the doctor. Their usual man was away and the new partner had assumed Hennessey knew much more than was, in fact, the case. His casually imparted phrases had sounded like the knell of doom in Hennessey's head. Lilian was schizophrenic, they had known it for years. A classic case really, hallucinating, obsessive and confused. When things reached a point such as this the only solution was long-term hospitalisation and drug therapy.

He had felt very calm afterwards, he had tried to put his arms round his wife and hold her, but she pushed him way. To her, he was a stranger. He knew how much she hated the hospital, she would have thought it worse by far than death. So he could not mourn her end. Instead he felt calm and sleepy, as if after many many miles he had at last set down a burden too heavy to bear. Life stretched ahead of him without form, without hope. He would not wait for Sheppard to sabotage his enterprise, he would do it himself, he was sick of the endless treadmill of work, worry and struggle, it made no damn money in any case. If it had Jenna might have stayed. Then he did feel like crying, he felt the sting of rejection all over again. It was a curse to love someone who didn't love you back, but there it was, he and Sheppard had something in common at last. He was too weary to think of it. Bed, that was what he needed, to sleep until the end of the world.

It was a week before he appeared again in the yard. The lads were working with hushed voices, asking each other if they should do this or that because without Hennessey there was no direction any more. When they saw him at last, to all outward appearances his usual lanky self, a wave of relief went through them.

'You OK, guv?' asked the head lad cautiously, and Hennessey grunted.

'I've got to go down to the police station, there are things to see to. And I've some calls to make. Keep things ticking over here will you, and for God's sake tidy things up. Looks a bloody shambles, this place does.' There was a water bucket looking lonely outside a door and a handful of straw blowing about, to him a bloody shambles. Through force of habit Hennessey began to go round the boxes, checking that all seemed well, then he stopped himself. Where was the point when it was all so nearly ended? He sighed and went instead to his car. It wasn't there.

'What the devil – oh yes.' Jenna had it. Damn it all, if she had to leave him flat it needn't be quite so literally, you might as well be on Mars round here if you didn't have a car. 'Can I borrow your car, Geoff?' he asked wearily. 'Mine has been abducted.'

The man handed over the keys to his battered Cortina with justifiable reluctance. Nobody in his right mind ever lent Hennessey a car, you might as well offer it up for the Monte Carlo rally. Geoff stood whimpering as the car raced away up the hill, its fragile gearbox double-declutching as Hennessey put two wheels on the verge to overtake a tractor.

The police were tactful and understanding, Hennessey felt that they expected him to break down and sob at any moment. There would be an inquest of course, but it was all quite straightforward. Mr Hennessey shouldn't blame himself, they knew how devotedly he had nursed her. He became suddenly embarrassed, wondering what they would say if they knew he had been carrying on a passionate affair for months. He quickly excused himself, which only confirmed the police in their view that the poor man was distraught. He sat in the borrowed car with the stuffing coming out of the seat and wondered what he should do next. Well, it was clear, he had to find his car. and if finding it meant finding Jenna that was purely coincidental. Besides, at long, long last there was nothing to be gained by restraint.

'What the devil are you doing here? Get out, get out of my house at once!'

Sheppard shook with rage and shock. Here was Hennessey, the man who had destroyed his life, calmly standing on his hall rug, being polite to his butler and nodding at his son. It was beyond belief! 'Get Stephen and the chauffeur,' he told George. 'We'll have him thrown out.' The butler took himself off.

'I take it she isn't here,' said Hennessey.

'Of course she isn't here, you said yourself she wouldn't be. Damn you, get out before I strangle you.'

Hennessey laughed. 'Not you, though you might pay someone else to do it. Look, I've got to find Jenna. For one thing she's taken my car.'

'You are worried about a car? I don't believe you.'

William was scathing. He looked dreadful, as if he hadn't slept in days, his skin blotched and the whites of his eyes bloodshot. Hennessey found it in him to pity.

'I want – to make sure she's all right,' he admitted. 'After all, there's the baby – don't you want to know where she is?'

William put a hand to his head and turned away, towards Tony, almost as if asking for help. The boy spoke in a low voice. 'You won't be happy till you've talked to her, Dad. I don't think you can go on hoping she's going to come back. But if you saw her and talked – she never meant to hurt you, I'm sure she didn't.'

'I did,' said Hennessey abruptly. 'I wanted to kill you a dozen times, you were so damned arrogant and look at you now. A jelly, that's what you are, Sheppard.'

'God damn you, shut up!' hissed William, a dull flush rising in his skin. 'I don't know where she could have gone and if I did I wouldn't tell you, if it wasn't for you she'd still be here –' his voice broke and when he spoke again it was with exhaustion. 'Go away and leave us alone.'

'I think she's gone to Denham,' said Tony on a swift, exhaled breath.

'Denham? Where's that?' Hennessey was avid, William disbelieving.

'She wouldn't go there,' he murmured. 'Would she?'

'It's a village by the sea. Jenna bought a cottage and took Rachel and me for holidays, but it's in the north-east and terribly cold. We didn't like it. So then we didn't go any more, but I don't think she sold it or anything.'

'Denham – I'd forgotten,' said William. 'I remember I was furious when she bought it. I didn't like her going with the children.'

'I never knew a man so jealous of his own son,' remarked Hennessey and turned for the door. He met Stephen Maynard and the chauffeur coming in. 'Too late,' he called. 'I'm leaving. Surprised to see you still here Maynard, your grovelling must be matchless. Get another job man, nothing's worth this. By the way, tell him he can take his horses any time he likes, I'm sick of feeding the bloody things.' He climbed into the decrepit old car and set off to find Jenna.

Denham is a little, windswept village in Northumberland. It has rocks and golden sand, cliff walks where you can count the heads of seals black amongst the breakers, but the cold bites almost to the bone. The people who live there are small and pinched, like the trees, like the clifftop grass, and they hurry to get in out of the wind. Even now, in summer, Jenna kept the wood stove alight all day. She went out along the beach in the evening, leaving the baby asleep, and collected the wood washed up by the tide. Left under the low hanging eaves of the cottage it dried and would burn quite well, and she could keep her money for food. There was a shop in the village that sold most of what she wanted, though she would have liked more fresh vegetables. The people here seemed to live out of tins. One day she bought a packet of lettuce seeds and planted them in a straggly line in the garden, but she did not know if they would ever come up. The wind lashed everything that grew.

For almost the first time in her life she found there was pleasure in eating. Here, all alone, in the quiet of the lonely little house she discovered the simple delights of bread, cheese, the tartness of a plum, and with no-one else around there was nothing to destroy the gentle ache of hunger before it could be satisfied. Besides, these days she was important and must take care, because without her there was no-one to look after Marcus. His presence had changed her forever, she stood in a different place and saw things differently. There was importance only in life.

Most of the time was spent indoors, alone with her baby. It was peaceful and ordered, the days marked only by the minutiae of babycare. Yesterday he was sick, today he has eaten twice as much, and wanted to play instead of going to sleep. Hours went by in which she stared at him and wondered that she had ever let him go. She treasured each gurgle and blink, saying to herself 'I would never have known about that.' There was no thought at all for tomorrow, there was only today and her small, safe world.

When the car drove slowly past, and then came back, she thought nothing of it. Only when it stopped and a tall, long-legged figure climbed out and stood looking at the cottage and its tangled mess of a garden did she know.

'Oh my God. Oh baby. Oh, oh.' She picked up the child and clutched him to her, shrinking back against the wall. He pushed through the rickety gate and gate to the door, knocking hard and then climbing over unpruned roses to peer in at the window. No help for it then. She went to open the door.

'Hello Dan. How did you find me?'

'You'd be surprised. Can I come in or must I stand in this gale till I freeze to death?' She stood aside to let him come in.

She was scruffily dressed by her standards but still elegant in jeans and a giant cream sweater. Her hair hung loose, a black cascade down her back, and there was colour in her cheeks, the colour of health, not embarrassment.

'You look well,' he commented.

'You look tired. I was sorry about your wife.'

'Were you? I doubt it.'

'Oh, but I was! Sorry that – she couldn't be happy, that she had to do it. She was always so frightened.'

'Yes.' He moved about the little room, the beams only inches above his sandy head. Then he held out his arms for the baby. 'Let me.'

Jenna hesitated, and he said, 'I'm not going to steal him. He's yours.'

'I only hope you mean that, because I'd tell William all about it if you took him.'

Hennessey looked stunned. 'Jenna – William does know all about it. I told him!'

'What? Everything?'

Hennessey nodded. Blindly Jenna thrust the baby at him and began to pace the room. 'You're an idiot,' she said tearfully. 'I go to all this trouble to save your precious horses and you throw it all away. What did you tell him for, he didn't need to know!'

'But – what were you going to say? You can't just walk out with a baby under your arm and expect your husband to take it all in his stride. Come on Jenna, be reasonable.'

'I left him a letter. I said that I had to get away, that I thought a separation would do us both good and you had asked me to look after the baby. Simple. I mean, I knew it would all need sorting out sometime but I thought if I didn't get you involved now – he wouldn't mind so much later.' She looked so tearful and confused that Hennessey started to laugh.

'I love you,' he chuckled.

'Don't say that, you know it isn't true. You like the sex and getting the better of William, but you don't want me. Not really.'

He was taken aback. He looked from the plump little boy in his arms to Jenna's sad face and didn't know what to say. Carefully he put the baby in his cot by the hearth. 'Why do you say that, Jenna?' he asked, making his words gentle and without threat.

'Oh, because – you think I'm mercenary. You want your horses more than me, when it came to it you wanted Lilian more than me, and I don't blame you for it, how could I, but – of two people I don't want to be the one that loves the most. I'm sorry you've lost your horses, I wanted to avoid that, and I know you're kind and probably think I'm pathetic and you ought to take me up, but it wouldn't be right. You can't help what you feel.'

He gazed in disbelief at this beautiful woman who was so much loved that two men would give anything to hold her, and yet thought herself unwanted.

'Jenna,' he said slowly, 'I don't know why you can't believe that people love you. You always think they don't know you, they're being polite, or they're in love with your face, you never think that it's you. When you finished with me, just before Christmas, I didn't know you were pregnant. I thought you were tired of me. I wanted to stop living, there didn't seem any point in going on. But I thought, there was a chance, if I wasn't demanding or difficult it might be all right. When I realised you didn't want me – that you'd actually have your baby adopted rather than turn to me – I didn't know what to do. But the baby was part of you, even now he's got your eyes, can you see that?'

'He's got your chin,' said Jenna shakily, 'and your temper.'

'I thought that was yours. Oh Jen, Jen, don't you know, can't you see how much I care? You knew I couldn't abandon Lilian, and it wasn't because I loved her but because I didn't. I never did, really. I married her for what I could get and by God I paid for it. We do such foolish things when we're young. I've always wondered if she knew how I felt and it made her worse. And now I've lost her and my horses, probably half the farm as well if Lilian's parents hear about us and change the will, I've got no money and no prospects, and you, the woman I did it all for, you say I don't love you! Jenna, your're driving me mad!'

She was starting to cry. She scrubbed at the tears like a

little girl and whispered, 'I'm sorry, I know I've spoiled your life. I didn't mean to, that's why I couldn't tell you about the baby. Oh Dan, I'm so tired of pretending. I'm so tired of trying to love the people I should and not love the ones I shouldn't.'

'Then stop.' He came to her and took her in his arms, rocking her to and fro against his shoulder. 'Do you love me, Jen? Will you come to me when I haven't a thing to offer? Or will you leave me the first Christmas you don't get a mink coat?'

She slid her arms round his neck and lay against him, letting the sure feeling of being home wash over her. 'I love you,' she murmured sleepily. 'Quite a lot. I think you're stuck with me, Dan Hennessey.'

He bent to kiss her in the tangle of her hair. 'Thank God for that,' he whispered.

They sat by the fire for a long, long time. Jenna fed the baby and put him down to sleep, then she wandered around the kitchen opening tins. 'I will learn to cook,' she promised. 'It can't be all that hard.'

'I've tried and I can't do it,' admitted Hennessey. 'I even burn toast.'

'That's because you are not bothered if you are useless at it. I am bothered so I will have to make an effort.' There was a sudden knock at the door. Jenna froze in the act of opening a tin of peas and looked anxiously at Hennessey.

'Who do you think it is?' she whispered.

'Three guesses.' He went to open the door.

William stepped into the untidy little room like a large, brooding animal, his black overcoat almost sinister in the fading evening light. 'Get out, Hennessey,' he snapped. 'I want to talk to my wife.'

'I'll not let you get your hands on her,' warned Dan. 'You won't be happy till you hear her scream.'

Jenna went to him then and caught his arm. 'Go for a

walk, Dan,' she urged. 'I've got to talk to him, it's only fair. I don't think he'll hurt me. I owe him an explanation.'

'Huh! You think all this can be explained?' Sheppard was veering between fury and tears, and at Jenna's pleading Hennessey went out into the garden. He hovered near the window, waiting for the scream that meant he had killed her. God help him if he did, he'd tear his heart out and feed it to the hounds! He caught the eye of the chauffeur watching solidly from the Rolls and he shivered in the freezing wind. If only he knew what was going on.

'You should at least have told me about the baby!' William was staring at her like a big, hopeless dog.

'I couldn't. You'd have made me have an abortion, you know you would. I wanted it.'

'Don't say that you loved him. If it was sex I can understand it, but not – don't say it.'

'It's true though. William, I'm so terribly, terribly sorry. I knew we should never have married, I knew from the time we first slept together, but Mother wanted it and so did you and I – I wanted to be safe, William. Out of it. The men frightened me. I'm sorry.'

'He – Hennessey – says I frightened you.'

'You know you did. And you meant to, if you frightened me enough I did as I was told. But I was fond of you William, in spite of everything. I still am.'

Why had she ever thought that it was enough? Everything had told her it was wrong, she had never once felt him touch her and welcomed him. She had blamed everything and everyone for her failure, and never once thought it was due to a simple lack of love. For Jenna, a woman so private and enfolded in a tight, protective bud, sex was an invasion. Dan had entered her heart before ever he entered her body, and with him the act was truly one of love. There was safety and reward in opening herself to him. With William she wanted only to keep him out, and caused herself and him such misery by refusing to acknowledge it.

William turned and went to glower at Hennessey, freezing in the garden. 'I'm going to ruin him,' he promised. 'He won't have a penny.'

Jenna was unimpressed. 'I knew you would. You never let anyone beat you.'

Suddenly William came to face her. 'If you came back – I wouldn't.'

'You mean – you want me back? After all that I've done?'

He took her hands, a more gentle touch than any she had known from him before. 'I love you, Jenna. You are my wife. For you I would do – anything.'

She freed herself with slow, final regret. The wind was mounting to a gale and through the window Hennessey, in his thin jumper, was visibly turning to ice. Beyond him was the Rolls, vast, luxurious, symbol of all she would never have again. But she had drunk from that cup and found it sour. She turned back to her husband, a look of softness on her face. 'William, I'm so sorry. All I want is that you should divorce me, I won't ask for money or anything. You made it after all, I only spent it. And I would like to see the children. I know you won't want that, but if you could let them – sometimes I almost loved you, William.'

He sighed, with heartfelt weariness. 'I won't hurt you. Him – I can't look at him. I think I'll go now, I feel very tired. Jenna – if you ever change your mind – if you ever did, even years from now – you can always come home.'

'Thank you, William. That is the most generous thing I have ever heard you say.'

He plodded silently to the Rolls, never once glancing behind him. Only when the car had drawn away did Jenna take her fist from her mouth and allow the sobs to come.

Epilogue

All over the world there are salesrooms devoted to the buying and selling of racehorses. At Newmarket they have statues and lawns, at Deauville white walls and glamour, but Doncaster is as plain and straightforward as the Yorkshiremen it serves. It was like a better class cattle market thought Jenna, trying to position herself on a bench under one of the inadequate heaters. Marcus wriggled in her arms, wanting to get down, but she hung on and pulled his hood close about his ears.

Wherever she looked people were staring, and she felt shy. Even after all this time they remembered the scandal and as for her, she had forgotten what it was to be gaped at after months in which she hardly ever left the farm. A woman across the ring raised a tentative hand and waved to her, and Jenna felt a shock. Someone knew her, someone from the old life who was prepared to risk acknowledgment as a friend. They had been few and far between recently. The woman was rewarded with a beam and a wave, but no more for the sale was about to begin.

William had made it his business to isolate Hennessey and Jenna, to find out who was in touch with them and make them the object of his spite. Lord Staveley, a staunch friend, found William had bought the field

329

behind his house and intended to build an estate of houses on it. Staveley was appalled, for he would lose his view of the hills and be faced with washing lines instead. 'It isn't even commercially viable,' he complained, but Jenna pursed her lips wryly and commented 'I bet it is.' Even with revenge in mind William seldom made mistakes.

As for the erring pair themselves, true to his word he had been kind to Jenna. The divorce had been slow but unbloody, William had saved his wrath for Hennessey. Within a month William was suing him for attempted fraud. Nothing had happened, there was nothing to prove, but by the time William's laywers had muddied the waters Hennessey was committed to a long and expensive courtcase, which he would win, but in doing so come near to bankruptcy. There was nothing for it but to sell the stables, his only worthwhile asset, but unlike Jenna he was not dismayed. The place held only nightmares and broken dreams. No Derby winner now. 'We'll buy somewhere else when we win the case,' he had assured her. 'They're bound to award us costs.' But she was not deceived. They had stepped off the merry-go-round and it was whirling on without them, it would not stop when they were tired of leisure and wanted to play again.

In the meantime they had moved on to the farm, to the delight of old man Hennessey who lost no time in taking himself off to a bungalow and breeding bantams.

'He's happy anyway,' commented Hennessey, and Jenna tried to smile. The house at least was wonderful, huge, rambling and needing her. This time the transformation would take time instead of money, but it was coming, she had found some lovely lacey nets on the market and when she draped them in swathes round the stark French doors the effect was super. And she had Dan, and Marcus, and in the holidays the children came to visit, largely she thought to impart tales of William's continued success and to return with doleful stories of the poor little farm. They were much closer to their father these days.

She wondered why William was being good about the children. Had she, by her concern, shielded him from the necessity for his? Or was it that now he had no-one else to turn to? No way of knowing. What she did know was that he sat there, brooding, and thought far too much about her and her life. William was not a man who had ever admitted defeat.

Oddly enough, she thought that Tony and Rachel had been damaged far more severely by this even than by the departure of their own mother. That had been so long ago, it had happened so swiftly and no-one had told them anything about it. This was something in which they were deeply, inextricably concerned, they saw for themselves that Jenna was as weak, foolish and deceitful as any one of them. They as much as William had believed in her perfection. Nonetheless they still came and they still talked to her, Rachel perhaps a little less readily than before, but then she was growing up. It was only to be expected.

As for Tony, he and William had come to terms at last, neither peace nor war but something in between. With Jenna gone there seemed less to fight about somehow, but it was noticeable that Tony did not like Jenna's baby. Truly William's son, he never took the easy path through life, he fought every inch of the way, changing only the opponents. And despite everything he still liked Hennessey, and valued his good opinion, a reassuring constant in a changing world.

William's horses had not done well since they left Hennessey's, and she could not pretend she wasn't glad. Fleece had lost what little enthusiasm he had and fretted himself to a lather before every ignominious outing, while

Sharps was over-raced and had leg trouble. To Jenna, it seemed only fair.

All it needed was for Dan to be happy, for while she had everything, he had lost his horses. Living as they did, with even their thoughts entwined, she could not pretend that he did not miss them. In racing the highs and lows are the sharp mountain peaks of life, in farming you live on hills that roll more gently. He was not a man for quiet fields and Jenna was deeply aware that she had condemned him to them.

Yet here they were today. The auctioneer was working hard, with a plethora of mediocre yearlings to deal with. Suddenly Jenna saw that Dan had slipped into the ring, and was leaning near the doorway looking bored. She knew him so well that it made her smile, and she was not surprised when she saw the covert nod and that meant a bid. Her stomach contracted with nerves, as never before at a sale. Never before had it been money for seed and fuel oil, clothes and, yes, food, that was on the line. He had to get him cheap, he simply had to. They had talked long into the night, scribbling figures on the backs of envelopes, and in the end it was she that insisted.

'If you don't buy it I will,' she declared. 'And the auctioneer will sting me, so you'd better.'

'You're always bossy when you're pregnant.' He rested a hand on the precious small swelling and she knew it was foolish to be afraid. He would take care of his family. He would not let her down.

The object of their heart-searchings was a spindly, under-developed colt with unfashionable breeding and ears like a donkey. 'Workmanlike,' was all Hennessey would say of him. 'And I'm sure I can make him win.'

Whether he did or not was of no interest to Jenna, all she cared about was that Dan should feel about his life the way she did about hers, that it was a warm, well-fitting coat. And if she had to do without real coats in order to provide this horse with a rug, then she would do it, and try not to complain. She had given up promising saintly forbearance. It wasn't in her.

'Fifteen hundred guineas. Any more gentlemen? Fifteen hundred then.' The gavel banged. 'Dan Hennessey.'

There was a ripple of interest and heads turned to look for him. Jenna got up and everyone watched to see where she went, but she and Dan exchanged only the tiniest smile.

'Cheap,' she muttered.

'Damned cheap, thank God. Let's go and have a cup of tea, you look frozen.'

'And you look – happy.'

They leaned against the wall in the shabby tearoom and wondered if Geoff Tunes might come back. He would have to help on the farm but he could do the horses as well and might even get the odd race. Almost without thinking they were talking in the plural, although today's purchase was the only horse they owned. A man came up to them, nodded to Jenna and said to Dan, 'Back in business again, Hennessey?'

'Looks like it. Yard needs a lot of work but we should have a few boxes ready by Christmas.'

'I – er – wondered if I could send you my yearling. Bit of a problem really, he's been a devil from the day he was foaled. By Le Duc. I remembered what you did with Fred Gainsbrough's colt, and I know it's asking a lot, because he won't be easy, but if you could take him –'

Hennessey looked dubious and it was Jenna's turn to look bored. Oh, Mr Man that I don't know, I could kiss you, I will carry your beastly horse home on my back if you'll only send us weekly cheques to pay for it. The tractor's so old they don't make the bits any more.

333

'I'll come and have a look,' promised Dan. 'I can't take too many till the yard's up straight, but I like horses with a bit about them. I'll probably have him.'

'Great!' You don't know what a relief that is, if I hadn't seen you I don't know where I'd have sent him. Good to have you back.' The man wandered off and Dan and Jenna exchanged glances.

'I thought you were going to bite his hand off,' murmured Hennessey.

'I was trying to look disinterested. Oh Dan, is it going to be all right do you think?'

The baby was wriggling in her arms and Dan took him, swinging him up and on to his shoulders. 'When will you learn, Mrs Hennessey that it's always all right? With you, and me, and this object, and whatever you're hatching inside there? It mightn't look a lot to anybody else – but to me it's what counts.'

She put her head on one side and looked at him, his hair being tugged by the baby's casual cruelty. 'It's better when you're brave, isn't it? Life I mean. You can't always run and hide.'

'Ouch! Stop that, you brat. Yes, it is better when you're brave. And the bravest ones of all are the ones who are frightened the most and don't show it. Which is you, my sweet. I want to kiss you, so let's go home.'

'We've a horse to load first.'

'You're not above snogging in a horsebox are you? Who do you think you are, a millionairess?'

And she slid her hand into the pocket of his coat, where it was warm, and messy and safe and simply said, 'Yes.'

Outstanding fiction in paperback from Grafton
Books

Nicola Thorne

A Woman Like Us	£1.25	☐
The Perfect Wife and Mother	£1.50	☐
The Daughters of the House	£2.50	☐
Where the Rivers Meet	£2.50	☐
Affairs of Love	£2.50	☐
The Enchantress Saga	£3.95	☐
Never Such Innocence	£2.95	☐

Jacqueline Briskin

Paloverde	£2.50	☐
Rich Friends	£2.50	☐
Decade	£2.50	☐
The Onyx	£3.50	☐
Everything and More	£2.50	☐

Barbara Taylor Bradford

A Woman of Substance	£3.50	☐
Voice of the Heart	£3.50	☐
Hold the Dream	£2.95	☐

Alan Ebert and Janice Rotchstein

| Traditions | £2.50 | ☐ |

Marcelle Bernstein

| Sadie | £2.50 | ☐ |

To order direct from the publisher just tick the titles you want
and fill in the order form.

Bestsellers available in paperback from Grafton
Books

To order direct from the publisher just tick the titles you want
and fill in the order form.   **GF4282**

The world's greatest novelists now available in
paperback from Grafton Books

Eric van Lustbader

The Miko	£2.95 ☐
The Ninja	£2.95 ☐
Sirens	£2.95 ☐
Beneath An Opal Moon	£2.50 ☐
Black Heart	£3.50 ☐

Nelson de Mille

By the Rivers of Babylon	£2.50 ☐
Cathedral	£1.95 ☐
The Talbot Odyssey	£2.95 ☐

Justin Scott

The Shipkiller	£2.50 ☐
The Man Who Loved the Normandie	£2.50 ☐
A Pride of Kings	£2.95 ☐

Leslie Waller

Trocadero	£2.50 ☐
The Swiss Account	£2.50 ☐
The American	£2.50 ☐
The Family	£1.95 ☐
The Banker	£2.50 ☐
The Brave and the Free	£1.95 ☐
Gameplan	£1.95 ☐

David Charney

Sensei	£2.50 ☐
Sensei II: The Swordmaster	£2.50 ☐

To order direct from the publisher just tick the titles you want
and fill in the order form: GF781

Crime fiction – now available in paperba
from Grafton Books

James Hadley Chase

One Bright Summer Morning	£1.	☐
Tiger by the Tail	£1.	☐
Strictly for Cash	£1.5	☐
What's Better than Money?	£1.5	☐
Just the Way it Is	£1.50	☐
You're Dead Without Money	£1.50	☐
Coffin From Hong Kong	£1.95	
Like a Hole in the Head	£1.50	☐
There's a Hippie on the Highway	£1.50	☐
This Way for a Shroud	£1.50	☐
Just a Matter of Time	£1.50	☐
Not My Thing	£1.50	☐
Hit Them Where It Hurts	£1.95	☐

Georgette Heyer

Penhallow	£1.95	☐
Duplicate Death	£1.95	☐
Envious Casca	£1.95	☐
Death in the Stocks	£1.95	☐
Behold, Here's Poison	£1.95	☐
They Found Him Dead	£1.95	☐
The Unfinished Clue	£1.95	☐
Detection Unlimited	£1.95	☐
Why Shoot a Butler?	£1.50	☐

To order direct from the publisher just tick the titles you want
and fill in the order form.

GF2781

he world's greatest thriller writers now
available in paperback from Grafton Books

Robert Ludlum

The Chancellor Manuscript	£2.95	☐
The Gemini Contenders	£2.50	☐
The Rhinemann Exchange	£2.50	☐
The Matlock Paper	£1.95	☐
The Osterman Weekend	£2.50	☐
The Scarlatti Inheritance	£1.95	☐
The Holcroft Covenant	£2.95	☐
The Materese Circle	£2.95	☐
The Bourne Identity	£2.95	☐
The Road to Gandolfo	£2.50	☐
The Parsifal Mosaic	£2.95	☐
The Aquitaine Progression	£2.95	☐

Lawrence Sanders

The Third Deadly Sin	£2.50	☐
The Tenth Commandment	£2.95	☐
The Second Deadly Sin	£2.50	☐
The Sixth Commandment	£2.50	☐
The Tomorrow File	£2.50	☐
The Pleasures of Helen	£2.50	☐

To order direct from the publisher just tick the titles you want
and fill in the order form.　　　　GF1881

Famous personalities you've always wanted to
read about – now available in Grafton Books

Dirk Bogarde

A Postillion Struck by Lightning (illustrated)	£2.50	☐
Snakes and Ladders (illustrated)	£2.95	☐
An Orderly Man (illustrated)	£2.50	☐

Muhammad Ali with Richard Durham

The Greatest: My Own Story	£1.95	☐

Fred Lawrence Guiles

Norma Jean (illustrated)	£2.50	☐

Becky Yancey

My Life with Elvis	£1.95	☐

Shelley Winters

Shelley	£1.95	☐

Stewart Granger

Sparks Fly Upward	£1.95	☐

Billie Jean King

Billie Jean King (illustrated)	£1.95	☐

Stephen Davies

Bob Marley (illustrated)	£2.95	☐

Pat Jennings

An Autobiography (illustrated)	£1.95	☐

Ann Morrow

The Queen (illustrated)	£2.50	☐
The Queen Mother (illustrated)	£2.95	☐

Pat Phoenix

Love, Curiosity, Freckles & Doubt (illustrated)	£1.95	☐
All My Burning Bridges (illustrated)	£1.95	☐

To order direct from the publisher just tick the titles you want
and fill in the order form.

GM581

A selection of sexology books in paperback from Grafton Books

Dr Harold and Ruth Greenwald The Sex-Life Letters	£2.50	☐
Anne Hooper (Editor) More Sex-Life Letters	£2.95	☐
Inge and Sten Hegeler The XYZ of Love	£1.50	☐
S G Tuffill FRCS The Sex-Life File	£2.50	☐
T H Van de Velde Ideal Marriage	£2.95	☐
Dr Sherman J Silber The Male	£1.95	☐
Richard Burton The Kama Sutra	£2.50	☐
The Perfumed Garden (translator)	£2.50	☐
'Walter' My Secret life	£2.50	☐
'J' The Sensuous Women	£1.95	☐
Avodah K Offit MD Night Thoughts	£2.50	☐

To order direct from the publisher just tick the titles you want
and fill in the order form.   **GF3981**

Crime fiction – now available in paperback
from Grafton Books

To order direct from the publisher just tick the titles you want
and fill in the order form.

Mystery and suspense from Colin Wilson

Ritual in the Dark	£1.95	☐
The Schoolgirl Murder Case	£1.95	☐
The God of the Labyrinth	£1.95	☐
The Occult	£4.95	☐
Mysteries	£4.95	☐

To order direct from the publisher just tick the titles you want
and fill in the order form.   **GF3481**

Bestsellers available in paperback from Grafton Books

Emmanuelle Arsan

Emmanuelle	£2.50	☐
Emmanuelle 2	£2.50	☐
Laure	£1.95	☐
Nea	£1.95	☐
Vanna	£2.50	☐

Jonathan Black

Ride the Golden Tiger	£1.95	☐
Oil	£2.50	☐
The World Rapers	£2.50	☐
The House on the Hill	£2.50	☐
Megacorp	£2.50	☐
The Plunderers	£2.50	☐

Herbert Kastle

Cross-Country	£2.50	☐
Little Love	£2.50	☐
Millionaires	£2.50	☐
Miami Golden Boy	£2.50	☐
The Movie Maker	£2.95	☐
The Gang	£2.50	☐
Hit Squad	£1.95	☐
Dirty Movies	£2.50	☐
Hot Prowl	£1.95	☐
Sunset People	£1.95	☐
David's War	£1.95	☐

To order direct from the publisher just tick the titles you want
and fill in the order form.

Outstanding fiction in paperback from Grafton Books

Raymond Giles

Sabrehill	£2.50	☐
Slaves of Sabrehill	£2.50	☐
Rebels of Sabrehill	£2.50	☐
Storm over Sabrehill	£2.50	☐
Hellcat of Sabrehill	£2.50	☐
Dark Master	£1.95	☐
Rogue Black	£2.50	☐

Edgar Mittelholzer

Children of Kaywana	£2.50	☐
Kaywana Heritage	£2.50	☐
Kaywana Stock	£2.50	☐

To order direct from the publisher just tick the titles you want and fill in the order form.

Outstanding women's fiction in paperback from Grafton Books

Mary E Pearce

The Land Endures	£1.95 ☐
Apple Tree Saga	£2.50 ☐
Polsinney Harbour	£1.95 ☐

Kathleen Winsor

Wanderers Eastward, Wanderers West (omnibus)	£3.95 ☐

Margaret Thomson Davis

The Breadmakers Saga	£2.95 ☐
A Baby Might Be Crying	£1.50 ☐
A Sort of Peace	£1.50 ☐

Helena Leigh

The Vintage Years 1: The Grapes of Paradise	£1.95 ☐
The Vintage Years 2: Wild Vines	£2.50 ☐
The Vintage Years 3: Kingdoms of the Vine	£1.95 ☐

Rebecca Brandewyne

Love, Cherish Me	£2.95 ☐
Rose of Rapture	£2.95 ☐
And Gold was Ours	£2.95 ☐

Pamela Jekel

Sea Star	£2.50 ☐

Chloe Gartner

Still Falls the Rain	£2.50 ☐

Nora Roberts

Promise Me Tomorrow	£2.50 ☐

Gloria Keverne

A Man Cannot Cry	£3.50 ☐

Josephine Edgar

Margaret Normanby	£2.95 ☐

To order direct from the publisher just tick the titles you want
and fill in the order form.

All these books are available at your local bookshop or newsagent, or can be ordered direct from the publisher.

To order direct from the publishers just tick the titles you want and fill in the form below.

Name _____

Address _____

_____

Send to:
Grafton Cash Sales
PO Box 11, Falmouth, Cornwall TR10 9EN.

Please enclose remittance to the value of the cover price plus:

UK 55p for the first book, 22p for the second book plus 14p per copy for each additional book ordered to a maximum charge of £1.75.

BFPO and Eire 55p for the first book, 22p for the second book plus 14p per copy for the next 7 books, thereafter 8p per book.

Overseas £1.25 for the first book and 31p for each additional book.